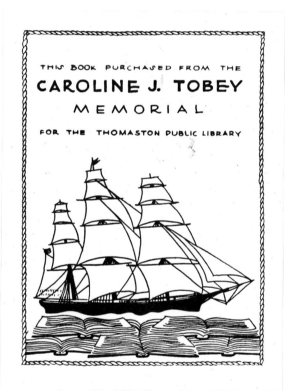

to Logan
and Charleston

9-22

Ream

Marcums Branch

#8

PEELCHESTNUT
MTN.

Annadel

Pliny Branch

x Slate Dump

Felco

#6

#5

Davidson

Jenkinjones

x
Spencers
Curve

Blackberry
Creek

#2

#10

Winco

#13

Raven

#4

Trace Fork

Tipple

Lloyds Fork

TRACE
MTN.

Daisy Creek

WEST VIRGINIA

DISCARD

Jolo

JUSTICE COUNTY
McDOWELL COUNTY

Levisa River

Marrowbone Creek

WV

KY

KENTUCKY

Cucumber Creek

to Welch

N

Henryclay

Kingdom Come

Grapevine

The Unquiet Earth

W · W · NORTON & COMPANY · NEW YORK · LONDON

The Unquiet Earth

DENISE GIARDINA

A NOVEL

Copyright © 1992 by Denise Giardina
All rights reserved
Printed in the United States of America

First Edition

The text of this book is composed in Janson Alternate
with the display set in Eve Light
Composition and Manufacturing by
The Haddon Craftsmen, Inc.
Book design by Antonina Krass

Library of Congress Cataloging in Publication Data
Giardina, Denise, 1951-
The unquiet earth : a novel / Denise Giardina.
p. cm.
I. Title.
PS3557.I136U57 1992
813'.54—dc20   91-46495

ISBN: 0-393-03096-2
W.W. Norton & Company, Inc., 500 Fifth Avenue, New York, N.Y. 10110
W.W. Norton & Company Ltd., 10 Coptic Street, London WC1A 1PU
1 2 3 4 5 6 7 8 9 0

For Gabe, Erin, Mary, and Sara Anne
and for Christine Reynolds Whitt

The writing of this book was supported by the Funding Exchange and the National Endowment for the Arts.

The story of the Blackberry Creek Food Co-op grows from events described in Huey Perry's book, *They'll Cut Off Your Project.* I am also indebted to the following books and authors: *Everything in Its Path,* by Kai T. Erikson; *Death at Buffalo Creek,* by Tom Nugent; and *The Buffalo Creek Disaster,* by Gerald M. Stern.

I appreciate the invaluable support and advice of Laurel Goldman, Alex Charns, Bubba Fountain, Elizabeth Stagg, Kathleen O'Keeffe, Dabney Grinnan, Mary Moore, Jay Mazzocchi, Martha Pentecost, Bill Hastie and the writer's workshop at Duke University Continuing Education. Thanks also to Buck Maggard, Anne Johnson, Jerry Johnson, Herb Smith, Andy Garrison and the other folks at Appalshop in Whitesburg, Kentucky, to Joe Szakos and Kentuckians for the Commonwealth, to the Institute for Southern Studies, Tom Campbell, John Valentine, Helen Whiting, Susan Southern and Randy Campbell at the Regulator Book Shop in Durham, North Carolina, to the Rev. Jim Lewis, Joe Hacala, S.J., and especially Jane Gelfman and Mary Cunnane.

Finally a thank you to the people of the Appalachian coalfields, especially in McDowell and Mingo counties, West Virginia, Floyd, Pike and Letcher counties, Kentucky, and the Massey and Pittston strikers of southwest Virginia and West Virginia, whose rich lives inspired this book.

The hand of the Lord was upon me, and he brought me
out by the Spirit of the Lord, and set me down
in the midst of the valley; it was full of
bones.

And he led me round among them; and behold, there
were very many upon the valley; and lo, they
were *very dry*.

And he said to me, "Son of man, can these
bones live?"

And I answered, *"O Lord God, thou knowest."*

—Ezekiel 37:1–3

Book One

THE ICE BREAKS

1930S

DILLON FREEMAN

When my daddy died I was an infant, lying on his chest with his thumb caught tight in my fist. I try to remember properly. I try to remember to hold on tighter to that thumb, to keep the warmth from seeping out. If I squeeze hard enough I'll recreate him, thumb first, then the rough hand, the forearm with its thick brown hair, the soft fold of skin over his throat, the chin stubbled coarse with beard. But I stop there because it is all I can bring to life. I don't know his face. And the quickening wanes again until only the thumb is warm, and then not even the thumb.

Me and Mom still live in the cabin where he died. She dragged the deathbed outside and burned it like a funeral pyre. He was already buried in the Homeplace cemetery with the rest of her people. But it was like she had to see something go up in flames. She wouldn't have

dreamed to throw herself on the fire, though, like Teacher says those women do over there in India. My mother, Carrie Freeman, wouldn't turn her back on life for nobody, not even a man she loved so desperate she slept with him and them not married and traipsed over mountains to be with him.

I am the child of that love. A woods colt, as we say in these Kentucky mountains. Nobody troubles me over it. Nobody dares because I am a steady fighter. People here don't get het up over such things anyway, except a few of the meanest church women. Besides, my mother was married to a preacher before she and Daddy made me, and I ended up with the preacher's last name, so that as good as sanctified the whole proceedings.

My daddy was a union organizer over in the West Virginia coalfields, and he was in a battle with the state police and company thugs and took a bullet that snapped his spine clean in two. That's how he came to die slow and in bed with me sprawled atop him. Rachel, who is my cousin, says she recalls him. I don't believe she could recall much, she was barely two. But she says she remembers being scared of the Aunt Jane Place because a mean man lived there. Mom says Daddy was bad-tempered for being paralyzed and Rachel was skittish of him. It does put me in awe of Rachel a little, it makes me jealous because I should be the one to remember him. I should remember grabbing onto that thumb. But I don't hold Rachel's memory against her. I just stay as close to her as I can.

Rachel gets uncomfortable when I talk about Mom and Daddy making me. She was raised more proper. Rachel is a Honaker, and she lives on the Homeplace just down Grapevine nigh to the shoals. We are first cousins—our mothers are sisters, Carrie and Flora. Me and Mom live at the Aunt Jane Place. It is all the same land, just two different houses, theirs the white wood farmhouse, ours the cabin that creaks in the wind and smells of woodsmoke. Uncle Ben says move down to the Homeplace, he'll build on an extra room and the older younguns will be moving out soon, but Mom won't hear of it. I think she wants to stay in the house of Daddy's last breathing.

Uncle Ben is worried about whether we can live on our land at all.

He says the taxes have gone up because the coal companies are buying land, and he has taken out a mortgage to pay them. Then he opened a general store at the mouth of Scary to help pay the mortgage but the store is not doing any good. Mom says Ben would pick the depths of the Depression to open up a store. Uncle Ben is a smart man but him and Aunt Flora have got no business sense, Mom says, and they give too much credit. In these times we are living in, lots of folks need credit. So the sacks of flour disappear from the dusty shelves as soon as they are set out, and Ben cannot keep the pokes of already baked-and-sliced lightbread that caused such a stir when they first arrived. A poke of sliced lightbread is prized, for it means you can afford to spend money to replace the biscuits and cornbread people bake themselves, but Ben even gives credit for lightbread, so everyone is the same.

At school Rachel has fried egg sandwiches on lightbread with store-bought mayonnaise or sometimes mayonnaise by itself which nobody else has. She doesn't take on about it. Mom will not have lightbread in the house, she says even if we had the money it's just as tasty as a handkerchief and she sends me to school with yellow cornbread. Some younguns who bring cornbread hide what they have because they are embarrassed to be poor but I won't do that because it would shame my Mom.

Mom says she gives the store less than a year, then she smiles and says, "That Ben, he'll feed the hollow while it lasts." There's things we don't get from the store. We grow our corn and vegetables and raise our own pigs and chickens and milk cows. We put up preserves in mason jars for the winter, or I should say the women do. They stand over the cast-iron stoves in the heat of summer and stir the great boiling pots of tomatoes and beans, dip their ladles into the roiling red and green liquid, and wipe the sweat from their faces with one corner of their aprons. They slice the apples and sun-dry them into leather-sweet strips. They take a needle and thread to the beans and hang them in rows to dry from the porch rafters. Me and Uncle Ben and his big boys plow and hoe and plant and haul. Rachel tends the chickens and cows.

But we get lard and salt from the store, and baking soda and flour, and nails and needles for piercing. And Goody's Headache Powder that Aunt Flora eats like it is candy.

Sometimes when the hens are laying good, Rachel has two eggs to trade at the store. Aunt Flora makes her trade even though the store is theirs, because she says it is proper. Rachel trades for a Three Musketeers. Each of us pops one chocolate Musketeer in our mouths and we break the third exact down the middle. I like to see the nougat heart. Or Rachel trades for a CoCola in a little green bottle, what some call a dope and others call a sodypop but Rachel always calls by its right name. Ben's store has a big metal sign nailed to the front wall with a raised red oval that reads Coca-Cola in curlicued white letters. The red paint has faded in the sun and there are dents where youn-guns throw pebbles to hear the clang. The best sodypops come from Ben's ice chest and you sit on the front stoop where the bottle catches glints of sunlight and you look at the green mountain that hovers over the store. It is best when your feet are dusty from the road. Rachel and I share sodypops and the neck of the bottle is warm and tastes the way I guess her mouth would taste.

A long time ago Uncle Ben was the teacher at the Scary Creek School. I am glad he doesn't teach anymore because I despise school and if he was the teacher I'd have to despise him. I am not a bad student, I learn what I am supposed to, but still I don't care for it. You have to hold your pencil a certain way even though it's cramped as hell and if you don't do it right, Teacher wraps your fingers around the pencil hard and like to breaks every bone in your hand. You learn spelling rules and grammar rules and that the way you talked all your life is ignorant even though it seems to suit most people fine, and when Teacher goes on and says we live in a free country it's just a little hard to believe. Nobody admits it but school is to teach you how to get bossed. I reckon I could read some books on my own and learn what I want, but my mom sets a store by school.

Rachel is the best student. She is sixteen and I am only fourteen-and-three-quarters. But I am right behind her at school. Rachel is very thin and has wavy light-brown hair that comes to her shoulders. She wears very nice clothes because Aunt Flora cuts pictures from the mail-order catalog and makes dresses to look like them. My mom says it's a good thing I'm a boy because she can't sew and she would send me to school in potato sacks. Most of what I wear is hand-me-downs from Uncle Ben's boys.

Once Aunt Flora got hold of some old window drapes and clothes from a missionary box. Missionaries from up North are always sending us boxes of old things like we aren't even Christian. I wouldn't touch a thing in those boxes nor my Mom neither, but Aunt Flora says why waste, she can make the things nicer than when they were sent. She took some drapes of slick red material and made Rachel a coat that looked like the Chinese wear. Then she cut down a big white wool skirt and jacket into a dress with a high collar and red buttons down the front. Rachel wore the red coat and white dress to school on Class Day when we all had to recite poems. Rachel's dress had long narrow sleeves and a long skirt down to her boot tops. When she stood up to recite, she looked like a queen.

RACHEL HONAKER

I wore the white dress and red coat on Class Day to impress the teacher, who was young and fresh from Transylvania College and in the mountains for some kind of adventure. He was a Bennett from Louisville and my mother said they were quality people. She knew about the Bennetts from the Society pages of the *Courier-Journal*, which she read faithfully even though we didn't know a soul in Louisville.

It rained on Class Day and we had two miles to walk to school. I carried an old umbrella but the wind blew the rain sideways and the umbrella went inside out. Dillon offered to throw his coat over me but I said no he would catch his death. It was November and the rain was cold and gray like the storm clouds had set right down on top of us. We walked and my dress got heavier and the mud pulled at my feet. By the time we got to school I was wore out.

Inside the wood schoolhouse we took off our coats. Everyone stared at me and I looked down. The coat had wept and left red splotches all over my white dress. It was like I'd been shot, like I'd been through bloody battle. My throat got hard but I was too old to cry. I put the coat back on. We crowded around the stove with our hands out, trying to get warm, and my damp wool dress smelled like an old sheep. I held my mouth straight and got madder and madder to keep from crying. Then Dillon whispered in my ear.

"Take your coat off. Nobody will dare laugh at you."

His breath warmed my frozen ear lobe. I couldn't look at him and went to my seat. But when it came my turn to recite the *Ode on a Grecian Urn*, I threw back my coat and stood in front of everyone with my back to the teacher. I faced Dillon.

I said,

> *Bold lover, never, never canst thou kiss,*
> *Though winning near the goal, yet do not grieve:*
> *She cannot fade; though thou hast not thy bliss,*
> *Forever wilt thou love, and she be fair.*

Dillon sat with his hands clasped on the desk in front of him. His straight brown hair was combed to one side and he had a small sharp nose that looked too delicate for a boy. He watched me carefully, his narrow eyes bright. I felt heat building under my armpits, between my breasts and down my backbone. My dress was still wet and sticky and I thought the steam must be rising from me.

My mother, Flora Honaker, never allowed me to call her Mom. It sounded country, she said. She was Mother. I used to ache inside when Dillon called Aunt Carrie "Mom." When he was little, he could fall and skin his knee and Aunt Carrie picked out the bits of twig and gravel with a needle, bathed the bloody skin with a cloth dipped in warm soapy water, and afterward kissed the mottled flesh before she bandaged it. When I fell my mother said I was too wild and turned back to peeling potatoes. Her hands looked white and cold from the rinse water. After a while, when I fell or was bee-stung, I walked all the way to the Aunt Jane Place, choking on my sobs, so that Aunt Carrie could bathe me and Dillon could kiss the wound.

But my mother made a house pretty. Our floors were rough wood but she scrubbed them on her hands and knees. She hung lacy curtains and brought flowers inside to stick in jars of water. She knew all the wildflowers and grew roses and pansies and snapdragons around the house. "You can tell there is love in a house when you see flowers," she used to say, and so I assumed neighbors with dirt yards always screamed at one another. Mother took the *Ladies' Home Journal* and *McCall's* and the *Pictorial Review*. At night, while we listened to Lum and Abner on the radio, she sat beside a lamp turning the pages slowly, her head bent reverently over the glowing photographs. Sometimes she would touch the page with her finger and look up as though about to speak, then drop her eyes quickly.

She learned out of her magazines how to fold a napkin, how to set out the silverware just so and lay the knife so the curved side faces the plate. "See here," she told me, "when you pick up the knife you don't have to turn it over, it is ready to cut your meat." She stood over me while I laid the table, until she could trust me with it.

I was her main project. My older sisters were gone, Mabel to Berea College, Jane married to a principal and teaching school in Danville. Mother longed for me to go to Berea, where she hoped the offending hillbilly would be whipped out of me and I would marry a future doctor or lawyer and live in Lexington or Louisville. I wished I could talk to my sisters about it, but they were far away.

When I was six, I'd said, "I'm going to marry Dillon when I grow up."

"You'll do no such thing," Mother said. "Dillon is your first cousin. You want to have babies that aren't right?"

"What do you mean, babies that aren't right?"

"I mean simple in the head. Deformed."

"Dillon says a man gives a woman babies with his peter. And Dillon's not simple, so if he gave me a baby, it would be all right."

She hit me so hard my mouth was bruised for days. I never recall her hitting me another time. I wept until I couldn't breathe.

"That wild boy! I'll speak to his mother. If she's not going to raise him properly, she can at least see he behaves around you. As for you, young lady,"—she always called me young lady when she was mad at me—"don't let me ever hear such filth come out of your mouth again. You aren't some trash from the head of the hollow."

Whenever the Kentucky Derby was run she sat close to the radio. While the announcer described the horses, she told me how the women present would all be wearing hats and what they would look like, to prepare me for the day when I would join them. Women who wore hats always had perfect babies.

So I grew up with the understanding I would leave the mountains, and as I got older the idea seemed more pleasing. But my ideas about leaving were different than my mother's. I listened to the radio and twice I had been to the movies in Shelby. I knew the way people in other places talked and I practiced sounding like them. I wanted to drink chocolate malteds when I was in one mood and martinis when I was in another, and wear silk hose with seams down the back and pierce my ears and smear the world's reddest lipstick on my mouth. I wanted to be a stewardess. A stewardess was the most glamorous thing a woman could be, next to an actress. That meant following in Aunt Carrie's footsteps at the nursing school in Justice, West Virginia, because in those days, stewardesses were nurses.

In the meantime I tended our cows in the pasture across the river. I used the time to dream about flying and going on dates with men who smelled like cologne. In good weather I would lie on my back in the hillside pasture, my arms spread wide, and feel the earth move and spin beneath me. Sometimes the clouds moved so fast it felt like the mountain would roll and hurl me right off it. I tried to imagine what the mountains would look like from the window of an airplane, over the shoulder of a man in a suit, a man with a clean-shaven neck. I would pour his cup full of rich, dark coffee, and the steam would rise and tickle my nose as I bent over his cup. I would take care of him and he would be grateful and ask me to marry him.

In winter I fetched the cows as quickly as I could to their shed. I rode my mule Mag across the ford at the shoals, tethered her to a tree, and climbed the hillside with a long switch like a magic wand in my hand. The cows knew me and I only had to tap at their ankles to move them down the hill, their moaning heavy with longing and relief, to the barn. With each tap of the wand I tried to change them into handsome princes, but they remained cows.

DILLON FREEMAN

I can tell when Rachel is ready to come home because the cowbells across the river sound clean and clear and then fall silent. Sound seems to carry even farther after a rain, it cuts the flat air like cracking ice with a hammer. I was on the riverbank the last February day of my fourteenth year, setting out lines for bass. The river was frozen gray but the edges of the ice were thin and transparent and had pulled away from the bank. I heard the cowbells across Grapevine, then the silence. Soon Rachel would cross the shoals downstream. I stuck chunks of tough fatback onto my hooks and tested the ice with one foot. The shelf gave way easily and I would have stepped in the cold water if I hadn't grabbed a birch sapling.

When the lines were set I scrambled up the bank. Then I heard a loud crack like an explosion farther upriver. I stood still. There was another crack, two more, then a long loud rattle like an avalanche of boulders.

I ran the half mile to the Homeplace over our mudspattered road. *The ice has broke! Rachel! The ice has broke!*

Uncle Ben and Aunt Flora were at the store so only my mother heard. She ran ahead of me, her skirt whipping around her legs until she caught it up and ran harder. When we reached the ford Rachel was halfway across, riding on Mag.

Rachel! The ice!

But she could already hear the gnawing tearing sound coming closer. She kept turning her head to look. The mule's ears were laid back and her teeth showed at the bit. The water rose in waves, lapped at Mag's belly, then to Rachel's knees. I plunged down the bank but Mom grabbed my arm.

Let me go!

I yanked my arm away but she grabbed me by the coat collar and hauled me down. I fought her but she held me so tight around the chest I couldn't breathe. Only a mother could be that strong to hold you back, and maybe only my mother.

"Pray God the mule will bring her over!" Mom was breathing short and hard. "You go in, you got nothing to keep you from being swept away."

A wave washed over the mule's back and Rachel slipped off. Her head went under but Mag surged forward, swimming now, and Rachel's head broke the surface. When Mag lunged again Rachel's finger caught fast in the ring on the mule's harness. Floes of gray ice bobbed around the bend of the river.

Goddamn you let me go goddamn you!

Then Mom let go of me so sudden I sprawled headlong. She waded into the shallows where Mag had found her footing, grabbed Rachel by the wrist and hauled her to shore. Rachel was gleaming wet and insensible. I slipped into the numbing cold water and wrapped my arms around her chest. I could feel the curve of her breasts. Mom put her hand on my arm.

"Don't touch me," I said.

She took her hand away and pointed at the jagged jostling ice floes. "You'd be drowned stone cold this minute if you'd gone after her."

What does she know? We carried Rachel to the Homeplace. Mom laid Rachel before the fire, stripped off her wet clothes, and now she is bathing her. I stand outside and watch through the window. Rachel is white except for her rosebrown nipples and the swatch of brown hair between her thighs. A towel covers her head like a turban. She shivers, opens her eyes and raises her head, then relaxes. She folds her long arms across her breasts. Mom wraps her in quilts.

The Ice Breaks, 1930s

I long to go inside and warm her with my breath, to take her fingers into my mouth until they are ruddy with life. Her index finger, the one that caught in the ring and saved her, is broken. No one notices until she wakes in a fever and complains that it hurts. Then Aunt Flora cries when she sees how bent and twisted it is. That finger will be crooked the rest of her life. It will ache when the weather turns cold. Every day I plan to tell her I love her, then I see her finger. I remember how I failed to save her and my tongue cleaves to the roof of my mouth.

RATS' ALLEY
1939–1944

RACHEL HONAKER, 1939–1940

The week before I was to leave for nursing school, Dillon sat on the edge of my bed while I mended a pair of underdrawers. I would have died before I let any other boy watch, but I was glad to have Dillon there that night. Lately he had been cold with us all, not cruel, but distant.

"Don't go to school," he said abruptly. "Stay here."

"Don't be silly," I said. "Everything's settled."

"Mom says we're about to lose the Homeplace. She says the bank's coming for it any day now. How can you leave at a time like this?"

I stopped sewing. "Dillon, if I stayed home from school it wouldn't change one thing."

Dillon got up and shut the bedroom door, then sat close beside me on the bed. "I love your daddy, but he's a weak man. If he had some

backbone, things wouldn't have gone as far as they have."

"That's mean of you to say. Daddy has put food on your table."

"And I'm beholden, even though I don't like to be. He's a good man. But he aint a fighter. Me and you, we're different. I got a hunting rifle. Anybody sets foot on the Homeplace to take it, we'll defend what's ours."

"You can't just shoot somebody!"

"I can if they try to take this land."

"You're talking crazy and I won't humor it. I'm going to school, and that's that."

He turned away. "If you leave, I'll never speak to you again."

His talk had alarmed me, but I thought he was mostly just letting off steam. His face, though, had grown so hard and stubborn that I became angry.

"It's my life, not yours," I said.

He came off the bed so suddenly I bounced and stabbed my finger with the needle. "You got no right to the Homeplace!" he yelled. "You don't deserve it!" Then he noticed the bead of blood on my fingertip. "It's the finger you broke," he said. He took my hand and gripped my finger tight so the bead grew larger, then put my finger to his lips and sucked. A shiver started in my toes and traveled the length of my body. When he stopped my finger throbbed but the flesh was white and the bleeding was done.

He dropped my hand. "That's the last thing I'll do for you," he said. He avoided me the rest of the week.

My sister Jane and her husband sent fifty-six dollars for uniforms and books, my father gave me two dollars spending money, and I set out over Johnnycake Mountain. I said goodbye to Aunt Carrie the night before, and she gave me her copy of *Gray's Anatomy* as a present. When I asked after Dillon she said, "He's squirrel hunting."

"I reckon I'll get no goodbye from him," I said.

She shook her head. "No. Dillon don't know how to say goodbye proper, not when it's something he cares about."

Later, Mother stood at the bedroom door and watched me pack.

"I want you to go," she said, "but not to that nursing school."

She'd made her feelings known to me on a number of occasions. Nursing was a common, nasty occupation, fine for Carrie who was always wild and headstrong, but the odors and sick, naked people could not be pleasant for the lady she wanted me to be. It didn't help when I said I wanted to be a stewardess.

"I read about stewardesses," she'd said. "Men take all kinds of liberties with them. What do you expect, a woman who will fly all over creation?"

"I can handle a forward man," I said.

"Can you? What do you know about it?"

"Aunt Carrie has told me," I said, and could have bit my tongue right off. I hastened to add, "I'm sorry, but I know you don't like to talk about such things, so I asked her."

"I love Carrie," she said softly, "but I hope you'll not do as she did. She picked a hard row to hoe, and she's still yet paying the price, alone, and raising a boy that's turned out wild as a buck. You don't want that, nor to traipse all the world round. You want to marry quality."

Then she proceeded to tell me about men, how they are only after one thing, and once they have it they will leave a girl high and dry.

"What about Father? Did he only want one thing?"

"Ben Honaker married a virgin." Her cheeks were flushed red, and I blushed too because I had never heard her use such a word. "Do you think he'd have married me otherwise, and him a respectable man? Most men will try to take advantage of you, it's in their nature, even the best of them. But if you say no, they'll see there's no choice but to marry, or else forget about you. A man of quality wants a girl who's pure."

And that was all we said to each other. Next morning she stood on the porch and kissed me on the cheek. She wiped her eyes on her apron, went back inside, and left me standing. Father had hired the postmaster's son to drive me to Justice, and they put my suitcase in the back seat of the car. Dillon was nowhere to be seen. I hugged Aunt Carrie, climbed into the car, and we drove away.

I did lose the Homeplace when I went to school, and it had nothing to do with banks or coal companies. It was the inevitable loss known by those who are not tied to the same patch of earth for all their days. I mourned but I could not say I had done wrong. Land is so fragile— it can be taken by flood or fire or a piece of banker's paper—that it is best to build a life inside oneself that can be planted anywhere and held onto until the last breath.

It was with this hope that I arrived at the Grace Hospital on the mountaintop above Justice town. The building was yellow brick with small dark windows and the look of the warehouses that lined Back Street along the Levisa. An alley that stank of garbage bins separated the hospital from the Nurses' Home, where the students lived. We gathered in the lounge for soda pops and sandwiches, frightened country girls from West Virginia and Kentucky away from home for the first time. Miss Kurtz, a short, stocky woman, was the new director of nursing students. She introduced herself by saying she was from Pittsburgh and had come to the mountains to do her mission work. She held a heavy book against her chest.

"This is Arnold Toynbee's *Study of History,*" she said. "Arnold Toynbee is a British historian, one of the preeminent scholars of our day. And why should young nursing students be familiar with Arnold Toynbee? Because Professor Toynbee has written about these Appalachian Mountains."

She looked around the room, then began to read. " 'The Scotch-Irish immigrants who have forced their way into these natural fast-nesses have come to be isolated from the rest of the World. The Appalachian Mountain People are at this day not better than barbarians. They are the American counterparts of the latter-day White barbarians of the Old World, the Kurds and the Pathans and the Hairy Ainu.' " Miss Kurtz shut the book. "If you are to make nurses, you must overcome your backgrounds. You must rise above the handicaps of inbreeding and the filthy living conditions you are used to. At this hospital, we expect you to keep yourselves clean."

I sat angry and shamed, wishing I could say something, but I had been taught not to backtalk a teacher. The girl beside me raised her hand. Miss Kurtz looked at her over her glasses.

"Excuse me, ma'am, but what's a Hairy Ainu?"

"Well," said Miss Kurtz after a slight hesitation, "I'm not sure I know or want to know."

"I just wondered because my cousins over on Greasy Creek, they're all inbred like you said, and they're cross-eyed and they got hair all over their bodies, even on their penises. I just wondered if they might be part Hairy Ainu?"

This was the first I saw of Tommie Justice, who was little and blonde and appeared to be twelve years old. You would look at Tommie and never believe she'd heard of a penis, much less say the word out loud to the director of nursing students. Some teachers would have taken her head off, innocent-looking or not, but Miss Kurtz acted faint. She said, "You will please not use the word 'penis' in that manner."

"I thought it was a medical term, ma'am," said Tommie.

"—and not to be used casually," Miss Kurtz said and changed the subject. But her voice held a tremor during the rest of her talk. We knew her then for a coward.

Tommie took other occasions to make her look like a fool. Miss Kurtz taught anatomy. She would stand beside the hanging skeleton and hold up its arm like it was an old friend, fingering the carpals and metacarpals familiarly while we called out their names. She had just explained that the narrow pelvis indicated the skeleton had been a man when Tommie raised her hand and, wrapping one blonde curl around her finger, asked what had happened to the bone in the piece of anatomy she wasn't supposed to mention casually. While Miss Kurtz turned red and we snickered into our hands, Tommie added, "Excuse me, ma'am, but it has to be stiff for a man to have sex. Medically speaking, of course, if it's not a bone in there, what is it?"

So Miss Kurtz had to explain in a strangled voice how a penis got hard. And Tommie, face solemn, said yes she understood now, and of course a bone made no sense anyway because how would a man put his pants on. Miss Kurtz would have loved to kick Tommie out, but Tommie made good grades and her grandfather gave lots of money to the nursing school.

Three girls left school the first week, and by month's end, ten were gone. Homesickness took them away. It is something you see often in the mountains, for we are tied to kin and land as closely as any people ever were. It is a belief we have, as strong as any religion, that home can be preserved forever and life made everlasting if we only stay put. And school was not like home. The teachers, even those kinder than Miss Kurtz, were there to goad us on, to judge and criticize, where many of us had known only petting and praise. I felt it myself, the sweet anguished longing for home and for those who loved me without judgment that made me cry in my pillow at night. But I never thought of going back. I could not return as only Rachel Honaker, daughter of Ben and Flora. I must be able to call myself by some other name. All I knew of nursing was what I knew of Aunt Carrie, that her work took her into homes up and down Grapevine and into the lives of other people, that it made her a party to a mysterious body of knowledge, like an initiate in a secret society. I wanted that life. I wanted to be Clara Barton and Florence Nightingale and Edith Cavell all wrapped up in one, to fly around the world and return to become the comforter of every sick soul on every creek in the mountains, and I wanted to be married as well, to a brave man whose face had not yet come clear to me. Silly dreams, but they kept me in school.

So I tried not to think about the Homeplace, tried to lose myself in my studies. We were dissecting cadavers sent up to us from St. Mary's Hospital in Huntington. The gray flesh wept clear liquid around the edge of my scalpel, and formaldehyde scalded the inside of my nose. But what bothered me was to think the gutted corpse on the slab had no people, no one to put it in the ground and weep hot tears, no one to shield it from the uneasy wise cracks of eighteen-year-old girls. Tommie Justice worked with me. She wrinkled her nose and said, "Lord, didn't you reckon a uterus would be bigger than that? It looks like an old woman's pocketbook that wouldn't hold a handful of change, much less a baby." And I wanted to stuff that flimsy uterus back inside that poor woman and haul her off to the Homeplace cemetery for a decent burial.

In the hospital I saw people dying, their loved ones gathered around them. Death would not come as a surprise; everyone was waiting for it, expectant. And yet when the chest stopped heaving and the arm fell limp, the cries of those left behind always held a note of astonishment. So I waited to hear that the Homeplace was gone, reconciled myself to it, but when I was called out of pharmacy class with the news that my father was waiting in the parlor at the Nurses' Home, I stopped in the alley and found myself trembling.

My father stood beside the coal stove looking small and thin and cold. He hugged me tight about the shoulders, squeezing then letting go then squeezing again.

"The Homeplace is gone, honey. It's gone."

I started to cry against his chest.

"It happened two weeks ago. I didn't write because I didn't want to upset you any sooner than you had to be."

I wished I'd known. It was two weeks I'd been thinking of home as though there still was such a place, dreaming on a lie. But it was like him to wait to tell me. He never was easy with pain and hated to inflict it.

"The store's gone too," he said. "Your mother and your Aunt Carrie are settled in a little house at Henryclay. It will do for the time being. I'm on my way to get work."

I wiped my eyes and led him to the settee. "Can't you teach like you used to?"

"No, honey. They've got different rules now. You need a college degree."

"You're not going in the mines?" It was the question I dreaded to ask. I couldn't imagine him in the mines. He was too gentle, with no hard edges to him. I thought the mountains would recognize such softness in a man and crush him as soon as he set foot in a tunnel.

"I thought on it," he said. "I can't do it. I can't go down in a hole. But there isn't much else around here. So I'm jumping a freight train, going to Norfolk."

"What's in Norfolk?"

"Shipyards. They're begging for men. That war in Europe, you know. I'll send for your mother after I get on my feet. I doubt your Aunt Carrie will move. By then I reckon she and your mother will be sick of one another. They've not got on well lately." He looked away. "There's no money for your train ticket at Christmas. Can you batch it here?"

My first Christmas away from home. But there was no home anyway. I nodded. "Don't you worry about me. I can go home with someone from school." Then I said, cautiously, "You haven't mentioned Dillon."

"It's what else I had to tell you. Dillon is gone, too. Run away the day before the bank foreclosed. He was talking crazy about standing off the bankers with a gun, so your Aunt Carrie took and hid his hunting rifle. Next morning he was gone. He left a note, said he'd not be there when it happened. Left a letter for you, too. I brought it."

He took the envelope from his coat pocket. The paper was wrinkled and smudged with ink. Dillon was never one for neatness.

"Rachel," he wrote, "you are a coward for leaving. And now I am as big a coward. I could have stayed and fought if you would have. But if you don't want it, why should I?"

He didn't say "Dear Rachel." He didn't say "Love, Dillon." There were only the hard words and the smudges. I crumpled the paper and put it in my uniform pocket. Damn you, I thought, I cannot even mourn without you adding to my burden.

Father was looking at me.

"He's feeling hard," I said.

"It's one reason your mother and Aunt Carrie have been at it. Your mother told Aunt Carrie that Dillon was brought up poorly."

"Mother doesn't care for Dillon," I said.

"No. He's kin so she loves him, but she'd rather him be at a distance. She told me there's something about him that frights her."

Me too, I thought, but I didn't say it out loud. I wasn't sure if I was frightened of him or frightened for him. We sat for a while. Father's hair was grayer than I recalled and the skin on his hands was spotted and loose. I talked him into staying for supper at the Nurses' Home and slipped him some extra fried chicken from the kitchen. Then he left for the railyard, passed under a streetlight, and disappeared into the darkness. I fled to my room. The mountains on the Kentucky side were black beneath a full moon, and clouds moved across the sky like spirits rising and departing from the land.

When Tommie Justice teased Miss Kurtz about penises stiff as bones, she spoke from experience. She had a weakness for the minor league baseball players who came to Justice town every spring and

summer, and to hear her talk she had seen every stiff penis that ever
wore Cardinal red. Tommie's grandfather owned most of the nearby
town of Annadel, West Virginia, as well as the Justice baseball team.
But it was her dead father who brought Tommie and me close. One
day I met her coming out of the five-and-ten downtown and we
walked back to the Nurses' Home together. We'd not said two words
to one another before, because I was shy and slow to make friends.
When we passed the stone county courthouse on the hill with its coat
of dark ivy, Tommie said, "My daddy was shot right there on those
courthouse steps. My mom was just pregnant with me, didn't even
know I was on the way."

I stopped walking. Aunt Carrie's stories, told before the Homeplace hearth, ran through my head. I could look at the stone steps
carved into the hill and see men in black suits and hats waiting at the
top with their hands inside their coats.

"Your daddy was police chief at Annadel," I said. "He was protect-
ing the miners' families from the company guards and killed some
company men in a shootout. The other company men shot him on
those steps on his way to trial."

Tommie's face quickened. "How did you know?"

"My Aunt Carrie was married to the preacher that was shot alongside your daddy."

So we had that between us, bloody family history. As we walked
up the hill she linked her arm through mine. "I aint known what to
make of you. You're such a pretty little thing but so quiet. I thought
maybe you had your nose in the air."

By November Tommie's roommate had left for homesickness and
I moved in with her. It was a corner room on the third floor of the
Nurses' Home. From our window we could see the rooftops of Justice like terraces descending to the stone and brick buildings downtown. Early in the mornings, the distant mountains of Kentucky
emerged from the fog like they were being born anew each day. Our
room held two narrow iron beds and two dressers painted black. The
window trim was black as well, for the trainyards in the bottom were
always busy with gondolas of coal switching tracks, coupling and
uncoupling, and each bang and crash sent clouds of black dust over

the town and up the mountain. Our windowpanes were streaked, and if we slept with the windows open, we woke to a fine dusting of black on our white pillows.

Tommie told me stories about her hometown of Annadel, which had once been a wild place famed for union politics and whorehouses, but she said it had quieted down considerably. The newspaper had been shut down by the government, her grandfather's hotel was closed, and only a few beer joints and one whorehouse were left to maintain Annadel's reputation. I told Tommie about Dillon, how a union organizer named Rondal Lloyd who'd lived in Annadel made Aunt Carrie pregnant out of wedlock.

"I heard my mommie talk about that man," Tommie said. "They say he was a devil with the women."

Then I talked some more about Dillon until Tommie finally said, "He sounds like a sweetie. Maybe you ought to spark him."

"He's my first cousin," I reminded her.

"Aint you heard tell of kissing cousins?" When I didn't laugh, she shrugged. "That's too bad, though."

Tommie teased me about being a virgin and kept asking me to double date with her. "I feel sorry for the fellow you end up marrying," she'd say. "You aint going to know diddley." She started me thinking. But while she talked, it was as though my mother heard, even at a distance, and wrote to warn me to behave myself and only attend the Methodist or Episcopal or Presbyterian churches as those were the places where gentlemen of quality worshiped. I read her letters fast and threw them in the trash, wanted to write her and say, "Mother, I am a grown woman, so please mind your own business." But I wanted a husband, and even more, I longed to have children. It was what every woman wanted, I thought. And Mother was older than Tommie and married and knew better how to get married and raise a family. So I wouldn't go with Tommie.

Then she got a new beau, one she seemed serious about. His name was Arthur Lee Sizemore, and he worked in the business office of the American Coal Company. I met him one Sunday afternoon when we were allowed to sit in the first floor parlor with our young men. He had a way of holding tight onto Tommie's elbow that I didn't care for, but Tommie liked him. She said he came up hard, one of twelve children from Jolo, and put himself through school in Huntington, so poor he ate only milk gravy for days on end. I thought that might account for his pasty complexion; Tommie approvingly called him "pale."

"He's a coming-on young man, everybody says so." She sat on the edge of her bed that night, black leather shoes dangling off the ends of her toes, and smoked a Lucky Strike. "You know, I aint even slept with Arthur Lee yet. I will, but not till he's good and hooked." So I thought Mother must be partly right after all. Tommie opened her mouth and swallowed some smoke. "He's got a friend. Want to go out with us?"

I sat slumped against my desk and idly flipped the pages of my chemistry book. "Who's that?"

"Bookkeeper for the coal company. Older man, twenty-seven. Dark and handsome." She grinned. "Italian."

"Italian! Good lord! I've never even met an Italian!"

"They say they're the sweetest men. Honey, you aint never heard tell of Rudolph Valentino?"

I had to admit I was intrigued. It was something different. "What's his name?"

"Tony Angelelli."

I think I said yes because of his name, it was that pretty. And maybe because I knew Mother would have conniption fits. He turned out to have black curly hair, a round fleshy face, and what Tommie called bedroom eyes. I decided if he had a mustache, he'd look like a short Clark Gable. We went to see *The Wizard of Oz* at the Pocahontas Theater and sat in the back row under the balcony. About the time Judy Garland stepped into full color he took my hand and scraped one fingernail across my palm. Tommie and Arthur Lee were already necking. Tony tugged on my hand, and I ducked my head toward him. "I don't know you very well," I whispered. He nodded and sat quietly, scratching my palm and seeming perfectly content with that. I had to admit he had nice fingernails and a backscratch would have felt just fine. I wondered if that meant I was falling in love.

He asked me out again, by ourselves. We went to see *Stagecoach*.

Rats' Alley, 1939–1944

After two dates and two movies we still hadn't talked much, just sat in expectant silence while the flow of light played over our faces, then he had to take me back to the Nurses' Home for curfew. Finally we went to *Gone with the Wind* and the line was so long we had to converse.

"Do you like your job?" I asked.

"Sure."

"What do you do?"

He smiled and his face glowed golden from the running marquee lights. "Look after the company's money." He explained a little about bookkeeping, then fell silent again. He didn't ask me about nursing school. That was all right, I thought, the woman was supposed to draw out the man. If he wouldn't talk, it was my fault. On the way home I kept trying, asked him more questions. He usually answered "yes" or "no," or, if that wasn't appropriate, he shrugged and smiled. His round face looked jolly when he smiled. At the front door I let him kiss me. It was my first kiss and I liked it.

After we'd dated for a month Tony took me to meet his mother, who lived in Number Ten bottom. I thought it would be an adventure, for the coalfields seemed exotic to me. Justice town, with its narrow curving streets and stone buildings decked out with carved gargoyles and other folderols, and the stone walls and bridges carved by Italian masons, reminded me of pictures of European hill cities I had seen in library books. At main Davidson there was a Russian church with an onion-shaped dome of gold leaf. And when we drove Tony's green Pontiac around the mountain above Number Ten, a sharp loop in the road brought a sea of headstones with floating stone crosses into view. We parked at the foot of the hill and walked past the graves at the edge of Number Ten bottom. The tombstones held photographs of people set beneath ovals of glass. I didn't see a word of English on the stones, and sometimes I didn't even recognize the alphabet for it was all cut sharp and turned backwards.

The house of Tony's mother seemed just as strange. It was dark inside, the windows hung with heavy brocade curtains and kept shut even in daytime. The walls were covered with dozens of crucifixes, calendars, and pictures of Franklin Roosevelt, the Virgin Mary, and the Pope. The wallpaper was peeling, the top layer adorned with roses the size of my hand and bright purple peeping from underneath. Heavy plastic covered all the furniture so that you stuck to it if you sat very long. I preferred the kitchen because of its odors. I had smelled nothing like it, and only later came to identify the garlic, the oregano, the olive oil.

Tony's mother was short and stout, with breasts that sagged to her waist beneath a yellow satin dress. She spoke little English, and so she chattered in Italian while we ate fresh bread from the oven with melted butter. Tony didn't talk much. His mother kept looking at me and I gathered she was not impressed. She never smiled and waved her arms while she held a wooden spoon, like she wanted to hit me with it.

"Capisce?" she said, after each long speech. "Capisce?"

"Yeah, yeah," Tony answered.

On the way home I asked Tony what she'd said about me.

He smiled. "She said you're too skinny. She said you must not know how to cook."

"She said more than that."

He shrugged.

"Is she a good cook?"

"Oh yeah," he said proudly. "She used to work at Ricco's Bakery in town, and before that she cooked for rich people in the old country. I take care of her now so she don't have to work. I got a good job."

"That's nice of you," I said.

"Yeah," he agreed. "She's scared if I get married I won't be able to afford to take care of her."

"I think your wife would understand," I said.

He smiled and squeezed my hand.

He wouldn't say much else about his family. But Arthur Lee Sizemore told me Tony's father and uncles were all killed at the same time in the big Number Six explosion, when Tony was a little boy. Tony's grandmother moved in with Tony and his mother, but she had lost her mind and kept scavenging coal at mine sites and piling it in the back yard, trying to move all the coal in the world off the never-found bodies of her sons, so she was finally sent to the state asylum. I decided Tony was kind, a good son, and if he was too silent it was because the gift of words had been shocked early from him.

Tommie wore saddle oxfords and a green fishtail coat with a skirt that swayed when she walked. When we went downtown sometimes I fell a step or two behind just so I could watch her coat. She'd turn her head and say "Come on, slowpoke," and I'd pretend to be interested in whatever was in the window of the store we were passing.

In those days there were plenty of stores in Justice town, for the mines were booming, thanks to the war. Nobody minded the war because we weren't fighting it, just making a living from it. According to what we heard from Europe, there wasn't much happening in early 1940 anyway. The streets of Justice were filled with endless lines of cars, and you couldn't walk without bumping into somebody. Barbershop poles twirled and neon beer signs blinked, the yellow lights on the theater marquee flowed like a waterfall, and red passenger trains clanked through the middle of town and pulled into the brick station at the foot of the hill. On a brisk March day when the air was like a sheet of ice about to crack, it was hard to stay inside and study.

On just such a Saturday afternoon we sat at a round table in the Flat Iron Drugstore and drank cherry cokes that Tommie bought. She always treated because I never had any money, and I paid her back by ironing her uniforms. We sat giggling and talking low to ourselves because we had just started giving baths to men and it was new enough that we thought it was funny. Then I heard my name and across the room Dillon stood up. I went toward him, not sure if I meant to slap him or hug him until he caught me in his arms and held me tight.

"How dare you?" I grabbed his shirt in tight bunches between my fists and buried my face against his chest. "How dare you worry us sick and blame me for it?"

"Don't be mad," he said. "Aint you missed me?"

"I thought about you every day," I said. He smiled.

I took him over to our table and introduced him to Tommie, who fairly twinkled at him.

"You're Rondal Lloyd's boy," she said.

"How'd you know that?" He looked at me like I'd let out some big secret.

"I told her. She's my friend. And Isom Justice was her daddy."

He looked at her differently then, softer. "Isom Justice was my daddy's best buddy," he said.

"I know," Tommie said. "I heard all the stories."

I'd had enough of small talk. I grabbed his arm and pulled him down onto a chair. "Where have you been?"

"I been with my daddy's people on Blackberry Creek. Over yonder's my cousin Brigham and his buddy."

We moved to a bigger table and waved for them to join us. They were miners. You could tell by their cracked and blackened fingernails and something about their skin that seemed rough and rubbed up in the light and the way they moved, tender and wary as cats. I knew because it was all we saw at the hospital, miners sick and miners hurt and miners visiting their sick kin. These two were older than Dillon, in their twenties. Brigham Lloyd was stocky, with thick black eyebrows at a slant and a V-shaped hairline. His buddy Homer Day was skinny with a shock of curly brown hair. They were smoking Camels and shared them with Dillon and Tommie.

"This is Rachel?" Brigham said. "You look like Ingrid Bergman. Homer, don't she look the spitting image of Ingrid Bergman?" He nodded at Tommie. "And you're Gladys Justice's girl up to Annadel. She's a good woman."

"I know you," Tommie said. "I see you in the drugstore at Annadel."

"That's right. And you'd see me in Ruby's Lounge if you went in such places."

"Maybe I do see you there," Tommie said. They laughed. I knew she didn't go in Ruby's Lounge, but she wouldn't be assumed about.

Dillon sat smoking and watching me. "You're not mining coal?" I asked.

"Naw!" said Brigham before Dillon could speak. "He tried to get hired on but I told the boss he wasn't old enough."

Dillon looked away and flicked his cigarette. "I'm pumping gas at Annadel. It's dull as hell. I'm thinking I might go off and fight in the war. I don't care for that Hitler."

"Time enough to go in the mines," Brigham continu
"Goddamn mines. Boy's smart he'll never go in."

"Aw, hit aint so bad." Homer Day grinned. "Good mone
now."

I wished that everyone else would go away. "Dillon, where are you
living?"

"I'm at Number Five. I'm boarding with Brigham. His wife just
left him and he's got room."

"It's not ten miles from here," I said. "I can't believe you've been so
close."

"I started once or twice to come see you. But I needed some time
first."

"Why?"

He shrugged and didn't answer.

Tommie was looking at her watch. "I got to run and get ready,"
she told me. "Arthur Lee's taking me dancing tonight. You going out
with Tony?"

"No. He's in Bluefield on business."

"I aint going back with you boys." Dillon looked at Brigham and
Homer. "I'll thumb a ride home tonight. Why don't you go on?"

"Suit yourself," Brigham said.

And then they were all gone and Dillon bought me another cherry
coke. "Let's go to a movie," he said. "Let's get a hamburger and then
go to a movie."

"I haven't got money. Not even for a postage stamp to write Mother."

"I got money. I make a dollar a day now and Brigham don't take
much of it."

The movie was *Wuthering Heights* with Laurence Olivier and
Merle Oberon. Tommie had read in a movie magazine that they hated
each other and Merle Oberon told Laurence Olivier he made her sick,
but you'd never have known it. When Cathy died standing up in
Heathcliff's arms, looking out that window, I cried. It was the best
movie I'd ever seen, better even than *Gone with the Wind.* Then when
Heathcliff died and found Cathy on the moors I glanced at Dillon,
and his eyes gleamed wet in the movie light. I never knew a boy to cry
at a movie, and I looked away quickly so he wouldn't know I'd seen
him.

Afterward we sat on a stone bench on the courthouse lawn high above the town, in the shadow of the trees. Justice showed so many lights it looked like a big city, at least I could imagine it was.

Dillon sat with his legs straight out in front of him and his hands at his sides, holding onto the edge of the bench like he might fall off.

"Who's Tony?"

"A fellow. A friend of Tommie's boyfriend."

"I mean what's his whole name?" When I told him, he said, "He's bookkeeper at Jenkinjones."

He sounded like a lawyer after a witness.

"That's right."

"I don't like him," Dillon said.

"Do you know him?"

"Not personal. But I know of him. I pump his gas. He's too soft. They aint nothing there that I can tell."

"I don't think it's fair to judge somebody you don't know. I like him. He's polite and he's never been nothing but a gentleman to me."

"He's got another girl. I seen them together in Annadel not two weeks ago."

My stomach turned over at that, because Tony had said there was no one else, but I tried to sound calm. "We don't have an understanding yet."

"Do you love him?"

I hesitated. It was a question I'd asked myself and not yet answered. "I don't know. He's hard to get to know because he doesn't talk much. But he's had a hard life and I feel sorry for him. And I like it when he kisses me."

"You can't let him kiss you!"

He grabbed my wrist. I tried to pull my hand away and he gripped it harder.

"You don't have to break my bones in two!"

He dropped my hand like it was red hot. "I aint meaning to hurt you."

Then he had hold of my hand again like he wasn't even thinking what he was doing. I could only see one side of his face. It was screwed up like he was in pain.

"You can't kiss nobody but me. I love you! I always loved you!"

I stared at him. "You can't," I whispered.

He leaned over and kissed me on the mouth and the tip of his tongue flicked mine, tasted fresh as a sprig of mint. He pushed against me, one leg between mine, pressed me against the back of the bench. I threw my arms around him and held on tight. He opened his mouth against my neck, tore the top button from my blouse and slipped his hand inside.

"I want to make love to you," he said in my ear and I felt my body molten like Tommie said it would be.

"Dillon, we're first cousins. We couldn't have babies, there might be something wrong with them. And we can't marry, it's against the law."

"Hell with the law and hell with marriage. We're above all that, me and you. We can make love this very night."

"No! It's trashy! It's sinful and ugly!"

"Don't say that!" He kissed me again. "Don't you like that?"

"Yes!" I turned my face away from him. "No!"

He put his hand under my skirt, between my thighs. I tried to run away, but he grabbed hold of my wrist and pulled me to my knees, twisting my arm and ripping the sleeve of my blouse, knelt beside me, and wrapped his arms around me. I struggled to free myself.

"Let me go!" I tugged at his arms. "Don't force me, Dillon, or I'll hate you forever!"

"Don't say that!"

He loosened his grip and I pushed him away, managed to stand up. I felt my body return cold and hard and unyielding, and a wave of shame overwhelmed me. I tried to catch my breath and started to sob.

"You got no right to do me like this," I said.

He stayed where he was, sprawled on the ground, his face covered by one arm.

"I only wanted to love you," he whispered. "I thought it was what you wanted too."

"You hurt my arm. You treat me like I'm someone cheap. You—" I searched for anything to say to keep me from running to him, "you're bad as any hillbilly trash from the head of the holler. Mother always said so."

He turned his face toward the moonlight. It was frozen into something like the cadavers I'd seen in the morgue.

"I don't care for nobody who says such things about their people," he said. "If you believe that, then go to hell."

I left him and walked up the hill. When I reached the Nurses' Home I looked back toward the courthouse. He was gone.

The first week in April I received two letters. One was from my father, postmarked Hampton Roads, Virginia. It was three pages long and between each page was a worn dollar bill, smooth and precious like a dried leaf.

The second letter was from Aunt Carrie. Dillon had gone to Canada and joined the British Army so he could fight in the war.

Don't blame me if you die, I thought. It will be your own fault.

CARRIE FREEMAN, 1940–1942

My boy Dillon joined the British Army, and he was stationed first near London. I could see him there for he has a face that is fine and sharp-featured like you would find in Dickens. His father was Welsh, a Lloyd, and I thought he might discover some of his people there. But before he could visit Wales, he was sent to Egypt and I could not imagine that. I kept a map of the world on my bedroom wall, and pins from Flora's sewing basket to show where he'd been and where he was. We listened to the radio for any mention of the British Eighth Army in North Africa. It was hard to get news. So many people did not care about the war except to keep America out, and Dillon's letters were censored, but I knew enough to tell he was suffering in the hot sun and in mortal danger. A mother knows that without being told.

· · ·

Rats' Alley, 1939–1944

We stayed in Kentucky while Ben worked the shipyards at Hampton Roads, but then Flora had her first stroke. I came back from delivering a baby at Kingdom Come to find her keeled over on the parlor carpet, her left hand drawn up tight beneath her chin and her eyes wide open. After a spell in the Grace Hospital with me and Rachel tending her, she came to herself but she will never talk and will have to sit a wheelchair the rest of her life. Ben came home and Rachel's friend Tommie Justice got him a job managing the company store at Jenkinjones coal camp in West Virginia. Tommie's fiancé was the new superintendent at the Jenkinjones mine, running the place for the American Coal Company. So we ended up on silkstocking row in a six-room house, much obliged for the kindness of younguns half our age.

The coal camps are strung along Blackberry Creek like beads on a necklace, and each looks much the same. Every house is painted white with black trim. Some of the houses hang from the hillsides, their fronts supported by fragile columns of brick and wood. Others sit in the creek bottom on streets of mud and red dog from the slate dumps, raised at four corners by short brick piles with space beneath the house for spare tires and sleeping dogs. Fences of wood and wire separate each house. In winter a truck comes from the mine and fills the coal houses in the corner of each yard so people can feed their stoves. Several times a day the black trains scream through the camps, and often the whistle at the mine blows for an accident. It is the same at Carbon, Davidson, Number Thirteen, Number Ten, Number Six, Number Five, Winco, Felco, and Jenkinjones. It has been the same since I can remember.

The first time I lived on Blackberry was 1917. Since then the main road has been paved for automobiles. There is a new coal camp called Number Thirteen on Lloyds Fork, and a country club on the hill overlooking it. It is strange to drive past the rusting tipple at Number Five, past the tumbledown camp at Winco, and come upon a nine-hole golf course taking up the bottom land. It is the only large patch of cut grass you see. The greens are shiny and clean like they've been washed. Men in bright plaid pants and caps stand on the greens. The golf course is built up both sides of Lloyds Fork between Number

Thirteen and Winco, and a curved white footbridge connects the two halves. The railroad runs along the mountainside beyond the golf course fence, and a towering bridge of wood and black steel siding carries the coal trains over the course where Lloyds Fork joins Blackberry Creek. I asked Ben who ever plays golf, and he said doctors and lawyers, store owners and coal operators from Justice town. Arthur Lee Sizemore told Ben he should learn to play, but Ben said he is too old and he cannot get used to the idea of working so hard to go home empty-handed.

Jenkinjones, where we live, is the poorest of the camps. There is no bottom land and the houses are squeezed together along a creek so narrow you can cross it in two strides. The paved road ends abruptly at a wall of steep mountainside. You can bear left past the company store and follow a narrow dirt road up the side of Trace Mountain past the tipple and portals. As you climb Trace you see the side of the mountain below is covered with black slate from the mine. Smoke rises from it, for slate burns when you make a pile of it. The fire will burn for years and cannot be put out. The black pile is streaked orange with charred slate, which we call red dog. It smells acrid, like singed raw sewage, and on a damp morning the stench fills the camp. You can only get away from it by rising above it toward the clean fog on Trace Mountain.

The company store Ben manages is red brick with stone steps and a wide porch. Inside it has a green linoleum floor, hanging ceiling fans, and a skylight. Clothes and shoes are on the left behind glass cases, and furniture is on the right. Groceries are at the rear, and a soda fountain. You can sit and sip your sodapop and smell the blood from the butcher's block. Ben seemed happy enough the first week, but on Friday he came home quiet, his face drawn and old looking. He sat and watched while I fed Flora her supper.

"I had to draw off the men's pay today," he said. I knew what was coming for I'd lived in the camps. I nodded and kept spooning mashed potatoes. "Had to go to that Italian bookkeeper with the store accounts and watch while he took what the men owed the store out of the pay envelopes. Lot of them envelopes was left empty. Ones that did have something in them, it was company money."

"Scrip," I said. They would be large coins with an American flag and "American Coal Company" stamped on each side.

"There're two families I can't sell groceries to this week. Owe too much on into next week's pay. It's the women come buy the food and I got to tell them they can't have it. The Italian bookkeeper says it's too bad but it's not our lookout." He stood up and walked around, sat back down.

"Reckon this is one store I won't ruin with loose credit," he said.

Ben still called Tony Angelelli the "Italian bookkeeper," even though he was courting Rachel and had come to dinner several times. It was a long time before Rachel brought Tony for a visit, because Flora didn't approve of her daughter keeping company with an Italian. Rachel asked me to talk to her mother.

"I can't argue with her now that she's crippled," Rachel said. "She wins without a fight."

I started to say, Rachel, you never could argue with her, but I let it pass. It was true Flora was even more difficult since her stroke. She had always been a gentle person on the surface, quiet and even tempered. But she had her own ideas she held to fiercely, her own notions of what was good and proper, especially where Rachel was concerned. She knew how to get what she wanted. Now she had lost her weapons. The sweet voice had been replaced by a hideous grunting rasp, the self-effacing gesture that invited compliance had become a withered shrunken arm that was hard to look upon. Flora responded to these changes with a bad grace and a stubborn, sour disposition.

I spoke to her about Tony while I was feeding her her breakfast. I had the upper hand, towering over her wielding spoonfuls of oatmeal. She knew it and resented it.

"It's not right to be prejudiced against Rachel's young man just because he's Italian," I said. "You ought to judge him on his own merits."

Oatmeal dribbled from the corner of her twisted mouth. I wiped it away with a damp cloth. She rolled her eyes like she had something to say and I gave her a pad and pencil. She wrote in a shaky left hand, "They are not clean people."

I started to say, How many Italians do you know? But Rachel was right. You cannot reason with someone whose every answer is so laboriously given and whose mind will not be changed because stubbornness is the last refuge of her strength. I gave it up.

Ben didn't care for Tony either. "There's something wrong with the boy," he said. "Although I shouldn't say boy, because he's ten years older than her. Too old."

"Age isn't important," I said. "It's love that counts."

"Love." Ben smiled a tight-lipped smile. "She doesn't love him."

I still thought he was as prejudiced as Flora until I met Tony Angelelli. Then I knew he was one of those damaged people who look perfectly fine on the outside, smiling and pleasant, but there is something missing inside. At first I thought him a person incapable of love. As time passes I see he is something even more tragic—he will care, on rare occasions in his life, but he cannot say it or show it or perhaps even acknowledge it to himself. He will hurt because he is not loved in return, but he will not know why he hurts. He is like a telephone whose cord has been cut and you scream into the dead receiver and hear only silence.

On the Sunday of Pearl Harbor, we were at the table eating fried chicken when Arthur Lee Sizemore telephoned, said, "Y'all turn on the radio," and hung up. As the radio voice, crying out above sirens and explosions, described the swarming Japanese bombers, the battleships become infernos, we stood up, left the table, and gathered around the dome of the radio. Only Tony sat, still gnawing the gristle from a chicken bone. He broke it in two and sucked on it. Ben turned to watch him.

"Son, is that all you can do?"

Tony laughed as though surprised. "Might as well." He moved his chair closer to the radio, chicken leg in hand, and kept eating with a foolish smile on his face.

Ben looked at me, then went out on the porch and sat in the swing.

I went to Rachel's room that night. She sat brushing her hair before the mirror.

"What do you see in Tony?" I asked.

She set down the brush and looked at her lap. "He's had a lot of sadness in his life," she said. "He wants looking after."

"You look after your patients and your younguns, when you have them," I said. "Don't marry Tony. You deserve better."

"Maybe I won't have any other chances. I don't see any other men coming around."

"Don't talk foolish. You've got your whole life ahead of you. Anyway, no marriage is better than an unhappy marriage. A woman can make a life for herself."

"A lonely life."

"Some of the loneliest people in the world are married women," I said. "Your momma's fancy magazines may not tell you that, but it's true."

She started brushing her hair again, with her head ducked down. "I was thinking of breaking up with him anyway. Dillon said Tony's seeing someone in Bluefield, and Tommie told me it's true. Arthur Lee told her. He said Tony proposed to the woman so she'd go to bed with him. I asked Tony and he denied it, but I know he's lying."

"It's just as well to find it out now. It shows what he is."

"Maybe all men are like that," she said coldly.

"No," I said.

"Wasn't Dillon's daddy?" She looked at me so straight and hard I had to fight back the urge to slap her. She knew it and grabbed my wrist. "Don't hate me!"

"I don't hate you, child. Not ever. I loved Dillon's daddy better than anyone in this world. Still he was a hard man to live with. If he hadn't been paralyzed I'd have kicked him out. No, that's not right, he'd have left on his own. He dreaded to be close to someone."

"Dillon's something like that. He'll try to hold someone so close he'll squeeze the life from them. But it's not because he needs them. He just wants to claim them."

"And when you pushed him away, he couldn't bear to be around you and he left to punish you."

"How did you know?" she whispered.

"Child, I've got eyes."

"It's impossible, what he wants. It's not right for cousins to love. I told him that and now he won't forgive me. He never writes. I don't know what's happening to him except what you tell me, and there's more I want to know but I'm afraid to ask."

"Ask me now."

"Does he have a girlfriend?"

"He hasn't mentioned a girlfriend."

"He'll find one," she said. Her voice was frantic. "I know he will. He'll forget about me."

"Isn't that what you want?"

Then she began to cry, not soft but loud and wild. I took her in my arms. Ben came to see what was wrong but I waved him away. When she could speak she said, "He'll get killed over there! I know he will!"

I touched her hair. "Pray God he won't." It was all I could say. He was still in Egypt and Rommel was closing in.

Pearl Harbor changed everything. Once we were into the war it was easy to forget that a lot of big shots like the president of American Coal in Philadelphia had been saying Hitler wasn't so bad, that he was fighting communism and the unions, and we might learn something from him. Once we were into the war, Hitler's buddies waved the flag and forgot they had said such things. Then I was proud of Dillon, because he got into the fight before such people. He hated the Fascists because that is the way I raised him and because it is his nature.

All the young people left. Arthur Lee Sizemore went into the army, and the old superintendent came out of retirement to run the mine. Tony Angelelli became an interpreter, stationed in North Africa until the invasion of Italy. Rachel claimed she didn't care he was gone. Tony had finally confessed about the girlfriend in Bluefield, and Rachel wouldn't see him anymore. Just as well, we all said, and breathed sighs of relief.

Rachel and Tommie graduated in the spring and signed up as army nurses. Together they caught the train for Fort Jackson, small and trim in new cotton suits, each clutching a suitcase. When a young woman is set for an adventure, a suitcase is a marvelous thing, so small yet full of all that is necessary for a life—clean underwear, earrings, a pretty nightgown, a book, and toothbrush and comb. I watched them stroll along the station platform, arm in arm, and I longed to go with them.

Rachel had not been gone a week, had just had time to send a postcard of South Carolina pine forests, when the yellow telegram arrived from the British Army. Regret to inform. Your son Dillon Freeman. Wounded in action. Will inform further.

I folded the telegram, laid it on top of the bureau, and waited.

Dillon came home with a limp from the bullet that shattered his leg above the knee. I met him at the train station in Justice. He was pale and thinner than I'd seen him since boyhood. He stumped along the platform on a single crutch, his uniform hanging on him like a sack. His first word, after he hugged me, was "Rachel?"

"Gone to the South Pacific. She's on a hospital ship this minute."

He clutched my shoulders and swayed slightly. "The Japanese have sunk hospital ships," he whispered.

"I know it."

"It's bad luck for her, water. She almost drowned at the Home-place."

"I recall."

He leaned back on his crutch. I thought he was falling and I grabbed his arm but he shook me off. Then he asked me how I was. I said there would be time to talk later, he was still weak and needed to get off his feet. I led him to the car.

The first week back he took to his bed with his face to the wall. He said his leg was not hurting terribly but he could not make himself get up. It had taken his mind's strength to get himself back across the ocean and he had nothing left. I coaxed him with chicken soup and cornbread. He ate a little but didn't say much.

I sat on the front porch swing on a new spring evening. A girl rode by standing on the pedals of a bicycle that was too large for her, bouncing over mud puddles and chunks of red dog. Dillon came onto the porch and sat beside me. He had a box of Falls City beer.

"First time you ever drank in front of me," I said. "I reckon my little boy is grown up."

"Ben brung it from the store. Wasn't happy about it but I reckon he figured a soldier is entitled to some vices. Want one?"

"No thank you. I never picked up a taste for it. Your daddy was the one for a beer."

I thought it pleased him that I mentioned his daddy, but he didn't say anything.

"Tell me what's wrong," I said.

He smiled briefly and sipped his beer, looked up and down the quiet street. "You can't sit here and know what it was like," he said.

"No. But I've seen some things in my time I don't like to talk about either."

"You never been in the desert," he said. "You don't know how the heat can make a man crazy, how he sees things that aint there." He shifted his weight and slowly straightened his bad leg. "We were coming off leave in Cairo, and they sent us to relieve a unit that had come under heavy fire and been pinned down for several days. When we found them boys, they was wild-eyed, hadn't had no sleep. While they was packing up, I went behind a burnt-out tank to take a crap. When I finished, next I seen was a fellow coming toward me. One of ours. His face was all black with grease and sweat and his helmet was gone. He was yelling stuff that didn't make no sense at all. He took his rifle off his shoulder. I raised my hand and said *Friend,* but he yelled, *Goddamn Kraut!* and aimed his rifle. I pulled my pistol out of my belt and dodged and took the bullet in my leg. Fired back and hit him in the thigh. Just wanted to stop him. He fell but then he raised back up and lifted the rifle again. So I killed him."

We stopped swinging back and forth and sat still. "No one would blame you," I said.

"Oh." He smiled. "I blame myself. He was an American, joined early like I did. But it aint him being an American that bothered me. Way I see it, an American aint no more valuable than any other human being in God's eyes. But I had a choice. It was him or me, him or me. I chose me." He drained the bottle of beer and opened another. "They said the fellow's best friend had his head blown off right in front of him, and he'd been on the verge of cracking all week. They was going to send him to the hospital in Cairo soon as they got some help. Nobody blamed me. I found out what I could about him. He was Ed McCamey from Centre Hall, Pennsylvania. Sounds like a damn estate, don't it, Centre Hall?"

"It happens in war," I said.

"Yes it does." He answered quick, like he was ready to agree with anything I said as a way to mock a mother's comfort. "And why did I choose me instead of him? Because that's the way people do, aint it? It's natural as breathing I should choose me so Carrie Freeman can sit on the porch with her son and Ed McCamey's mother can lay the flowers on the grave. You'd rather be setting right here, wouldn't you?"

I resolved to say nothing else. He finished another beer quickly and opened the third.

"You know what I done while I was laid up in the hospital? I read the Bible. Now that's something you aint known me to do, is it? You never thought of me as religious, and I aint in the church-going way. But I believe in God, and I believe they's a fire running through everything that lives. When that Bible starts throwing rules at me, I laugh, but when it tells how sin burns and says turn the other cheek and when God gets hung on that cross, buddy I'm right there. I chose me and that's sin. I aint no better than a goddamn Nazi. That's what they do, choose themselves. And the rich people that keep what they got, they do the same. It's sin and the only way you burn it out is to die. Only it don't work if you just die for yourself, it's got to be for somebody else."

I sat quiet. He drank two more beers without a word, and the dusk turned to heavy darkness.

"I'm going in the mines," he said.

"Why? To punish yourself?"

"You can call it that if you want to. I want to work with buddies that are like to die at any time, and me with them. I don't want to get separated from them. That's what happened to me in that desert. I got separated. That's Hell, don't you know."

"What about your leg?"

"It's healing. They'll take me, they're begging for men right now."

He found a cigarette in his shirt pocket and smoked it, looked at me sideways with his eyes at a squint like he dared me to talk him out of it. He should have known I was too practiced at letting go to take him up on it.

"Your cousin Brigham has married again and just got on at Number Thirteen mine," I said. "It's a new camp built since the war started. That union local is full of troublemakers because all the miners expect to make money now." I smiled. "Sounds right for you. You ought to get on there."

"I done asked," he said.

DILLON, 1943

In this place there is barely room to stand, and only four feet between us and a wall of rock. We were ready to load bone when a rumble like a train ran above our heads and long shards peeled off the roof. We just had time to make this hole. You can only see one wheel of Homer's buggy, mashed flat so it looks sculpted from a section of the floor. The buggy has been crushed beneath the roof fall.

I sit with my back against a seam of coal and my knees drawn up to my chest. Brigham sits beside me, so close our arms and legs touch. Beyond Brigham is Homer Day, our buggy man, Brigham's buddy from way back. To my left is a Negro name of Sim Gore. None of us know him. He has only worked Number Thirteen a month and just started loading bone in our section. Bone is slate. The company has no use for it, so Sim loads it and it goes out of the mine to be dumped over the hillside. There is a bone pile at the head of the hollow above Jenkinjones that is near as high as the mountain.

When Brigham and Sim breathe, their arms move against mine. I wish they would breathe at the same time, the unevenness puts me on edge. The light on Homer's cap bobs up and down. The dust is still flying, it clots the beams of the lamp and smothers the light.

"Hit's all closed off," Homer says. "All closed off. Aint no place big enough for a piss ant to crawl through." He sniffs loudly. "All closed off," he says again.

"Shut the hell up," says Brigham. He digs an elbow into Homer's rib cage. Homer grunts.

"Got to be quiet, breathe slow," says Sim Gore. "Got to conserve the oxygen."

"Shut up, nigger," says Brigham.

I feel Sim's body go stiff against mine.

"We dug our own grave," Homer says. "Just like the songs say. Dug our own grave."

I say, "They'll be coming for us. I been in the army. This aint so different from being trapped in a foxhole. The Nazis has dropped a bomb on us, see. But our boys will be in to dig us out. In the meantime we got to be calm."

"Calm!" Brigham coughs. "God, I'd love a shot of whiskey."

I crawl away on my hands and knees, scrabbling over chunks of bone. I find one of the dinner pails Brigham and I brought in.

"Homer, where was your dinner pail?"

"With the buggy."

"Tuna fish pancakes if you can find it," says Brigham.

Sim Gore doesn't say a word. I can't blame him. I crawl back.

"We'll get out," I say. "We're already goddamn lucky. Could be us instead of the buggies. Y'all know the procedure. We got to take turns banging with something. Maybe they'll hear us."

I prize open the battered dinner pail, dump out its contents. Homer has me in his lamplight.

"Your head's bleeding," he says.

"Must not be bad. I don't feel nothing." I hold up two fried baloney sandwiches. "Half for each of us. But not just yet."

"Who says when?" Brigham asks.

"I do."

"Who appointed you?"

I ignore him and hold up a can of Vienna sausages and a package of chocolate cupcakes.

"One Vienny apiece right now, and we'll save the crackers. Half a cupcake apiece, but not now. Two sips of coffee. We'll save the water for later."

"Who appointed you?" Brigham says again. "Hit's my bait."

"I been in the war," I say. "I had practice at this."

"Leave the boy be," says Sim Gore. "He's making sense."

I give Homer a hunk of bone because he is still sobbing and needs something to do. He shifts to the front of our place, bangs three times against a boulder, waits, bangs again.

I hand out the Viennas, sit back against the coal face. A glob of jelly clings to my sausage. I catch the jelly on my tongue and hold it until it melts. I eat small bites, try to make it last. We sit in silence and listen to Homer bang.

Bang. Bang. Listen. *Bang. Bang.* Listen.

Brigham says, "That pounding is driving me nuts."

"You do it a while," I say. I am thinking Homer is getting tired anyway.

I lean against Sim Gore. "Where you from?"

"Live at Jenkinjones," he says. "Was raised up yonder to Annadel."

He doesn't say anything else. Brigham keeps pounding.

Rachel is heading toward the Philippines from Corregidor. She is on the ocean where there is nothing but air and water. I want to be with her on a boat and swim with her and after she dries in the sun I will lick the salt from her skin I want to spread her legs and taste the saltiness there

I read the letters she writes Mom. She writes, "There was a full moon over the ship tonight but it was wasted because we aren't allowed to talk to the sailors and they're all awfully nice and sweet."

I can't stand it because those sailors are taking care of her and I'm not.

She can be so damn silly. In the middle of an ocean in the middle of a war she writes, "You should see the tan I'm getting. My legs look like I have leg makeup on."

She never writes me. She wouldn't dare write me that crap.

I can reach out and touch the limit of my world. I measure each slow breath and wait to die. But nothing in the world has tasted so good as the Vienna sausage I just ate. It's a good thing we will die or life would be worthless, we wouldn't even know what it is. Except I don't want to die this soon.

Sim and Brigham and Homer sleep, and I crack the bone against the wall. Our hands have worn the bone clean and smooth.

Sim wakes and takes the bone. I lie down beside Homer. It is cold and I fold myself into the curves of his body.

We eat the rest of the Viennas, and I hand out a Saltine apiece because it is our big meal.

"How long you think it's been?" Sim asks.

"Ten hours," says Brigham.

"Got to be more," Homer wails. "Hit seems like eternity."

Silence.

"Jawbone seam," says Brigham. "Good seam of coal to work. High coal. Pretty coal, got a little whorl in the grain."

His voice has a flow to it like when he tells a story. Brigham tells a good story.

"Keep talking," I say. "Why's it called jawbone seam?"

"Jawbone of the Devil." Brigham coughs, spits. "Don't you know we're digging the Booger Man's bones, boys?"

"Why the Booger Man's bones?" asks Sim.

"Because they're black as pitch."

"I'm black," says Sim—his voice with an edge to it—"and I got nothing to do with the Devil."

"Don't you?"

They lean toward each other over me.

"My daddy hated a nigger," says Brigham.

I push my arms against his chest. "What I heard tell, your daddy hated everybody and everything," I say. "Probably hated you, too."

"You son of a bitch," says Brigham. "You didn't know him."

"He was my daddy's brother."

"You didn't know your own fucking daddy."

I suck in my breath. "I heard the stories," I say.

"Brigham's daddy was a mean one," says Homer. "Would cuss you out soon as look at you. Used to split Brigham's skin with a strap."

"Sons of bitches." Brigham leans back again. "I'd beat the shit out of all of you if they was room."

Silence.

"Booger Man a-laying in the ground," Brigham says like he's

chanting, talking real low, breathing short breaths like he's not even inhaling. "Poor feller digs up the Booger Man's big toe, thinks it's a 'tater, poor starving feller. Takes that toe home, cooks it, and eats it. Booger Man comes that night and claims the feller's soul. Devil's bones in the ground."

"That don't mean this is the Devil's Bones," says Sim, sipping the air. "Could be God's bones. God's bones a-holding up the world, and we got a powerful nerve to be messing with them."

"What kind of God would do that way?" I ask. Answers fill the inside of my head. A dead God who raged against dying and left his cursed bones behind? A God who knows that death is the spice of life, who lives on our dying and sucks our sorrow for sustenance?

"God's ways is not our ways," Sim says. "His time is not our time, his reasons is not our reasons. God have a majesty."

"I'm saved," says Homer. "Brothers, I hope you are all saved. We will be going from this hole to live with Jesus."

I have the bone. *Bang. Bang.* Then we hear it, away off in another world. Two answering taps.

We listen.

Brigham grabs the bone from me. *Bang. Bang. Bang.*

Tap. Tap. Tap.

"Lord Jesus, they hear us!" Sim cries.

"Long way off," says Brigham. "Long way."

We piss in the empty dinner pail and close it to keep down the smell. We squat and crap and cover the shit with chunks of bone, like we are big cats. The smell comes anyway and at least reminds us we are alive. We lay huddled together because the cold is in our bones.

"I was borned in a whorehouse," Homer says. "Yonder to Annadel. My mommy was a loose woman. Ruby Day was her name. She run off to Cincinnati and left me. Then she got pregnant with my brother Hassel down there and sent him up to me. Vernon Finley took us in and raised us like we was his own. We kept our last name though, Day. I was seventeen when I was saved. Was bad to drink before that but Jesus set me right. He struck me down while I was setting a timber in the mine. I seen his face in the wood by the light of my lamp. I come back away to kneel and pray, and the roof fell where I'd been standing. I knowed right then Jesus had me in his care."

I want to say *Stop talking, you are using the air,* but I don't because the stories are important too. I pick up the bone and bang. The taps answer. "They sound closer," I say. "Talk, Sim. Tell a story."

"You ever see that monument at the Davidson cemetery?" Sim says. "Monument to all them miners blowed up at Number Six. Got a list of all the names carved in stone, says they give their lives for American Coal. Some of them names got the letters COL after them. Time I ask my momma what that meant, she say Colonel. She say it meant they was all officers in the army. Didn't want to tell me what it really was, Colored. Didn't want me to know they marked us different like we was leftovers. I wanted to know it. And I wanted to know they was Negroes in that mine. This is my place too."

"Colored man blows up just like a white man," Homer says.

"My daddy was shot when I was a youngun," Sim says. "Killed when the coal operators run a machine gun through the camp on a train car. Him not even a miner. Him a bartender for old man Ermel Justice."

"Jesus I'd like a drink," Brigham moans. "Did your daddy make a fine drink?"

I can feel Brigham trembling against me.

"It's hard to breathe," he says. "Hard."

And I notice my chest hurts like someone is setting on it.

"Air's bad," I whisper.

Sim sits up and strikes a match. It sparks and then flicks out.

"Jesus," he says. "Jesus."

Brigham cusses, "Goddamngoddamnsonofabitch."

Sim staggers to his feet toward the wall of bone. I see the spark of another match. Nothing. The orange sparks move to the right. Nothing. Nothing. Soon Sim will be out of matches. I grope through my pockets and I don't have any.

Then a tiny pearl of orange flame catches with a puttering sound, high up on our right. "Here!" Sim calls. "Here!"

I reach him first, stand on tiptoe, and stick my nose in the narrow crevice. A cold clear blast of air freezes the inside of my nose. We scrabble at the bone with our bare hands, but we can't make the opening bigger.

"They's just room for three," Sim says. "Step up, y'all, put your nose to it. When I can't go no more I'll tell you. We'll take turns."

I stand on tiptoe between Brigham and Homer, our arms around each other's waists for balance. The air is so cold it burns all the way down.

"Can't go no more," Sim says behind us.

Brigham lets go of me and stands back. Sim is too short to reach the crevice so Brigham finds a hunk of bone for him to stand on. Sim's cheek rubs mine, the stubble of beard dry and scratchy. We breathe. Brigham pulls me away and takes my place.

I keep count of how many times I step back but lose track after ten. The pounding beyond the wall is loud, you can breathe to its rhythm. But the bouts without air weaken me. I see red stripes then white ones and my ears buzz. I don't want to bother Homer any more Homer has a new wife he doesn't need me to bother him I lie down because my head is pounding the others are breathing and I will let them.

"I aint told my story yet," I say. "I fought in the war I killed a man point blank I killed a man I should never have come out of Egypt."

I can hardly hear my voice for the pounding.

I didn't save Rachel I didn't save the Homeplace I killed a man I should have saved him I should have died in the river I should have died in Egypt.

The bars of light blind me the angels lift me up and bear me away.

GOD'S BONES
1945–1946

In the army, you have to have a story. Everybody looks the same from the neck down, and from the forehead up. You have only your eyes nose and mouth to say who you are and that is not enough without a story.

Tommie and I had no problem. Every place we went—Fort Jackson, Camp Anzio, Corregidor, Leyte, Manila—we were the only nurses from the mountains. People kept saying, How funny your accents are, Does your father make moonshine, Are those the first shoes you ever had on? At first we laid it on good. I said our family mule slept in the living room, and Tommie told one GI that she never saw a pair of panties until she joined the army. It was fun for a while but then it got old.

The GIs came around all right. In the Solomons they were so

grateful for a woman's company they didn't seem to mind if you said you only wanted touching and wouldn't go all the way. They looked strange with their scalps shining through their close-cropped hair, but they were cute with their caps or helmets on. Tommie had her boyfriends wear their helmets when they made love.

Tommie was engaged to Arthur Lee Sizemore, but she still had lots of boyfriends. Arthur Lee was in Italy, so who knew when she'd see him again. Life goes on, she said, and there are good looking men in the world who never heard tell of Arthur Lee. I always felt sorry for Arthur Lee when she said that.

I dated around a while but in Manila I settled on one boyfriend. His name was Fred Sullivan. Fred grew up rich in New Orleans where his family owned a jewelry store, and he told me things I'd never heard of—like people eating the tails of crawdads and dead people buried above the ground and mulattos and octoroons. And wearing tuxedos to dinner sometimes. Fred said I was dainty and trim and had delicate hands like a lady should have, which he didn't expect to find in a girl from the mountains. This last made me mad, but I feared to argue for I had written to my mother about him. She wrote back, "Your new friend sounds so nice. I know you have been taught to behave properly and I'm sure he appreciates that. I'm very proud of you." The letter was short and her writing was large and shaky, for her right side was paralyzed and she was still awkward with the left. She was more precious to me for being halfway around the world. I kept the letter because she had touched it.

Fred was a first lieutenant in charge of the colored troops. The Negroes lived in their own compound and Fred was the only white man who stayed with them. All the barracks were built on stilts because of the floods, and Fred's little wood house sat on the highest stilts of all so he could see out over the compound from his window. He had a Filipino cleaning woman, and he told her "his boys" were really white men who had been injected with dye so they could fight at night without being seen.

Fred didn't like the Filipino cleaning woman or any other Filipinos. He called them gooks. I'd never heard that word until the army, and I didn't think there was anything wrong with it because everyone called the Filipinos gooks. Fred said anybody with slant eyes was one except for the Japs, who were a breed apart, "really nasty devils." When I wrote Dillon I told him what Fred said, thinking it was interesting. He wrote back and said I should be ashamed, and what was I doing spending time with someone like Fred, and didn't include a single kind word for me, not even to wish I was safe. I was so hurt I tore up the letter and decided not to write him again.

When I asked Fred how he liked being in charge of the Negroes, he said, "Honey, it's like teaching first grade. You've got to tell them every little thing. The guys at the Officer's Club say I've got the patience of Job. But I can't complain. They only trust my outfit with the easy jobs, and I get to watch. It beats wading around in the jungle getting my tail shot at."

I didn't know any Negroes, but Tommie said there were lots of them at Annadel, where she grew up, and they were not at all the way Fred claimed.

"I aint sure I care for your Fred," she said.

"You don't know him."

"So introduce us. Or are you ashamed of your hillbilly friend?"

"I'm from the mountains too."

"And from what you've told me, he likes you because you're different from the rest of us. You getting above your raising?"

We were sitting on my cot. Tommie held my foot in her lap and was painting my toenails bright red. The rush of air against the wet nail polish made my feet feel cool. I sank back on my pillow.

"I get tired of being different," I said. "I get tired of people thinking I'm stupid just because of the sound of my voice. Nobody knows us here."

"It don't help to hide where you're from. If Fred don't like it, it's because he's a snob."

"You sound like my Aunt Carrie, always criticizing the men I date."

"Rachel, I think the world of you. But honey, you got bad taste in men."

"I dated Tony," I said. "Tony is Arthur Lee's friend."

"He's Arthur Lee's puppy dog, that's what he is. You wasn't in love with Tony and you aint in love with Fred."

"Is that so?"

"I'll tell you who you're really sweet on. It's that cousin of yours."

I sat up so fast that Tommie painted a streak of red nail polish across the top of my foot. I grabbed a towel and tried to wipe it off. "That's a damn lie!"

"Ooh! Rachel's cussing!"

I scrubbed harder at my foot. "I love Dillon, but not like you think."

"How is it, then?"

I thought a minute. "I love Dillon because he's my flesh and blood. Kin will love you no matter what. But Dillon wants to know every little thing I'm thinking and wants it to be just like what he's thinking. He's bossy and he doesn't have one bit of a sense of humor. He gets mad and sulks if he doesn't get his own way. He's—"

Tommie put her hand over my mouth. "You're crazy about him," she said, and smiled a wicked smile.

Then my eyes filled with tears and she moved closer to me. "Rachel, I didn't mean to upset you."

"When he was wounded I thought I'd die from worry and it was the same when I got the letter that he'd been trapped in that roof fall. All I could think was what if he'd died before they got him out and I never got to see him again. I miss him so bad. But he's my cousin, so we've got no future."

"That makes it more romantic! It's like in a book, star-crossed lovers. Do you write him?"

"No. He wrote me a mean letter because I told him some things about Fred and I won't write him again."

"Well of course he got mad," Tommie said. "If you're trying to run him off, you're doing a good job."

Then I stubbed up and wouldn't talk about Dillon any more. I wanted Tommie to meet Fred. I was determined she would like him better than Dillon. The next time he took me walking, Tommie went along. We went to Manila Harbor. Green foam like moldered candy floated on the cloudy water. A crowd of ragged brown children had followed us, tugging at our sleeves crying, "Chocoletto, Joe!" We didn't have any candy bars so we gave them all the gum we had and a nickel apiece, then Fred waved his arms at them like he was shooing chickens out of the barnyard and they fell back. They sat on the sea wall twenty feet from us, their naked legs dangling and their jaws working hard at the gum.

"So did you tell Fred what happened to your cousin Dillon in the coal mine?" Tommie said. She had this glint in her eye like she was trying to provoke something.

"Rachel doesn't talk much about her family," Fred said.

Tommie poked me. "Tell him."

I told him how Dillon had been trapped by a roof fall and nearly died. I was getting to the part about how he was rescued when Fred said, "Your cousin didn't go on strike back in forty-three?"

"No. He was still in the service when that happened."

"Good. They should have lined up those miners and shot them for treason."

Tommie turned red and reared back. "That's a terrible thing to say!"

"They went on strike while our boys were dying over here."

"They're dying too," Tommie said.

"Lazy bums. Unions are full of Reds anyway. They damn near took over the country in the thirties." Fred spoke to me as though Tommie wasn't there. She kept kicking me in the shin like she wanted me to say something and I knew I should but the words wouldn't come. After a while she left us and walked home on her own.

"Your friend has a big mouth," Fred said, watching her go.

"She's entitled to her opinion," I mumbled and looked at the ground.

"Is that so?" He studied me for a moment, then laughed and kissed me on the forehead. "You're cute when you get mad."

"Am I mad?"

"You've got this look on your face."

"I don't feel well," I said. "Maybe you better take me home."

When I got back to the barracks, Tommie was sitting on her cot reading a magazine.

"Fred is a bastard," she said.

I turned my back and started to undress. "You can't expect him to know about the coalfields," I said. "He's never been there."

"It don't matter. You can tell how a person treats people, no matter how much they know. And you sat there like a bump on a log and let him say those things."

"I didn't like what he said, but I didn't know what to say back. I don't know enough about such things to argue."

Tommie lit a cigarette. "When I first met you, I thought you was a shy little mouse. But I learned that you're strong underneath all that. You don't let women push you around, not if something's important to you. You don't let Dillon push you around, that I can tell. Why can't you stand up to Fred?"

"My mother says men don't like a pushy woman."

"Rachel, your mother aint always right."

Neither are you, I thought. I got in bed. "I'm really tired. Let's talk about it some other time." I pretended to sleep. But I lay thinking about Tommie and how loose she was with men, about Mother and the way she had taught me to be. I thought that Mother was my true flesh and blood, not Tommie, and I recalled my mother's smell, like dried flowers, and missed her. I wanted to make her happy so she could forget she was bound to a wheelchair and wouldn't worry what would become of me. And Tommie was my friend, but there were some in the barracks who whispered about her behind her back and called her a tramp. I always defended her if I heard them, but I didn't want to be like her.

In Manila we sewed evening dresses from parachutes and mosquito nets. We dyed the dresses purple with gentian violet from the hospital laboratory, and yellow with Atabrine, the tablets we took to keep away malaria, filched from the mess hall tables. We went dancing in nightclubs in our mosquito net dresses, ate carabao steaks at candlelit tables, while girls sang love songs in cracked English and Tagalog.

At night we slept under the mosquito nets. It was like having our very own screened-in porch, a tiny house in the country just large enough for one. Beneath the mosquito net I dreamed of home and it was always the Homeplace I saw. The air was soft and the mosquitoes grew large and benign and turned into lightning bugs.

We rose before dawn to go to the wards at Pasay, walked a mile and a half past the long canvas bags hung from iron poles that collected rainwater for drinking. The hospital was a string of long wooden buildings, walls open at top and bottom so the air could circulate. From the outside you could see the white shoes of the nurses and their white caps, as they walked the length of the wards.

We dressed lots of bayonet wounds, for the jungle fighting was close, nursed men gutshot with rifles, with jaws shot away, with arms and legs ribboned into bloody strips by grenades. The soldiers lay beneath the mosquito nets like a long row of white cocoons. We raised the nets and draped them over our shoulders, leaned close into a private world of suffering. A sharp smell of carbolic acid permeated the wards, but beneath the nets the odor was sweet with blood and sweat.

We worked twelve or more hours at a time and were exhausted. Once I went from the wards to dance with Fred and fell asleep on his shoulder as he moved me around the dance floor. But we were young.

While we worked at the hospital, Filipino women came to make our beds and clean the barracks' toilets. They stole us blind. I tried not to care because I knew they sold things for food. I thought about buying food for them, but I recalled the mission boxes we received at home, how angry Aunt Carrie would be and the shame I would feel, the way my mother convinced herself she was superior to the givers because she could make do with what others cast aside.

One Sunday I went for a drive with Tommie and her latest beau to a slum where people lived in houses of cardboard and plywood and corrugated tin. They were like the wood and tarpaper houses up the hollows at home, only all gathered in one place and jumbled close together instead of spread out along the creek. Most of Manila was a pile of stone from the bombings, but at least the houses of the poor were makeshift and easily rebuilt. We parked our jeep and walked past vendors hawking stunted green bananas. It was the only food we saw for sale. When we returned for the jeep it was gone. I was glad. I knew how a man at home could take an old car, set it in his yard, and use it forever. Dillon said an automobile carcass was a poor man's auto parts store. I saw the jeep stripped and dispersed, its metal innards reborn as rice and fish balls. I decided it is better for a person to steal what they need than be given it, because when they steal they are at least doing for themselves.

In August, America dropped the bomb and the war was finished. We didn't think much about what had happened to Hiroshima, only that we were going home. We drank, we danced in the summer heat until we were sticky with sweat, we strolled arm in arm along the streets of Manila like good-hearted children. The nurses stayed to tend the men released from the prison camps, so Fred left before I did. On his last night he wanted me to go to bed with him, but I wanted to lose my virginity in a nice hotel on my wedding night, the way ladies did. So I said no. Fred promised he would write in care of my parents, and as soon as I returned to the States he would come to West Virginia and marry me.

I packed his suitcase for him because he said a woman was neater than a man, and it seemed a wifely thing to do. He pulled a box from under his cot. While I sorted pairs of socks he snuck up behind me and dropped a skull in my lap. I jumped but I didn't scream out or act silly because a nurse who has been through a war has seen everything.

"Jap skull," said Fred, and grinned. "Buddy who was on Bataan got it out of a big pile of them."

I started to hand it back but he said, "Keep it to remember me by."

Some of the other nurses had Japanese skulls their boyfriends had given them. On Halloween, Ellen Standish lit hers with candles like a pumpkin and set it in the barracks window. Then her boyfriend's ship went down in Subic Bay after it was hit by a kamikaze and she threw the skull in the trash. *Life* magazine said the Japs were not like other people, that savagery was bred into them and you could tell it by the narrowness of their foreheads. I held the skull against my belly and felt the forehead. The bone was smooth beneath my fingers. Fred took off his cap and set it on the skull. Then he took a picture of me holding the skull in my lap. When he reached California he wrote me in Manila and enclosed the photo. On the back he wrote, "I lost my head over you."

Tommie was dating a cargo pilot from Pierre, South Dakota. He planned to take his plane for a joy ride and invited Tommie and me to go.

"Won't Billy get in trouble?" I asked.

"The war's over," Tommie said. "Nobody gets in trouble any more."

When we reached the airfield outside Manila we found two planes parked side by side. They were dark green and had swollen bellies like they were pregnant. Billy and a friend loitered beside the planes.

"We're both going up," Billy said. "Rachel can ride with Ed."

I smiled at Ed, who was cute, blue-eyed, and from Wyoming, but I didn't flirt because I was practically engaged. Billy had his arm around Tommie's waist. "You girls are in for a treat. We're going to show you how we run buffalo out West, right Ed?"

Tommie giggled.

It was my first time to fly. When we took off I gripped the sides of my seat and held my breath, because the plane was shaking like it would fall apart and it is not often you do something that makes you think you could die that very moment. Then the heaviness drained away and we lifted as though we were made of feathers. Ed reached over and pried my fingers loose. "You can let go," he said, and winked. We floated above Manila. The piles of rubble looked like mounds of brown sugar spilled beside the bluegreen ripples of Manila Bay. A jagged shadow moved over the surface of the city and then I saw Billy and Tommie were flying ahead of us.

"Over there." Ed pointed. General MacArthur's mansion stood unscathed, its swimming pool like a gemstone set in a ring. "Those Nips wouldn't touch old Mac's house," Ed yelled above the roar of the engines. "They think he's a god or something." And so were we like gods, American gods, as we passed beyond the suffering city and over an ocean of trees and green grassland.

"Water buffalo!" Ed yelled. His radio crackled, and Billy's excited voice answered, "Round-up time, cowpoke!" Ed whooped and grabbed the throttle, and we dropped out of the sky. There were only a dozen of them, a make-believe herd. They were running, they seemed to be beside us, then we leveled out and passed over the terrified carabao, so close I could see the muddy splotches on their backs. We soared again. I clutched the seat and hoped I wouldn't throw up.

"Your mouth's wide open!" Ed pointed and laughed.

I clapped my mouth shut and looked out the window. Tommie and Billy were far below us. They swooped down, wing at a tilt, then straightened to make a run. The frenzied carabao bore the cross-like shadow of the airplane on their backs.

"He's damn low!" Ed yelled.

In my mind Tommie sat forward in the cockpit, screaming for joy. I tried to call a warning, pressed my hand against the window as though I could reach through and pull her to me, hold her close for safety. The airplane skimmed the grasses, tipped its wing, and disappeared in a plume of gray smoke that gathered itself, then opened and spread like the petals of a bright orange rose.

RACHEL, 1946

I came back from the war with a new suit of clothes, a suntan, an album full of photographs, and a Japanese skull. I came back without Tommie.

She tried to follow me around. When the train rocked and swayed up the Levisa and the mountains, ragged and unkempt, closed in on me, she whispered, *Aint four years a long time to go without mountains? How can you leave them again for New Orleans?* When I saw my parents and Aunt Carrie at the train station in Justice, Father nearly bald now, Mother hunched over and gray in her wheelchair, Tommie was looking in vain over my shoulder for her own mother. I missed her, but I wanted her to leave me alone. I thought she died from too much wildness, and I was anxious to avoid her fate. So after we'd hugged and cried together and were settled in the car, the first thing I asked for was the letter that would carry me safe into the arms of a well-off man. Tommie disappeared.

"Letter from New Orleans?" Father said. "We aint had any such letter that I know of. Don't believe we have any mail for you at all."

I sat in the back seat beside Mother and tried not to show that anything was wrong. She gripped my arm with her one good hand and leaned close against me. "He'll write," I said to her. She smiled on one side of her face.

I never asked about Dillon because I was hurt he hadn't met my train. But while she fried the pork chops, Aunt Carrie said, "Dillon lives at Winco and he's working at the Number Thirteen mine. They're shorthanded so it's hard to get away, but he'll be by soon as he gets off work."

When I was upstairs in my room taking clothes out of my suitcase, I heard a tap and he stood there so tall his head nearly touched the doorframe. I dropped the blouses, and next I knew he swept me up in a hug and I was hugging back as hard as I could. It was a while before we stood back from each other.

"You're beautiful," he said. "You're a woman now."

I blushed. I was getting a nervous rise in my stomach and to quell it I said, "A woman, and engaged to be married."

A change came over his face. I talked on, fast. "I wrote you about him once. He's from New Orleans. His family has money but he's not stuck up. I'm just waiting to hear from him to set the date."

He shut the door and stood by the bed. His long fingers strayed over the pile of clothes. "I still love you. Always will. Stay here and love me."

"We've been through this before. It's wrong and people would talk."

"Who cares what anybody thinks?"

"It's not just what people think. It's what I feel. It's how I feel." I was shaking all over.

He pulled me to him. "What do you feel?"

I tried to pull away but he held me tighter.

"I love Fred."

"No you don't." He kissed my neck. He unbuttoned my bra and slipped his hand over my breast, pressed me against the wall. I felt him hard against my belly. He kissed my mouth and I opened it.

"I'll tell you how you feel," he said "You want to take your clothes off and make love to me. You never made love with any Fred, because you didn't want to." He raised my skirt and pulled down my panties. He touched me.

"You're wet," he said.

It was too much. I pushed him and was surprised at how easily he stepped back.

"How dare you in my mother's house!" I pulled up my panties and tried to cover my breasts.

"What are you afraid of?"

"I'm afraid of you, because of what you just did and because of what you just said. You run right over top of me and there's no place to hide from you."

"No, it's your mother that scares you. Does she rule your life, that old woman in the wheelchair yonder?"

"Don't you speak of my mother like that!"

"She's a cripple and she'll make you one."

He stepped closer again. I slapped at him and caught him on the cheek with the heel of my hand. He stumbled backward, his fingers pressed against his cheek, and knocked a box off the dresser. The Japanese skull tumbled onto the floor. Dillon looked at it like someone waking from sleep.

"What the hell—"

"Fred gave me that," I said. "It's a Jap skull."

He stooped and picked it up, touched the top of the skull. "It was a person. You can't carry a person's head around like this."

"I told you, Fred gave it to me."

"Fred can go to hell! You don't give part of a dead person's body as a present!"

"In case you don't recall, we just fought a war against the Japs and they acted like animals!"

"They're people, goddamn it!"

"You're so self-righteous. You always have thought you were better than anybody else."

"I am better than the sonofabitch who gave you this skull. And if you can't see it, you can go to hell."

He yanked the door open.

"Where are you going? Give me back that skull."

"No."

"My fiancé gave that to me. You can't take what's mine."

"It aint yours. I'm giving it a proper burial. If you got any decency you'll come with me."

Even as he spoke the skull took on flesh and veins and hair and a body and stood beside him a whole human being, a mother's child, and accused me. But I could not bear the two of them ranged against me, to have Dillon's part taken by a ghost.

"If you walk out with that skull, don't you ever come bother me again."

"I won't. Don't think that I will."

He went out with the skull and left me alone.

DILLON

The Rachel I knew would not treat a person so. War changes people, even those who don't pick up a gun. Maybe my Rachel died in the Philippines and another has come back in her skin. My Rachel would not cart a person's head halfway around the world in a box like a pair of old shoes.

I'm driving so fast I barely make the curves. The road is black. I am tempted to straighten up and take a tree, but I keep leaning on the wheel. I don't know how she could push me away in favor of some rich sonofabitch with no respect for the dead.

No, she always was shallow. She wanted to be a stewardess, Jesus Christ. I don't love her, never did. It's my childhood I love, living on the Homeplace and being a boy with my mother. It's my daddy I love. I only thought I loved Rachel because she remembers him.

The car clips the shoulder of the road, kicks up gravel. I fight the wheel and keep control, the back end skips when it hits the pavement but I keep going.

A streak of orange flashes past my headlights and disappears with a thump. I pull off the road onto a wide shoulder and sit breathing hard, listening to the motor. Then I turn the truck around and drive back, hoping to find the road empty. But a red fox is there, stretched full length across the black pavement. I drive past twice more, hoping it will be gone, a bad dream, but I catch it each time in my headlights. I marvel at how its coat burns fire, even in death. I haven't seen a red fox since I left the Homeplace, they do not much come around the coal mines. There is just this one.

I pull onto the shoulder again, turn off the motor and get out. I pick up the fox by the legs. It is heavy, things take on heaviness when they are dead. I lay it carefully in the back of the truck and drive to my house at Winco. In my mind I see what might have been, the red fox slaking its thirst at the edge of Blackberry Creek, comforted by the murmuring of the water and the sound of its own drinking, calmed by the rustling of leaves in the night breeze. It slips up the bank, across the road and safely up Trace Mountain to its den, alive because I was driving slow and careful and sane, because I didn't let a woman hurt me.

At Winco I dig a hole beside the fence in my yard. I wrap the fox around the skull and bury them together. I don't know what religion the skull is so I say O Buddha O Christ O ancestors O God. The red fox died for our sins.

TRACE MOUNTAIN
1946–1951

RACHEL, 1946

I never heard from Fred. After a while I swallowed my pride and wrote to him, but he didn't answer. Mother and Father didn't say a word to me and treated me as solicitously as if I had a disfiguring disease.

I went to Aunt Carrie to cry out my hurt. But the first thing she said, after she comforted me, was "Does Dillon know?"

I straightened my back and dabbed at my eyes. "What difference does that make?"

She didn't say anything.

"He'll be happy," I said. "I don't like someone being happy about something that makes me so sad."

"Did you really love that boy?"

"Of course I did."

"I just wondered. When you talked about him, your eyes didn't light up."

"I don't show my feelings so easy," I said.

She just smiled. I turned away, angry, sat down at my dresser, and started to brush my hair.

"Dillon hasn't been by the house lately," she noted.

"That's because he's off sulking." I tugged hard with my brush, ignoring the tangles. "It's what he does whenever he doesn't get his own way."

"I figured you all had a fight," she said. "Anything you want to talk about?"

I had invited her to my room, but now I wished she'd leave. "It's nothing to do with Dillon," I said just for spite, "and nothing you can do anything about." I was putting bobby pins in my hair. "I ran into Tony Angelelli today." I watched her face in the mirror to see how she'd take that. She wasn't pleased, so neither would Dillon be. Good. When she left I smiled into the mirror.

I was glad to see Tony again, in his little office in the Jenkinjones company store, with the huge black safe and the bars on the window. He looked small, a man who was once free to roam the world but has been cast back in his prison cell. He had been with the army in Italy, an interpreter. It must have been pleasant for him, repeating the words of others, not having to think of his own. I had expected he would bring back a docile, grateful Italian war bride, but he was still single.

Our marriage was all my fault; it wouldn't have happened if I hadn't pushed for it. Tony would have drifted on by me. But my fear was growing. A woman was nothing without marriage, fit only for a lonely, unhappy life, to be shunned and talked about behind her back. Girls younger than me already had children, and when I went to church I thought they looked at me like they felt sorry for me. I watched their children and longed for a baby of my own to fill my empty spaces. I had lost time during the war; while other girls were courting I was nursing soldiers. Lots of nurses caught husbands in the army, and I thought I had too. But I'd come home and learned I was unlucky. That was life, and I must do the best I could.

Tony still had a round face with a sweet, gentle expression, still had black curly hair that I knew other women admired. He agreed to go to a movie with me and didn't seem to think me forward for asking him. He tried to feel my breasts and asked me to go to bed with him but didn't mind when I refused.

"I been talking to my mother about you," he said. "I told her you wouldn't sleep with me and she said you're a lady."

"Lady or not, you cheated on me one time," I reminded him.

"Aw." He laughed. "It wasn't nothing serious. She wasn't the kind of girl you marry."

Within a month we were engaged. To my surprise, Mother didn't protest when I announced my plans. She watched Tony, who sat beaming at the kitchen table, eating a slab of Aunt Carrie's apple pie and saying nothing. That night, Father came to my bedroom and said he'd talked to Mother. They both agreed the army might have been good for Tony, would have "straightened him out," as Father put it. "We know it's hard on a young girl these days, finding a husband. It's the times, all the young men dying in the war."

"I want your blessing."

He hugged me. "You'll always have our blessing."

Then it was only Aunt Carrie and Dillon who stood opposed, and they were silent. Aunt Carrie knew better than to say anything out loud, and Dillon avoided me. The few times we did meet, he was distant and superior, as though it was beneath him to converse with such a backward person. He didn't come to the wedding, and I was glad.

I took my vows in a white wool suit with fake pearls around the collar and sleeves. Tony went against his mother for once and agreed to be married by the Methodist preacher. He was pleasant and didn't seem the least bit nervous. We spent the night in Huntington at the Hotel Pritchard. I undressed in the bathroom, terrified of what was to come, and didn't look at Tony when I got in bed. But it wasn't much worse than going to the doctor. He pulled up my nightgown, stroked my body a few times, then laid on top of me and pushed. I felt numb, dug my fingers into his shoulders and held on. He kept pushing and I thought that nothing must be happening, that he would give up. But finally he relaxed, sighed loudly, and patted the top of my head. Then he fell asleep. I reached down cautiously and touched the insides of my thighs, felt something sticky. I turned on my side, wrapped my arms around myself, and lay awake for hours.

We moved into a five-room house at Jenkinjones, just down the road from my mother and father. I didn't take a job because everyone said it was time for women to settle down and rebuild the home. I sewed curtains and cleaned and learned to cook Italian food, to measure out oregano and basil, pour olive oil in the boiling pasta, slit a squid and remove the thin clear backbone. Tony never said the house looked nice, never complimented my cooking, but complained if the spaghetti stuck together or the bread was too hard.

I told myself it didn't matter; I didn't need someone patting me on the back all the time. We spent quiet evenings together, Tony listening to the radio or reading newspapers, me with a book. Then Tony bought a car.

We'd been without one because cars were in short supply after the war; every dealer had a waiting list. Blackberry Creek had a bus line and passenger train, but it was hard to go anyplace at night. Then Tony brought home a black Ford. Soon he spent every evening at the Moose Club in Justice town. He stayed out later and later until one night I fell asleep over a book, sitting up in an easy chair. When I woke it was midnight and he still wasn't home.

I paced the floor, felt sick to my stomach. At one o'clock I called the Moose Club. No one answered. I found a piece of paper and wrote in large letters, "Two can play this game," and laid the note on the nightstand beside our bed. I turned out every light in the house and watched out the window.

Around two-thirty his car pulled in front of the house. I ran to the clothes closet and hid behind the coats and long bathrobes. I heard his key rattle in the lock, heard the creak of the door and the snap of the light switch. He walked slowly through the dark to the bedroom, turned on the light, and walked to the closet. I held my breath while he hung up his coat, left the door standing open. When he stopped near the bed I parted the clothes and peered out. He was reading the note. Then he dropped it in the wastebasket, undressed, stretched, turned off the light, and got in bed. A few minutes later he began to snore.

I slipped out to the living room where I curled up on the couch, wrapped in an afghan I'd just made, and cried myself to sleep. The next morning I cooked his breakfast in silence, waiting for him to speak. He just ate and read the morning paper as though nothing had happened. Finally I said, "Didn't you wonder where I was last night?"

He looked up. "Nah! I knew you was all right."

"Didn't you wonder if I was out with another man?"

He laughed. "I knew you wouldn't do that." He went back to reading his paper.

He continued to stay out most nights. After he was gone I'd walk the quarter-mile to my parents' house. Sometimes Dillon would be there, visiting Aunt Carrie. We were polite to one another. Sometimes, if I saw his truck parked out front, I'd turn around and walk back home. Aunt Carrie said he was dating a waitress in Justice town but he didn't seem serious about her. I was relieved when she said it and angry at myself for being relieved. I longed to talk to Aunt Carrie about Tony's absences, but I was too proud to admit anything to her. My own mother was no help. She sat silent and forbidding in her wheelchair like a statue in a pagan temple.

Tony and I fell into a routine. He stayed out late on the weekends and I tried not to think about what was going on. On week nights he came in around ten and I knew he had only been playing poker. His reverence for money kept him from wagering large sums, so his losses never amounted to much. For Tony, gambling was a chance to watch money change hands, to fondle it and see it fondled by the coarse hands of other men. If he won, he let me alone and went silent to bed, satisfied. If he lost, he berated my cooking, my housekeeping, my family, and after haranguing me to tears demanded sex as though I owed him compensation. When he was on top of me I held tight to the bed frame behind my head and tried to think of pleasant things. Mostly I thought about children. I spent the daytime thinking about them as well, hoping and praying for fat babies smelling of milk and talcum. I even asked Tony for sex at certain times of the month, because I wanted children so badly, but the babies never came. I sought out doctors as far away as Charleston. They could find nothing wrong with me, although one was not pleased with the way my heart sounded and said it would bear watching, especially if I got pregnant.

"The problem may be with your husband," another suggested. "He may have a low sperm count or even be sterile. He should be checked."

I waited for a winning poker night and raised the subject with Tony as we were getting ready for bed. He laughed. "You're crazy," he said. He proved his point with an hour of sex, poking and prodding, then said, "Nothing wrong with that, was there?"

Arthur Lee Sizemore came back from the army to be superintendent of the Jenkinjones mine. He was the youngest superintendent in the state, American Coal's boy wonder. His first year back he ran for County Commission with the company's blessing and money, and of course he won. Arthur Lee also played poker with the other coal men at the Moose Club, and rumor had it he was overly fond of liquor. One evening he had car trouble and Tony drove him home from the card game. When they entered our living room for a late cup of coffee, Arthur Lee brought the sweet smell of whiskey with him.

I was already in my bathrobe. I made the coffee as quickly as possible and tried to slip into the bedroom but Arthur Lee said in a loud voice, "Where are you going, honey? Sit down here and visit. I aint seen you in a 'coon's age." He patted the couch beside him. He was sprawled out so I'd have had to squeeze up close to him. I sat on a chair instead, perched uncomfortably on the edge.

"Tony, that's a pretty wife you got," Arthur Lee said, his voice slow and wet-sounding.

Tony was smiling. He didn't say anything.

"Always did think she was pretty. Bet she's good in bed." He leaned toward me, shaky like he might tip over, and put a hand on my knee. "Are you, honey? Do you like to fuck?"

I stood up and retreated to the kitchen. "Tony," I said.

Tony was still smiling, his face red. "Now, Rachel." he said. "Now."

"Tony, get him out of here."

"Aw," Tony said. "It's Arthur Lee. You be nice to him."

Arthur Lee spread his arms wide. "I didn't mean nothing!"

"See," Tony said, relieved. "He didn't mean nothing. She knows you don't mean nothing, Arthur Lee."

"If Dillon was here, he'd lay you low," I said. "Both of you."

I went in the bedroom, slammed the door, and leaned against it, breathing hard.

I was loading groceries in our car at the Jenkinjones company store when Arthur Lee stepped out of his office.

"I'm sober," he said. "Can I talk to you?"

I looked away.

"Please," he said. "For Tommie's sake if not for mine."

I slammed the trunk shut and faced him. "What do you want?"

"I want to apologize. I was way out of line. You're a lady and I know that. It was the drink talking. This aint no excuse, but I been tore up ever since I lost Tommie. You can't believe how much I loved that girl. When I'm drinking, she comes to me real clear. When I'm sober she's just a blur. Don't excuse it, I know. I got to learn to control it."

He looked so pitiful I couldn't stay angry. I accepted his apology.

"Can I ask you a question? Did she love me?"

"Yes," I said.

"She had other boyfriends, I know she did. She said as much in her letters, said she didn't take them serious, that it was something fun. I thought maybe she didn't love me, that I was something fun too."

"She loved you." I thought a minute. "Tommie never knew her father. I always thought she was looking for him with all those men. But she would have married you. It's what she planned on."

"It aint supposed to be this way. It's the man supposed to get killed in the war and leave the woman behind. Maybe that's why it's so hard."

"I'm sorry," I said.

"Me too. Life goes on. I'm seeing someone in Bluefield now. It's okay." He shrugged. "Well, I won't keep you."

He called me a week after our conversation and offered me a job with the county as a health nurse. I would give shots to children in one-room schools and visit the homes of tuberculosis patients and elderly shut-ins.

"I told the other commissioners they wasn't a better nurse in the county than you," said Arthur Lee. "Interesting work and pays good. Put some money of your own in your pocket and get you out of that house. Tony won't dare fuss if the offer comes from me."

I said yes, and whatever else Arthur Lee Sizemore did, I would remember that kindness.

RACHEL, 1950

It is a different world on Trace Mountain. There are two ways to get back in. You can go up the Pliny Branch past the slate dump at the head of Jenkinjones hollow, or you can drive past Number Thirteen camp on Lloyds Fork and go back up on the mountain at Raven. Any way you go is dirt road and ruts where you would not take a car. I drove an army surplus jeep provided by the county.

People on Trace Mountain make a living tending apple orchards and honeybees. Some make moonshine on the side, and a thin gray line of smoke hanging in the sky can mean a house chimney or a still. Other people live down over the ridgetop in little coves where their houses of wide boards blend into the landscape. They have chickens in the yard and slatted-wood pig pens—or let the pigs forage—and 'coon dogs and patches of potatoes and corn, and beans growing up round the cornstalks. Some of them are descended from people who couldn't abide the coal mines and took to the hills to avoid them. Others are disabled miners or miners' widows put out of their company houses and forced to squat on whatever piece of land they could find that was out of the company's eyesight. They are people you might see twice or three times a year in town and then never again unless you went looking for them. Looking for them was my job.

Tuberculosis was common on that mountain, and polio. One March day, I visited a one-room school, Trace Ridge, to check the children from consumptive families. It had been warm for the time of year and yellow crocuses bloomed alongside the wooden building. The children were outside on recess when I drove up. The younger ones crowded around, wrapped their arms around my legs and waist. I savored the closeness of their small bodies and tried to make the visit last as long as possible.

From the school I drove three miles around the ridge to see Shep and Bertha Ingram. It took me an hour to reach them, for the spring rains had cut ridges two feet deep and sharp-edged in the road. I left the jeep on the ridge road, pulled on a pair of boots, and hiked the quarter-mile down to the Ingram's, who lived at the bottom of a slick muddy track. Shep was paralyzed with a back injury from the mines and Bertha had TB. She should have gone to the sanitarium in Beckley, but I didn't push for it because Shep needed her and she never got out to infect anyone else. Bertha moved slow, walked without lifting her feet from the ground, but she said the house was so small it was easy to clean and she had all day to tend the garden and put up her preserves. Her niece brought groceries and a neighbor boy chopped wood for the stove and brought a mule for springtime plowing.

While Bertha cooked Shep's dinner I checked him for bedsores, bathed him, and changed his bed linens. We listened to his bedside radio while I worked. When the CBS News came on at noon, Shep said, "Dinner time."

"Almost done with you," I said. "Just in time for Bertha's cornbread hot from the oven."

The radio announcer talked about the war in Korea, then said, "Actress Ingrid Bergman was denounced from the floor of the U.S.

Senate today. The international star of such films as *Casablanca* remains at the center of a storm following the news that she is expecting a child by a man not her husband."

Shep nodded at the radio. "Hit's a shame the way they carry on these days," he said.

The announcer said, "Senator Edwin Johnson of Colorado told his colleagues today that Bergman's wanton behavior was 'an assault upon the institution of marriage.' Johnson called the actress 'a powerful influence for evil.' Bergman is in seclusion with the father of her child, Roberto Rosselini, amid reports that her actions have brought an end to her fabled film career."

"Her daddy ought to horsewhip her," Shep said.

"Now Shep," I said. "What about that man she ran away with? Nobody's fussing about him."

"Fellow's got to have his fun," Shep said.

I was glad to finish with him and go back in the kitchen. I took Bertha's sputum sample to send to the state lab and climbed the hill to the jeep.

My last call was to Granny Combs. Granny lived seven miles in and two miles from her closest neighbor. She was eighty-seven years old and spry, still able to pluck a chicken or render lard. My supervisor thought I should talk Granny into a nursing home. But if you took Granny off that mountain she would have collapsed and vanished like a long-buried body that is dug up and disintegrates when it is exposed to the air. Granny's face was wrinkled and ridged as the mud road and she smelt faintly of wood smoke and urine. She had strength in her grip and her eyes were clear and active. I figured she'd go until something busted inside her and she keeled over and that would be that.

Granny had a cold in February but the March warmth had dried her up. I listened to her thin chest with my stethoscope and heard her breath come in a clear rush.

"Dosed that cold with honey and corn liquor and camomile tea," she said.

I drank a cup of her camomile tea myself. It is still the best thing for a cold, so soothing for a cough and clears the sinuses too. They will not teach that at nursing school and call you a hillbilly if you recommend it, but they will suffer the colds.

I finished the tea and went back to the jeep. I turned the key and the ignition clicked but nothing happened. I twisted the key harder and pumped the gas pedal. Nothing. I sat back, shut my eyes, and listened to a pair of jays screech. When I opened my eyes Granny stood by the jeep.

"Is your vehicle poorly?"

I nodded. "Worse than a stubborn old mule, isn't it?"

She looked scornfully at the jeep. "I wouldn't have one."

"Where's the closest telephone, Hatfield's Orchard?"

"That would be it. They're on a party line."

It was over two miles to Hatfield's. At least I had my boots and the day was fine. I accepted a square of cornbread spread with molasses and set out to walk. It was four-thirty by the time I reached the orchard. Troy Hatfield gave me a cold CoCola and pointed out the telephone on the wall of a storage shed. I sat on an empty packing crate and called Tony's office.

"Where are you?" he asked twice and twice I answered Hatfield's Orchard. I knew he wouldn't come after me. Tony had never been back up on Trace, had a knack for getting lost, and knew nothing about fixing cars.

"Can't someone there fix it?" he said.

"Troy Hatfield knows cars," I said. "But I think it needs a new starter. He'd have to go off the mountain to get one."

"I was going to the Moose Club," he said.

"Fine. You're always a big help."

"I don't know what to do. I was going to the Moose Club."

"Of course you were. You go right on." I hung up the receiver, quiet, before he had a chance to answer, not slamming it but trying to hurt him with my patience. It wouldn't work. He was impervious to such things. Other men would feel guilty and bring the part. Tony would go on and not think another thing.

Troy Hatfield came over, a chain saw in his hand. He was clearing brush. "I can drive you off the mountain," he said. "You could bring a mechanic up tomorrow."

Of course he could, and Junior Tackett would come up from Arthur Lee's new Esso station and fix the starter. But Troy had work to do, and Junior would have work to do. Besides, they were not my people.

"I hate to put you out," I said. "Let me make one more phone call."

Dillon was just home from the day shift when I rang. After I told him what had happened, he said, "Why'd you call me? Don't you have a husband?"

I started to hang up. I pressed the phone to my chest. Then I listened again. The line was silent.

"Dillon?"

"I'm still here."

"I'm not begging you. I didn't beg Tony and I'm sure not begging you. I thought you might help me. You're kin."

"So you kept telling me."

I did hang up then, slammed the receiver hard and wished I could tear the phone out of the wall. I went to look for Troy but I heard the whine of the chain saw off in the woods and I hated to bother him. It didn't matter. I didn't need help from Troy or anyone. I would get off the mountain under my own power. I set out to walk. I would do for myself, do everything in this world for myself.

DILLON

The sun is behind her as she walks down the mountain. I put my hand to my forehead. When I finally make out her face it is set and angry. She walks past my truck so I have to stop and put it in reverse. It is rough, backing down that road, but when she sees I will follow her, she stops.

"I can walk," she says.

"I know you can."

"I don't need to be rescued. And I sure don't need you."

I rub my chin, which is rough with stubble because I didn't take time to shave this morning.

"You want to fix the jeep or not?" I say. "I brought a starter from the Esso."

"Why'd you decide to come?"

"Why'd you call in the first place?"

She turns away.

I say, "Rachel, you asked for help. I'm sorry I was smart with you on the telephone. When you need help, you know I'll always be here for you."

The truck door creaks when she pulls it open and the seat squeaks when she sits down. She may be crying but I can't say for sure because her face is turned away from me.

"That's why I called," she says.

I let off the brake and ease up the rutted road.

It is the starter, all right. Rachel always had good sense about cars. I squint in the evening light and make quick work of it. In the house Rachel and Granny Combs are cooking soupbeans and cornbread and creasy greens. Rachel comes outside and picks wild onions. Lightning bugs rise from the spargrass, like bits of lost moonlight seeking their source.

"Almost done?" Rachel asks. She stands beside me with a bunch of onions in each hand.

"Just about."

I hop in the jeep and turn the key. The engine jumps and roars, then settles into a low rumble.

"Good," she says, and goes in the house.

I can still smell the onions, strong and tart, and I am thinking Homeplace, the years are rolling away and we are children on our land. I know she has been thinking it too. I know Rachel though she does resist my knowing.

I wash my fingers at the pump. Cold water will not much cut black grease, so I wipe my fingers on my T-shirt. In the house Rachel has the table set and Granny dips the beans. I ask Granny if she gets company.

"Yes sir," she says. "I get company here. Course I don't want folks around all the time. I like to run around in my nightie."

Then she hollers laughing.

"Granny!" Rachel pretends like she is shocked.

"Tell this fellow what I told you, first day you come here."

Granny is still laughing. She tugs on Rachel's sleeve.

"You tell it," Rachel says. "You tell it better."

"This here little girl," Granny says, and pats at Rachel, "comes and asks me if I ever been sick. And I say oncet or twicet. And she says, 'Granny, have you ever been bedridden?' And I say, 'Law yes, child, and oncet in a buggy!' "

Granny cackles and I laugh until I choke on cornbread and Rachel is giggling, although it is an old joke, it is not even Granny's, she stole it from Minnie Pearl. Or maybe Minnie Pearl stole it from Granny. Rachel is laughing into the back of her hand while a kerosene lantern flickers behind her.

We sit quiet for a spell and then I say, "Granny, I had a great-uncle come up on this mountain to live, years ago. Sixty year, maybe. Lived a hermit's life. You heard tell of such a fellow?"

"Name of?" Granny says.

"Name of Dillon Lloyd."

"Yes, now. Dillon Lloyd. That man was crazy as a bedbug."

Rachel snickers, but this time I ignore her.

"He was my daddy's uncle," I say. "I'm named for him. I heard family stories about him. You know where he lived?"

"I do for a fact. Aint far from here."

She says how to get there and I listen careful. "Used to be but a footpath up in," she says. "Not that I ever took it because he didn't welcome company, Dillon Lloyd. But my daddy pointed it out to me many a time. Now they's a two-tire track. Must be the coal company or maybe the power company been in there."

"Must be," I say.

"I don't care for no electric myself," she says.

We wash Granny's dishes and then we leave. It is full dark outside.

The jeep starts just fine so I drive away in my truck and Rachel follows behind. We go a mile or so, then I stop. Rachel pulls in behind me. I walk back, open the passenger side of the jeep and get in. Rachel shuts off the motor.

"You really ready to go back down this mountain?" I ask.

I can't see her face.

"Tony will worry," she says.

"Is that so?"

"What do you want to do?" she asks.

"Let's leave the jeep here. Let's take my truck and see if we can find Dillon's cabin."

"It's dark," she says.

"Moon's out, and I got a flashlight."

She looks down at her lap, then opens the door and gets out.

"Let's go," she says.

I stop twice and grope around with my flashlight before we find the track Granny described. There is a white metal sign—POST-ED NO TRESPASSING PROPERTY OF THE AMERI-CAN COAL COMPANY. I rip down the sign with a crowbar and toss it into the weeds.

It is a sharp, uphill climb and tree limbs lash the truck. Then we top out onto a bald. On the other side, clear in my headlights, is the outline of a cabin. I shut off the engine.

"What do you know," I say.

"We can't get to it," Rachel says. "It's too growed up."

"I aint sure I want to get to it. Just want to look at it. I'm scairt if we touched it, it would disappear."

It is dark beyond us but I can feel the mountains falling away. I turn on the radio. The dial lights orange.

"You'll run down the battery," Rachel says.

"Wouldn't be a bad place to be stranded," I say. "We could spend the night here."

"It's getting chilly," she says.

"I got a sleeping bag stowed under the seat."

"One sleeping bag?"

The Unquiet Earth

Voices come to us clear as the angels spoke to people in the Bible, only it is Mother Maybelle singing "Wildwood Flower" from Bristol, and just as sweet as anything Abraham heard

> *O I'll twine with my mangles and waving black hair*
> *With the roses so red and the lilies so fair*
> *And the myrtle so bright in the emerald dew*
> *The pale and the leader and eyes look like blue.*

"What does it mean?" Rachel says. "That first verse of 'Wildwood Flower?' It doesn't make sense the way the Carters sing it."

"The Carters always change words around till they don't make sense," I say. "What's important is how it makes you feel."

"How does it make you feel?"

I don't say anything, just cover her hand with mine. She doesn't pull away. Her head is laid back against the seat.

She says, "You been following what's happening to Ingrid Bergman?"

"I heard it on the radio. It's a shame the way they're doing her. Narrow-minded prudes."

"You would think that. You're the only person I know who would, you and Aunt Carrie."

"Most people are scared of life," I say. "You are too. Except when you're with me."

She turns over her hand so our palms touch.

"There is something I want to feel at least once before I die," she says.

I take her hand and hold it to my mouth. I can still smell the wild onions on her skin. I tickle her soft palm with the tip of my tongue.

"I should be careful," she says. "I've made a mess of things with Tony."

I pull her close and kiss her. Her mouth opens.

I want to see you naked and pale and the lilies spread over you, and the myrtle draped

I undress her slowly and then I take off my own clothes. We leave the cab and wade through the moonlight to the back of the truck. I let down the gate and spread the sleeping bag. The air is turning cold. Rachel's arms are wrapt tight across her chest and when I touch her arms I feel the goosebumps. But then I lay her down and zip the sleeping bag around us and cover her with my body, praise her with my hands until she warms and melts and I do what I want.

───────────────────────────────

RACHEL

You see the world differently on top of a mountain. Up there you might think that you are safe.

We sat in the back of Dillon's truck, our legs and arms twined, and watched the white banks of morning fog run at us, so thick we could have stepped out and been carried off to the next peak. The smell of him was all over me, I could taste him inside my mouth.

"Is this the end of it?" he asked.

I shut my eyes and pressed my face against his neck. "I don't want it to end. But I'm scared."

"Scared of what people will think?"

"Yes. And scared of you."

"Me?"

"You're too strong for me and you want too much."

"I only wanted one thing," he said, "and now I've got it."

"No," I said. "You'll want more."

He brought my hand to his mouth, ran his lips along my crooked finger, the one I broke when I was a girl.

"Do you love me?" he asked.

"Yes."

"And I love you. Can you turn your back on that again?"

"No. I can't turn my back on it."

"Then you'll leave Tony and move in with me?"

"Don't ask me any more hard questions, Dillon. I can't think straight right now."

I followed him in the jeep, back down the mountain. I barely watched the road, kept my eyes on the shape of his head in the truck's rear window. It was strange to see him so close yet out of reach. We passed the slate dump that loomed over Jenkinjones. I didn't want to see the ugly slate or the coal camp. I wanted to carry a piece of the mountain back with me, under glass, store it away for safekeeping, and bring it out now and then to live on.

At my house I stopped the jeep and walked back to the truck. Dillon's window was rolled down and his elbow rested on the door. I touched his arm and he took my hand.

"Leave Tony," he said. "Climb in the truck right now and come with me."

"I can't," I said. "It would be fine for you, but I'm the woman, Dillon. I'm the one who would suffer."

He squeezed my hand hard. "For God's sake, Rachel, don't turn away from me again."

"No," I said. "I'm not strong enough for that. I could see you Friday night when Tony's at the Moose Club."

He relaxed and smiled. "Friday night," he said. "Come to my place."

"Yes," I said. I walked toward the house.

"Rachel!" he called. "Can we at least tell my mother?"

I smiled. "We won't have to. She'll figure it out."

By Friday night I'd had time to sort things out. I had dreamed of Dillon all week and each time I dreamed, I accused myself, called myself an adulteress. I had always considered it the worst sin, next to murder. If I went to him again, I would have no excuse, could not claim to have been swept off my feet on a moonlit night. When Tony left for the Moose Club I sat alone and listened to the ticking of the kitchen clock. Then I bathed and put on a fresh dress and drove to Winco.

I parked behind Dillon's house, well out of sight of the highway.

There were no other houses close by, no one to mark my coming and going, and if we were seen, no one would think ill of a relative paying a visit. He took me by the hand and led me straight to the bedroom with hardly a word. At first I was nervous and awkward but he soothed me and I forgot everything except to hold him and love him as fiercely as I could.

Later he brewed a pot of coffee and we snuggled on the couch in bathrobes and sipped from steaming cups.

"I almost didn't come," I said.

"I worried about that," he said. "I would have come for you."

"It's adultery, Dillon. It's a sin."

"It's love," he said. "Sin is a puny thing to speak of when two people love. Anyway, it wouldn't be adultery if you'd divorce Tony."

"It would still be sin because we can't marry."

"At least you'd be free of Tony. I can't stand to think of you having sex with him."

"It doesn't happen often. But what if I stopped sleeping with him and then got pregnant? He'd know I was having an affair. Everyone would know and I'd lose my job and my parents would disown me. And the baby. What would I say to the baby?"

"There are other jobs and other places," he said, but he didn't say anything about family because he knew there was no answer to that. Some people are made to throw over the bonds of kinship but I am not one of them.

We were quiet for a while and then I said, "I do want a baby. I've tried with Tony but I think maybe he's sterile."

"I'll give you a baby," Dillon said.

"Do you think it would be all right? It wouldn't be deformed?"

"It won't be deformed." He smoothed my hair back from my forehead. "It would be a perfect baby."

I missed a period soon after and the morning sickness came on fast. I should have been pleased but I was terrified. I'd had sex with Tony only two days before Dillon and I spent the night on the mountain. When I told Dillon the baby might be Tony's, I thought he would put his fist through his living room wall.

"Goddamn it, Rachel, I thought you said he's sterile!"

"His sperm count may just be low. He won't have it checked so I don't know for sure."

"Jesus Christ!" He paced the floor, raked his fingers through his hair. Then he stopped. "I'll know," he said. "I'll look into that youngun's face and I'll know if it's got his blood or mine."

"You can't be sure." I started to cry. "Dillon, I want you to love this baby."

"I can't love Tony Angelelli's baby," he said, his voice so cold it like to froze my blood.

"It's my baby too," I said. "Whoever the father is."

I went to the door. He grabbed my arm.

"Don't leave," he said, and pulled me to him.

When I told Tony I was pregnant, he laughed and went to tell his mother. He never touched me.

When Jackie was born, I counted her fingers and toes as soon as I saw her, studied her face, pleased at the even features, the alert eyes that promised intelligence. She had dark hair, like both Tony and Dillon. Tony didn't come to the hospital until after the delivery, and I forbade Dillon for fear it would look suspicious. When Tony finally came to take me home and pushed my wheelchair to the car, I saw Dillon's truck parked down the street. He held a cigarette out the window, but I couldn't see his face. I lifted Jackie as though I was changing positions, but I was really holding her for Dillon to see. After we passed by his truck I heard him gun the engine and drive away.

THE CHILD
1959–1961

Jackie, 1959

I am almost eight and I am an insomniac. That is the biggest word I know. The doctor calls me it and he says I am young to be one but girls are sensitive and it's just a phase. Mommy says that means it won't last forever.

I live in Jenkinjones and when I was real little I thought there were bad things living outside my house. It is a wood house like a box and there is a wire fence around it but I thought the bad things might get in anyway.

I had an orange cat named Tiger who went outside and one time I heard Tiger scream and I heard lots of growls and Mommy said don't look outside. I was afraid to go in the yard for a long time.

I had a playhouse. It was made of heavy paper and you put it around a card table and you could go in and out the door and live in it.

It had windows with flower boxes and red flowers painted on. It looked like our house. Mommy and me went to town and left the little house in the yard and when we got back the sky was dark and growly and the little house was shreds of paper that didn't look like a house anymore.

There are snakes outside too, fat gray snakes, and I have seen them. One time Mommy dug up a snake in the garden and it tried to bite her but she killed it with her hoe. The snakes can run and they grab their tails in their mouths and turn into big hoops that roll fast and catch you. I dream about the snakes and they almost are on my front porch and I can't get in the house because my dad is inside holding the door and then I wake up.

My dad eats bacon and eggs for breakfast. When he finishes he gets up from the table and says, Now I have to go make some wampum. He says wampum like it is something you chew but Mommy says wampum is money.

Today when I come home from school my mommy isn't here and I go in the house all by myself. I am watching Mr. Cartoon so I won't have to worry about her. My dad comes home. He says, You know Mamaw Honaker? like I don't know Mamaw Honaker, even though she is my grandmother.

He says, Mamaw Honaker is real sick. Your Mom took her to the hospital and she won't come home until Mamaw dies. When you get off the school bus tomorrow, you go to my office instead of here.

I don't want Mamaw to die but I want my Mommy to come home soon.

My dad's job is keeping books. After school I have to sit in his office and I look for the books but I can't find any. The office is made of dark wood, and the floor smells like behind a bus because they put oil on it and the coal dust is ground in and the cigarette smoke. The green pad on my dad's desk is the only color in the room.

My dad says today is pay day when the miners get their money. He hangs out a sign that says NO WORK TOMORROW. One by one the miners look in at the bars of a window cut in the door. Their faces are black and shiny and the whites of their eyes look at me, then at my dad. They look like they are mad at him. Some of them read the sign and say bad words.

The Child, 1959–1961

We eat round steak for supper but my dad doesn't know how to make french fries and he makes me go to bed early. He stands in my bedroom door and he doesn't have any clothes on. His private things are fat and brown like big rotten fruits. I lie on my back and make a tent out of my blanket so I don't have to see.

I have to get up and go to the bathroom. He is in the living room watching Jack Paar and smoking cigarettes. I try to slip by without him seeing me but I have to go right behind his chair. I go so close by the chair I can smell the hair oil on his head. He says Aint you asleep yet? He sounds like he is mad at me. When I get back to bed I make the tent again.

The telephone rings and it is morning. My dad talks into the phone while I eat my cereal. When he hangs up he says, You know Mamaw Honaker? Mamaw Honaker's still real sick.

He says it like he is trying to remember something else but can't. I cry on the school bus because I miss my Mommy and I am afraid she will die too.

My dad takes me to the Moose Club. The Moose Club won't let us in until an eyeball watches us through a hole in the door, then we go inside. I think this is the place where mooses live but I don't see any, only one's head on the wall. The men are drinking from dark bottles at a bar like on TV.

Hey, Tony! the men say. They act like they like my dad.

He leaves me alone in a room with three pool tables. I poke at the colored balls with a big stick until I knock over a lamp. So I put up the stick and just roll the balls as hard as I can across the green table. Sometimes I roll a lot of balls at once and they hit each other. It's pretty fun.

Mommy is at home when we get back and I start crying and she starts crying. She yells at my dad, Where have you been? I called and called. It's a school night my mother is dying and can't you do anything to help? He says I don't know how to take care of her. You know I like to go out.

My dad gets mad and goes to spend the night at his mother's house. Mommy talks on the telephone and cries. Then she comes in my room and puts my clothes in a suitcase.

Dillon is coming from the hospital, she says. He's going to take you to his house.

Dillon is tall and skinny and has dark hair that gets in his eyes. He wears big brown shoes with dirt on them. I only see Dillon at Mamaw and Papaw's house. He watches me close and sometimes he lets me ride on his back like a horse. He doesn't come to our house because he and my dad don't like each other. Mommy goes to see him but she won't ever take me and sometimes she says don't tell daddy where she's going because he'll fuss. I don't like him to fuss so I never tell.

One time I asked Dillon how he was kin to me, and Mommy said, Cousin, real fast. She said, Dillon is your second cousin. Dillon said, Hellfire, and looked real mad and went home in his truck so I thought he didn't like me to be his kin.

When he comes Mommy talks to him in the living room. They talk real quiet but I can hear them if I lay down and put my ear against the door.

Are you sure? Mommy says.

Sure I'm sure. The mine's shut down until the end of the month so what else do I have to do except sit with you all in that hospital? I'm useless there. I love Aunt Flora, but you know she never cared much for me.

I don't want to impose, Mommy says.

How long do you want to keep punishing me? Dillon says.

Until you can love her wholehearted, Mommy says.

I told you I can't tell, Dillon says louder. How can I tell when she's being raised by that sonofabitch.

Mommy says, Ssshhhh, little pitchers.

After Mommy leaves, Dillon stands in the middle of my bedroom with his hands in his pockets.

Anything you want to take with you besides clothes?

Will you play a game with me?

What game?

I get a blue and gray box off the shelf and open it. It's a game about the Civil War. It has a map of the United States with rivers and it has plastic men, horses, and boats. I am afraid Dillon will laugh like Papaw did when I took the game to his house.

Papaw said, Lordy, Rachel, that's no toy for a little girl.

Mommy said, It's her birthday and that's what she wanted.

This is cavalry, I tell Dillon. That's different from the place where Jesus died. That was Calvary. Cavalry is horses. This is infantry. This is gunboats. Gunboats can only move on the rivers.

I wait for him to laugh.

Dillon bends over the board. He looks at me with his eyes real narrow like he is thinking hard. Who plays this with you? he says.

Nobody will play it. Mommy tried once but she didn't like it. So I just move things around myself and tell stories.

Dillon folds the game board and puts it in the box. I'll play it with you, he says. He puts the game under one arm and my suitcase under the other and we go to his truck.

At Dillon's house we drink Cokes in little bottles, eat popcorn, and play Civil War. I am blue because I like the North and they freed the slaves and gray is an ugly color. Dillon says he likes to be the South because the South lost and he loves a loser. This is a silly thing to say but I don't make fun because he doesn't make fun of me. Then he says a loser knows things about this world that a winner will never know and is better for it. We roll dice and move infantry and shove gunboats up and down the rivers. I win right before bedtime so Dillon will be happy.

Dillon lives at Winco. He doesn't have much furniture except a couch and chair and television and kitchen table and one bed and boxes for his clothes. He doesn't have any pictures on the wall. I sleep on the couch because I am little. We eat oatmeal for breakfast but on Saturday he makes pancakes with hot chocolate syrup to go on top of them.

Mommy calls on the phone and Dillon lets me talk to her. I tell her I'm having a good time and she doesn't say anything for a while. Then she says, I'm glad. Tell Dillon I appreciate him.

When I tell him he smiles and takes the phone. I love you, too, he says. Then he hangs up and winks at me.

Dillon has a brown pickup truck. He takes me for a ride because it is more fun to ride in a truck even if you go places you've already been. But Dillon says we will go someplace new.

I wear my cowboy boots and corduroy jacket. Dillon has a baseball cap that says UMWA on the front. He has a thermos jug of coffee and a lunch bucket with baloney and mustard sandwiches and Hostess cupcakes. He has a little thermos of milk for me and four spoons of coffee in it. He plays country music on the radio, Roy Acuff singing about car wrecks.

Good driving music, he says, and smokes a cigarette.

At Annadel we take the right fork to Jenkinjones. We go slow under the railroad trestle where the road is always full of water from the creek and the other trestle where the road curves so sharp you honk the horn to let other cars know you are coming through. It is a fun road to Jenkinjones. We pass the row of little Negro houses, then the road forks again as the hollow narrows and we go left where my house is but we don't stop, we keep on going.

I never been past the store, I say.

You never been up on Trace Mountain? Your mommy goes up here to work. There are people living way back in here she goes to nurse, but I doubt she'd take you unless you ask her.

Are you taking me to see those people?

Naw. I'm taking you someplace special.

We pass the company store. The road turns into dirt and goes up the mountain. The slate dump is burning and smells like where someone went to the bathroom.

I used to think bad things live here, I say. I thought they used the toilet at the slate dump and that's why it stinks so bad.

I expect him to smile and shake his head but he looks serious.

You were right, he says. There are bad things living here.

That scares me because Mommy said the bad things were figments but Dillon believes in them and he is grownup so maybe they are real after all. Then I am not scared again because Dillon takes my hand and holds it but his hand doesn't feel scared, it is quiet and warm. His hand has rough places like plastic all underneath. We go on the dirt road and then we turn onto a skinny road with a high hump that goes straight on up the mountain. Dillon puts both hands back on the steering wheel. He says this is a bear track we're driving on.

I can't hardly hear him because the truck rattles so loud. I bounce around on the hard slick seat and branches switch the truck. Then the road ends and we get out and walk for maybe ten minutes or a half hour. The trees move away and there are tall weeds tangled up like hair. Dillon stops and points. Then I see the log cabin. The weeds reach up its walls, the roof is sideways, and the logs look chewed on like the bad things have been having them for lunch.

I had a great-uncle, Dillon says. I was named for him. When the coal company come in, long time ago, he moved back up in here on Trace. He become a hermit, didn't see many people. I like to think this was his cabin but I don't know for sure.

It's real old, I say. I never seen nothing so old.

I keep thinking of what a hermit is. All I can figure is an old man with a long dirty beard like John the Baptist.

Did the hermit eat grasshoppers? I ask.

Dillon smiles. Lordy, I reckon he ate a little bit of everything. Grasshoppers and dandelion greens and groundhogs and possums.

Can we go inside?

Naw, that's something I won't do. Don't know if he's in there or if the animals has scattered his bones. Rather not know. There's some bones wasn't meant to be gathered in.

He looks at me. He says, Your mommy is the only other person I ever come here with.

She never told me, I say.

It was a long time ago. Before you was born.

We find a long flat rock to sit on. The stone is cold through my pants and my rear end goes numb. My face feels raw. We can see the tops of mountains, one after another, whipped up like the peaks of a gray mud pie. The mountains are scratched with the brown lines of strip mines so that the tops of the mountains seem to set crooked. Dillon opens the lunch pail and puts the thermos bottles on the rock. The mustard on the sandwiches makes the edges of my mouth burn. Dillon pours more coffee in my milk to warm it. The heat fogs my glasses.

Don't tell your mommy I give you coffee, he says.

I sit up straight and say, Hey, I know some things.

He smiles. I know you do.

·   ·   ·

At Dillon's house we eat hot dogs for supper and a can of pork and beans. Dillon says he can't feed me fancy because there's not much money with the mine closed. Then we walk to Uncle Brigham's house at Number Thirteen coal camp. We have to walk the railroad track because the Number Thirteen car bridge washed away. The water got high and when people woke up one morning the bridge was gone.

Uncle Brigham is Dillon's cousin but on his daddy's side so he is not my cousin. Everybody calls him Uncle Brigham even if he isn't their uncle. Dillon's buddy Homer Day is there and his brother Hassel Day who is skinny and Hassel's friend Junior Tackett who is fat. Hassel has a little mustache like Zorro and Junior has a crewcut so you can see freckles on his scalp. We watch West Virginia play California in basketball. Dillon says it is for the national championship. Little gray men in shorts run back and forth. The TV voice says Jerry West Jerry West Jerry West. The basketball falls through the net like water splashing and the ball is gone from the face of the earth and then it is there again and they grab it and run with it.

Uncle Brigham's wife Betty makes popcorn and me and Uncle Brigham's two kids eat it all up so she pops some more. Jerry West! the voice yells. But West Virginia loses the national championship by one point and Uncle Brigham cusses, and Uncle Brigham's boy Doyle Ray cries until Uncle Brigham shames him out of it. Dillon sits back like he is satisfied and not a bit surprised. I know what he is thinking about losers, and it makes me happy because there aren't many people I know what they think.

Mamaw Honaker is dead. She has been wooled and worried until there was nothing left and she had to go to Heaven. I'm not too sad. She always sat in a wheelchair and couldn't move or talk and just looked at me. Her right arm laid in her lap and the meat of her arm was so loose it looked to slip out of her skin and plop right onto the floor.

Papaw Honaker will go to live with Aunt Carrie and they will move back to Kentucky which is where they come from. Dillon says Aunt Carrie will take care of Papaw and it will give her something to do. He says Papaw Honaker is sick too and missing Mamaw and will not last long. So Mommy will be an orphan.

Mommy cries a lot but she is glad to be home. Dillon comes to see me at our house. Mommy says he shouldn't come but he says, Tony's at the Moose and me and this girl want to visit. I ask Mommy why she doesn't like Dillon and she says, I like Dillon, now do your homework.

Dillon has been to Charleston on union business. He has a white bag with the words Major's Book Store in red letters. Inside is *Charlotte's Web*.

The woman said it's for fourth grade but I said this is a real smart second-grader, Dillon says.

I have never had a book belong to me. Mommy takes me to the library every Saturday but I have to give the book back no matter how much I like it. Sometimes I want to hide the book instead of give it back.

I take *Charlotte's Web* to my room. I turn on the light so my dad won't fuss about buying me new glasses. I smell the book. Charlotte is a spider and she writes messages into her webs. Dillon is like a spider, his hair hangs over his forehead and he looks out from under it like Charlotte looking out from her web. He doesn't say SOME PIG but he is trying to tell me something.

JACKIE, 1961

My dad killed my spiders. They lived in the living room window, on the outside so they weren't hurting anybody. They were twin brothers named Harold and Darold and they each made a web shaped like a tunnel in the corners of the window behind the flower box. I hit flies with the fly swatter and took them outside and dropped them in the webs. I could just reach if I stood on the lawn chair. Harold was bigger and he had two white stripes down his back but Darold only had one stripe.

My dad said, "Those spiders will get in the house and bite us."

That is silly because spiders can't go through glass but my dad is too stupid to know that and he is afraid of spiders. Besides, he knew I liked Harold and Darold better than him. He took the broom and killed them right in front of me. I screamed and screamed but he still killed them. I will hate his guts forever.

My mom hates my dad too. She tells me everything awful about him. Mom says I am her best friend and she can tell me anything. She says she wants us to be close because she and my mamaw weren't. So she tells me about things like sex. It doesn't sound like much fun.

I don't know how mom can stand to have sex with my dad, but if you want babies you have to have sex. Now my mom has heart trouble and the doctors won't let her have any more babies. They tied her tubes. The baby goes up the tubes like CoCola up a straw, but if the tubes are tied the baby can't get by and it will die so it can't hurt my Mom. I'm glad because I would hate a baby that killed my Mom.

Mom doesn't have many friends, just Dillon and the nurses she works with, but she only goes to the movies with Dillon and me. Dillon says she should have more friends but she says we are enough. We don't tell my dad when Dillon goes to the movies, we say it is just me and Mom. The best we went to see was *Old Yeller* at the Pocahontas Theater in Justice. We sat in the balcony in front of the wall that marks off the Negro section. The Negroes don't go in the front door and I don't know how they get in. We can't see them and I wonder how they can see over the wall but I guess they can see because when Travis gets ready to shoot Old Yeller, I hear them call out and rustle around like they are anxious.

My Mom is a public health nurse during the day, but she works one night a week at the hospital in Justice, Friday nights, and my dad goes to the Moose Club. I'm supposed to have a baby sitter. But tonight my dad has the flu so he stays home. Mom heats a pot of leftover chicken soup.

"Maybe I should stay home," she says. She acts real nervous.

"Go on," says my dad. "You can't miss work."

After Mom leaves, I try to pretend my dad isn't there. I read *Little House in the Big Woods.* He says the light is bad and I will go blind but I ignore him because that is the way you have to do him. He lies on the couch, wrapped in a blanket, and watches the news. A blonde-headed woman says how exciting Washington is since Kennedy is president. My dad makes me get up and switch channels because he wanted Nixon. Then I ask, "Can I watch *The Wizard of Oz?* It's on tonight, and it won't be on for a whole nother year."

"They's a fight on," he said. "Friday night fight at nine."

"*The Wizard of Oz* comes on at seven-thirty," I say. "Just let me watch part of it. It's only the best movie in the world."

He shrugs. "Go on." He shuts his eyes like he will take a nap.

I know if he wakes up, we'll have our own fight and I'll lose, so I watch the first part of the movie as hard as I can. It's the only movie I know where a girl is the main character and does most everything right. Dorothy acts silly when she falls into the pig pen, but after that she is all right. I wrap my thumbs in my white undershirt while she runs away from home, and I wait for the tornado with a knot in my stomach. The house takes off. When Miss Gulch turns into a witch and hollers and carries on while she rides her broom, my dad opens his eyes.

"What's that?" he says.

"*The Wizard of Oz.*" He is really slow sometimes. The house falls out of the sky. It is made of wood and its paint is peeling off, just like our coal camp house. When it thumps down without breaking into a million splinters it is my favorite part of the movie.

"Turn it off," my dad says. "It's too scary. You'll dream."

"It's not nine o'clock!"

He gets up, walks to the set with the blanket trailing behind him, and flicks the button. The screen spits a white spark and turns gray.

I cry and kick the couch and he sends me to bed. After a while I can hear the donging of the bell and the fight announcer yelling through his nose. I can't sleep or dream.

·   ·   ·

I am surprised when he says he will take me to the carnival on Friday night because he never takes me anyplace. I want to go to the carnival, but not with him.

"He won't let me ride the big rides," I tell Mom.

"Yes, he will," she says. She is pulling on white hose and hooking them onto her garter belt with the snaps like little rubber pills, getting dressed to go to the hospital. "I'll tell him to let you ride the big rides."

Big deal. He never listens to Mom.

The Thomas Joyland Carnival is in Number Ten Bottom. You can look down on the lights and the going-around rides from the road on top of the mountain. The carnival shows up one week each year, then disappears like Brigadoon in Scotland that I saw on TV. Even in the dead of winter I can look in Number Ten Bottom and remember the tents and red trailers. The camp houses on the hill keep a watch with their windows dark like big sleepy eyes while they wait for the carnival.

I ride the merry-go-round first. My dad keeps looking around while he buys the ticket. I ride a purple horse while an organ plays music like they dance to in a fancy movie. I have read that some merry-go-rounds in special places have brass rings to grab. That must be the difference between a plain old merry-go-round and a carousel. I pretend I am on a carousel and reach out for the ring each time I pass my dad. He is talking to a woman.

When I get off the merry-go-round, my dad says, "Come over here and meet Jean."

Jean has curly brown hair pulled up on one side with a barrette and wears a purple and white checked dress. "What a beautiful little girl," she says, and smiles.

I wouldn't believe anybody who calls me beautiful. I turn to my dad. "I want to ride the cars." I have decided to start slow and work up to the big rides.

I ride the cars and a caterpillar that goes over humps. Then my dad buys me a candy apple. He doesn't mind buying me food. He says I'm too skinny.

He talks to the woman. "Doc the Fish died. You heard about Doc the Fish?"

Jean looks at him like she doesn't know what he's talking about.

"Doc the Fish," he says again. "He's this big fish they found way back in the mine under Trace Mountain, in a pond about four miles in. No telling how long he'd been underground like that. Since caveman times maybe. He turned white after they brung him out."

"I never heard of that," she says.

"It was in *Ripley's Believe It or Not*. Old Mister Denbigh used to keep him in a tank in his office, and then Arthur Lee got him."

It is the longest I've ever heard my dad talk to anybody. But I don't care about any Doc the Fish. I tug his sleeve. "I want to ride the Scrambler."

"Naw," he says. "That's too dangerous."

"No it aint. Nobody ever gets hurt."

"Jackie, I know what I'm talking about. They're a bunch of drunks that works for carnivals. They take them rides down every week and put them back together too fast. Half the screws is loose. That car might fly right off of there."

"Everybody gets to ride it. Mommy rode it with me last year. You ride it with me."

Now I've made him mad. "I aint getting on one of them rides." He looks at the woman. "It's silly."

But I know he's scared of the rides, like he is scared of spiders.

Jean is still smiling. "I'll ride with her," she says. "She'll be my little girl."

I run to buy a ticket. When we climb in the car, Jean puts her arm around me and holds real tight. "Now you won't go anywhere," she says. Her skin is warm under her dress and I can smell her stinky deodorant. I am already figuring how I can get back at my dad for Harold and Darold.

I tell my Mom everything. She says, "Your father is visiting your grandmother this afternoon. We'll just go over there and see about this."

As soon as we get to my grandmother's house, Nona Teresa comes on the porch. She has a bowl of tomatoes that she holds against her hip. She doesn't like Mom. Mom tries to keep on her good side because she says my grandmother tells my dad how to wipe his bottom.

When Mom sees Nona on the porch, she gets out and stands beside the car, says, "Hello, Nona." Nona throws a tomato at her but it misses and splats all over the windshield. Mom gets back in the car real fast and says, "I guess your father already told her."

When my dad comes home, they fight right in front of me.

"Her brother is one of my Moose buddies," my dad says. "She's a friend. Can't I have friends?"

"If you have an affair, that's your business. If you want a divorce, I'll give it to you. But why was that hussy making up to my daughter?"

"Aw," says Dad.

Then Mom sends me to my room. I shut the door and laugh my head off. I know she will ask him about sex. If I lay down flat on my stomach I can hear them under the door. The rush of air from the kitchen makes my ear cold.

"You're sleeping with her."

"Maybe."

"I don't care, do you understand? But you don't bring my daughter into it."

"She's my daughter too," my dad says.

And there is dead silence in that room.

After a while my mom says, "You never acted like it before."

"That ain't true. I pay the bills, don't I?"

"I pay half of them."

"I pay for the food that goes in her mouth. I correct her when she needs it."

"You've never been a father to her."

"My mother don't like you," my dad says. He's good at changing the subject that way. He's not trying to be smart, he just can't think in a straight line. "I took Jean to see my mother. This Sunday I'm taking Jean and Jackie to see her."

"The hell you are," Mom says, and when she cusses you know she is mad. She comes through the door so fast I have to roll out of the way. She turns on the light and stares at me, sprawled on the floor beside the bed.

"Pack a bag," she says. "We're leaving."

· · ·

We go to stay with Aunt Carrie. Aunt Carrie used to live at Jenkinjones but now she lives on Kingdom Come Creek in Kentucky. In Kentucky there are mountains and coal mines just like West Virginia but it is different because the license plates on cars are white instead of blue and gold, and the names of towns are on white signs instead of green ones. After we cross the Levisa Mom asks, "Would you be upset if I divorced your father?"

"No."

"You wouldn't miss him?"

"I'd like it better."

"We won't have much money."

She holds the steering wheel with both hands. I think what a good driver she is, and how I am never afraid to ride in the car with her.

"I don't care," I say.

"We'll have to move, but I promise we'll stay on Blackberry Creek. You won't have to switch schools." She glances at me. "When Dillon hears about it, he'll want us to live closer to him."

I bounce up and down and say "Yea!"

"You like Dillon, don't you?"

"I wish Dillon was my dad."

She doesn't say anything for a long time. Weeds grow thick in the ditch beside the road. We cross a high mountain and I can't see the bottom of the hollow below us. If we went off the road we'd fall forever.

"Dillon's wild," Mom says. "I want you to love him but I don't want you to be like him. Don't you tell him or Aunt Carrie I said so. You hear? It would hurt their feelings."

I say yes because I hardly ever disobey her, not when it is something important. Mom is all I have and if I don't act right, maybe God would take her away to punish me. When I read in the newspaper about kids whose mothers have died, I wonder how they keep from going crazy.

Aunt Carrie lives in a white farmhouse with an open porch around two sides and a screened-in porch at the back. She has a well with wire over the top to keep you from falling in, and a hand pump. Next to the house is a falling-apart barn where the milk cow lives. I don't like the milk from the cow because it has big globs of fat in it and hairs floating on top. When I come visit, Aunt Carrie buys real milk from the store.

We take our suitcases inside and then Mom makes me go out to play. I can tell she is about to cry. Aunt Carrie puts her arm around Mom's waist and guides her through the kitchen door. "Does Dillon know?" she asks. I can't hear what Mom says back.

Later Aunt Carrie comes outside and sits on the front steps. She sits easy even though she's so old. All the skin on her arms and neck is loose and empty.

"Your mama is lying down," she says. She sits still and looks out over the yard like she comes from someplace else. "Are you all right?"

"Sure."

"Tony Angelelli's all wrong for your mother," she says. "I don't want you to blame yourself. Hit's one of those things should never been, but good may come of it yet."

I nod. "I'm glad she left him," I say. Then I start to cry too. She puts her arms around me. She smells old and musty like a suitcase that has been shut up for a long time.

"Law, child," she says. "They's so much I'd like to tell you."

After supper I look at Aunt Carrie's photo album. I love the pictures, all faded and brown and pasted on the black pages of the photo album with white stickers at each corner. Aunt Carrie and Mom sit on the couch while I stretch out beside the fireplace with a plate of peanut butter fudge. The room is quiet because Aunt Carrie won't have the TV on when she has company.

The names under the photographs are familiar. *Carrie and Flora, 1938.* Two women wearing dresses with their arms around each other. They stand in front of the old Homeplace on Grapevine. *Dillon on crutches, 1944,* from where he got wounded in the war. All the pictures are of Mom's family, brothers, sisters, cousins, aunts, and uncles. They are tow-headed, all except Dillon who takes after his daddy. I don't look like Mom's people either because my dad has black hair.

"I want my maiden name back," Mom says. "I'm going to be a

Honaker again. And I want to change Jackie's name too. Jackie Honaker. How would you like that, honey?"

"I'd like it fine," I say. It will be fun at school. I will fool everyone.

I try to wish myself into the pictures, fall asleep, and wake up when the telephone rings. Aunt Carrie, sounding far away, says, "Dillon will be here tomorrow morning." Mom carries me upstairs and lays me on the featherbed. I burrow deep beneath the quilt so that I lie in a black spider's tunnel that leads backward. When I wake up I will be inside the pictures and hold hands with all my kin.

RACHEL

Dillon was forty years old the year I left Tony. He was still thin but he had a chest like a barrel, the way miners do after they've worked underground for years, like he had been pumped full of water. He sat at his mother's breakfast table and cut his fried eggs so the yolk ran into the red-eye gravy from the country ham, made yellow and red swirls with his fork, and sopped the whole thing up with his biscuit.

"You could move in with me," he said.

Jackie clapped her hands.

No," I said sharply. I kicked him under the table and he looked at me with his eyes narrowed. "I've been bullied by a man for fifteen years, and I want to be on my own."

Aunt Carrie kept frying eggs and trying to pretend she wasn't interested in the conversation.

"Well then, the doctor's house in Number Thirteen has been empty for a spell," Dillon said.

I'd been waiting for this too and was determined to put up at least a show of resistance. "Number Thirteen is a hard place to live with that bridge out. Jackie would have to walk a mile to the school bus. Anyway, I can't afford to buy a house on my salary. I was thinking about renting an apartment in Justice town."

"Only four thousand dollars," he said.

"Four thousand—You mean down?"

"I mean four thousand period. Company's unloading all its houses or else tearing them down. This one would have been only three thousand, but your boss Arthur Lee is tacking a thousand dollars on everything he sells. Says it's his reward for faithful service to the company. Maybe Arthur Lee will cut you a deal since you're such good buddies."

"You won't convince me by giving me a hard time about Arthur Lee," I said. "He gave me a job back when I was desperate to get out of the house."

"I wouldn't mind walking to the school bus," Jackie said. "I like that house. I could have the doctor's office for a playhouse. And we could walk to Dillon's real easy."

"I hear you," I said.

Dillon was smiling. I pulled him aside while Jackie helped Aunt Carrie with the dishes.

"I know what you're thinking," I said. "You think we'll be together every night."

"I can walk to Number Thirteen if you don't want to come to Winco," he said.

"I won't have it. I won't sleep with you and my daughter in the same house. She'd know."

"Maybe it's time we told her."

"Told her what? That her mother doesn't even know who her father is? That her mother has been pretending to work at the hospital on Friday nights while she carries on with her first cousin? I'm trying to raise her properly, Dillon."

"And you're doing too damn good a job," he said. "You'll make a little nun out of her.

"That's for me to say. I'm her mother."

His jaw was tight like always when he is angry. "Let's get blood tests. We'll settle this once and for all."

"No. Maybe when she's grown up. Then she'll know enough to

keep a secret if she needs to, and if things don't turn out the way we want, she'll handle it better. But not now."

"I want to know for me, not her. If I knew that girl was mine, I'd have run Tony Angelelli off a long time ago."

I didn't answer him.

Aunt Carrie wanted Dillon to cut weeds at the Homeplace cemetery, so she packed fried baloney sandwiches and dried apple pie into a paper poke. We squeezed into the cab of Dillon's pickup. Jackie rode in the bed, perched on the spare tire. Dillon rarely got out of third gear, for the roads were pocked with potholes gouged out of the asphalt by coal trucks. It was early April and the trees were dotted with green buds. Here and there sprays of white dogwood and sarvice quickened the gray mountainsides. At the mouth of Scary we crossed a one-lane bridge and parked beside the railroad track.

"Train track wasn't here when we was younguns," Dillon told Jackie. "They brung it through in the forties. We'll walk it on up Grapevine. You sure you're up for it, Mom?"

"I can still yet walk you into the ground," Aunt Carrie said.

Dillon carried a sickle and the paper poke with the sandwiches. Jackie walked on the track rail, arms out, pretending she was on a circus tightrope. I felt suddenly lighthearted, watching her, enjoying Tony's absence and knowing it was permanent. I joined Jackie, balancing on the rail.

Aunt Carrie showed Jackie where the Aunt Jane Place had been. "Dillon and me lived here," she said. The bottom was dense with ironweed, blackberry bushes, and untended canebrakes, and the cabin was gone.

Dillon kept looking off to the left, his eyes narrow against the sun. "Nobody's been on this land yet," he said.

"No," said Aunt Carrie. "Last I heard the bank had sold the mineral, but nobody's come for it, thank God. Still, it's only a matter of time."

We found the cemetery path but I said, "Let's walk on a tad longer. I want to show Jackie the shoals." So we went on another quarter mile until the bottom narrowed and disappeared at the curve of the river. Beyond a stand of birch saplings, water purled in white ripples. I told Jackie how Dillon and I had fished here, and Aunt Carrie and my mother before us. Once there was a pool above the shoals for swimming, and a ford. Now the river was shallow and black with sludge. Pieces of tires and rusting metal drums littered the bank.

"I nearly drowned here," I told her. "I got caught crossing the ford while the ice was breaking upstream. My mule saved me. I caught my finger in the bridle ring and broke it." I held up my crooked finger for Jackie to see. "I loved that old mule and I never forgot how it saved my life. I cried when your Papaw had to put it down."

Dillon had already turned and was walking back up Grapevine. He appeared to be in a huff, the way he walked so fast and left us, but I couldn't tell why. We followed him back to the mouth of a narrow ravine that climbed a low shelf of the mountain. A path twisted up between the trees, its steps sculpted from roots and rocks. Then a clearing opened beneath the pine trees. Dillon was waiting, standing quiet and watching us climb. He talked to Jackie, acted like his mother and I weren't there. "If you want to find a cemetery, always look for the pine trees. They fancied evergreens around a burying ground."

The graveyard was surrounded by a wire fence, rusty and sagging on one side. Brambleweed and broomsedge grew around the tombstones, which were jumbled together as though dropped from the air and planted where they landed.

"These are your kin," Aunt Carrie told Jackie. She turned in a slow circle, pointing. "Aunt Jane. Aunt Becka. My mother Tildy. Papaw Alec May that was killed during the Civil War. Your Mamaw and Papaw Honaker, new graves. And them two—" she nodded at two old headstones set side by side. Albion Freeman, 1889–1921. Rondal Lloyd, 1890–1922. "My husband that give Dillon his last name, and Dillon's true father."

I'd told Jackie that Carrie had not been married to Dillon's father and that she was not to ask about it. She didn't say anything, just looked at the graves.

"My mom and dad wasn't married," Dillon said. "Does that make them bad people, Jackie?"

"Dillon!" Aunt Carrie said, sharp and low.

I wanted to smack him. Jackie looked at him, then at me, and I saw the confusion on her face. I'd taught her it was wrong to have sex outside of marriage. I knew it was hypocritical, but I wanted her to act better than I had, to be a lady the way my mother had taught me.

"Dillon's just teasing you, honey," I said. "Don't pay him any mind."

I looked hard at him. He knelt and wiped the graven letters on the stones with his handkerchief. Clumps of dirt and cobwebs clung to the white cloth. Then he set to clearing the weeds from the graves, swinging the sickle wide like he was cutting slices of air, ignoring the rest of us.

"Dillon keeps this place neat," Aunt Carrie said, trying to sound cheerful. "He always liked a burying ground."

"Not me," I said. I kept looking hard at Dillon. "I don't care for dwelling on the past nor to think on death. It makes a person tedious."

"I like a burying ground," Jackie said. "I wish all them people would stand up so I could see what they looked like."

"You wouldn't care for what they look like now," Dillon said.

I said, "Stop it! You're scaring my daughter to death!"

"And you're being self-righteous. As usual."

Aunt Carrie sat on the ground and leaned against a fencepost. "If they's some reason why you all are at each other's throats, I wish you'd figure it out and leave me and the child in peace." She opened the poke and handed Jackie a sandwich. "Us two are the only ones with a lick of sense. We're going to eat lunch."

JACKIE

I always thought they liked each other, but maybe they were just pretending. Me and Aunt Carrie are sitting right here and they seem like they forgot.

"Tell me you don't give a damn about the past," Dillon says. "Why'd you show Jackie the shoals?"

"I wanted her to see the shoals. I don't want her to wallow in them."

"And because I care about this place and my flesh and blood that's buried here, I'm wallowing?"

"You act like I don't care. I care too. But sometimes I think you'd dig up a grave and dance with a skeleton. And not for any reason except to lay claim on it."

Dillon stabs a tree trunk with the sickle, so deep the point sticks and holds. Aunt Carrie looks at me. "Dillon, you are scaring this child," she says.

"You see," Mom says. She sits beside Aunt Carrie and eats a sandwich. Nobody says anything for a while. Mom and Dillon don't look at each other.

Aunt Carrie says, "I wish Jackie could see the house."

"The foundation might still be there," Dillon says. "But that bottom is awful grown up. I don't know if we could find it or not."

"I can see the willows from here," Aunt Carrie says. "The house was near the willows. Why don't you younguns go? I wouldn't mind a spell by myself with these graves."

Mom tries to act like she isn't interested, but I can tell by her face that she is. We leave the railroad track and aim for the green willows. Beggar's lice sticks all over my clothes and briars scratch my arms and legs, but I keep going.

We reach a bunch of thick stalks that Mom calls a canebrake. Dillon is in front. He parts the cane with his sickle and stops to hold it back for us. Mom tells how Papaw and the neighbors made molasses from the cane at the wheel and the pan, how she and Dillon ate the meat of the cane stalks for the sweetness. Dillon breaks off a stalk and I taste, try to imagine him and my mom being kids like me. The cane isn't as good as a candy bar. I throw it down, cut ahead of Dillon, and head toward the willows. I want to be the first one to spy the foundation.

Then I feel a board under my foot and it snaps with a loud crack when I step down on it. I drop so fast it is like my stomach jumps up to my throat. My arms hit the board and I try to hold on, but my right arm slips and I kick out. My legs are hanging in space. My arms hurt and I slip farther, splinters bite the skin above my elbow, the board sags. I kick again and scream. Then Mom grabs my arm, Dillon throws himself flat on his belly with his head stuck down in the hole, reaches out, and catches hold of a belt loop on my jeans. Mom leans over and slips her arms under mine. They drag me up and we fall in a heap.

Mom holds me tight. Dillon gets up slow and finds a rock. He drops it in the hole. It gets real quiet and then we hear a faraway splash.

"It's the old well," Dillon says.

"It almost took my baby," Mom says. "So much for living in the past."

"I suppose it's my fault."

"I want to leave."

"Fine. We'll leave. We're only ten yards from where the house set, but if you're going to be pigheaded about it, we'll leave."

"I don't think I want to move to Number Thirteen."

They have forgot about me again.

"Fine. Why don't you go back to that sonofabitch Tony?"

"I'm making a big change in my life and I almost lost my daughter down the Homeplace well. It's not a good sign, it doesn't bode well."

"Jesus Christ, you yell at me for living in the past and here you turn superstitious on me. You want a sign, I'll give you a sign. We pulled that girl out of the well together and here we stand, just the three of us, on our land. Tell her what she needs to know. This is where she should hear it."

They look at me for the first time.

I dance around yelling "Tell me, tell me," but something hard in Mom's face stops me cold.

"I'm going back to Aunt Carrie," she says, and pushes her way back through the canebrake. Dillon picks me up and sets me on his shoulders. I can see above the cane, across the bottom to the mountains on the other side of the river.

"One thing I want you to know," Dillon says. "This is your land.

They's a piece of paper at the courthouse in Shelby says otherwise, but don't never believe a piece of paper. Land belongs to them that love it. I want you to love this land."

"I do love it," I say. I want to make him feel good after Mom has been so mean. He pats my knee.

Mom waits beside the railroad track. Dillon stops when he sees her and sets me down. "Run on ahead," he says. I skip down the track, bouncing from one cross tie to the next, pleased that I have had an adventure on my land. Someday I will come back and look down the well. I stop once and glance back down the track. They are standing with their arms around each other and Mom puts her head on Dillon's chest and starts to cry.

On the way home, we stop at the Grace Hospital in Justice so Mom and Dillon can give blood. Mom says it is to help people who are sick but I hate needles so I think they are crazy. Then I have to get my finger stuck to make sure I don't need iron pills, even though the doctor did that when I had my checkup. Afterward we stop at an office on the first floor and Mom talks to a woman.

"Wanda's mother is one of my patients," Mom tells Dillon. "She'll look at Tony's records for me."

We walk down the hill to the Flat Iron Drugstore and Dillon buys us chocolate sodas. I tell him about my baseball cards while Mom talks on the phone. When she comes back she stirs her soda with her straw.

"I'm O positive," she says. "You're A positive. Jackie is A positive." She bites her fingernail. "Tony is A positive. So it doesn't prove a thing."

Dillon's knuckles are white where he is holding onto the table. I am scared because I have been reading about leukemia in *Reader's Digest*.

"Is somebody sick?" I ask.

Mom puts her hand on my head. "No, honey. Nobody's sick."

Book Two

THE ROVING PICKETS
1 9 6 2

JACKIE

When we first moved into our new house at Number Thirteen, I figured I would be a writer. The new house has got white bookcases built right into the wall. It has a bedroom downstairs where Dillon sleeps sometimes, with a bed that Mom says is oak. The doctor left the bed with ugly white paint all over it but Mom took the paint off and she says it is an antique. The house has got big bedrooms upstairs with sloped ceilings. You can walk right into the closets and there are smelly old trunks the doctor left behind. There's nothing in the trunks but they look like what you would take on a sea voyage in a wooden ship or strap onto the back of a stagecoach. When I looked at the trunks I started to think up lots of stories about princes and princesses in faraway lands.

There is a boy in Number Thirteen named Toejam Day. His father

works at the mine with Dillon. Toejam isn't real smart, and his family is poor. Toejam's teeth are so rotten they have got black streaks all over them and Mom says when he gets big he will have dentures.

Toejam delivers the newspapers for Number Thirteen and sometimes I help him. I let him borrow my bicycle and he doubles me. Toejam is little but he is strong. He stands up and pumps the pedals while I sit on the seat and throw newspapers on the porches. The streets are made of mud and chunks of red dog from the slate dump, so it is rough riding but Toejam has never wrecked us. He only wrecks when he is by himself.

While Toejam pedals I tell him stories I made up about the people who live in the houses. They aren't good stories because you can't tell good stories about people around here, but it is what Toejam likes. His favorites are about the people who live on Hunkie Hill. They are Hungarians, Russians, and Czechoslovakians. Toejam can't even say "Czechoslovakians."

There is a church with a gold dome in main Davidson for the people from Hunkie Hill. Mom says it was an Orthodox church but now it is closed up. I tell Toejam they still go there and they have got a secret radio transmitter in the dome with a direct line to Nikita Khrushchev. Sam Chernenko is a real old man who lives in the last house on the hill and he still speaks English with an accent so strong you can't hardly understand him. He whitewashed the rocks and tree trunks in his yard. Mom says Sam Chernenko is eccentric. I told Toejam that Sam has witch ceremonies at midnight and dances around the painted rocks in a white gown and sacrifices groundhogs with a curved sword. Toejam is scared to death of Sam Chernenko.

They are just silly stories I tell Toejam, like the dumb old hillbilly story Uncle Brigham Lloyd tells. Uncle Brigham and his family live just across the street from our new house. Uncle Brigham has a big chest and skinny legs. He leans forward when he walks, like a stiff chicken. He comes onto his front porch every blue evening in the summertime, leans over the rail, coughs a while, and spits out icky black gobs that Mom says is coal dust from his lungs. Then he sits on the metal glider with the faded green plastic cushions and leans back with his legs straight out in front of him.

I like to sit on our front porch swing and read Nancy Drew mysteries from the library. Nancy Drew is real smart, smarter than anybody in Number Thirteen.

But Uncle Brigham will holler, "Hey, Jackie, come on over here, gal!" I hate to interrupt Nancy Drew and it is nice on our porch with the ivy and rose bushes and flower boxes all around, but I don't like to be rude. So I walk across the red dog road to his bare old porch. I pull open the gate that is almost off its hinges in the wire and wood fence and sit on the front stoop. When Uncle Brigham leans toward me, I can smell his breath sweet with alcohol.

He tells the story of the Big Toe like this:

"Once upon a time, they was a man put in a potato patch right over yonder in the bottom by Lloyds Fork. He lived in that big old house of yourn. And this feller lived all by himself, no wife nor younguns. One night he had a hankering for fried taters and wild onions. So he goes out to his garden and he hoes and he digs him up the finest big tater you ever did see. That feller pulled him some wild onions and went back to his wood stove and fried himself up a whole mess of taters. And after he et all that, he didn't feel like doing nothing but sleeping. So he dragged himself up the stairs and went to bed.

"Hit was sometime around midnight he woke to a thumping noise, coming from the kitchen. He set right up in that bed.

" 'Who's there?' he hollers.

"First he didn't hear nothing. Then they come a low moaning. 'O-o-o-o-h!'

" 'Who's there?' he hollers again.

"Then he hears a faraway voice. 'I—want—my—big—toe.' "

Uncle Brigham stared over my head like he saw something horrible in the dark. Lightning bugs floated by.

" 'Hit's the devil at your door and I want my big toe. I'm on the first step. I'm on the second step.'

"Now that feller was shaking so hard his bones rattled.

" 'I'm on the third step. I WANT MY BIG TOE! I'M ON THE FOURTH STEP!'

"Feller tried to hide under his bed but hit was built too low to the floor.

" 'I'M ON THE FIFTH STEP!'

"That feller was back in the bed with the quilt pulled plumb over his head.

" 'I WANT MY BIG TOE! I'M ON THE EIGHTH STEP! I'M—'

"GOTCHA!"

I almost did scream when he grabbed a hold of my neck.

"I scared you, girl."

He started laughing like it was real funny. I have to admit I was a little nervous but I was younger then. I wasn't that scared. But he kept teasing me while I rubbed my bare feet back and forth in the gritty coal dust on the floor and wouldn't look at him, I was so mad.

Then he had to quit laughing because he started coughing. He wiped his mouth in a red bandana, then said in a wheezy voice, "They aint no escaping the Booger man, youngun. Hit's a waste of time to try."

I ran across the road and settled on our front porch swing. And every time I go to Uncle Brigham's, he tells the same dumb story about the Booger man, and no handsome prince to rescue anybody. It's not a real story like you would hear someplace else.

When I got back from his house I'd get a notebook and figure I would write a real story with a happy ending. But it never worked. I'm not a real writer. Real writers live in New York apartments or sit at sidewalk cafés in Paris.

Sometimes I study Number Thirteen from my front porch. The houses used to be white, but now they are faded gray with coal dust and their paint is peeling. They sit all close together. In the dusk I can pretend it is not Number Thirteen, it is the German village where the Grimm brothers told their stories, and the coal camp houses are really cottages like where Hansel and Gretel lived, cottages lit with candles and lanterns instead of cheap lamps from the five-and-ten.

But it is still the same old Number Thirteen. In one house Homer Day reads the Bible while his wife Louella heats up bacon grease for the wild greens Toejam picked for supper. It is all they will have to eat. Nearby Homer's brother Hassel and his friend Junior Tackett sit on a vinyl couch outside Hassel's trailer. Across the street, Uncle

The Roving Pickets, 1962

Brigham Lloyd is getting drunk and I can hear the TV turned up loud through the open screen door. Betty and the kids are watching "Bonanza" and Uncle Brigham is hollering at them to turn down the goddamn noise. My mom is working her half-acre in the camp garden, trying to finish hoeing the tomatoes before it gets dark, and Dillon is walking the railroad track toward her. She stops hoeing to watch him come on.

So there is not a thing to write about, only hillbillies, and nobody cares to hear about hillbillies. I go inside to watch TV.

I don't know what I'd do without my mom. One day when she was late from work, I was sure she was dead. I imagined a car wreck. I stood in the screen door watching down the hill and pictured the glass scattered like shiny popcorn and red sticky blood puddling with the coal dust in the road. I am a Christian. I was saved when I was ten at the Felco Methodist Church Sunday School. So I got down on my knees and promised Jesus that if my mom came back safe I'd go off to Africa and be a missionary. I was sorry for that promise as soon as she walked in the door and said she'd had a flat tire.

I knew I'd have to figure something out. Louella Day says when people break promises to God, He squashes them flat. But I wonder if God can be got around. Like the story where God tells Abraham to sacrifice Isaac. Sure Abraham went through the motions, laid his son on the altar, and even raised up the knife. But who's to say he would have gone through with it? Abraham had to have an eye cocked toward Heaven waiting to hear 'Don't Bother.' Anybody who hears a lot of stories could see it coming. I considered that maybe God didn't want any more missionaries in Africa and was aggravated at me butting in. Or maybe I could convince Him I'd be a second-rate missionary and He'd want to fire me. I decided to test my call on the Lloyds. If I succeeded, there'd be more souls in Heaven, but I'd also have to find another excuse for not going to Africa. I wasn't too worried, though. The Lloyds would be tough nuts to crack, and God would understand that I was a failure.

The Lloyds never go to church. Neither does anyone else at Number Thirteen except for the Days, since Homer pastors the Holiness church on the hill and his congregation walks in from up Lloyds Fork. It's not that people here are heathens—they all believe in God. But Dillon says they don't like to be preached at unless they're ready to die and need to be whipped into shape for Heaven. Everybody reckons to go to church some day. It is just something they'll get around to when they're too old to have fun. It's the preacher's job to remind them that some will be caught unawares.

There were four Lloyds for me to save, and I decided to go after one of the kids. Doyle Ray, the oldest, is the most obnoxious person in Number Thirteen, always picking fights and throwing red dog. At school he hit me in the face with a hunk of red dog and broke my glasses. The doctor said I was lucky I didn't lose an eye.

Doyle Ray needed saving, but I couldn't muster enough charitable feeling toward him to do it. The Bible says to return good for evil, but after Doyle Ray hit me in the face I gave him a glass of Kool-Aid made with creek water. The creek is full of mine acid and sewage, so it wasn't very Christian of me.

That left Brenda.

Brenda is in my class at the Felco Grade School. She sits at the desk in front of me, so she would be easy pickings. Besides, I like Brenda and thought I would enjoy saving her. She is real short and skinny. Her black hair is cut straight across in bangs and she has a mustache of little black hairs on her upper lip. She wears short-sleeved cotton dresses that her mother makes off the same pattern, no matter what time of year it is.

Brenda is the best arithmetic student in the school, which means she is also the fastest. Miss Cox, the fifth-grade teacher, believes in speed. She taught us the steps of long division and sends us to the blackboard in teams—boys against girls, one row against another—to see who can get the right answer the fastest. Brenda always finishes first. When she works long division at the board she has to reach high because she is so short. Her dress rides up her back, the material pulled up by the belt, until her panties almost show. Her long skinny arm skips across the blackboard like a monkey looking for bugs on tree bark that I saw on "Wild Kingdom."

I decided to save Brenda a little at a time. I would start by asking questions like "If Jesus knocked on your door this evening, what would you be ashamed of that you done today?" That is Preacher Johnson's favorite line.

But every time I had a chance, like walking home from the school bus, the words stuck in my throat. I did manage to ask Brenda if she'd like to go to church.

"Not really," she said.

I felt awful uncomfortable trying to save Brenda, like I thought I knew more than she did. I talked to Dillon about it, and he said anyone who tried to save someone else was a snob and he wished Mom wouldn't take me to such a narrow-minded church. So I didn't have to fool God into thinking I would be a wash-out as a missionary. It was an actual fact, and I was off the hook.

Mom doesn't like the Lloyds. Uncle Brigham is Dillon's first cousin, but from his daddy's people. Mom says the Lloyds are Dillon's rough side. Uncle Brigham's face is wide, and he has a big fat nose with a wart stuck on one side. He's got a blue scar he calls a coal tattoo on his forehead where he was hit by a chunk of falling slate. Mom feels sorry for his wife Betty, because Uncle Brigham stays drunk. A long time ago, he ran off his first wife with his drinking. Sometimes he and Betty fight with dishes and brooms and frying pans. Dillon lives too far away to help, so the kids run across the street to Mom and beg her to make the peace. She comes back after half an hour, shaking her head, and is in a bad mood the rest of the day. Usually she does our ironing after she's been to the Lloyds and smites our clothes with a strong right arm like God did the Philistines.

Once after she came home from the Lloyds, I snuck across the street and found Uncle Brigham slumped on the front porch glider.

"Uncle Brigham, how come you drink so much?"

"Hey, Jackie." He stared into space.

I felt real brave so I asked him again.

"Aw," he said, "hit aint as final as a bullet and tastes better than rat poison." He rocked back and forth, smiled in a way that made his lips go thin. "My back hurts, youngun. Broke it in the mines oncet, you know." He waved his hand slow and tired like. "Come up on this here porch. Let me tell you a story."

I sat on the floor, my back against the glider, my fingers tracing patterns in the coal dust on the floor. He told the story of the Big Toe again but he didn't grab me. I pretended like I was scared but he didn't laugh.

HASSEL DAY

I am the mayor of Number Thirteen. It's what I tell them at that county courthouse. It's what I tell anybody that asks. Now Hassel, they say, you know you aint never been elected mayor. That's because we don't have no election, I tell them. If we had one, I'd be elected. So there.

American Coal owns the land and they used to own the houses until just here a bit ago. When they let things go, somebody had to look after folks, and I like to do that. I never finished the ninth grade and the mines won't take me because I was working under a car in Junior Tackett's yard and slipped a disc. Company is afraid I'd hurt my back again and they'd get the blame, so they won't hire me on. It was touch and go for a while how I'd make a living. Lucky I got kin and I could eat off my brother Homer and his family. Or Junior would help. Junior stays at the trailer sometimes. Then we will fight and he'll go back to his mommy's for a while. But he generally comes back.

Arthur Lee Sizemore opened his Esso station at Felco, and Junior got me a job pumping gas. Junior is the best mechanic on Blackberry Creek, he could fix a motor with Band-Aids and rubber bands, so his word counts for something with Arthur Lee. It is nice work pumping gas because you see the world pass by, but they aint no mental exercise to it except counting out change. I like a challenge, so in my spare time I look after Number Thirteen.

Number Thirteen was built sturdy, but coal dust and hard living will wear a place down. We had a company store but American shut it up and boarded up the windows. Our houses all got four rooms and a porch, except for the double houses around the hill and the big house where the doctor used to live. The outsides of them houses is peeling, and aint nobody can afford a can of paint. Still yet it is a fine place. I know every man jack that lives here, know their wives and younguns, know the insides of their houses like I know my own trailer. I set and drink coffee with everybody and they tell me their troubles. Wouldn't you know, the folks that has the most problems makes the best coffee. It's funny the way life works out.

My trailer sets on the Free Patch. The Free Patch is five acres between Number Thirteen and the ninth hole of the golf course that don't belong to the coal company or the land company or the railroad. Nobody knows who owns it. I tried once to look up the title, but a heavy feeling come over me while I turned the pages of the deed books and I got short of breath, so I stopped. Some things is best not known or searched out.

My trailer is old, green, and round at the edges and looks like a submarine that took a wrong turn at the beach. I built me on a little porch, and I got a vinyl couch in the yard that I put the plastic on when it rains. I got my own private CoCola machine propped against the trailer under the porch awning. Since the company store closed, everybody uses my Coke machine and I make a little money off it. In the evenings, when it's warm enough, I open my door and turn on my record player. Then the kids come a-running. I got over a hundred 45s. They aint the real thing, like I got Harvey Frolic singing "Ring of Fire" instead of Johnny Cash, but it sounds good and if you get to laughing and carrying on, you can't tell the difference.

I only make twenty dollars a week at Arthur Lee's, but I got a car that I share with my kin. It's a 1951 black Studebaker and Junior Tackett created its innards from scratch out of three old junkers in his yard. I call it the Batmobile. Louelly says the Lord give us the car. She took red paint and printed GOD IS LOVE on the front bumper and THE END IS NEAR on the rear to witness and to cut down on tailgating.

Louelly is tall and bony, and has a long ponytail she pulls back with rubber bands. When Homer is at the mine and the younguns are in school, she drops me at the Esso and goes off in the Batmobile looking for pop bottles. She will get right in the ditch with a gunnysack, sorting through the weeds. One time a copperhead bit her on the hand and she drove herself to the Grace Hospital. She claims she seen Jesus in the rearview mirror, setting up in the back seat while she drove, ready to grab the steering wheel in case she fainted.

One time Louelly had me to drive her up Peelchestnut Mountain. When we got to the top she said, "Now stop right here."

I pulled over onto the wide shoulder. They was trash all over the place, tin cans and cigarette packs and candy wrappers. And lots of bottles.

"The Lord told me about this here place," Louelly said. "This is where the sinning goes on. This is where they park with their girls, and neck, and drink beer. The Lord said, 'They have made this place a desolation, but the righteous shall gather up the manna in the wilderness.' "

I will go to hear Homer preach, but I aint religious in some ways myself. Still I will never question them that are. You never can tell what somebody else has seen or heard, especially Louelly. I put on the emergency brake and we each grabbed a gunnysack. Wasn't long before we had the trunk half full of bottles. I started to shut the lid but Louelly said, "Not yet. They's more down below."

"Down below?"

She motioned down over the hill. "That's why I brought that there rope in the back seat."

She told me to tie the rope to the back bumper beside THE END IS NEAR and the other end around her waist. Then I braced myself against the Batmobile and let her slowly down over the mountain. She went backwards, with her legs held straight and wide apart and the gunnysack over her shoulder. She had on some brown polyester pants and one of Homer's plaid hunting shirts for a jacket, and she went slow to watch for briars and to search out the bottles. Lucky it was the fall of the year. Everything was stripped to the branch and the snakes was asleeping. I let her down as far as the rope would reach, maybe a hundred-fifty feet, and she picked up bottles along the way. Then I got in the Batmobile, started the engine, and hauled her back up. When she come over the edge she was on her knees but she still had hold of that gunnysack. She went down twice more and we filled the trunk and part of the back seat too. Then we took the bottles to the Pick-and-Pay at Annadel that Arthur Lee Sizemore owns, where they fetched eleven dollars worth of groceries.

Now I'm working at the Esso, I can help look after Homer's family. They got it rough. The mine is only working one day a week, union scale is twenty-four dollars a day, and Homer has a wife and two younguns to feed. Ethel is thirteen and she's already tall as a grownup and eats like one. Her momma is big-boned too. Ethel likes to play baseball. When Ethel is catching you have to take care about stealing because her throw to second will come in head-high and she don't care who she hits.

Jewell is the young one but we call him Toejam. He is skinny like his daddy and me. Toejam's got a blue pump knot on his forehead where Doyle Ray Lloyd hit him with a hunk of red dog. Toejam's got the toughest feet in Number Thirteen. All the kids go barefoot in warm weather. You got to walk tender at first, roll your ankles and shift your weight around where the red dog cuts. It takes two weeks to get toughened up. But Toejam, he walks straight from day one, like he don't feel a thing. His feet's the only part of him that don't get hurt though. Toejam is what you would call accident-prone. He is always pounding his thumb with a hammer or stepping into yellow-jackets' nests or falling on the red dog and cutting open his knees. Louelly says Toejam shouldn't never work in the mines because he wouldn't last a day.

It was Toejam that got me determined about the bridge. We lost our car bridge at Number Thirteen back in 1958—flood took it out. So folks have got to leave their cars in the bottom below Dillon Free-man's house at Winco, then walk the mile along the railroad track and up Lloyds Fork. You can drive along the railroad right of way, but it is steep and your car will ride sideways. When a coal train come by while old Sam Chernenko was driving the right-of-way, he edged too far from the track and his car turned over. So folks walk most of the time.

All that's left of the old bridge is a steel girder from bank to bank.

It's only a foot wide and people stay off it except for the younguns, and you know how a youngun will do. But when Toejam was nine, he took on that newspaper route for the *Justice Clarion.* They always leave Toejam's papers at the golf course clubhouse across the creek and Toejam's first day he walked across the girder because it is that much closer. He didn't stop to think it would be different coming back over with a bag full of newspapers. He was just a little ways across when he fell twenty feet and landed near the bank where the water is still yet shallow. His left leg and wrist was broke and he fractured his skull. The doctors at the Grace Hospital said it was the bag of newspapers he landed on that saved him, and Louelly claimed it was Jesus. We went and tore that girder out so no other younguns would get hurt on it.

I have had some fine accomplishments as mayor. One of the biggest was when me and Dillon and Brigham and Homer hauled a TV antenna all the way to the top of Trace Mountain so Number Thirteen could get all three stations. But after Toejam fell into the creek, building a car bridge become my main goal.

Rachel

I saw what was happening. Dillon would claim later that I was blind to it, but that wasn't so. Who better to see than a nurse?

I knew the machines and strip mines had taken the jobs of the miners, who were getting only one or two days' work a week. Every day I drove past the empty houses they left behind when they moved to Ohio or Michigan. I saw the weed-choked fields where entire camps were torn down to the foundations, saw the boarded-up stores and movie theaters in the smaller towns, the loaded coal trucks from the new strip mines rumbling through Justice like great iron elephants and shaking the buildings, as though the town was being ground to dust. I was sad that Jackie would miss the Italian bakery, the fish market, the tailor shops and little groceries, the dark maroon passenger trains with elegant white window shades. There had been wonderful things in the world, and they were no longer.

And I saw the people. I saw as much as Dillon saw, and more. I talked Arthur Lee into letting the county set up a free clinic one day a week at the Felco company store, now closed and empty save for a row of empty display cases with broken glass. I don't know where Arthur Lee got the money; I suspected it was from some funds he'd skimmed off the county coffers for his own use or taken from the coal companies to do their political bidding. I didn't ask, I just bought the medicines and supplies.

People came to the clinic who had worked all their lives, who had paid their own way and never taken charity. They came because their children were hungry and sick, because they were hungry and sick, the men in work clothes, the women in shapeless polyester dresses, the children with swollen bellies beneath thin T-shirts. They sat on hard folding chairs or stood against the wall when the chairs ran out, waiting for hours to spend ten minutes with me. They were unused to leaning and they did it awkwardly, as though afraid to trust the wall they rested against.

I saw them in their homes, old people who wheezed and coughed while I laid a cold flat stethoscope on their chests, who slept in camp houses where the wind whistled through the cracks, with coal stoves for heat only the company no longer provided the house coal, and so they picked up the leavings shed from the fast-moving trains and overloaded trucks. They were men who had worked in the mines until their lungs filled with dust or their backs gave out, women who had cooked and scrubbed the coal dust from kitchen floors and listened for the accident whistle to blow, who finally depended upon their children for food only now their children had nothing to give.

I also watched the television. I heard President Kennedy talk about stamping out poverty in America and learned for the first time that I lived in a place called Appalachia. It was a strange feeling to think my home had been named without asking anyone who lived here, but I was glad someone was paying attention. Dillon called me naive. I didn't care. When I finished with my patients they moved to the next line to receive the white-wrapped blocks of commodity butter and cheese sent from Washington. Of course it was demeaning; of course it wasn't enough. Of course Arthur Lee gave cheese and butter to all his buddies, would have given it to me if I'd taken it. But children don't care for all that, and a cheese sandwich will fill a child's stomach.

I was a good nurse. I could diagnose as well as any doctor and I didn't panic in a crisis. I kept county medical supplies at home in the old doctor's office because people in Number Thirteen would come to me in the evenings. I even did veterinary work, sewed the hind leg back on a black tomcat that had been caught by dogs. The leg was dangling by the bone but Hassel Day wrapped the cat's head and body in a thick towel and held it while I sewed with a plain needle and thread, careful to match the layers of fat and sinew, like piecing a quilt. Later the cat walked without a limp. I could have made a surgeon, if women had thought to do such things in my day.

One summer evening I sat down to a glass of iced tea and the newspaper. I heard Jackie outside yelling, "Mom! Mom!" and went out to the front porch. Jackie and Toejam Day were beside Brigham Lloyd's house, standing in the middle of a pile of old lumber Brigham was using to fix his porch. Toejam was perched on a small board, his legs close together, and Jackie had her arms around his chest.

"Toejam's stuck!" Jackie called. "I think he stepped on a nail."

Toejam didn't say anything. His face had gone white and the blue pumpknot stood out on his forehead like a robin's egg. When I reached him, he clutched my arm and tottered on the board.

"Lift your foot a little," I said.

He raised his foot an inch and the board came with it. I knelt and grasped the board gently.

"Pull again."

This time his foot came away. A wet, rusty nail stuck up from the board. Toejam tottered on one leg, his eyes shut, and scraped my arm with his fingernails. I held his ankle and leaned over to look at the bottom of his bare foot. The hole was perfectly round, its edge crusted with dust. For an instant I thought I could see far up the miniature tunnel past the moist tissue to the white bone. Then the hole filled with blood.

By that time Louella Day had heard the commotion and come running from her house. She held the foot up and looked. "Oh, law," she said, her hand over her mouth, "hit's just like when they nailed Jesus to the cross."

Toejam's eyes grew wide. Then he began to shriek.

We carried him up the hill to the doctor's office. He kept up a steady sobbing, his cries gathering in intensity when I cleaned the wound with stinging alcohol and filled a syringe with tetanus vaccine.

"Hush now," Louella said. "You want to get that there lockjaw? You want your jaws to grow together and you won't never be able to get them apart nor eat again and you'll die slow that way?"

He didn't want it but he didn't want the shot either. It didn't help when Louella said he was too big to cry, trying to shame him. He was still in tears when Jackie took him to the kitchen for cookies and milk.

I gave Louella a glass of iced tea in the living room. "What do I owe you?" Louella said.

"Nothing. The county provides tetanus free. But you ought to take him to the Grace and get it checked."

Louella sighed. "Leastways it happened now. Pretty soon we may have to come to that clinic of yourn when we take the sickness. I aint sure we'll have the union medical much longer."

I was surprised. "Why ever not? Homer's still got his job even if the mine is working slow."

"Aint you heard? The union has cut a deal with American Coal and we might get dropped. So even if Homer has a job, hit would be nonunion."

"Dillon hasn't said a thing about that."

"Don't know why. Hit's all the talk at the bathhouse." She stood up and called, "Come on, Toejam. Me and Hassel got to wag you down to the hospital."

Toejam wailed.

·   ·   ·

The longer Dillon and I spent together, the more clear our differences became. I have never cared much for politics, nor thought deeply about why the world works the way it does, why some are rich and some are poor, why the coal companies do what they do. Dillon is obsessed by such things, will watch the evening news and get so angry you think he could throw something through the TV screen.

On the other hand, I am more practical than he is. He would have loved me openly, with never a thought for what people might think, of what that might do to Jackie. Tony had remarried and moved to Logan County, and he never bothered us. But I heard from Arthur Lee that his new wife was having trouble getting pregnant. Suppose he heard I was carrying on with my first cousin and tried to get custody of Jackie? But Dillon would never think of such a thing.

And my parents were dead, but what of my standing in the community? I was well thought of by my patients, and I took Jackie to the Felco Methodist Church every Sunday. No one knew the sin I was engaged in. For I was certain it was sin, all my raising told me so, and the Bible told me and the world around told me. Dillon did not care a whit for sin, he was the kind to laugh in the face of it, but I must be ashamed of it, even though I couldn't stop. For I could no more send him away when he came to the house in the evening than I could stop breathing. He had the bedroom downstairs, and no one thought anything, neither Jackie nor the neighbors. It was natural that a woman by herself would like a man around now and then, and Dillon was my only kin. When Jackie was asleep, I slipped down the back stairs and into his bed. I told him it was better that I come to him, I could walk more quietly and we didn't have to worry about the sound downstairs waking Jackie. Still I had nightmares in which Dillon and I lay naked in my living room, and I would rise up to find Jackie watching me, and then Jackie turned into Tommie before my eyes. But I still went to him, I went to him of my own free will. I had no excuses to offer for what I was doing, and someday I shall pay. I hope God will be merciful, because I did love Dillon.

I loved his strength and passion, the life in him that seemed to warm me like a fire. But I knew I could never live with him, even if it had been legal, for he is not a man to relax with in a bathrobe and slippers and watch a silly TV show. He grew restless and bored, retreated to the kitchen to drink coffee and read a book or brood. He wanted me to sit across from him and fret over the crumbling of the coal camps or upheavals in Africa or Mississippi. I wanted to sit on the couch and embroider pillowcases and laugh at Lucy on the television. He accused me of being shallow and unsympathetic, baited me about working for the county, about staying friendly with Arthur Lee. I told him he was bossy and smothering. After an argument I would lie in my bed, flat on my back with fists clenched, and vow I would not go creeping down the back stairs to him.

Once I kept the vow, left him alone, and he was silent at breakfast until Jackie went out to play. Then he said, "I don't mean to hurt you. I'm harder on myself than I am on you but that's no excuse. I wouldn't blame you if you hate me sometimes."

"There's just too much of you," I said. "And I don't know what you see in me. I'm not like you at all."

He came behind me as I stood scraping bits of sausage from the frying pan, put his arms around my waist. I set down the pan.

"I'm too much for myself sometimes," he said. "You're my peace. You're my home."

He stayed a second night and I went back downstairs to his bed.

On his first visit after Toejam stepped on the nail, I sent Jackie to spend the night with a school friend in Felco. I fried some chicken and baked a chocolate pie. We ate quietly. Dillon had worked the hoot owl shift the night before and he always had trouble sleeping in the daytime. I sensed his fatigue in the slow scraping of his fork across his plate. His mood would be bad, but he always told me more when he was tired.

"Louella Day says something's happening at the mine," I said.

He set down his cup. "Did she?"

"You haven't said a word to me, Dillon."

"You usually aint interested in union politics."

"I am now, and it's a funny time to spare me. You usually talk about it whether I want to or not."

"Well," he said, "it does involve your good buddy Arthur Lee."

I tried not to show I was irritated. "Tell me, Dillon."

He sipped his coffee. "We heard that American Coal has cut a deal where the union will drop the membership of everybody at the smaller mines and cut off the medical cards. That means Number Thirteen. The company will take part of what they would have spent on us and kick it back to the union officials to put in their pockets. The company will run Number Thirteen nonunion, wages half scale and no benefits, the union will go along with it, and we'll take it or leave it."

"What on earth makes you think the union would do a thing like that?"

He shrugged. "It's already happening in Kentucky. If you'd paid any mind to what I've said this past year, you wouldn't be surprised. It's a new gang in Washington, a bunch of crooks that are in bed with the operators."

"What are you going to do?"

"Don't know yet. But when I do know, I won't tell you."

I felt like I'd been kicked in the stomach. "Why ever not?" I said.

"Because Arthur Lee Sizemore is running this end of things for the company, and he's a good buddy of yours. Because he gave you the kind of political job people have to kiss ass to get."

It was the first time he'd spoken disparagingly of my work. "I thought you admired my nursing," I said.

"I do. I just don't admire who you do it for. Lie down with dogs and you start to smell like one."

His words brought tears to my eyes. "Do you know how much that hurts? And to know you don't trust me enough to tell me what's going on?"

"Quit that job, Rachel. You can be a nurse at the hospital and not work for the county."

"I love my job and I don't want to be cooped up in the hospital. Besides, I see people that can't afford to go to the hospital. I'm not a crook and I didn't do anything wrong to get this job. I'm qualified for it and I'm going to do it."

"Then don't expect me to tell you what's going on at the mine.

And if this thing gets as ugly as I reckon it will, it will make things damn hard between us. I may not be able to be seen with you."

"Why? Are you ashamed of me?"

He shook his head and looked away. "Rachel, there aint been a bad strike for a while. You don't know what it's like. It gets bitter. Quit the job."

"No. You don't boss me, Dillon."

He left without staying the night.

DILLON

I walked the track in the dark, following the gleam of moonlight along the rail. I kept stopping and looking back. I could hear my own voice demanding, *Quit the job*. I did hate the sound of it. She should have poured the coffee pot over my head.

I knew I ought to go back and apologize. But I stood still, covered my face with my hands, and breathed deep, smelled the fear on my breath. I know about a strike. My daddy comes to me sometimes and whispers in my ear, says I have obligations beyond the hold of any woman. Rachel is adrift among the ice floes, calling to me, and this time a bitter ghost, not my mother, holds me back.

But in the daylight it seems different, and I do apologize. Rachel accepts my apology but she is uneasy and quiet. She doesn't ask me any questions about the mine. When we are together, we are peaceful but somber, as if one of us is terminally ill and each of us tries to avoid what we know, to be strong for the other.

JACKIE

The television people have come to Blackberry Creek, right to my school at Felco. They're making a news show about Christmas in Appalachia, and they have cameras with those eyes painted on them. I keep looking for Walter Cronkite but Mom says he didn't come with them. Mom brought them to the school because they spent the morning at her clinic. She is aggravated, I can tell by the way she holds her mouth shut tight like her teeth are stuck together with bubblegum. She talks to my teacher, Miss Cox, while the television men make noise in the hallway.

"What are they like?" Miss Cox asks.

"They make me feel like a specimen in a jar," my mom says. She waves to me and leaves, and a television man comes in the room. He tells Miss Cox his name is Phil Vivanti. He has black hair cut like someone drew around the edges with a pencil before they trimmed, and he's wearing a turtleneck shirt.

"We need a place to set up," he says. "Where's the cafeteria?"

"We don't have a cafeteria," Miss Cox says. "We serve the children at the kitchen door and they eat at their desks."

"Then where's the library?"

"There's no library either. We keep books in each room." She points at our bookshelf under the window.

"That's no good," says Phil Vivanti. "We need lots of space to give out the shoes. I guess we'll just have to film in the hallway."

"It's okay, Phil," says a bald man who comes in the room. "The hall has a nice bleakness."

"What shoes?" Miss Cox asks.

"A shoe company in Paramus, New Jersey, heard about your problems here. They sent several boxes of their product for Christmas. We thought we'd film the distribution."

He goes back out in the hall and the TV men come in and out with cords and plugs and lights on tall metal poles. Miss Cox tries to teach about the planets but we keep looking at the door so she gives up and says that people want to see television shows about Appalachia because they think we are stupid and backward and they can't figure out why. She says we are not stupid or backward and are just as good as anybody, but she says it low and keeps glancing at the door like she thinks someone might come in and take her away.

We line up to get our lunches, corn dogs and macaroni and cheese and carrot sticks and pineapple slices. Toejam Day trips on a fat black TV cord and spills his lunch but Miss Cox gets him another one. Toejam usually doesn't eat the school lunch because he can't afford it, but the principal said everyone gets a tray today. It is a present from the Board of Education. The TV men sit on the staircase and eat their lunch. They hold the corn dogs sideways and look at them before they take a bite.

After lunch we carry our trays back to the kitchen. The TV men have stacked lots of big boxes on the stairway. The boxes say Parkway Shoe Company. Phil Vivanti tells the bald man to turn the boxes sideways so the name won't show. "No free advertising," he says. He makes Miss Cox sit at a table with a pile of shoes beside her. The shoes are ugly. Some are pink tennis shoes, others are square boy's shoes that look hard as rocks. We go back to our desks but Phil Vivanti comes in and tells us to line up. Brenda Lloyd, who sits beside me, whispers, "I don't want any of them shoes." I raise my hand.

Phil Vivanti says, "What is it?"

"Some of us don't need them," I say. "And some of us don't want them."

He looks at me like if he was a teacher he would spank me. Then he glances around the room. "How many of you need shoes?" he asks. No one raises their hand. Lots of them do need shoes but they would rather have their tongues pulled out than say so. "Great," says Phil Vivanti. He looks at his watch. Then he says, "How many want to be on TV?" We all raise our hands. "Good," he says. "Line up."

We line up and Miss Cox asks our shoe sizes. She fishes in the boxes and hands each of us a pair of shoes. Toejam gets a pair of white tennis shoes and holds them close to his chest. He looks happy. Brenda

Lloyd gets bright pink. She makes a face at me as she walks by. Miss Cox gives me a pair of sandals made of hard purple plastic that look like they would take all the skin off the top of your foot. She whispers to me, "I know you won't mind because you don't need them anyway." I am proud of what she says and I swing the sandals high over my head as I walk past Phil Vivanti. I am tempted to give them to him and say, "Take them home to your little girl," but that would be sassing a grownup so I don't say anything.

After the TV men leave we are still too stirred up to pay attention in class, so the teachers send us outside for early recess. Brenda is with her brother Doyle Ray, who is a year ahead of us in the sixth grade. He has a pair of black Sunday shoes.

"Mine are ugly," Brenda says. "I hate pink."

"Never mind," Doyle Ray says. "They're big enough to grow into."

"I don't want them. I want to pick my own shoes."

"I don't need any shoes," I say. "I think I'll just throw these away." I fling the sandals against the side of the school.

Doyle Ray wheels suddenly and shoves me against the brick wall. I step away and he shoves me again so that the back of my head hits the wall. Brenda comes close and hits me hard in the stomach. I am too surprised to cry out. They are still hitting me when Miss Cox pulls them off me. I get my breath and start to cry.

"What brought this on?" she demands. "Jackie, why were they hitting you?"

"I don't know." I hold my arm up and sob against it. "I just said I was going to throw my shoes away."

She grabs Doyle Ray and Brenda by an arm and shakes them. "Why were you hitting Jackie?"

"I don't know," Doyle Ray says. Brenda is crying too. She has never fought anybody or been in trouble with the teacher. "I don't know," Brenda says.

Dillon comes to our house to watch the show about Blackberry Creek. We see Mom listening to a man's chest and I point and holler, "There's Mom!" "Poor health care," says a voice. Mom sighs loud like her feelings are hurt. We watch children lined up for shoes and I see Brenda Lloyd and Toejam Day. I don't see me. "Children who go barefoot," says the voice. "Schools and houses in terrible condition." The TV shows empty falling-down coal camp houses. Phil Vivanti looks at us from the TV set. He stands in front of a camp house. "There is another America hidden away in these hills," he says. "Like something out of another century," he says, "a land time forgot, a life most Americans will never experience. Why do people want to stay here? How will we bring them into the mainstream of American life?"

We sit downhearted like we have been beat on. Then Dillon gets up suddenly and flips off the TV set. "Mainstream of American life! Sonofabitch! Coal companies been shoving the goddamn mainstream of American life down our throats since my papaw's day."

"Don't cuss in front of Jackie," Mom says.

Dillon goes in the kitchen to smoke a cigarette. I follow him, looking for a CoCola in the refrigerator. Instead he pours me a cup of milk with coffee in it, like he does when Mom isn't around.

"We're in for it now, Jackie," he says.

"How come?"

He throws his head back and blows smoke at the ceiling. "You know what the old fox says. Fox says, 'Poor chicken, he was looking puny anyhow.' Then he eats the chicken for supper."

I can tell he's glad I came in the kitchen.

DILLON

I have never been a regular churchgoer, not even when I was in the war and expecting to get my head blown off any minute. The God I believe in doesn't take kindly to people sitting around in buildings feeling pious. I fancy a God that would as soon level a church build-ing as look at it.

But on Blackberry Creek there is one building where you are free of the coal company and that is a church—unless it is a church Ameri-can Coal built, like the one in Felco where Rachel takes Jackie, that looks just like a company store with a steeple stuck on. But the Holi-ness Church at Number Thirteen is not like that. It is a tarpaper building stuck on the hill across the railroad track from the Free Patch. You can't see it half the time because the company parks a line of coal cars in front of it. When the track is blocked, the people have to climb between the gondolas to get to services, or else walk half a mile to get to the end of the train and then back.

When word came down that the union had cut us free and taken our medical cards, I called the first meeting at the union hall up to Raven. It was just going through the motions. When I showed up early at the cinderblock building, the lock had been changed. From then on we met at the Holiness Church. The boys that lived up the creek didn't like walking all the way in to Number Thirteen, but it made me feel safe.

The Holiness are also called Holy Rollers, and Homer Day is the pastor. He must have a powerful call to preach, because Homer is quiet and shy, and it is hard for him to stand up in front of all creation and spout off in some foreign language. But when the congregation prays, the Holy Ghost grabs him and he is off and babbling in the lost tongues of the ancient Amorites, Perizzites, and Hivites. At least it is what he claims, and I am not one to dispute it.

The church has a red neon JESUS SAVES sign above the altar. Homer plugged in the sign when I arrived for the meeting.

"Reckon anybody will mind if I plug that in?" Homer asked.

"Hell, we need all the help we can get," I said. Then I realized I had cussed in a church, but I decided not to apologize for it. I am of the belief that God cusses more than anybody.

The men straggled in slow, some of them straight from their shifts and bone tired, others on their way to the mine but figuring they might not get there. They wore their work clothes, recalled they were in a church, and pulled off their caps that said Mail Pouch and

Caterpillar and Cincinnati Reds. They didn't talk loud or joke like they usually did before meetings, but studied the JESUS SAVES sign or stared out the windows at the kids playing baseball across the tracks on the Free Patch.

I called the meeting to order from the pulpit. I said, "Well boys, some fellows up in Washington say we don't have a union no more."

Brigham Lloyd stood up and cleared his throat, said, "Hell with the United Mine Workers, pardon me, Homer, for my language. That union has done been took over from within. Hit's just like the Communists, how they work."

They talked one after another, getting the anger out. Byrum Hoskins said his wife was facing heart surgery and now he couldn't pay for it. Ralph Bays said, "You know what I hear tell? I hear tell Arthur Lee is going to work the mines five days again. I hear tell they could work ever thing on this creek five days, and they will once the union is busted all over. But they'll pay half union scale."

Stanley Cawood said, "Don't know why they bother to bust the union. One day's work a week union scale aint feeding my youn-guns."

"I'll tell you why they bother," I said. "Them bastards in Washington won't be in charge forever, and the company will try to break us before we can get that union cleaned up. But I'll tell you what. There was a day on this creek when there was no union. And the boys working the mines here, they made the union. It was them done it for theirselves. And no sonofabitch in Washington tells me if I'm in the union. I am the union. You're the union."

They listened hard. I stood quiet a minute and looked out at them. The air was tight like something was ready to bust loose. Then Brigham said, "Son, what are you saying?"

"I'm saying strike. I'm saying strike like they aint seen since my daddy's day. I'm saying pull out all the boys at the other mines that's been kicked out of the union. Any mine that keeps working, union or not, we'll shut it down. We'll do what has to be done. They'll not put us out without us pulling this place down around their heads, like Samson pulled down the Philistine temple."

I am not used to talking from the Bible like a preacher, but it seemed the time and place for it. They were yelling all at once, saying "That's it. That's it right there."

"Who's with me?" I said.

They all raised their hands.

I hit the pulpit with a little gavel.

"Local Union 555 is now on strike," I said. "I want a picket line up at Number Thirteen tipple five-thirty tomorrow morning."

They were standing and clapping. I watched their faces and wondered who would go that night and squeal to Roger Jennings at the union office in Justice.

I kept Brigham and Homer after the meeting. Brigham rubbed his hands, said, "You want us to haul a picket shack up to the tipple?"

I smiled and said, "Sure, but we aint going to be spending much time there."

Sim Gore is the president of the local at Jenkinjones, the first Negro to get elected. I drove to Jenkinjones that night and parked my truck across the road from his house in Colored Bottom. I reckoned he would have heard and that the boys at the union office in Justice would be keeping a close eye on him. Jenkinjones is the biggest mine on the creek, and it is part of the deal that it will stay union and keep working. The company and the union would both want the coal to keep running out of Jenkinjones.

I got out of my truck, shut the door, and lit a cigarette behind my cupped hand while I leaned against the cab. Sim's house was dark and I reckoned he would be watching out a window. There would be others watching too. I strolled across the road, my boots loud on the gritty pavement.

The door of the house opened and a voice said, "Hold it right there!"

"You got a gun, Sim?"

"You damn straight," he said.

"I aint got mine. Left it in the truck."

"That's your lookout," Sim said.

"I just want to talk."

"I aint interested in talk," he said. "It may be two in the morning

but you can be for damn sure I aint got the only ears in this bottom
that heard you pull up."

I thought he was meaning keep talking but be goddamn careful. I
said, "Sim, I know you shoot basketball sometimes down to Annadel.
They say you're good. I recall you took Excelsior High to the colored
state tournament back before the war."

"Yeah. I may shoot ball tomorrow evening after my shift. So what?
That don't make you nothing to me."

"We was trapped together oncet. We swapped breaths at an air
hole."

"And I recall you got a peckerwood cousin that called me a nigger.
He raising hell with you now?"

"Me and you, we're union brothers, Sim."

"You the one seem to forgot about that. You aint in no union, from
what I hear tell. Now get away from my fence before I call some of
my boys."

"Company suck," I said. I gave him a mock salute, got in my truck,
and drove back home to Winco, watching in my rearview mirror the
whole way. When I got to my house, Brigham was waiting on the
front porch.

I said, "What the hell are you doing here?"

"Making sure nobody don't mess with your house that aint supposed to," he said.

We went inside but didn't turn up a lamp.

"What'd he say?" Brigham asked.

I lit a cigarette and grinned in the flare of the lighter. I said, "Called
you a peckerwood."

"Sonofabitch! They's white boys in that mine at Jenkinjones, more
than half. Will you tell me why they elected a goddamn nigger president of the local?"

"Because he's smart," I said.

"Don't give me that," said Brigham. "Shit, sometimes I wisht I
lived in Alabama."

I tapped my ashes into an empty beer bottle, leaned back on the
couch, and smiled and said, "Get the hell out of here. I need a good
night's sleep. I'm shooting basketball tomorrow."

· · ·

There's no net in the goal at the town playground in Annadel. A clean shot whips through the iron with just a whish of air. The court used to be asphalt but it has been ground to hard-packed dirt. I stood beside my truck and watched Sim Gore send three straight through the hoop. He was ignoring me.

"Air ball!" I called.

The others, there were twelve in all, stopped to look at me. Sim said, "You aint got eyes, asshole."

"What's the score?" I said.

"My team's winning," Sim said. He drilled a shot from the side.

I said, "Am I on your team?"

He flipped me the ball so suddenly I almost dropped it. My shot bounced high off the back rim and over the backboard.

"Off the court," Sim said. He jerked his head sideways. "Bad as you shoot, you ought to try tomorrow morning early when they aint nobody around to watch you. Now get on away from here."

I got back in my truck and drove away. A Negro in a tan Plymouth followed close on my bumper as I left Annadel. I recognized him for an active union man. I held my breath and waited to see what he was up to, thought I might have got the message wrong. But he just followed. When I reached the mouth of Lloyd's Fork, the Plymouth pulled off the road and turned around. I held my fist up to my window and stuck my thumb up. The man did the same. I smiled at myself in the rearview mirror and drove on home.

I never could stand to get up in the morning. But you can't help notice how everything smells better in the dawn. The brewing coffee fills my kitchen with a rich odor, and the back door is open to let in the damp air. In two hours the sun will crest the hills and burn off the dew. We have to be on the mountain before that happens.

I rub my eyes and watch Hassel fry baloney.

"You sure you want to come?" I say.

He half turns. "Wouldn't miss it."

We pack fried baloney sandwiches in a poke and go out to the Batmobile. I curl up in the floor behind the front seat and Hassel covers me with a rug. I can smell motor oil and coal dust ground into the plastic flooring.

The Batmobile travels Lloyds Fork and on up the dirt road that winds up the back side of Trace Mountain. Hassel doesn't say anything so I reckon no one is following us. My back starts to hurt because I am draped over the axle hump, but I fall asleep anyway.

I wake up when the Batmobile stops. "We're here," Hassel says. He sounds far away. "Hit's all clear. Brigham and Homer done beat us, and looks like they's ten or twelve with them."

I get out, trying not to straighten my spine too quick. The boys are lounging around their vehicles. They are all from Number Thirteen mine. Brigham is standing spread-eagled beside his Ford and Homer is perched on the hood.

"First time to shut down a union mine and we got to trust a nigger," Brigham says.

His voice sounds soft and I know he has been drinking.

"Shut up," I say.

"I don't trust a goddamn one of them."

I go and stand right up against him. "You'll keep your voice down," I say. "And if you call one of them a name I'll poleax you myself."

He shrugs and tucks a plug of tobacco under his gum. I walk away from him, along the edge of the dirt road that leads back down the mountain past the tipple. We are high up in the fog. Late in the day you can see a lot from here, the rooftops of Jenkinjones, the curled smoke rising from the slate dump that fills half the hollow. The entrance to the Jenkinjones mine is above us, farther up. I feel good while we wait. If they have been watching for us, it would be along the main road, but I doubt they know we have come over the hill on them. The entrance to the Jenkinjones mine is up to our right. The hoot owl shift will still be inside.

"Deputies up there?" I ask.

"Nary a one," Homer says. "We reckon they'll come in with the day shift and bring the hoot owl out."

"And if you're wrong about your Nee-gro," Brigham says, "we're stuck between a rock and a hard place, aint we?"

We hear the car engines pulling up the hollow below us. The fog has burned away a hundred yards down the mountainside.

"Hit's a convoy for sure," Homer says. "They're expecting something."

"That's all right," I say.

The boys behind us fold up their penknives, stick their whitrocks in their back pockets, and move up. Their cheeks bulge with chaws. I find my pouch of Red Man and fill my own jaw. The cars are close now, we can hear their tires chewing up the road. Then gray bulges rise out of the fog. The first three are county deputy cars with round lights on top. Behind are the miners. Their cars and trucks are beat up, their engines rough and rattly like ours. Nobody can afford anything new. I hate to do some of them like we might have to do.

The deputies get out, six of them. The one in front is from down below Justice town, I have seen him around.

"You boys are blocking the road," he says like we don't know it.

"Turley," I say, "we can't let you bring them boys by here."

All down the line the cars and trucks stop, doors open and slam shut. Men climb up the hill. I recognize Sim Gore but he is too far away to say anything.

"We got a shift here wants to work," Turley is saying, "and the union aint called no strike. We can't let a bunch of troublemakers keep these boys away from their place of employment. You got one minute to get in your cars and move them out of this road or we'll move them for you and take you in to Justice."

Sim is within shouting distance now.

"Yonder comes the president of this here local," I yell. "Sim Gore, ya'll come to work today?"

Sim comes on up the hill, his arms moving at his sides.

"We aint here to work," he says. "We here to shut down this mine until American Coal quit fucking with our union brothers"—then he smiles real big, pats Turley on the shoulder—"and we do appreciate the escort."

You have never seen such a surprised bunch of deputies. They turn quick and stare at Sim. "What the hell—" Turley sputters. "You just said—"

Some of the miners look confused too.

"I'm here to work," one says.

"Naw," Sim says. "No work. I done polled the most of the membership. This here local is on strike."

"Any man don't agree," I say, "his car goes over the hill."

Turley has been looking around wild-like and now he puts his hand to his gun.

"Don't do it, son," I say. "You got to live in this county. Look around you here. You know all these boys. They know you."

Turley keeps his hand on his pistol and licks his lips.

"Listen to him, Turley," says one of the deputies. "This here is too big for us."

"Tell that to Arthur Lee," says Turley.

"You tell Arthur Lee to keep you boys out of this or he'll need some new deputy cars," I say.

"What you aiming to do?" Turley asks.

"We're aiming to call out the hoot owl shift and send them home. And then we're claiming that tipple. Come back this afternoon you'll see what we done."

Turley squints at me. "You'll do time for this," he says.

"Bud," I say, "only if you make an identification. And only if Arthur Lee and somebody's army come to arrest me."

"It may end up somebody's army," says Turley.

"May be. Until then, I reckon you ought to just leave them deputy cars here and walk on back to town. You get started now you ought to be able to thumb you a ride and get to the Tic-Toc in time for a cheeseburger and a piece of pie."

Sim and his boys stand aside to let them pass.

"Anybody aint with us, go on follow them," Sim yells.

"And let you topple my car?" says the one that spoke up before. I knew his daddy that got killed at Number Ten in 1949 and left his mommy with ten younguns. He is a fellow that aint had two nickels to rattle together in his pocket.

"Ray," I say, "you may not be with us, which is why Sim aint said nothing to you before. Just don't get in the way and it will be all right for you."

Ray shakes his head but he doesn't leave. Him and a few others stay by the cars since they can't go anywhere. The rest of us go up to the mine. The boys from the hoot owl are coming out. Some of them join us, the ones Sim has reached. The others cuss but they just stand by and smoke their cigarettes because they are outnumbered.

First we tear down the fences and raid the supply shed where they keep the dynamite. Me and Sim see to placing the charges, and he is a good man to work with, he knows his job and will say what is what. At noon we blow the tipple. It is a tall metal tower several stories high. Sim Gore stands beside me and flinches at the sound of the explosion, watches the girders holding the main structure buckle as though the tipple has taken a bowlegged step, then it collapses in a cloud of dust.

"It's a shame on this earth," Sim says.

"You want out?"

"Naw. The Bible say they's a time to build up and a time to tear down. This here's a tearing down time."

They join us by the hundreds, all the men in the little mines who've been cut off and some of the miners who've been kept in the union but know they might be next, who are tired of working short and going home to hungry younguns. We go all over the county, hitting a different mine each day, and no one but me and Sim knows where we will show up next. We blow tipples, burn buildings, and tear up track, throw up picket lines and stop the coal from moving.

The *Justice Clarion* carries the story under a thick black headline that looks heavy enough to fall off the page: COMMUNISM COMES TO JUSTICE COUNTY.

They call us the Roving Pickets.

The Roving Pickets, 1962

ARTHUR LEE SIZEMORE

I am a Kennedy man. Wasn't always. Early in that 1960 election, used to support Hubert Humphrey. Familiar as an old hound dog, Hubert. Knew how things was done. Wasn't so sure about Kennedy. Didn't care for how he played up his religion, making out how if dumb ignorant hillbillies would vote for a Catholic, anybody would. Made him look good when he won. Hell, that is politics. But Kennedy had all the network TV cameras poking around here looking for "poverty," like it had ever been lost. That disturbed the peace and quiet.

Then the Kennedy people called from Charleston and asked why all they ever saw in Justice County was Humphrey signs.

"Because it's my county." My feet was up on my desk.

"I'd like to send someone to see you," said this Yankee-sounding voice.

"Waste of time."

"He'll bring money to help with your local campaigns. But only if you promise to take down every Humphrey sign in the county and shut Hubert out."

Chewed on the end of a pencil for a while. "How much?"

"How much do you need?"

"Thirty-two." Always think big.

"Twenty-eight," said the Yankee.

Know how it is when you're fishing and that bob takes a dive and you feel the tug?

"Thirty-one."

"Twenty-nine," he said. "That's my last offer."

"You got a deal. Twenty-nine."

"Good. I'll send my man down on Monday. If he sees one Humphrey sign, he heads back to Charleston with the cash."

Told my buddies on the Democrat committee. Hollered laughing and I said, "Boys, twenty-nine hundred dollars is twice what Hubert's paying. But that aint the point. They know how it's done and this proves it. And they got more of what you need to do it with, so why not?"

They got the general drift. Come Monday, man in a pinstripe suit showed up at the coal company office with a briefcase.

"Like the scenery?" I said.

"Lovely. Coal mines and Kennedy signs. But we expect more than signs."

"I know what you expect. Told you it's my county."

"Good." He set the briefcase on the floor and left. I locked the office door and opened the briefcase. Stared at the stacks of cash, new and crisp, you would not expect old bills from a Kennedy. It took my breath away and my fingers trembled when I started to count.

Called my Democrat vice-chairman. "Herman?" I said. I was so tickled I wanted to drag it out. "Herman? You setting down? You know that twenty-nine hundred? It's twenty-nine thousand!"

That one called for a cigar. Cuban, one of the last I ever smoked. Slickered people often enough, but that was the first time without trying. I became a born-again Kennedy man, from admiration and from pity.

So they owned me and I thought I owned them. When the Roving Pickets burned that first tipple I got hold of a middling ass-kisser in the Justice Department.

"We delivered," I told the ass-kisser. "It's payback time. Pass that word on."

"You're one little hillbilly county," said the ass-kisser. He sounded bored.

"One little hillbilly county with a bunch of armed reds running wild up the hollers and half the cameras in the country filming every little tarpaper shack they can find and crying over poor people and talking to every troublemaker that wants to get on TV and tell the whole world about it. I bet they're watching in goddamn Moscow. I bet they're showing it to their people and laughing up their sleeves."

"I hear you. Calm down. It can't be that hard to handle."

Goddamn prick, like the paper pushers I saw in the army. Had a better idea. Called my boss who is the president of the American Coal Company, got houses in Philadelphia and Georgetown and Miami Beach and eats his lunch at the Cosmos Club. Took me there once. Food aint as good as what you'd think, but the men who eat there, you see their faces and you know what they know. Boss is a coal man who will not say a thing about little hillbilly counties, and he knows nothing in this world comes easy.

DILLON

I don't turn on a light in my house anymore. At least the days are long so I can see to get around for a while. I turn the TV to the wall, away from the window. I read with a flashlight. I love to read. Just now I have a Sam Spade mystery from the library. I have to limit myself on mysteries or I will finish all the library has and there will be nothing left.

I stand in the shower, washing off the sweat and dust, rinse out the shampoo and slap on some Old Spice because I am going to Rachel's. When I throw back the shower curtain it is twilight and the house is falling into darkness. The world seems quieter at twilight, as though the darkness soaks up sound.

The glass breaks in the front window, falls, and a zingpingwhine rackets through the house. I drop flat in the bathtub and hold my breath. Off on the highway I hear a motor race and grow faint, then the silence again, only this time there is a buzz beneath the surface of soundlessness. I turn on the flashlight, its beam like a round yellow eye, and find shattered glass on the living room floor and the front porch. There are three rips in the window screen, and I dig two bullets from the kitchen doorframe with my jackknife. I drop the bullets in my shirt pocket and they jingle harmlessly.

Outside I walk the railroad track a hundred yards in the wrong direction and watch, hunkered on the track, to see if anyone is following me, before I go on to Number Thirteen. I stop first at Brigham's to tell him what happened, and since he is not drinking I say, "Keep an eye on Rachel's," then I cross the street.

It is like she knows. She has fixed pork chops and fried potatoes and blackberry cobbler, my favorite supper. After Jackie goes to bed, we make love, kick back the sheets and let the air from the window cool our damp bodies. Now is the cruelest time to tell her, and that is my only hope. I reach for my shirt, draped over a chair beside the bed. I hold her hand open a moment, run my thumb along the soft flesh of her palm, then place the bullets there and close her fingers over them.

I say, "I dug these out of my door post. Somebody shot at me tonight."

"Oh, God," she says. She raises her hand like she will throw them away, then stops, but one bullet falls on the bed. I grab her hand and make her hold the bullets tight.

"This is what's real," I say. "I'm not coming back here after tonight. It's too dangerous for you and Jackie right now. Besides, I'll be moving around at night."

"How can you fight the company and the union both?" she says. "You don't even know who's shooting at you."

"They're the same right now," I say, "so it don't matter."

"Can't you back off? Is it really worth it?"

I drop her hand and sit up. I feel sick.

"That's just the opposite of what I needed from you," I say.

She turns her head away. "I can't be what you want," she says. "You want me to be pleased someone tried to kill you."

"No. I want you to be upset. But I want you to say you'll do what it takes to stand by me."

"You want to stand alone. You love it. You've waited your whole life for it."

"That aint true."

"Don't deny it, Dillon, I know you. Nobody knows you better."

"You know me," I say, "but you don't understand me."

"So," she says, "we've got a problem, then."

The Roving Pickets, 1962

She stands up and looks out the window.

"Get away from the window!" I say.

She shrinks back.

"Brigham's keeping an eye on the house," I say, "if he aint drunk. Be careful just in case."

She starts to cry. "If you get killed," she says, "I don't know what I'll do."

I wrap my arm around her waist and draw her back to the bed.

"It won't last forever," I say. "These fellows that have got hold of the union now, they're thugs doing the company's dirty work. That kind never lasts."

"It won't matter if they kill you first."

"I'll be careful as I can. Just be patient."

"For how long?"

"I don't know."

"And what will you be doing in the meantime? How many tipples will you burn? Who will you shoot at? Number Eight tipple burned last week. You were behind it, weren't you?"

She lays her hand on my cheek and turns my face toward her. "Weren't you?" she asks.

I look at her, staring back a warning.

"I'm afraid of how I'll feel about you when this is all over," she says.

"If you stand back from it," I say, "I'm afraid of how I'll feel about you."

In the morning I find Jackie on the back porch playing with her cat.

"I got to go soon," I say. "Can't hang around this morning."

She jumps up and hugs me. I set my hand to her forehead and tilt her head back.

"Can we talk just a minute?"

"Sure," she says.

I sit on the porch steps. "I won't be coming by here for a while. I won't be seeing you. And I don't want you coming around my house, not for any reason. You understand?"

She stares at me. "Don't you love me any more?"

"Of course I love you. This has got nothing to do with you, honey. I'm in trouble right now and I don't want you messed up in it, that's all."

"How come you're in trouble?"

"It's hard to explain. But I'm trying to help people around here, the miners and their families. Only the coal company don't want me to."

"Can't you come and play a game sometimes?"

"No, I can't do that for a while. Maybe not for a long time."

"How long?"

"Don't know. Maybe a year. Maybe even longer."

Her mouth goes tight and her chin trembles.

I say, "I know that sounds like a long time to a youngun. But it will go fast."

She ducks her head, picks up the black-and-white cat, and sets it on her lap. The cat purrs and raises its chin. Jackie won't look at me.

"Jackie, I'm sorry."

She rubs the cat's ears.

"Socks is going to have kittens," she says.

"Is that right?"

"I'll be real busy taking care of them."

"I reckon you will."

"I'd probably be too busy to play games anyway."

"All right," I say. "We'll play games when this mess is over and the kittens are grown up."

I kiss the top of her head. She doesn't move. I go back in the kitchen. Rachel has been watching out the window.

"You're as bad as Tony," she says.

"That's damned unfair. It's different altogether."

"Whatever the difference is, it doesn't matter to her."

"One of these days she'll understand," I say. "Even if you don't."

"I'm trying," she says. "Are you?"

She cooks breakfast but I barely taste the food. Jackie disappears before I am done eating.

On the way home I get a wheelbarrow of scrap metal from Junior Tackett. That afternoon I build a three-foot-high wall of sheet metal around my bed.

· · ·

I am frying potatoes and I hear the car pull up beside my house. I shove the iron skillet off the burner and drop to the floor. A car door slams, feet tromp up my porch steps, and comes a hard knock on the door. I get to my knees and peek out a window, see the back end of a white Chevrolet with federal plates, say "Shit."

The man has on a gray suit. I know before he opens his mouth and says my name that he is FBI. Your regular run of government men do not have that kick-ass look. He has a square head, and short black hair, and a scar on his forehead.

He says, "Agent Temple, Federal Bureau of Investigation," flips open a leather folder and flashes a badge and snapshot, snaps the folder shut and puts it back in his coat pocket before I have time to open my mouth.

"Hold on," I say. I won't be run over by them, it is what they want, to talk fast and loud, to keep you off balance. I say, "Let me see that again. I want to make sure who I'm dealing with."

"Don't get smart with me," he says.

I grab hold of the door frame in case he gets rough, I say, "If you're FBI, show me and I'll talk to you. If you aint, then get the hell off my porch."

We stare like it is some kind of contest, then he takes out the folder slow, pretending to be real polite, polishes the plastic, and sticks the badge under my nose. I step back and study the picture, unmistakably that of FBI Agent Shirley Temple.

I look up, say, "Shirley Temple?" I choke back a giggle, try to cover by taking a cigarette out of my shirt pocket and sticking it in my mouth.

Agent Temple glares at me. "You want to see something funny? I'll show you something funny if you don't shut your trap."

I stare at my feet and chew on the cigarette. I am shaking scared and the tension seems to make me drunk. I giggle again, can't help it, and almost drop my cigarette.

Temple grabs my shirt, pushes me against the door, and sticks his face so close I can smell his Dentyne chewing gum.

He says, "I came to tell you one thing, tough guy. The FBI is on this case now. We got no proof yet, but we know you've been behind all the trouble. One false step and we'll arrest your ass in a New York minute. Maybe you'll find something to laugh at in a federal penitentiary. And by the way, we've got an injunction. Tell your boys anybody caught shutting down a mine will be up on federal contempt charges."

Temple pushes me away and walks down the steps. He looks around, says, "Some little shack you got here. Looks like a goddamn firetrap to me."

"You better be careful who you threaten," I say. "I got friends on this hollow."

Shirley Temple smiles, says, "Is that so? I'd like to meet them. I'd like to point out to them that I'm the law now, Mr. Freeman."

HASSEL

When the FBI come in with that there injunction, the boys decided to lay low for a spell, see if things cooled off. We was still yet feeling good since hardly any coal was moving, not even from the union mines. Everybody just stayed home. Only the strip miners kept at it, and they was brought-in men from Kentucky and Virginia.

So I was laying in bed at my trailer early one morning, but I am a light sleeper, and I had the window throwed open to take the cool breeze. I heard the footsteps tromping down the railroad track from the coal tipple, walking hard like an army, and I heard a man giving orders in a low voice. It sounded like a TV show, like it wasn't real. But when I set up and peeked out the window I seen about twenty of them heading into Number Thirteen and they was each toting a rifle.

I pulled on my pants and run right outside without a shirt on. The men was already past my trailer and didn't see me come out. Turned out they wasn't interested in me no way, because I aint a miner. They passed right by Rachel Honaker's big house and ignored old Sam Chernenko's on the hill. But when they come to a miner's house they went right in the front door. Most folks here don't lock up at night, but if them men come on a locked door, they bashed it right in with them rifles.

When I seen two of them go in Homer's, I hid around the corner of the house and looked for what would happen, wondering if I ought to go back to my trailer and fetch my pistol. I heard the younguns screaming and hollering inside like they was scared to death, and then them fellers come back out on the porch with Homer at the end of their rifles. His hair wasn't combed and his shirttail was hanging out like he'd just throwed on his clothes.

I pressed flat against the house and hollered, "Big brother, what's going on?"

The men stopped and turned toward me but they kept them rifles flush on Homer.

"If you got a gun," one of them said, "I'd advise you not to use it."

"I just want to know where you're taking my brother," I said.

"This here is company business. These boys has been playing hooky," one man said. "We're the truant officers come to make sure they go to school." He poked Homer in the back with the rifle. "Let's go."

"Go on back home," Homer said. "They're taking us to the mine to work."

"You aint even got your dinner pail," I said.

"It aint our fault if his old woman won't cook for him," said the other man. They headed off. I hollered after them, "Hit's a damn shame, going right in a man's home like that!" They ignored me. The street was filling up with men marching off at gunpoint. The doors of all the houses was throwed open and I felt right then like I wasn't the mayor of Number Thirteen, and the company could see right inside my head.

When Homer come home that night, he said the air inside had been close because the fans had been shut off so long. He had put in a twelve-hour shift with nothing to eat and he said the guards would be back every day.

"Every day!" I said. "You wasn't working every day before all this happened."

"Wasn't working half pay neither," he said. "But don't you worry. Dillon will figure out something."

Louelly was setting in the corner reading the scriptures. She looked up. "While Dillon's figuring," she said, "I got an idea of my own."

And I listened close because Louelly don't often get an idea, but when she does, hit's generally a good one.

The scab coal truck drivers is from out of state like the scab strip miners. The West Virginia scabs is over in Kentucky breaking up strikes and the Kentucky scabs is over here doing the same thing. It is the way the companies like it. They know it is hard for a man to live with his next-door neighbor if he takes food out of his mouth.

In summer, the coal truck drivers have got their windows rolled down and their radios on loud. They sing along with their arms hanging out the window and pat the sides of their cabs in time to Hank Williams. They run between the new strip mine up on Trace Mountain and the cleaning plant at the Number Thirteen tipple. The drivers are plenty happy because the company pays big money to haul scab. They drive like they are plenty happy, fast around the curves when they are empty, running cars off the road, and tearing up the road when they are full to overloaded. I can set in that vinyl couch outside my trailer and hear them brakes squeal as they come down the last grade off the mountain onto Lloyds Fork two miles away.

Now I am standing at the foot of the grade with a crowd of women, so many they fill Lloyds Fork road all the way to the curve. They are all miners' wives, around three hundred of them, that Louelly has rounded up. They have on shorts and T-shirts and tennis shoes with holes in the toes. Some of them are toting baseball bats, but most of them have got thin peeled-off switches stripped from green saplings, like you will wear out a youngun's legs with if he misbehaves.

Three trucks loaded from the strip mine are coming toward us, so close I can read the names painted on their cabs—Captain America, Big Bertha, and Bucket of Guts. They will keep pistols in their cabs, but I am hoping they will not go for them because they know the men are in the mines and they will think they are not afraid of women. They stop their trucks, stick their heads out the windows, and call to one another, laughing, but they look a mite worried to me. Then Bucket of Guts hollers, "You broads want to move it?"

Instead the women go closer. Louelly stands right up against the truck door. She is so tall she can almost see in.

"You better dump this here load of coal," she says.

Bucket of Guts laughs. "Sure, sister. You girls know about the injunction?"

"Injunction says miners," Louella says. "We aint miners."

He laughs again but it is real high and nervous. He looks around, then lets off the brake a little like he will try to ease forward but there are women as far as he can see, they wrap their arms across the radiator and press against the humps over the front wheels, and he will have to crush forty or fifty of them to get anywhere. They are banging on the truck with their baseball bats, with their fists. He pulls on the emergency brake, leans sideways, and hollers over the racket, "Goddamn bitches, you all gone crazy? Get out the motherfucking road!"

"Boy, that aint no proper language to use," Louella says. "We're here to teach you what your mommy didn't."

She wrenches open the truck door before that surprised Bucket of Guts can think to lock it. Ten or twelve women have got a hold of him and haul him out. He scrapes his knees when he hits the ground and then he is so covered up by women I can't see a scrap of him. Comes a high singing sound when the women start to whipping him and Bucket of Guts twists and turns and squalls, so I know his legs and backside must feel like they are on fire. But he can't fight clear of the women—there is nowhere to go except into the arms of more mad women—then they haul him up like a sack of flour and dump him in the ditch.

Big Bertha's driver has rolled up his window, but them women climb right up on the cab and smash the windshield with baseball bats until he opens the door and slips out with his arms over his head, and him and Captain America end up beside Bucket of Guts in that green scummy ditch water. Big Bertha has lost his cap and his face is scratched and bleeding up one side. The truck cabs is full of women, pushing buttons, pulling levers. The truck beds rise up slow and we scatter away as all them tons of coal pour into the road. Meantime more trucks is backed up since the road is blocked, and the women are moving down the line.

RACHEL

When the guards marched the men at gunpoint to the mine, I heard the commotion, the men cussing and the women yelling out the windows after them. I ran to Jackie's room and she was just sitting up in bed.

"Don't look out the window, honey," I said.

"What's going on? Is it something bad?"

"There are company men outside who've come to take the miners to the tipple, only they don't want to go so everyone is angry." I shut her window and sat on the edge of her bed.

"Why can't I look?"

"Because I said so."

I didn't want her to know how frightened I was and how worried, didn't want her to see the guns pointed at Uncle Brigham across the street, to see Betty Lloyd standing on her porch, face twisted with hate, shouting obscenities. I thought, a child should not grow up in a place where such things happen. My child should not. And if it weren't for Dillon, I might have moved to a town with neat brick houses and white picket fences. But Dillon—

"Where's Dillon?" Jackie asked. "He'll get away, I bet."

"I don't know," I said. After making sure Jackie would stay in the house, I walked across the street. Betty Lloyd, still mad and red in the

face, said she hadn't seen Dillon among those taken to the mine. I
called the health department to say I would miss work that day, because I didn't want to leave Jackie in Number Thirteen with Louella
Day, who usually babysat for me in the summer. I decided to get
away, to take Jackie swimming at the pool in Justice town. First I
called Arthur Lee's office. He would know if Dillon had been hurt or
arrested. But Arthur Lee was out. We listened to the radio on the way
to the pool, but there was no mention of Dillon or of the armed
roundup.

He called that night, while I was washing the supper dishes.

"Where you been all day?" he said.

I glanced at Jackie in the living room, stretched out on the couch
with a book. "I could ask you the same thing," I said in a low voice.

"You know they took the boys to work at gunpoint."

"How could I miss it? It was happening right under my windows."

"They didn't get me because I wasn't home. I was sleeping in the
back of my truck up at our hermit's cabin."

"Is that so?" I tried to sound calm, distant.

"Brought back memories," he said. "I wished you were there."

I ignored that. "Where are you now?"

"Pay phone up to Annadel. Rachel, can I come by tomorrow
night?"

I waited a moment before I answered, wanting to make him worry
and suffer as I had. "I thought you were going to stay away."

"Is that what you want?" I could hear the hurt in his voice.

"It's what you wanted, not me. I don't want it unless your being
here is going to put my child in danger."

"I have to talk to you one more time. I'll slip in after dark and be
real careful. No one will know I'm there."

"All right," I said. "I'll have supper for you."

Later I stood in the door of Jackie's bedroom and watched her
sleep. I wanted to see Dillon, wanted to see him badly. But it wasn't
talk I wanted. I dreaded the talk. What I wanted was for him to take
me in his arms. And I hated myself for wanting it.

·   ·   ·

The next day I had paperwork in the health department office at Justice. Arthur Lee called at ten o'clock.

"I'm coming into town today. Can we have lunch? I want to talk to you."

So does everyone, I thought. I said I'd meet him at the Tic-Toc Grill. He was already there, looking tired, when I arrived. We ordered cheeseburgers and fries.

"I'll come right to the point," he said. "You see much of that cousin of yours?"

"You mean Dillon?"

I was having trouble getting the catsup to come out of the bottle and he took it from me, smacked it hard with the butt of his hand. A bright red stain spread across my plate.

"Your cousin's in trouble," Arthur Lee said. "The FBI is building a conspiracy case against him. That means time in a federal penitentiary if they make it stick."

My stomach was turning over but I forced myself to eat a French fry. "What do you want?" I said.

Arthur Lee laughed. "Want? Honey, I aint in a position to want nothing. My mines are shut down, I got thousands of dollars in equipment and building losses. Those boys are in charge. They're calling the shots."

"What do you want?" I said again.

Arthur Lee leaned over the counter. "I want you to tell that bone-headed cousin of yours that he won't be a free man much longer unless he calls a halt to all this foolishness. Tell him the Justice Department won't be fooled with. And tell him we can work something out."

"What can you work out?"

"I can keep him out of jail. And I can make sure his buddies at Number Thirteen aint treated too bad.

"You mean you'll keep the union?"

"Union." Arthur Lee laughed. "It's the union is messing over those boys. Why do they want to worry with the union anyway? I mean, I'll take care of them personal. Will you tell him?"

"I'll tell him," I said. "I don't think it will make a difference."

"There's something else." He put his hand beside mine on the table. "I been watching you for a while, Rachel. I like you, always have. For a long time I thought it was because of Tommie. You know how I loved her. But it's been years, honey, years. I try to recall what she looks like and I can't picture her. Terrible, aint it? We think we'll remember and save the dead thataway, but it don't work. When I try to recall Tommie these days, I see your face."

I put my hand in my lap. "I'm not Tommie," I said.

"No. You're something better, a flesh and blood woman. I'm asking you to court me, Rachel. I'd ask you to marry me right out, but I don't want to go too fast for you. I spoke to Tony, by the way. Me and him are still buddies, and I didn't want to make him mad. You know he's living in Logan now, took a job over there, married to that Jean. He won't mind if we keep company. I'll be good to you, honey. And I'll love that little girl like my own. I can send her to any college she wants to go to."

I wanted to get up and run away. I tried to drink my CoCola so I wouldn't have to look at him but my hands were shaking so bad I set down the glass and hid them in my lap.

"You know I had a drinking problem," Arthur Lee said. "I licked it, though. Go to AA meetings at the Methodist church once a week. I aint touched a drop in four years. I knew I'd not find a good woman to marry unless I quit, so I done it."

"I'm glad you quit," I said.

He lit a cigarette, blew the smoke away from me, waved away a fly that tried to light on the remains of my French fries.

"It was hard to quit," he said, "but I can do a thing like that if I set my mind to it. I am strong willed, Rachel. I generally accomplish what I set my mind to. I thought you'd appreciate that."

"I do," I managed to say.

"You aint eating," he said.

"Oh." I grabbed my cheeseburger and nibbled at the edges of the bun. "It's a lot, Arthur Lee. I'm flattered. It's a lot to take in, what you're saying."

He was watching me with a smile on his face and a hard look in his eyes, not mean but determined.

"You want these mines to be union?" he said suddenly.

"I don't know much about it," I said. "It's what these men want. Dillon says the union is corrupt but he thinks the miners can fix it. If it's gone, he says there's nothing to fix."

"I got nothing against a union," Arthur Lee said. "Sometimes it even helps if you know who you got to talk to. These big boys in Philadelphia, they don't understand that. They don't talk to nobody, not even me. Sometimes I think I need my own damn union." He smiled and tapped his cigarette against the ash tray. "Tell you what. You talk to Dillon, I'll talk to the union and the big boss in Philly. Honey, don't look at me like you seen a ghost. They aint no catch and no promises either way. You got a little girl needs a daddy and a cousin you want to keep out of trouble. This community needs peace and quiet. Think on it for a little while, then we'll talk again. Okay?"

I nodded my head. He stood up and laid a ten dollar bill on the table. "Got to run," he said, patted my hand, and strode out the door of the Tic-Toc like he was entering a world he owned.

He came late, after Jackie was in bed, ate cold fried chicken and potato salad and green beans I heated on the stove. When I carried his dirty dishes to the sink, he followed me, stood behind me and put his arms around my waist.

"It's been lonely," he said.

"For me too," I said. "Louella and Betty see their husbands."

"Nobody's singled out Homer or Brigham."

I turned around and leaned against him but didn't hug him. "You said you wanted to talk."

"You know what the women did day before yesterday, stopping the coal trucks? They'll do it again. It's not some big strategy, it's just what they'll do when they have to."

"I can understand it," I said.

"I want more than that from you. I want you with them."

I pulled away and poured him a cup of coffee. "You know I can't do that. I'd lose my job. I wouldn't even get on at the hospital because they've got coal people on their board."

"You'd find something. I'd help you out meantime."

"You? Dillon, you haven't got two nickels to rub together right now. How are you going to help me pay my bills?"

"You're living high. Look around you, what people are going through. They're starving, Rachel. You were raised poor. You can give up something."

"And Jackie? What do you want her to give up?"

"She doesn't have to eat steak twice a week like she is right now. She doesn't need new clothes and new toys every time you turn around. You spoil her rotten."

"That's my business. She's my daughter and I want her to have nice things. I also don't want her mixed up in this strike, and she would be if I got involved. What if I got put in jail?"

"She's old enough to handle it. She needs to know what the world is like."

I shook my head. "I don't understand you, Dillon. I thought you were staying away because you didn't want us involved."

"I don't want you involved with me. If those bastards decide to take me out, it will be with a bullet or a bomb, and anyone close by is liable to get hit too. But that doesn't mean you can't support the strike. It would mean so much to me, knowing you was involved."

"I am involved. I nurse the families of those men every day. I keep the radio on everywhere I go, listening for the local news, praying to God they won't announce that somebody has shot you. But I can't wear out a truck driver with a switch. You're asking me to go against my nature and I just can't do it. I'm not a miner's wife either. I don't even spend much time with them."

"So I noticed. You keep to yourself too damn much, like you're above them or something."

"If you don't like the way I am, then what are you doing here?"

"I'm here because I love you. And even though you aint my wife in the eyes of the law, I think of you like you are. I want my wife on the picket line, not sucking up to Arthur Lee Sizemore. That's all."

"Did you ever stop to think that Arthur Lee Sizemore might be able to protect Jackie and me or that he might help all three of us?" I heard the catch in his breathing and I tried to talk fast to head off his anger. "Listen to me, Dillon. Arthur Lee told me the FBI is after you and they'll put you in a federal prison if you don't call this off. He says if you calm things down he'll work something out."

"Sure. What's his price?"

"He just wants to run the mines like usual. He'll take care of you personally and everybody at Number Thirteen."

Dillon smiled. "Rachel, you are so damn naive."

I looked away. "I'm telling you what he said. And he said a union isn't necessarily a bad thing. He said he'd talk to the company."

Dillon put his hands on my shoulders. "You don't understand. Arthur Lee can talk until he's blue in the face. If the same crooks are running the show, it don't help a bit unless we're all willing to look the other way like we always done, while the crooks bleed the union dry and the companies tear Blackberry Creek apart." Then he noticed something in my face. "Is that all Arthur Lee said?"

I shook my head.

"Did the sonofabitch threaten to fire you if I didn't go along with him?"

"Of course not. He wouldn't do a thing like that."

"Hell he wouldn't. He's capable of anything."

"He asked me to marry him."

I looked down so I couldn't see his face.

"You told him to go to hell?" Dillon said in a choked voice.

"I couldn't tell him that! He was serious, Dillon. The man has feelings like anyone else, and I can't be cruel to him."

"Rachel, I thought you loved me."

"Of course I love you. But I don't hate Arthur Lee. I like him. And he can bring the union back to Number Thirteen. He can keep you out of prison. The FBI—"

Dillon threw his coffee cup across the room. It shattered against the door frame and a brown stain spread across the wallpaper. "Fuck the FBI! And fuck you if you're even talking to Arthur Lee Sizemore!"

Jackie called from her bedroom, "Mommy!"

I held the back of my hand against my mouth and turned toward the stairs. Dillon grabbed my arm and yelled, "No way that bastard is putting a hand on you. I'll see him dead first. And you can't stop what's happening on this creek, do you hear, it's the only thing they understand. If you're not for me, you're against me. You got to decide, Rachel, you got to decide right now."

"Mommy!" Jackie cried again.

I pulled away and ran up the stairs to Jackie's room. I held her to me. The floorboards creaked in the hall, and I knew he was there but I wouldn't look at him.

"Now, Rachel," he said. "Tell Arthur Lee to go to hell, and quit your job."

"Dillon—"

"Mommy," Jackie said, "is Dillon mad at us?"

"Rachel. Do it." He walked down the stairs. The front door slammed.

Arthur Lee stuck his head in my office door.

"Talk to your cousin?" he said.

I stopped writing my report and looked away. "He won't listen."

"Then I can't account for the FBI, Rachel. I just can't account for them."

I couldn't speak, pretended to write.

"You thought about us?" he said.

I started to sob. "It's too much! You're all asking too much!"

"Honey, honey." He came over and put his hand on my shoulder. "They aint no rush. You're worth waiting for."

DILLON

I lie on my back in my bed with the iron wall around it. I feel like I am in my goddamn coffin. I hear the car motor, the tires crunching across the red dog in Winco bottom.

I climb over the iron barrier and pull on a pair of pants, peer outside with my pistol in my hand. Agent Shirley Temple is sitting in his white Chevrolet. All the lights in the house are out, and the car is idling but it is dark too, except for the inside light. I can see Temple is smoking a cigarette. Another man is in the car with him.

I light a cigarette, go outside, and stand on the porch. We watch each other and smoke and listen to the car grumble. After a while, Shirley Temple lights another cigarette but he doesn't smoke it, he tosses it lit toward the house, backs up and drives to the end of the bridge, where he waits.

I understand. It is the most I can ask for, really, and I feel like thanking the sonofabitch. I ransack my drawers for pictures of Rachel and Jackie and my mother, grab a shirt, a change of underwear and my wallet and toss everything into a paper bag.

HASSEL

I am setting up to Homer's playing rook and we hear the dull boom of the explosion and the windows rattle. When we go out on the porch we can see the tops of the flames flicking at the sky beyond the lower slope of Trace.

By the time we run the mile to Winco bottom, Dillon's house is about burnt up. All we can do is stand and watch while the roof beams fall and throw out flames like orange foam. Then Rachel Honaker comes a-screaming down the railroad track, and I have to grab a hold of her to keep her from going too close.

"His truck aint here!" I holler in her ear, over and over. "His truck aint here!"

Louelly gets a hold of Rachel then and takes her to set in the Batmobile. When the fire burns down I go closer, walking careful. I can feel the heat through the soles of my shoes, so I find a long stick to reach in and poke around with.

After while I come back and tell Rachel, "They aint nothing in there that could have been a man. Nothing at all."

"You can't tell," she says. "Not with that heat." She aint crying now but her voice aint got a bit of feeling to it.

ARTHUR LEE

I live in the big red brick house on the hill at Annadel that used to belong to Tommie's family. They were the Justices, had more money than anybody except the coal companies. Admired the hell out of them. All dead now, Tommie in the war, then her momma took cancer and went in a nursing home in 1956. Talked her into selling me the house before she died. Always loved this house. Old lady knew it, knew I loved Tommie too. Said she wouldn't have sold to nobody except me.

Threw out the knickknacks but kept the furniture. Old furniture, comfortable. Aint much of a housekeeper, but I hired a colored girl to come up from Spencers Curve and do for me. I like things neat.

Keep the front room for company, which I don't get much of. Got a den at the back where I watch the TV and work late at night, got a fireplace and desk and couch with big pillows. Got a fat old cocker spaniel, Baby, likes the rug in front of the fire. Baby has started to smell bad in her old age. If you rub her belly, which she dearly loves, you can feel her tits have turned hard as rocks. Sometimes she piddles on the floor, never used to. Alberta that does for me complains about Baby ever chance she gets. Had Baby since just after the war, though, hate the idea of putting her to sleep.

Baby can't climb the stairs any more, so sometimes I sleep on the couch beside her. I like to do that. Funny when you live by yourself, how you can sleep in a different place in the same house and feel like you're not you, like you took a vacation or got a new life. Wake up and feel refreshed.

I was asleep on the couch and the banging on the front door woke me up. Baby didn't even hear, she is stone deaf. Got my flashlight but didn't turn it on, got my pistol. Crazy miners running around, don't always feel safe. Deputies drive by the house regular.

But when I reached the living room, saw it was a woman. Porch light showed her outline through the door glass. Went back and put away the pistol, pulled on my robe, and tied the belt. Opened the door and it was Rachel.

"What do you know about this?" she said first thing.

"Know about what? Rachel, good lord, it's near two in the morning."

"Dillon's house. What do you know about it?"

Scratched my head, knew I'd been stupid. Should have expected her to come at me. "Dillon's house? What about Dillon's house?"

Her face is yellow in the porch light. "Somebody blew it up tonight," she said.

I said, "Was he inside?" And for a minute I was scared, I thought, *Those idiots have fucked up. They wasn't careful and this woman will be hating my guts.*

"We don't think he was home," Rachel said. She started to cry.

"Honey, don't stand out there all upset," I said. "Come on in and I'll make some coffee."

"I better not. What if your neighbors see me go in?"

"Hell with my neighbors. Come on in."

She eyed my robe. "You're not dressed."

"Aw, come on, we been buddies a long time. We'll just set and talk, that's all."

Started to set her down in the front room, but I decided a woman will talk more easy in a kitchen. My dirty dishes were in the sink where I left them for Alberta to get in the morning. Rachel sat down at the table and rested her elbow on it, then raised it up and looked down. Bread crumbs stuck onto her bare elbow.

"Sorry," I said. I grabbed a dish towel and wiped the table. "Aint cleaned up proper after my meal. Need a woman around here, I reckon. Been a long time since one set at that table." She didn't seem to notice, just looked away. I said, "I really am sorry about Dillon's house. Reckon the union just had enough of him."

She stood up quick. "Goddamn, you, Arthur Lee. I didn't come here for bullshit. I know the union is working with the company on this one."

"Honey! Sit back down!"

She didn't move, just stood beside the table. I'd never heard Rachel even come close to cussing. I turned away in case she could see the swelling under my robe, poured coffee into two red cups. "Them FBI boys have been chomping at the bit too. I told you I can't control them."

She still stood. "You sent armed men to Number Thirteen to take the men to the mine."

"That's right," I said, my back still to her, "because the old man in Philly told me to. I tried to talk him out of it. It's pouring salt on a wound, my very words. He don't know how stubborn these boys can be. He said fight fire with fire, intimidate them just like they intimidate us."

She sat down. I carried the coffee to the table and sat down across from her, awkward and one foot stuck out straight. I touched myself with one hand under the table and sipped coffee with the other. Coffee was strong and rich, one thing I know how to do in the kitchen.

Rachel sipped slow, eyes down. Must be forty and still yet a handsome woman, younger looking than some you will see at thirty. I could picture her on my arm when the governor invited me to the Mansion in Charleston.

She said, "You asked me to marry you, Arthur Lee. I can't do it and I came to tell you why. You can fire me if you want to."

I drummed my fingers on the table and felt a little sick. "Why would I want to fire you? You're the best nurse in the county. Only don't turn me down yet, honey. Think on it until this trouble is over. I don't want that between us."

"It doesn't matter. I don't love you."

"You like me?"

"Yes," she says. "I like you a lot."

"It's liking that counts," I said. "You can love someone and have a hell of a life together."

She is so still and looks so scared I know I have hit a nerve.

"What is it?" I asked. "Is there someone else?"

"Yes," she said, and bit her lip.

"Who?"

She changed the subject. "I don't understand why you have to do these miners this way. You can be kind when you want to be."

I leaned forward. "Honey, I'm all that stands between these miners and Philadelphia. If I go, it'll be some smart ass from Harvard running the show from away off somewhere."

"And how would things be different then?"

I grinned. "I'd be poorer."

"That's just it."

"Rachel, I'm honest with you. You want me to be honest, don't you? It won't help the world or me if I lose my job. That's the long and short of it." I reached out and touched her hand. "Now you be honest. Who is it you're in love with?"

"It's Dillon."

"Dillon?" I laughed. "Dillon's your first cousin, honey."

"Yes," she said.

I stared at her.

"I haven't told anyone else," she said.

Leaned way back in my chair, dick getting bigger and harder. Woman with the hots for her cousin, Jesus Christ.

"I expect you'll be wanting my resignation," she said.

Narrowed my eyes and looked at the ceiling. "Honey," I said, hoped my voice sounded normal, "the last thing I would do is send you away."

"I don't want him hurt," she said. "You hear me, Arthur Lee? If you care about me at all, you keep them off him."

"I hear you."

"I'd better go," she said.

"Okay," I croaked. When she reached the kitchen door I was still in my chair. I said, "You'll be at work?"

"If you want me there," she said.

"You'll be doing me a favor," I said.

RACHEL

Maybe it was stupid. Maybe I am as naive as Dillon thinks. But I held him more precious for nearly losing him. If Arthur Lee had a shred of decency, if he cared for me at all, he would protect Dillon now. And I had declared myself. I would let Dillon take me some place where we could be married, would come back and face with him whatever gossip, whatever persecution, there might be. Only I would not whip a coal truck driver and I would not quit my job. I was clear about everything and drove back to Winco bottom with a sense of relief.

Outside my car the air was crisp, an early touch of fall, and still smelled of wood smoke from the ruins of Dillon's house. I turned on my flashlight and let the beam play over the ruins. The embers were charred and cracked like petrified wood.

I walked the track to Number Thirteen, stopped at Brigham's house to pick up Jackie. Brigham came out on the porch while Betty roused Jackie from sleep.

"Have you heard from him?" I asked.

"Not yet," Brigham said. "Aint no one heard nary a word."

"If you hear from him, tell him I have to talk to him. Tell him it's important."

"You'll hear before I do," Brigham said.

"No. He's mad at me right now. That's what I need to talk to him about."

"I'll tell him. But blamed if I know where he is."

"Brigham? Are you all going to win this strike?"

He laughed and lit a cigarette. "Law, no. Not with injunctions, and the FBI in here, and them marching us to work every day on the end of a rifle. Coal's running again. It's going on out of here. Even old Dillon has run out of ideas, I reckon."

DILLON

I have kept the box at Junior Tackett's, under the bottom shelf of his tool shed beside the old car batteries. No one knows about it except Hassel and Junior. They're the only ones I trust not to talk: It is something they have learned together, I think.

Inside the tool shed I stumble against a barrel. Junior's hounds set up a racket in their pen but they quiet soon enough. They know my scent. I find the box without striking a light, set it on the table and reach inside, touch the caps, the jars, the rolls of baloney dynamite. I cradle the box against my belly and walk slow and easy. When Rachel was big pregnant with Jackie she walked with a rolling gait and her shoulders thrown back. Now I understand why.

Junior's house is near the riverbank. I climb down carefully by a path near the old bridge site and wade into the water. I am wearing my hip boots, like a fisherman, and I go out until the water reaches above my knees. The bottom is slippery with silt: Sometimes my feet sink to the ankles and sometimes I slip to my knees, so I might as well not have the boots on. When I slip, I raise the box to keep it dry. It is like lifting weights, and after a while my arms ache.

The sky is filled with clouds that pass over the face of the full moon so that waves of light throb across the black water. I slosh out of Lloyds Fork into Blackberry Creek and the water is above my waist, deeper than I expected. I hold the box above my head, pain shoots through my arms as I edge toward the bank, haul the box onto the ground, and rest near the end of the golf course fence. It is still a ways, a quarter mile to Winco and another half mile downstream. I am tempted to walk the railroad track, but I am afraid of being seen by company men or the FBI or railroad detectives. I rub my arms until the muscles relax, then I pick up the box and step back into the water. When I pass beneath the car bridge at Winco, I think of the Japanese skull and the red fox buried beside the ruins of my house. I say a prayer.

Finally the railroad bridge is ahead. It is black and rests on great piles of brown stone that carry it over the highway. I recall Rachel saying Jackie was scared of the bridge when she was little, she would cover her eyes with her hands when they drove under it.

I wait until I am under the bridge and then I climb the bank. I rest again, then crouch and look and haul myself up on the track.

The gravel between the ties gives way to empty space and I hear the rush of water below. I straddle the rail with my legs dangling between the ties like I am riding the bridge and work by moonlight.

The jars of nitroglycerin slosh a little when I take them out of the box. I wedge them with the dynamite between the track and the steel frame of the bridge, bite down on a cap and taste bitter metal, and string out the fuse, fumbling with it a little.

There're no houses nearby and rarely a car on the road this time of night, but I stop to listen. A breeze kicks up and whistles in my ears. No other sound except night creatures up on the mountain. I strike a match, light the fuse, and run, head down. When I reach the track I keep running toward Winco until the ground throws me.

RACHEL

I climbed into bed for the few hours of sleep left to me, but it was no good. Dillon should have called or sent word, he should have let me know he did not die in that fire.

If he didn't die.

I lay on my back and stared at the dark ceiling. I hated him and wanted him.

The window shattered. I rolled off the bed and lay on the floor. At first I thought someone was shooting. Then I heard it, a long faraway roll like thunder,

I stood up slowly. Splinters of glass littered the floor, and one long shard lay like a clear dagger across the foot of my bed.

DILLON

I think I know where I am. I am sitting on the railroad track, waiting.

He is walking toward me. His gun is in his hand but his arm is down at his side.

"Hands behind your head," says Shirley Temple.

I lace my fingers together. My middle finger is swolled stiff and hurts like fire. I put my hands behind my neck.

"You got here fast," I say. My voice sounds thick.

"No wonder," says Shirley Temple. "Heard you all the way to Justice."

The Roving Pickets, 1962

"Is it gone?"

He says, "Appears you took out the entire midsection."

I smile. "We're even," I say.

"Mr. Freeman," he says, "nothing is even in this world."

Book Three

NUMBER THIRTEEN
1963–1968

RACHEL, 1963

I was sitting in my jeep on top of Trace Mountain, eating a cheese sandwich and listening to the radio, when a news bulletin said President Kennedy had been shot. No one knew if he was dead, but they thought he'd been hit in the head and I knew what that meant. I threw my sandwich out for the birds and drove down the mountain. It was a cold, rainy day, and a skin of yellow leaves covered the road. The jeep took a curve too fast, slid like it was on ice, and spun half around, finally stopped up against the bank. I hunched over the steering wheel, breathing hard, and then I started to cry.

By the time I reached the foot of Trace, the voice of Walter Cronkite, solid and solemn as a tolling bell, said the president was dead. I wondered if Dillon had heard. I pictured the federal penitentiary in Atlanta, endless rows of stone corridors and iron bars, men locked

behind the metal doors, pacing, or lying upon low cots in fetal positions, staring at the wall. Would some of them have radios, would they pick up a signal behind those thick walls? Would the guards walk the corridors calling out the news like a town crier, "The president is dead, long live the president"? Would Dillon care? Or would his bitterness extend even to this? I couldn't know. He never wrote.

I took Jackie to his trial in Huntington. We sat on the second row in the federal courtroom, on hard wood pews beneath a gold seal set like an amulet against a dark blue wall. Dillon looked around once but he turned away without smiling or acknowledging us. When he was sentenced to five years he didn't turn to look again. Jackie huddled in the back seat on the way home and pretended to sleep, but I could hear her quiet sobs. I vowed I'd never forgive him for that.

But I wrote anyway, for Jackie's sake. I begged him to write her, even if he was angry with me. I told him how I'd turned down Arthur Lee. The letter came back by return mail.

Sometimes I heard of him from Sim Gore's wife, Remetha. Sim had been arrested the day after Dillon blew up the bridge and charged with conspiracy. So Sim was in Atlanta with Dillon, serving a three-year sentence in the same cell block. I gave Remetha news of Jackie and she passed it on in her letters. Sim wrote Remetha that Dillon kept to himself, mostly reading and writing in a diary or working in the prison laundry, ironing and folding. I could not imagine him doing that day after day.

The talk at Number Thirteen was that Sim had been railroaded by American Coal because Arthur Lee wanted the strongest union leaders out of the way.

"Arthur Lee seen his chance and took it," Brigham Lloyd told me one day.

I didn't answer him, but wanted to defend Arthur Lee. When he came by the health department I asked him about it. He laughed. "Don't believe everything you hear," he said. "What would I get out of putting that boy in prison? Miners still got their union, aint they? Company even brought back the local at Number Thirteen mine, and the union boys in Washington didn't care for that. It was my doing, you know. Over in Kentucky the union's gone. But I told them in

Philadelphia I couldn't run a mine with all them shenanigans going on." He winked at me. "And I sure can't run coal out of a hollow that don't have a railroad bridge. That cousin of yours got some attention, that's a fact. Can't say much for his methods, though."

So the men had their local union and their benefits, even though they were back to only one or two days work and more people left to look for work in Ohio and Michigan. And Arthur Lee sent me flowers on my birthday and always had a kind word. I began to think more of him. But I wouldn't encourage him, not while Dillon was in prison. I couldn't do that to any man, no matter how he hurt me.

I reached Winco just as Jackie was getting off her school bus. The children were subdued as we walked toward Number Thirteen, even Doyle Ray Lloyd, whose eyes looked red from crying. Ethel Day said, "Mrs. Honaker, did you hear about President Kennedy? What are we going to do? He taken an interest in us."

I thought of the FBI and of the picture of President Kennedy on Louella Day's kitchen wall. I said yes, he did. Jackie walked along silently, sometimes kicking gravel along the railroad ties. She went so slowly that the others were soon ahead of us.

"Honey, are you all right?"

She nodded. "I don't care about it," she said.

"What?"

"I don't care if he got shot."

"Jackie! That's a terrible thing to say."

"I don't care! He didn't do a thing for nobody. Not a thing. He just talked big." She kicked the gravel. "He put Dillon in jail."

"That's not true."

She stopped walking. "I heard what they said at the trial. They said it was the United States versus Dillon Freeman."

"Dillon went to prison because he blew up a bridge," I said. "He never denied that he did it."

"He did it to help the miners," she said. "They shouldn't put him in jail for that."

"He still had to pay for what he did. He didn't help the right way."

"I don't care. I don't want him to pay for it." Then she started to cry. "Why doesn't he write me? Doesn't he love me anymore?"

How do you explain spite to a child?

"He does love you," I said. "But some people are prideful and stubborn. They don't want any dealings with people when they're hurting because they think it makes them weak. Dillon is like that."

Jackie sniffed and wiped her nose. "I wish he'd escape," she said. "Why doesn't he escape?"

HASSEL, 1963

The night the picture fell, Homer set at the kitchen table. His forehead was so wrinkled that his scalp looked like it had stretched out too big for his head.

"Hit's different at the mine with Dillon Freeman gone. Dillon kept the company off our backs."

I knew what he was talking about. Me and Junior has heard Arthur Lee talking to his buddies up to the Esso station. They hang around the office on Saturdays for a hobby, smoking cigarettes and drinking coffee and watching us work. They act like we aint even got ears to hear. Arthur Lee said, "You don't break a union, you tame it. Easy as pie. Put 'em back to work union and starve 'em out. Then where do they go?" So the boys are back to working short weeks, and the union safety man is a company suck.

Louelly was at the sink washing dishes. Homer leaned way over his coffee cup and talked low like he didn't want her to hear. "My roof aint safe."

That's when Toejam come through the back door, slammed the screen door hard, and the picture fell off the wall. We all jumped like we'd been shot. It was the picture of President Kennedy, the only one with glass over it because Louelly said a president ought to have glass over his picture to keep the coal dust off and bought a frame from the Murphy store for ninety-nine cent.

"Mommy, I'm sorry," Toejam said, and his face screwed up like he was about to bawl.

Louelly's arms was fuzzy white with soap suds up to the elbows. "Don't fret," she said. "Now go on back out to the coal house and bring me a bucket. It's a-getting chilly."

Toejam went and Louella still stood, not even wiping the suds from her arms. "Hit's a bad omen," she said. "Picture falling off the wall means somebody will die. I didn't want to say it in front of Toejam else he'll blame hisself." She looked fearfully at Homer. "Dad, don't go to work tomorrow. I got a bad feeling."

"Aw, honey, it's just a saying. If Jesus means to call me home, I'll go, whether I'm down in that mine or sleeping in my bed. Besides, we aint had but one day so far this week. I got to work."

Now I didn't say a word, but I put a store in omens and bad feelings, especially Louelly's. Homer went on to work the next day and nothing happened. But they aint no law says an omen has to come to pass on schedule. It was two weeks later I was under a Chevy draining the oil when Junior come out from the garage at the Esso.

"Get cleaned up," he said. "Hit was Louelly on the phone. Homer's hurt and carried to the hospital."

I sat up and rubbed my hands on my pants. My stomach hurt like I'd swallowed an ice cube. "Bad?" I asked.

"Sounds it."

I walked past him toward the washroom and he grabbed my arm. "Send the younguns around to Mommy's if you need to," he said.

I nodded and patted him on the back.

They had Homer in a ward, last bed on the right. One side of his skull was stove in and he had white bandages wrapped all over. His eyes was the only thing that showed and they was shut so tight the lids had turned dark blue. Louelly set beside the bed, her hands a-hold of his arm, and Ethel and Toejam shared one chair in the corner, so close Toejam was almost in her lap.

Louelly looked up at me and I seen she was too shocked yet for tears.

"Roof?" I said.

She nodded. "Like he said. I hoped he might just have a coal tattoo like Uncle Brigham got that time, but I reckon hit caught him more than a glance." She looked at Homer. "He don't wake up. I keep talking to him but he don't wake up."

Toejam started to whimper from the chair. Louelly said without looking at him, "Don't you fret, son. Ifn the Lord calls your daddy home, we'll just have to accept it."

An elder from Homer's church come with about twenty more of the faithful and had the prayers. They was a man in the next bed with a hernia so we tried to be quiet, and the "Yes Lords" and "Thank You Jesuses" was soft as sobs. Louelly still yet didn't cry, only the youn-guns, who couldn't stop and held tight to each other. Once in a while Toejam said, "Oh, please Daddy." The church people left and the man with the hernia turned on the television. The "Beverly Hillbil-lies" was on.

Junior come along later and took the younguns to his house. Homer passed on in the morning around three. His chest stopped heaving and Louelly peered over the rail of the bed. "He's gone on home," she said. Then she set to bawling and would have tore down that rail and laid on top of him but I held her off. I was crying myself, my throat all clogged up to keep from yelling. I wanted to pull off the bandages and see his face but there was only the blue eyelids.

Homer laid a corpse in the front room of the house. All the neigh-bors come by with food, hams and fried chickens and deviled eggs and potato salad and chocolate pies, until Louelly had to send some of it to Rachel Honaker's house to put in her big freezer. It was enough food to make do a month on, and that is the way folks are.

Arthur Lee Sizemore come to pay his respects. He brung a big ham from the company, and Louelly made him eat a plate of food. After he eat and picked his teeth, he pulled some papers out of his jacket.

"Louelly, I'm real sorry," Arthur Lee said.

Louelly kind of ducked her head and didn't say anything.

"Hassel, you can have off work a week and I'll still pay your sal-ary," Arthur Lee said. "I know this family needs you right now."

"I'm obliged," I said.

He handed me the piece of paper. "I come with a form for Louella to sign. It's just a formality."

I read the paper quick as I could. It had lots of long sentences like lawyers use to take up room, and then it said that the American Coal Company was in no way responsible for the injury or accidental death of said employee, Homer Raymond Day.

"It's what we always do," Arthur Lee said. "It just means this was an accident and there are accidents in coal mines. You know that, Hassel. Always have been and always will be." He looked at Louella. "I'm just as sorry as I can be. Homer was a good man and a hard worker."

Toejam was setting on the floor beside the coffin, taking in every word.

"Hit weren't no accident," he said.

Arthur Lee looked at him funny. "Now, son," he said.

"Jesus took my daddy," Toejam said. "Jesus don't make no accidents. Hit's all a-purpose with Jesus."

Arthur Lee kind of laughed and looked relieved. "Louelly," he said, and held out his hands.

Louelly had her arms folded acrost her chest like she does when she's feeling muley. "Toejam's right," she said. "I can't sign."

"Hassel," said Arthur Lee, worried again. "You see that casket your brother's laying in. That there is the best casket money can buy, courtesy of the company."

"We're much obliged," I said.

"You're a good worker," he said again.

"Thank you," I said.

Arthur Lee looked like he couldn't think what to do. "I'm sure Homer would want Louella to sign," he said, looking at me instead of her.

"I won't sign," said Louelly. "Hit were a bad roof."

And I thought Arthur Lee would faint dead away. "Now, Louella," he said, "you got no proof of that."

She nodded toward the casket. "It's what he said. That's my proof. But don't you fret none. We won't file no claims. The Lord settles such like."

I could tell Arthur Lee was relieved at that, but some people will not fear the next world until it is right up on them.

We did appreciate that there coffin from the company. It was silver and so smooth that when we shut it to carry Homer out of the house to the church, Louelly threw herself on it and slid right off. The coffin had white satin insides, and Homer was laid out in his best brown suit. The bandages was off and his head and face was puffy like he'd gained a lot of weight, so you wouldn't have knowed him. We had a fine preaching and the church was full. Brother Ed Marcum from Daisy Creek preached the sermon and saved two people at the altar call. Then I heard a coal train clanging and banging outside, and I knew they'd be trouble.

The church sets on the hillside behind the tracks, and trees and underbrush all around except where the wood steps go up. Sometimes the trains set on the track waiting to be loaded at the tipple. Mostly the train just sets still, but this one was taking on coal.

After the preaching, the pallbearers talked what to do.

"Why not walk this side of the track?" said Brother Marcum.

I told him how folks could walk that side but it got close to the hillside and would be rough going with a coffin. "Maybe we ought to wait," Junior said.

"They might be an hour or two," I pointed out. "And that hearse is a waiting up to Winco bottom and we got that long walk ahead of us with this here coffin. I reckon we ought to start on and climb over while the train is stopped."

So we carried Homer out of the church and down the steps to the train. It was moving slow and then it jerked to a stop with a loud clang and boom all up and down the track.

"Come on now," I said. "Hit will stay still while they load a car."

We hoisted the coffin on our shoulders. Uncle Brigham and Brother Marcum climbed over the train hitch and waited.

"You be careful," Louelly called. "His head might fall off the pillow. He always did have a stiff neck and he couldn't abide to sleep without a pillow."

We had just started to poke the coffin through, resting it on top of the hitch, when the train took another jerk forward. The coffin slid back toward us too fast to catch hold of, and we just did get out of the way. One end of the coffin fell on the track and the old greasy train wheels ran right over it. Hit looked like a tube of toothpaste that has been squeezed from the bottom.

Louelly took a shaking fit so bad she had to take some nerve medicine before she could go on to the cemetery. I stood beside Junior and watched that squashed coffin put in the ground.

"Junior," I said, "if we had that car bridge, it wouldn't have happened."

"If we had that car bridge," he said, "we still yet would have had to get past that train."

"But we wouldn't have tried to hurry so much," I said.

I could see it, even if he couldn't. And I took another vow to get it built, and call it the Homer R. Day Memorial Bridge.

Jackie, 1963–1964

Something awful happens between sixth and seventh grade. In sixth grade the boys will like you because you're smart and because you can tell a joke and you can step in at first base and dig a bad throw out of the dirt. Then you get to seventh grade and the girls you haven't seen all summer have bumps on their chests and giggle behind their hands, and the boys hang around them instead. The boys don't care any more if you can catch a baseball or make them laugh. If you haven't turned all lumpy and silly, you are a loser.

The girls are mean, too. They can tell when you don't know what is going on, and they will cut you dead. It is like they formed into groups during the summer and had secret meetings to grow their breasts and figure things out, only I never knew about it. So I tried to see where I fit in, but it was too late. I even begged my Mom for a training bra, even though it is the most uncomfortable thing in the world, like a T-shirt that is too short and tight. It didn't help.

Brenda Lloyd was in the same fix. She sat by herself on the gym bleachers where we wait for the school bus and studied her math book. We all have to wait for the bus in the gym, it's a school rule. Davidson High School has lots of rules, like you can't go to the bathroom without a hall pass and everybody has to join two clubs but nobody can join more than that. There is a fence all around the building with barbed wire strung along the top, and if you could escape over the fence you would land in the river. Adolf Hitler would have loved our school.

In the gym, the boys sit together on the top bleachers and the girls are at the bottom. The girls giggle all the time and look up at the boys, then look away real fast. Brenda sits by herself near the door with her head in her book. I sat with the giggling girls but I couldn't figure them out so I just watched them. Mostly I watched Lila Cummings who has blonde hair and makeup and red lipstick that looks really stupid except to boys.

At the end of the first quarter, I got five A's and a B in math. Brenda got straight A's. None of the other girls was even close. While we waited for the bus, Lila Cummings kept looking at Brenda and talking to the other girls. They didn't giggle and they talked so I couldn't hear them. After a while they moved in a bunch to where Brenda sat. I straggled along behind.

"Your grades are too good," Lila Cummings told Brenda.

Brenda looked up, her mouth open.

"The teachers are grading on a curve," Lila said, "and you're keeping everybody else from making good grades. If you don't stop scoring so high"—she stuck a piece of hair under her pink knit headband—"no one will ever talk to you again. And the boys already hate you."

They marched to the other end of the bleachers and dissolved into gales of high laughter. Brenda had closed her book and ducked her head. The corner of her mouth tugged down like she was fighting tears. One of the boys at the top of the bleachers threw a paper wad at her. It hit her shoulder and bounced off. She didn't look around. The girls had their heads together, whispering, and Lila looked at me.

I wouldn't give them the satisfaction. I climbed the bleachers and sat beside Brenda, all the time looking daggers at Lila Cummings.

"They're idiots," I said. "You don't need them. You and me are still friends."

She opened her math book. "I don't care about them either."

I opened my book too and we studied, right there in front of them. I reckon it's the bravest thing I ever did. We both made 100 on the next test, studying extra hard for spite so we could mess up the grading curve. The class treated us like lepers in the Bible. Now we are in the eighth grade and nothing has changed. I still don't have any breasts or periods either. Me and Brenda have our own group, just us.

I don't care how the girls treat us because they are stupid anyway. And I don't care about the boys either because they are stupid for liking the girls. So maybe I will never have a date in my life. I've got pictures of Paul McCartney on my bedroom wall, but he isn't real. I don't understand flirting anyway. The way it should be, somebody likes you or they don't. If I like a boy, I tell him so. It worked in sixth grade. In junior high, it doesn't.

I have kissed a boy once, but he was not from around here. He was Betty Lloyd's nephew from South Point, Ohio. It was the only time I ever tried to flirt. The kids were playing baseball, but I wouldn't play because I didn't want him to think I was a tomboy. Then I pretended I didn't know about baseball and asked him what a squeeze play was, but he didn't know and I couldn't stand anybody to be so dumb so I had to tell him. He didn't even seem interested. Later on we stood close together under the train trestle and he stuck his tongue right in my mouth where it took up all the room. It was real messy, like using somebody else's toothbrush, and I got away from there as fast as I could.

I learned from a Dear Abby book for teenagers that this is called a French kiss. I guess they are not too clean in France. I wanted to ask Mom about it but I didn't want her to think I am bad. I am all she has and if I am bad she won't have anybody. I can't ask Dillon because he isn't here. I don't care to ask him anyway. He never writes us. He was real country, and he was always listening to hick music. Sometimes his face will flash by in my mind like when you change TV channels fast, but mostly it's hard to remember what he looks like.

HASSEL, 1965

Some youngun name of Tom Kolwiecki has showed up like he dropped out of the sky and calls hisself a VISTA worker. He told me what that VISTA stands for but I can't keep it in my head, although I can recall anything important. Nobody could figure out what Tom was here for, so I come right out and asked him. He said the VISTA is something the government thought up like the Peace Corps, only for this country. The VISTA is supposed to help end poverty. I got a hoot out of that. "No, really," said Tom, and he started laughing too, like he didn't believe a word of it. That started me to really wondering about him.

Uncle Brigham is offended by the VISTA. He don't like to think we need help like they do in Africa, and he says, "Here I am a growed man getting grayheaded and some shirttail youngun is supposed to save me? And him sent by the government and what if hit's the government I need saved from?" He asked Tom how come he didn't just stay in New Jersey where he was from, and Tom said the government likes you to go someplace different from where you grew up so you can learn new things. I reckon that is fine for the VISTAS, but I don't see where it does us much good.

I reckoned it was my mayorly duty to find out more about Tom, about his people and such. Besides that, I figured if the government was going to all the trouble to send a fellow to Blackberry Creek, they might be something useful in it.

So I set Tom down on the vinyl couch outside my trailer with a Falls City beer. The summer sun was disappearing behind the mountains and the heat was getting softer.

I said, "So you're from New Jersey?"

"Yeah," Tom said. "Paterson, New Jersey." He said it "Juisey."

"You look like you're from someplace like that," I said. Tom has got black hair a little longer than a crew cut, and a nose with one of them crooks in them like the Italians do, even though he claims he's Polish. "I reckon it's a whole lot different from here."

"Oh yeah," he said, "but we got some things in common.I heard you guys had a big strike a few years back. We had lots of strikes in Paterson, big strikes. Lots of factories. My grandfather was a shop steward in a shoe factory. My mother's father. He was Greek. That's where I got this nose."

"And your daddy was one of them Polish people?"

His face got all sad. "Yeah, his people were from Katowice. My dad coached football at Rutgers when I was a kid. He died of a heart attack when I was thirteen."

He jiggled his beer bottle and looked around like he didn't care to say anything else about it.

I said, "You one of them college boys?"

"Just graduated from Boston College. I had a football scholarship, caught twenty-three passes last fall and got all my front teeth knocked out." He grinned and showed his teeth. "I've got bridgework."

"You can't tell it," I said. I do admire a good set of teeth, and I know they cost some money. "So how come you didn't get a fancy job somewhere? How come you joined up with this VISTA?"

Tom leaned back. "In a couple years I'll be going back to school. But first I wanted to work with people, you know, not sit at a desk all day. See if I could raise a little hell. After VISTA, I'm going to become a Catholic priest. I've just been accepted by the Jesuits."

That set me up straight. "And you're drinking that beer?" I nodded at the bottle he was about to open.

"Don't you know?" he said. "Catholics love a good beer."

I ought to have remembered that. There is a Catholic church down to Davidson, but nobody this far up the hollow goes to it. I recall the Catholics, they can drink and carry on as long as they tell the priest about it afterward. Still I was confused. "You been around a week," I said. "If you're going to be a preacher, how come I don't see you praying and talking about Jesus?"

Then he laughed right out. "Don't you remember? Jesus said to pray in a quiet corner and don't show off."

I said, "Don't tell Louelly that. She is Holiness and they pray out big and loud."

"That's all right," he said. "They're in their own church. That's like their home."

So he seemed like he was used to thinking on things and polite and a Christian on top of it. I reckoned they wasn't a thing wrong with Tom and told Uncle Brigham so. He weren't impressed, but Brigham will be hardheaded. I said, "Treat him right, Brigham, he might get us a bridge built."

I'd done asked Tom about it.

"I don't know," he'd said. "Look at the people that don't have enough food to eat. Maybe that's more important than a bridge."

But I reckon there is plenty of time to talk him into it. Tom will be around a spell, and I am a patient man.

Arthur Lee has come by the Esso and asks me real close questions about Tom. Like where he's from and what he does with his time. Mostly he sets around, I say. Tom says he's supposed to set around and get acquainted with us.

"Where does he do his setting around?" Arthur Lee says.

"Lots of it in my yard," I say.

"Is that so? Who else sets in your yard?"

"Most of the younguns."

"I knew it!" Arthur Lee pulls a pamphlet out of his shirt pocket and smacks it with his hand. "That's just what it says right here!"

"What's that?" I say.

"*Dusseldorf Rules.* It's a secret Communist document they found in Germany after the war. Corrupt the young people. It's how them Commies do it."

"Aw," I say.

Arthur Lee has got big old thick eyebrows and they hump like woolly worms when he gets mad. If they was an eyebrow hall of· fame, Arthur Lee would be in it along with John L. Lewis and that Leonid Brezhnev that just took over Russia. But I'd never tell Arthur Lee to his face that he looks like a Communist.

He waves them Dusseldorf rules under my nose. "Let me tell you something, Hassel. You stay away from that VISTA."

"Be hard to do," I say. "He's renting my spare bedroom."

I think Arthur Lee will swallow his false teeth. I am cleaning the windshield on a Buick and he keeps following me around. "Hassel," he says, "do you like this job?"

"I like it fine," I say, "but if it comes to that, he's paying more rent than you are salary. It's the government pays his keep, you know."

Arthur Lee sticks out his chin. "Is that right?"

"That's right," I say.

"Is that right?" He turns around and walks to the door of the Esso. "Just who by Jesus do you think you are? Have you turned Communist too?"

"Lord, no. I aim to be a businessman."

He laughs right out.

"It's true. Tom says the government is giving fellows money to start them a business. I reckon he can help me get some of that there money. That makes me a capitalist, don't it?"

Arthur Lee's lip curls up. "You take money from the government, you aint no capitalist," he says.

"Why," I say, "I don't aim to take as much as you do."

That tears it. He fires me right on the spot. I been expecting it, so I don't much mind. I know he'll not fire Junior, because he won't find another mechanic near as good. Besides, Junior is not living at the trailer right now, he is staying over to his mommy's again. I told him keep out of Arthur Lee's way and don't go to none of them meetings Tom sets up. So if folks wants to go to Tom's meetings, Junior looks after their younguns.

It turns out one thing a VISTA does is organize us into groups. Tom says there will be the Blackberry Creek Concerned Citizens, and we will have our own chapter at Number Thirteen that meets at the Holiness church. He goes to every house in Number Thirteen and tells people why they ought to come to the meeting.

The next night we walk to the church. Brother Marcum from Daisy Creek comes to lead the service on Sundays now, but I look after the building. I plug in the neon JESUS SAVES sign above the altar. The meeting is supposed to start at seven o'clock but nobody comes until seven-fifteen and by seven-thirty we only have six people. That includes me and Louelly. Tom stands at the back of the church, and I can tell he is disappointed.

He says. "Twenty-five people swore they'd be here."

"Don't you take it personal," I say. "Folks hereabouts wouldn't come out to watch Jesus Christ ride a bicycle."

"I thought at least Betty Lloyd would be here. She seemed real interested."

"Uncle Brigham's laying drunk again," Louelly says. "He smokes a lot when he's drunk, and Betty don't like to leave him for fear he'll set hisself on fire. Besides that, people at the county been saying don't go to them meetings or we'll take away your food stamps. It scared off some."

Tom says, "I dare them to touch anybody's food stamps. If they try it, we'll kick some ass. Maybe that should be the first thing on the agenda."

Tom is good at talking like that. He wants to move along, get things done. But I'm glad I got elected president of the Concerned Citizens. One thing I figure, you could do your business in maybe two minutes if everybody bears down and speaks plain. But people won't come to a meeting for that. They will want to visit, so you have to let them and don't worry if somebody starts in to fuss about a spoil bank sliding into their vegetable garden and ends up asking Louella how she puts up her mixed pickles. You just don't write up the mixed pickles in the minutes.

What we do, in between the visiting, we stick a sheet of paper up beside the JESUS SAVES and write down our goals. One goal is to get a car bridge built. I make sure that gets on the list. The other thing we decide is to start what Tom calls a food cooperative. That is because the company stores are all closed and the prices at the Pick-and-Pay in Annadel are high as a cat's back. And if you take twenty dollars of food stamps to the Pick-and-Pay you will only get ten dollars of groceries. Tom says, "If we're successful with this, people won't have to buy from the Pick-and-Pay any more."

We get back to the trailer at nine. Tom sets on the couch and drinks a Falls City.

"It's a good thing you enjoy a cold beer," I say. "Hit'll comfort you after you get in trouble with Arthur Lee Sizemore."

"Who's that?"

So I tell him Arthur Lee is a boss for American Coal and that he's on the county commission. "And that aint all." I pop open a beer bottle, lean back, and stretch. "Arthur Lee owns the Pick-and-Pay."

JACKIE, 1965

Tom Kolwiecki is the cutest thing in this world. He's got a sweet face just like Paul McCartney and he's real smart. None of the girls from Davidson know him and he wouldn't like them anyway.

I'll never forget when I first set eyes on Tom. All the kids were watching TV at Hassel's trailer. We hang out there because it's like a secret clubhouse, dark and mysterious and full of neat junk. Hassel's got calendars on the walls from every funeral home in Justice County. He's got shoe boxes stacked up that he keeps things in, and a grass-green ashtray from Myrtle Beach on top of the TV. Hassel doesn't smoke but Junior Tackett does and the ashtray is always full of squashed cigarette butts.

Hassel also collects weird lamps. One of the lamps is a big fat pig with a skirt on and a light bulb in its belly. Another one is shaped like a ship with sails, and the lights turn so it's like the waves moving. Hassel keeps the lamps on in the daytime because the trailer is always dark inside. There's only one window with glass in it, beside the stove, and it's covered with grease from where Hassel fries his food. The other windows are broke out and there is plastic over them that you can't see through. Hassel keeps the door open unless it's cold outside.

We were watching the "Andy Griffith Show" when *he* walked in the door. Hassel said, "Younguns, this here is Tom Kolwiecki. He's staying with me for a spell."

And I thought I would die because Tom is so cute.

Toejam Day said, "Whereabouts you from?"

"New Jersey, stupid," said Doyle Ray Lloyd. "My daddy told you that yesterday when you was over to the house."

Then Toejam, who is too slow for words, points at the television and says, "My favorite character on 'Andy Griffith' is Ernest T. Bass. Who's your favorite character?"

"I don't know," Tom said. "I don't watch much TV."

On the TV, Barney Fife yelled "Nip it in the bud!" and everybody giggled. I didn't laugh. Tom sat on the floor beside me. I said, real low so the others wouldn't hear, "I don't like TV either. But nobody wants to do anything else."

"What do you like to do?" Tom asked. He looked straight at me, and I felt real jumpy in my stomach.

"I like to go to movies and listen to music," I said.

Then I realized Doyle Ray was listening in. "Jackie reads lots of stupid stuff," he said. "That's why she's four-eyed."

Doyle Ray always makes fun of my glasses because they are thick. I felt like crying but then Tom said, "Put a zipper on it, kid. There's nothing wrong with glasses."

Doyle Ray looked real surprised, because nobody ever talks to him that way. "Oh, yeah?" he said.

"Yeah," Tom said. "You play football, big guy like you?"

"I'm going out for the team next year," said Doyle Ray. He was still real mad and looking Tom over like he was trying to figure out if he was too big to hit.

"Defensive lineman on my college team wore glasses. You call him four-eyes, he'd pop you one."

"Yeah?" said Doyle Ray.

"Yeah. He had a trick for moving the center off the ball. I'll show you tomorrow."

Doyle Ray sat up. "Sure," he said.

Everyone started watching TV again, but Tom leaned over to me. "Do you like poetry?"

I wondered if he was making fun, but he looked serious.

"Yes," I lied, guessing that was the right answer. It wasn't a total lie because I do like Shakespeare.

"T. S. Eliot is my favorite poet." Tom said it loud and looked at Doyle Ray like he dared him to make fun.

I never met anyone who had a favorite poet except Miss Meade my English teacher who likes Robert Frost. Then I knew Tom Kolwiecki must have made good grades in school and wouldn't care if anyone made fun of him for it because he wasn't scared of anybody.

Mom says I can have a party to welcome Tom to Number Thirteen. Once I saw in *Seventeen* magazine where you can't be a successful teenager until you have a party and I don't know anybody who has had one, so I will beat them.

Mom says, "Are you going to invite your friends from school?"

I say no, real fast.

"Not Vicky or Tammy? You haven't mentioned them in a long time."

"They're dating," I say. "They don't have time for girlfriends any more."

I don't miss those girls. I don't even care about them. Brenda is my friend, and I love Tom and Mom so that is enough.

"Do you want pizza?" she asks.

"And little Cokes and potato chips and onion dip."

I send written invitations on pink construction paper cut in the shape of stars with silver glitter at the edges stuck on with Elmer's glue. I buy a new blouse at Watson's and six new 45 records at Murphy's in Justice town, and a *Seventeen* magazine for last minute advice. One article is "Create Your Own Summer Party." It has a big color picture of food I never heard of, like tacos and guacamole. I don't know how to pronounce them or what is in them, but the guacamole is green and looks really gross. The tacos are in little baskets with red and white checked napkins. I shouldn't have looked in *Seventeen*.

I model the blouse in my mirror. It is blue and white striped with lace around the collar. It looks OK with my navy blue shorts. The

Seventeen magazine is open on my bed. There is another article in it called "Inner Beauty." It says, "Believe in yourself and let the true you shine through." I clean my glasses and try to see what I look like without them, but I have to stand so close to the mirror that the breath from my nose clouds the glass, so I can't tell if the inner beauty is shining through or not.

The party is in what used to be the camp doctor's waiting room. I have a green stereo that will hold five records at one time, and the wall has posters of the Beatles. The cups and napkins are on my mom's card table in the corner, and the kitchen is next door with the CoCola in the refrigerator. I have made the Chef-Boyardee pizzas and Mom is watching them in the oven. She isn't supposed to come in here except to tell me when they are ready.

Everybody except Tom comes to the party right at six o'clock, which is when I said on the invitation. Toejam has his invitation with him like he thinks I won't let him in without it. We sit on the waiting room benches and look at each other. I am sick to my stomach because the pizzas will be done and getting cold and I know Tom is not going to come because he thinks this party is the stupidest thing.

Toejam keeps looking around like he is nervous. "I used to come here and get shots," he says.

Doyle Ray Lloyd laughs. "What for? Being brain diseased?"

"You shut your mouth!"

"Shut it for me!"

They are both standing up. They fight about three times a week and Doyle Ray always wins. It is Doyle Ray who put the pumpknot on Toejam's head.

"Don't you fight at my party or I'll kill you!" I am ready to cry.

Doyle Ray sits back down. "So where's the food?"

"Everyone's not here yet."

I pass around a bag of Fritos. We eat the chips and it is so quiet you can hear people chewing. Doyle Ray says, "What do you do at a party, anyhow? You got any games?"

Mom sticks her head in the room. "Not yet," I say, and she goes away. I get out Chinese checkers and Doyle Ray and Ethel start to play. Tom arrives at six-thirty. He's got on a tan T-shirt with green letters that says Robin Hood Was Right. I run to the kitchen for the pizza, which Mom has kept in the oven so it is still sort of warm. When I get back I notice Tom is eating pretzels, so I will save the bag for a souvenir.

He eats two pieces of pizza. It has pepperoni and green peppers on it. "You make this yourself?" he says. "It's good."

"Play some music," Brenda Lloyd says. She knows I like Tom. When I go to the record player she follows me. "Maybe he'll dance with you," she says.

"No, he won't."

"Want me to put him up to it?"

"Don't you dare!"

I put on "Woolly Bully" by Sam the Sham and the Pharaohs. Nobody gets up to dance, they just sit and look at their feet.

"You guys better dance," Tom says. "That's what parties are for."

"Don't know how," Toejam says.

"Haven't you ever watched 'American Bandstand'? It's easy."

Tom gets them all to dance, even Doyle Ray. He is so cool. I try to stand behind him when I dance because I'm not very good and I don't want him to watch me. When the record stops he turns around and smiles at me. I smile back. Then "Cherish" drops on the turntable and it is slow.

"How do you dance to that?" Toejam says.

"You have to slow dance," Tom says. "Watch up."

He takes my hand and puts his arm around my waist. We sort of walk around and sway a little. I try not to touch him so he won't think I'm fast, but sometimes I bump him when I step the wrong way. My blouse is damp where his hand is on my back. When we turn I see Brenda grinning at me. I make a face.

"Boring," Doyle Ray says.

"Let's go down by the creek," Ethel Day says. "I got some cigarettes off Junior this morning."

She leaves with Doyle Ray. Brenda looks uncertain, then says, "I just remembered something," and winks at me so I know she is leaving me alone with Tom on purpose. Only Toejam stays, watching us from a bench. Tom is humming along with the music and my ear buzzes. I can smell him. I thought from the TV commercials that men aren't supposed to smell, but Tom smells like soap and sweat and something I can't figure that is sort of pleasant like warm bread.

The record stops and we stand apart. Toejam is squirming on the bench. "Tom, you going to kiss that girl?"

"*Toejam!*" I cover my face with my hands.

"Cause if you do can I watch?"

I want to cry. I try to think how a *Seventeen* girl would handle the situation but I figure a *Seventeen* girl wouldn't know Toejam.

"We were just dancing," Tom says. He is still smiling. "You can dance with someone who's a friend, Toejam, and you don't have to kiss them. Dancing's one of the social graces."

"Oh," Toejam says.

"Speaking of social graces, I better not overstay my welcome. Looks like the party's breaking up. I'd better get back to Hassel's."

"I'm glad you came," I say. I am afraid to look at him.

"Me too. Do it again sometime."

He leaves and it is all over. Nothing will be so wonderful, ever again. Toejam is still here. "Jackie, will you dance with me? Slow like that?"

"No way!"

"Why not?"

"You're too young."

"I'm eleven."

"That's still three years difference. Ask me again when you get out of grade school."

That will take a while. Toejam is only in the third grade, since he's been held back almost every year. "Aw," he says, scuffing his feet on the floor.

"Go on home," I say coldly. "The party's over."

I know I am being mean, but I don't care. I have been wounded by love. I go in the house. Mom is watching TV with the sound turned down low. I sit beside her on the couch.

"Have fun?" she says.

I am about to cry so I don't say anything. She puts her arm around me.

"Tom's twenty-two," she says. "He's a grown man. Besides, I've heard he's going to be a Catholic priest."

I sob against her shoulder. He can't be a priest. Only old ugly men should be priests.

"You don't want to rush," Mom says. "You'll meet the right person when you're older."

I won't ever get older. It's too far away. And by that time Tom will be a priest. If I could grow up before he became one, I could change his mind. I go upstairs to my bedroom but I can't sleep so I turn the light on and get out my notebook. I write

> J. H. + T. K.
> J. H. loves T. K.
> Jackie loves Tom
> Tom loves Jackie
> Jackie Kolwiecki
> Mrs. Tom Kolwiecki

all over three sheets of note paper.

RACHEL, 1965

Brenda Lloyd ran up the steps to our house, her bare feet smacking the rough wood. When she saw me standing in the screen door she stopped.

"Mrs. Honaker! Dillon's at our house! They let him out of jail on parole and he thumbed all the way from Atlanta!"

I held onto the door frame and felt my heart flutter like it was trying to leave my chest.

"You want to come down and see him?" she said. "Mommy's baking a chocolate cake."

"No," I said. "Tell him I'm glad he's home. Tell him he's welcome up here."

"Yes'm." Brenda looked around me to see if Jackie was in the living room.

"Jackie's upstairs reading," I said. "Tell Dillon she's here if he wants to see her."

I went back to the kitchen and started a pot of coffee, then went upstairs. Jackie was stretched out across her bed, her chin almost touching an open book.

"Jackie, Dillon's back from prison."

She sat up quickly. "Is he downstairs?"

"No. He's at Uncle Brigham's. I guess he's going to stay there until he can find his own place."

"He doesn't want to stay with us?"

"I think he would have come here first if he did."

She turned back to her book.

"I sent word by Brenda to invite him up."

"I don't care," she said.

Then I heard the knock at the door. My heart was still pounding, and I had been feeling short of breath for a while, so I took my time going down the steps.

He looked thinner than I recalled and his hair was streaked with gray. He wore jeans and a blue cotton shirt with the sleeves rolled up.

"Rachel," he said.

"Dillon."

I opened the door and stepped back away from him. He came inside but didn't try to touch me.

"Sim's last letter from Remetha said you weren't feeling well." His voice was distant, polite.

"I've felt run down for a while," I answered, and thought, *Damn you for asking after nearly three years. Goddamn you.*

He looked around. "Where's Jackie?"

"Upstairs."

He glanced up, then looked at me like he expected me to call her.

"You never wrote," I said. "Not even on her birthday."

He walked to the bookcase, restless, then turned back toward me quickly, eyes wary, as though he didn't trust what I'd do behind his back. "I didn't know if you'd want me to write. Some people wouldn't care for their daughter getting letters from prison."

"I'm not just anybody, Dillon, and neither is she. Besides, you never wrote me either."

"I was alone," he said. "I went out on that bridge knowing I was alone. And I didn't want your pity after."

He had brought the stink of prison with him, the fear and anger. Suddenly I wanted him out of my house.

"She's only a child," I said. "She loved you. Punish me if you want to, Dillon Freeman, because I can't live up to your expectations, but when you punish my child, you make an enemy out of me."

"I wasn't trying to punish her. Matter of fact, I did write her, but I tore the letter up each time. You know why? Because I wrote things you wouldn't let her hear. I told her whose daughter I think she is. I couldn't write a letter that left that out."

"I was ready to tell her," I said. "And we would have written every week, we would have come to visit. If you were alone during the strike, if you were alone in prison, it was because you wanted to be."

He shook his head. "If I'd had a letter from you saying you quit that county job and told Arthur Lee Sizemore to go to hell, I'd have written you back in a minute. But I never heard that from you. So I finally stopped needing you. I decided to be strong and not need anything from you ever again."

"You were practicing that before you went to any prison," I said. "You want all the world to need you and you not need a thing. It won't work, Dillon. The world will pass you by. I've learned to do without too."

We could have gone on like that, coming at each other from awkward angles, probing and poking and doing nothing but harm. I didn't have the strength for it and I was the first to turn away. There was no sense in either of us asking if we still loved one another and if Dillon had not gone to prison it would still likely have come to this. Love is different when you are older, it is not something to die for but rather a comfort, and a hot wounding passion will be a solace to no one.

He stood beside the staircase, looked up. "I want to see her."

"Go on up," I said coldly. "But don't expect her to be excited to see you. And if you tell her anything about us, I'll deny it."

I watched him climb the stairs, hesitated, and then followed. Dillon stood in the doorway of Jackie's room.

"Jackie," he said. "It's been a long time. You're grown up."

I heard her say, "Are you going to live around here?" trying to sound like she didn't care one way or the other.

"I'm going to put a trailer on the Free Patch near Hassel's. I wanted to put it where my house used to set but the company won't let me."

"Oh. You going to work in the mine?"

"They won't hire me back right now, and I'm on the union black-list too. Don't know yet what kind of work I'll get."

"Are you going to move away if you can't find a job here?"

"No. I'll figure out a way to stay."

"I thought you wouldn't want to come back here any more. You didn't write."

"Jackie, I don't know if you'll understand this. I was shut in like an animal in a cage, without a friend except for Sim and I couldn't see much of him. The people there didn't care if I lived or died. I could hear them screaming in their cells at night. In prison you learn to depend on yourself for everything you need in this world or else you don't make it."

I stood in the hall and fought against the desire to strike him, wanted to cry, *Honey, don't listen to him!*

"Prison sounds even worse than my school," Jackie said. I couldn't see her face but I heard the hurt slip away in the rising of her voice. "You could stay with us until you get a job."

"I don't think I better. Sim's got a spare bedroom at Jenkinjones and we need to do some serious talking. We're going into business together. It's something we talked about in prison. Don't worry. You'll see a lot of me after I get my trailer in."

"What kind of business?"

"Sim's got an idea for a car wash. One of them automatic kind. Plenty of dirty cars around here with all the coal dust."

I turned and went back downstairs. In the kitchen I poured a cup of coffee. Jackie's room was above me and I could hear their voices, low and indistinct. I didn't want to understand them. After a while Dillon came back downstairs. He stood beside me and touched my arm, as though speaking with Jackie had warmed him some. I pulled away.

"A child forgets so easy," I said. "Don't expect me to. Nothing will be the same as it was."

"No," he said.

"Let me tell you about Arthur Lee," I said. "That night you blew up the bridge, I'd already been to tell him I couldn't marry him. I guess that wasn't enough for you. Anyway, he's kept on proposing. He asks once every three or four months. I always turn him down. But he never gets mad, never tries to force himself on me. He's kind to me. And you needn't have thought I'd give up a job I enjoy and my daughter's financial security just because you're jealous of Arthur Lee."

"I gave up everything," he said. "You wouldn't give up a goddamn thing. I don't know why you didn't marry the sonofabitch while I was in jail if financial security is so important to you."

"I wouldn't accept him until you came back. I had to know for sure that we were done with each other."

"Sounds like we are."

I blinked back tears and shook my head. "You've never understood or appreciated when I've tried to be loyal to you. I'll tell you something. There's some that would save the world and think nothing to hurt those around them, and you're that way. There's some would be damned for their politics will be saved by their human kindness. Arthur Lee's that way."

"Goodbye, Rachel." He walked out. I heard the front door shut. My chest hurt. I sat down and started to sob until I shook and it was hard to breathe. That night I lay in bed on my back, thinking about Jackie. My chest still hurt.

I stopped at Arthur Lee's office in Jenkinjones on my way up Trace to work. He smiled when he saw me and pulled up a chair.

"Dillon's back and he's trying to open a car wash with Sim Gore," I said. "I'm thinking they'll try to get a bank loan and I know they'll get turned down, unless you help—behind the scenes, of course. Dillon would die if he knew."

Arthur Lee stuck his lips out and narrowed his eyes.

"There's something else I've come to tell you," I said. "I'll marry you. But only if you promise to take care of Jackie if anything happens to me."

His face softened and he smiled. He reached across his desk and took my hand in his. "I'll treat her like she was my own," he said.

DILLON, 1965

In prison I thought about going someplace where not a soul would know me. There are places where a man can go and be bitter, where it has been done before. There's Key West, where you can work a fishing boat in the hot sun and knock back liquor in salt-rimmed glasses. Or a big city like Chicago. I would take a little room no bigger than my jail cell, lock myself inside, and never come out except to get groceries. Rachel and Jackie would look for me but they wouldn't find me.

I came back here instead. I knew it was right when I stood in what once was my yard, beside the ruined wire fence where I buried the skull and the red fox. I have come back to watch over them and to keep company with the ghosts of my people who lived on this land, my Papaw, my great-uncle Dillon the hermit, and especially my daddy. I have come back to dance with the ghost of my love for Rachel, who drowned in the ice-swollen Levisa when we were children only I would not see it. And I want to watch this skinny, brown-haired girl who may be my daughter, to learn by knowing her what blood tests will not tell.

Number Thirteen, 1963–1968

I hitchhike over to Kentucky to see my mother. She is seventy-two now, the only person I wrote from prison. I walk the last two miles up the hollow to her place and she is sitting on the front porch. She spies me from a distance, stands up, and watches me come on with her hand over her mouth. When I reach the porch steps I stop. She has been stringing green beans and the pan sits beside her chair.

"Got enough beans for two people?" I ask.

She nearly stumbles when she comes down the steps and I catch her to me. She clutches my arm with one hand and pats my chest with the other.

She says, "I dreamed about you last night, and when I woke up, I knew you was either dead or coming home."

Then she steps back. "Rachel?" she asks.

I shrug and say, "I seen her. Whatever we had is over."

My mother says, "Whatever you had, you killed. And the way you done it, it's a sin in this world."

I sit on the porch step and say, "You think I shouldn't have blowed that bridge?"

"That aint what I'm talking about," she says. "You done what you had to do. It's your coldness after that I mean."

"She wasn't faithful. What would you have done? If it was my daddy leading that wildcat strike, if it was my daddy blowing up that bridge?"

"I would have been by his side," my mother says. "Wild horses wouldn't have kept me away."

"See there," I say. Then I hunch my shoulders against the pain but it is no good. I grab her and cry against her shoulder. "Why wouldn't she do that for me, Mommy?"

"I'm me," she says, "and Rachel is Rachel. Who's to say what's best. There's plenty to admire in Rachel, only you won't see it now."

"No," I say. "I won't see it."

I cry myself out. Then she takes me to the garden and I hold a bowl while she picks cucumbers and tomatoes and ears of yellow corn. She slices the tomatoes thick as steaks, lays out the cucumbers, the corn with butter and salt, the beans cooked with ribboned fatback and chunks of steamed potato, and the crusty hot cornbread. She won't let me do anything except set the table, talks while she gets the food, tells me her second cousin has kept the weeds cut in the Homeplace cemetery, that she has the arthritis in one knee but she takes a hot water bottle to bed, that she still delivers a baby now and then and visits shut-ins, asks, "How are you going to live, son?"

"Me and Sim Gore are going to open one of them Robo car washes between Davidson and Justice town. We already got us a loan. Fellow at the bank thinks they'll be lots of trade for a car wash, and it don't take but a scrap of land to set it on. I'll be able to help you out."

"I don't need help," she says. "I got my Social Security and my garden, and now and then folks pay me for the nursing. You look after yourself."

She sets a plate of vegetables in front of me. Then she takes a blackberry cobbler from the pantry. "Baked it this afternoon because of that dream," she says.

I stay the night in her spare bedroom, in the same featherbed I slept in when I was a boy.

HASSEL, 1966

So we have our Concerned Citizens and we are going to start a food co-op but we need some money to buy the first batch of groceries. We figure the best way is to have a road block, but Tom don't know what that is. You'd think that there government would teach a VISTA such a thing, but I have to do it.

"You stand in the road at a turn where cars has to stop," I say, "and you hold out your tin can and wave your sign. Then folks drop their change into the can."

"Does it work?"

"Sure. They just raised two hundred dollars for Little League uniforms with a road block up to Annadel."

So we go on up to Annadel, me and Louella and Betty Lloyd and Tom in the Batmobile. The road block lasts ten minutes and we raise less than two dollars between us when the Annadel town cop drives up. It is Luther Beasley who used to work the Jenkinjones mine before he got half his foot cut off. Luther keeps some white ointment smeared all over his nose because he gets the sunburn real bad.

"Y'all got to move on," Luther says. "Hey, Hassel," he adds so they's no hard feelings.

"How come?" I say. "Y'all had road blocks before."

"That's different. Them was fund raising. This here is panhandling. It's a public nuisance."

Louelly steps up. "Who says? Arthur Lee?"

"Now Louelly, you know I can't engage in that kind of speculation." Luther squints his eyes at Tom. You can tell the sun is bothering him. "You that VISTA I hear tell of?"

"That's me," Tom says.

"I heard tell you was a Communist. You do look Communist."

"It's the nose gives me away," said Tom.

Luther grins. Then he pulls a straight face like you see them TV cops do. "What would that be you're passing out?"

"It's information about our food co-op," Tom says. "We're giving one to everybody who donates."

"Food co-op? What's that?"

"Well, we'll buy food together and sell it cheap. It's nonprofit."

"Sounds Communist to me. You're under arrest."

Tom is so surprised he just stands there, and I throw my Cincinnati Reds cap right in the road. "Luther, what the hell are you doing? You can't arrest a man when he aint done nothing."

Luther gets all testy. "Don't tell me how to do my job, Hassel. I got my orders."

"From who?" says Tom.

"Just never you mind."

So he takes Tom to the Annadel city hall and charges him with panhandling, obstructing traffic, and handing out seditious literature. Tom is mad as hell. It is a hot day and the little beads of sweat are all over his forehead. He claims he gets one phone call, but instead of calling a lawyer, he calls his supervisor in Washington. Then they put him in Annadel's one cell that is the size of a broom closet until a deputy sheriff can carry him down to the county jail at Justice town.

It's Arthur Lee's doing, of course. When Junior comes home from the Esso, he says Arthur Lee stopped by and was laughing about it on the telephone, talking so loud his voice carried all the way out to the gas pumps. "Yeah! Seditious activities! Yeah! They was planning on selling red tomatoes, hee, hee!"

So Tom is in jail and his supervisor in Washington calls me because Tom give him my number. The supervisor says he is very concerned. He says Arthur Lee has called his senator and his congressman that American Coal always gives lots of money to, and the senator and congressman called Sargent Shriver and then they all called the supervisor. The supervisor is talking real fast and I have to listen fast to keep up. He says, What the hell is going on down there? I am all excited to think Sargent Shriver has been talking about us but I don't want to get Tom in trouble so I think real hard before I say anything. I say, "What does Arthur Lee say is going on down here?"

"Mr. Sizemore claims there are food stamp recipients picketing the county courthouse and intimidating public officials in their offices. He claims there have been complaints filed against the American Coal Company because of their strip mining practices. He claims you're starting a food cooperative on the Soviet model that will drive private merchants out of business. He says he's got nothing against Tom Kolwiecki personally but he wants him out of Justice County. And he suggests that we need bright young men like Tom in Vietnam where they can do their country some real good."

I listen so long I have to keep changing ears with the phone. "That last don't sound too good," I say.

"No, it doesn't," says the supervisor. "What the hell is Tom doing to get that kind of reaction?"

"He's doing just what y'all said to do. He started him some groups."

"Yes, but what does he have those groups doing?"

"He don't have us doing nothing. We're doing it our own selves."

"Doesn't he give you any direction?"

"We don't need no directions. We know this place better than he does."

There is this noise on the phone and then the supervisor starts to talking real slow. "You don't understand, Mr.—ah—"

"Day," I say. "Hassel Day."

"Yes, Mr. Day. Part of Tom's job is education. And he's supposed to be addressing the problems of poverty. I can hardly see what strip mining has to do with poverty. Tom can't just turn people loose to harass government officials and business leaders. Those are the very people in the community you should be cooperating with."

"Naw," I say. "That aint the way it works down here."

"Mr. Day, I believe I know my job."

"Yessir, but you aint never lived in a coal camp, have you?"

"Mr. Day, I have a master's degree in sociology from Brown."

"I don't know no Brown," I say, "but I know Arthur Lee."

"Mr. Day. Thank you Mr. Day. Tell Tom I want to talk to him. And you might inform him that Mr. Sizemore has called the president of the American Coal Company about the situation, and that gentleman is an active member on the national draft board."

"Yessir, I'll tell him that for you."

I am sure glad to get off that telephone. That is the kind of fellow that could have said what he had to in a minute or two and look at the time he wasted. Not to mention the taxpayer's money for that phone call.

They let Tom out of jail just as sudden as they arrested him, and he hitchhikes up the creek to Number Thirteen. He has got a growth of rough beard on his chin. I tell him about the president of American Coal and the draft board. When he don't say a thing, I say, "Well?"

He goes to the icebox and takes out a cold beer, rummages through the drawer for the bottle opener.

"I don't worry about the army," he says, "or the government. I answer to God and the Jesuits. That's it." He pops off the metal bottle cap. The mouth of the bottle smokes. "They can't touch me, Hassel," he says, and smiles. "I'm beyond their reach."

•   •   •

Louelly says we are having problems because it is 1966. She says 666 is the number of the Beast in Revelation, and even though they's only two sixes in 1966, a nine and two sixes is enough to give Satan a leg up. When we go to the county commission to ask for a new car bridge at Number Thirteen, Louelly says she don't expect much. But she is dressed up anyway in her yellow Sunday school dress and a hair bow in her ponytail. She has been picked to give our speech and she has practiced at our meeting and in front of the younguns at home, but she is still yet nervous. We have called around and the TV station in Bluefield has sent a camera to the meeting. When Louelly stands up they shine that bright light right in her face. She speaks so soft nobody can hear her. Arthur Lee sits all reared back in his chair at the front of the room with the other two commissioners. He don't even look at Louelly while she's talking, he just keeps staring at Tom. Tom sets in the back with his arms folded across his chest and stares right back.

When Louelly is finished Arthur Lee says, "This is all fine and good, but where's the money going to come from?" He turns to the TV camera and smiles real big.

Nobody says anything, then I stand up. "The state gives you money for the highways, don't it?"

"That money is done took up," Arthur Lee says and he sounds like he'd purr if he was a cat.

Louelly had set down but she stands back up. "Hit's took up all right," she says, loud this time. "You paved your driveway with it!"

Arthur Lee's mouth drops open.

"I was picking up bottles at Annadel when I seen the truck at your house," she says. "I followed it in the Batmobile all the way to the county parking lot. I even wrote down the license plate and I'll give it to these TV men after the meeting."

"You'll shut up that kind of talk!" Arthur Lee says.

But now the TV man is sticking a microphone right in Louelly's face and she is testifying.

"I been sitting here praying to the good Lord above. I was scairt to speak before, but He has opened my mouth like he done for Moses."

Number Thirteen, 1963–1968

She sticks her hand in her pocketbook and fumbles around. "Tom Kolwiecki setting yonder that you throwed in jail has been sent to us from the Lord. He got me into the adult education up to Annadel and I learned to read and to write poems. I wrote this here about you, Arthur Lee. I weren't going to read it but the Holy Ghost is calling me to it." She smoothes the rumpled up sheet of paper and clears her throat.

> I think that I shall never see
> A politician mean as thee.
> A politician with a look
> That says he is a great big crook.

"Now you stop that!" Arthur Lee calls out.
Louella bulls on ahead.

> A crook that has his dirty hand
> In more bad deals to beat the band.

Tom has his hands over his face.

> Poems are made by fools like me
> But a bigger fool is Arthur Lee.

We don't get the bridge.

JACKIE, 1966

The longer I'm a teenager, the more I hate it. I have done some catching up. I'm not what you'd call stacked, but my breasts stick out a little and I can wear a two-piece bathing suit without the pants coming off in the water. But I still hate being a teenager because everything has changed too fast. Goblins used to hide in the coal tipples, fairies lived in the basements of the company stores, and the mountains were magic. Now they're just tipples and closed-up buildings and Trace Mountain is being stripped. When I was a kid I thought Trace Mountain was too powerful to be stripped, that anybody who tried would be cursed for all time. I wish I still believed it.

Arthur Lee thinks a strip mine is the greatest thing. He says it is the wave of the future, that soon they will be tearing the whole tops off of mountains and scooping out the coal like eating a soft-boiled egg. He talks all about strip mines at dinner.

Mom says, "There are still people living up on Trace."

Arthur Lee says, "We won't bother nary a one of them. They won't even know we're there. Since old lady Combs died there aint a soul living on the end of the mountain we're stripping."

I don't say a word, just eat as fast as I can and leave the table. I don't even say "excuse me" and Mom doesn't fuss when I leave. These days she knows it's better just to leave me alone.

I can't stand Arthur Lee. He is a big turd. Mom says I have to talk civil to him because he is good to us. I keep a count in my diary of how many words I have to say to him every day. My record so far is three, and I am aiming for minus one.

I asked Dillon once why Mom married Arthur Lee. He said, "For meanness," and he sounded so mad I was afraid to bring it up again. Dillon is mad a lot and it is hard to talk to him. I don't think Mom likes it when I visit him, but she never tells me I can't. She thinks I am with Dillon whenever I'm at Number Thirteen and she is mad at

Dillon because he doesn't like Arthur Lee. But I don't hang out with Dillon when he gets all stubbed up, which is often. I mostly visit Brenda or Tom Kolwiecki. I don't mind not dating any of the boys at school because Tom is so cool and cuter than any of them.

Sometimes I talk to Hassel Day. Hassel is such a hick but he's funny too. He used to work for Arthur Lee and he doesn't like him either, so I can say anything I want around him. Hassel says Arthur Lee is not naturally mean but he has got a mind like a high straight creek bed that never floods. I wrote that down when I went home and at first I couldn't figure it out, but then I started to notice how Arthur Lee is all tight like he is tied up in knots, how he looks at my Mom like he wants to make out with her and then gets on the telephone and starts yelling at somebody instead. Arthur Lee likes money, just like my dad did, only he is good at getting it and my dad wasn't. Hassel says Arthur Lee knows how to make himself necessary, and if you want to be rich in the coalfields you have to be necessary.

Arthur Lee says Hassel used to be a hard worker but he has taken notions brought on by welfare. I think Arthur Lee is jealous because Hassel has got his own business and Arthur Lee can't boss him around anymore. Hassel and Junior Tackett tore out the inside of a house near the Free Patch and put up black aluminum siding on the outside. The siding salesman said there wasn't much call for black and he sold it half price, and Hassel says it won't show coal dust. Hassel calls his place the Dew Drop Inn. He started it with money from the War on Poverty. "Economic Opportunity loan," he tells me. "Ten thousand dollars."

Hassel calls the Dew Drop Inn a restaurant, and he sells hot dogs with chili and slaw and onions on them, and popcorn, but that is all the menu. The Dew Drop is really a beer joint. I can't go in there when it's open because I'm not old enough, but Hassel showed me what it looks like right before it opened. There's one little room with a pool table that just barely fits. Hassel and Junior tore out the rest of the inside walls to make one big space. The bar is dark, with rows of smoky bottles like at the Moose Club. There are two neon signs above the mirror, plugged in and glowing red. One says Falls City Beer, the other says Hassel.

"Place that made the JESUS SAVES for the Holiness church done them signs for me," Hassel said. He flicked a switch and a silver ball hanging from the ceiling started to turn and sprinkle colored lights across the floor. "Even got me a psychedelic light. I'm going to bring in live bands on weekends. And I'm going to run this thing tight. No fistfights in my place. Louelly insists on that. She don't hold with alcohol either, but I say if Jesus turned the water into wine, why not? Now if we can just get that there bridge built, I'll have to beat the customers off with a stick. Although one good thing about that long walk, it will sober up some of them."

I never cared for the long walk along the railroad track but I missed everything else about Number Thirteen. In Number Thirteen you could go right in someone's house without knocking, just sit on the couch and watch what was going on. No one would think a thing of it. Out in the world you will be by yourself, but not at Number Thirteen. I miss Dillon too, or at least the way he was. Hassel says they did something to him in prison. I think it is me and my Mom that did it. Dillon says I am spoiled and he doesn't like that. Sometimes that makes me cry and sometimes I don't give a damn.

I still think about Dillon a lot. My school bus stops at Winco bridge to pick up the kids who have walked the track from Number Thirteen. I try to sit on the left side of the bus so I can see where the cars are parked at Winco and maybe watch Dillon get in his truck to go to work at the Robo car wash. I also like to sit in the front of the bus because the back gets full first and the Number Thirteen kids have to sit in front. I save a seat for Brenda Lloyd and we talk about Tom Kolwiecki. Brenda is not sweet on him. She likes a senior from Number Six who doesn't like her, and she tells me everything about Tom. Toejam sits behind us and listens in. I have told him if he lets Tom know we talk about him, I will put a new pumpknot on his head.

Toejam is twelve but is still in the fourth grade. His grades are mostly F's, and he brags that he makes C's in penmanship but it's because he writes so slow he has to be neat. One morning he got on the bus holding a paper bag and declared he would make an A in science that day.

"Tell Jackie what's in the poke," Doyle Ray Lloyd said.

Toejam looked at me with his chin up in the air. He said, "My science project."

"Show her!" Doyle Ray said.

I could tell by the way Doyle Ray was acting that it was something disgusting that he expected me to scream at because he thought I was a silly girl. I couldn't wait to see it and disappoint him.

Slow and awkward, Toejam took the paper bag off a gallon jar with holes punched in the lid. Inside was a skinny pointy-nosed brown rat. A bunch of hairless pink rat babies were piled on a rag wadded up in the end. Their skin was all wrinkled and you could see the blue veins in their sides. The mother rat ran back and forth real fast. She kept stepping on the babies and they would squeak.

"Toejam," I said in my most bored voice, "you are really cruel."

"Make her hold them," Doyle Ray said.

I smiled patiently at Doyle Ray and tried to take the jar from Toejam before he could offer it, but he clutched it to his chest.

"No way," he said. "You might drop them."

"So where'd you find them?" I asked. "In your bed?"

Doyle Ray laughed. Toejam sat up straight. "They was under the house," he said. "I was looking for a spare tire for Junior and I found them with my flashlight. Hassel took me to the library at Justice and I wrote down everything there is about rats. So I'm going to get an A."

Then I felt bad that I had teased him, because I reckon Toejam never got an A in his entire life. I watched the way he rubbed the jar while he held it in his lap, like it was a genie's lamp, and how his adam's apple jumped up and down. He was dreaming about that A, could see what it looked like on top of his report, and how Louella would cry when he took it home to her.

He got off the bus with the other grade school kids. When I watched him go down the steps, his skinny shoulders hunched tight, I had a premonition. I could feel the jar slip inside the paper bag, feel it roll off his fingertips. I glanced away and when I looked back out the window, I saw it had happened just as I expected. Toejam stood in the middle of the road, the bag dangling in one hand. The mother rat was gone. Broken glass glistened in a pile at Toejam's feet, and the fat pink rat babies were scattered all over the asphalt.

Toejam just stood there and cried. One of the other boys started laughing, picked up a rat baby and threw it as far as he could. Toejam stomped his foot and cried harder. The coal trucks and cars going to work were lined up and waiting for Toejam to move. "Get on out of the road!" the bus driver yelled at him. Toejam scurried out of the way. The bus driver waved his red flag and got back on the bus. The traffic moved forward and the tires of the coal trucks squashed the baby rats flat.

When it comes to dating, I feel just like Toejam. I'm just turned fifteen and nobody ever asks me out. Sometimes I go to the movies with a friend named James from Carbon who is in the school choir, but he never tries to hold my hand, much less kiss me. Doyle Ray Lloyd says James is queer. Doyle Ray is such a jerk. Mom says that is an ugly word and not ever to say it. She says James doesn't try to kiss me because me respects me, but I don't know. She is always telling me I'm too young to date. Sometimes I think she's glad James doesn't try anything because she wants me to herself, and sometimes I'm glad he doesn't try because it might be gross or I might do something bad and Mom wouldn't like me anymore.

Mom goes lots of places with me, to all the high school football games and to the movies, and she says I am her best friend. But when she took me to *Dr. Zhivago,* some girls from school came in and sat in the front row. I watched them giggle and tilt their heads back to eat popcorn. When Rod Steiger raped Julie Christie, Mom started twisting around in her seat, then she whispered, "Let's leave. I'm not very comfortable with you seeing this."

I stared at the screen. "Why do you always come with me?" I said. "Nobody else comes with their mother."

Even in the dark I could tell she had gone all stiff and then I heard her sniffle.

"I didn't know you felt that way," she said.

I felt like the most evil person in the world because she is the best mom and I don't know why I acted like that.

"I didn't mean it," I whispered.

"Yes you did," she said, "or you wouldn't have said it. Don't worry. It's the last time I'll come with you."

The Bible says an ungrateful child is sharper than a serpent's tooth and that is me. I wanted to put my arms around her but it was like a cartoon when a crack opens in the ground between the Road Runner and the Coyote and the Coyote knows he will never get across, never, and he can't stop running before he falls in.

We didn't speak all the way home. I stayed awake at night seeing it all happen again like a murderer who keeps watching the knife go in. It was a while before I got up the nerve to ask Mom to go with me again. We both knew something had changed. Maybe if she wasn't mad at Dillon things would be different. Maybe if she hadn't married Arthur Lee and moved us to Annadel. I never wanted to leave Number Thirteen. It was my happiest place.

Every day after school I get off the bus at Winco and walk to Number Thirteen. Tom has a program for all the kids where we play chess and ping-pong and talk about things. Arthur Lee doesn't like me going to it, but Mom says it will broaden my horizons and I need someplace to go until she gets off work. We meet at the Dew Drop Inn until four-thirty when we have to leave because that's when Hassel starts serving beer. Then I go to Dillon's trailer to do my homework until it is time to walk back to Winco where Mom picks me up. Dillon usually isn't home because he works late at the car wash but the trailer is never locked. He leaves Cokes for me in the refrigerator, and I sit on the couch with my books open and the TV on.

The cold dark of winter is when folks do foolish things, Hassel says, because they are bored and don't get much sunlight. "It's like in Russia," he says. "I seen in the *National Geographic* where they make their younguns stand under light bulbs all the time in winter, so they won't go stark raving mad."

In winter, houses are shut tight against the cold, so the gunshot wasn't much noticed. I heard it, stretched on Dillon's couch with my algebra book, but it was faraway and flat like a balloon popping. I didn't think it was anything. Then I heard somebody screaming. I looked out the window. Betty Lloyd was on the porch with her hands over her mouth turning round and round in circles.

I ran down the street. Betty saw me and started waving her arms. "Brenda!" she cried in a voice that sounded like she was sucking up the air. "Oh God, it's Brenda!"

I looked around. Neighbors were coming out on their porches. Tom and Hassel appeared in the door of the Dew Drop. I ran up the plank porch steps. Betty Lloyd gripped my arm tight enough to punch holes in the flesh.

"What's wrong with Brenda?" I said.

"She's shot! Oh God, help my baby!"

She dragged me through the doorway. Brenda was lying all twisted up in the middle of the floor. Her head glistened like someone had spilled red paint on her, and streaks of blood ran down the face of Bob Barker on the television screen. I grabbed hold of the door frame. Betty was on her knees, tugging at Brenda's shoulders, and then she rocked back on her heels and wailed.

Then I saw Doyle Ray. He was huddled in the corner cradling a rifle to his chest like it was a doll, the barrel pointed toward the ceiling.

"Doyle Ray," I said.

"Hey, Jackie," he said. He talked real slow. "Please help her."

I moved to the telephone and dialed, watching the gun the whole time. Tom and Hassel came through the door and froze.

Then I heard the voice on the phone say, "Fanning Funeral."

I said, "We need somebody from the funeral home at Number Thirteen. A girl's been shot and we have to get her to the hospital. We'll meet you at Winco Bottom."

Then I stood and held the telephone, suddenly afraid to move. I became aware of Uncle Brigham hollering and cussing from the kitchen.

"Doyle Ray," said Tom, "put down the gun."

Doyle Ray's face was pale and he was shaking. "I got to hold onto something," he said.

"Put the gun down," said Tom. "You can hold onto me."

Doyle Ray laid the gun down. Tom went to him and held him around the shoulders. "Jackie," Tom said, "call an ambulance. Brenda may not be dead yet."

Hassel said, "They aint no ambulance so we always call a hearse to carry folks to the hospital. Jackie's done the right thing. We'll have to get Brenda to the bottom somehow."

He felt Brenda's wrist.

"She's still yet alive," he said.

Doyle Ray started to sob.

Hassel went to the kitchen and came back with some towels. He covered Brenda's head with a towel. When it soaked through with blood he tossed it aside and used another one. He said, "Uncle Brigham's setting in the kitchen yonder holding his arm. Look's like it's broke."

"Betty, what happened?" Tom said.

She rocked back and forth, holding Brenda's hand. "Brigham's been drinking. He started in to beat on Doyle Ray for not doing his homework and we couldn't get him calmed down. After a while Doyle Ray grabbed the rifle. But he couldn't just shoot his daddy so he swung the stock at him, hit him in the arm. Only it went off and Brenda—my baby was—"

"Jackie," said Hassel, "you hold these towels. Press down some but not too hard. Junior has got an old wreck he's working on up to his house that I think will run. We'll drive her down the railroad track."

I felt dizzy but I took a deep breath and held the towel. I turned my head so I couldn't see the red streaks on the TV and the wall. Tom was watching me. "You all right?" he said.

"Yeah," I said.

"You're doing fine," he said. "Damn fine."

Doyle Ray slumped against Tom. "Are they going to put me in that electric chair?" he said.

"Nobody's going to put you in any electric chair," Tom said. "We know it was an accident."

They loaded Brenda into a beat-up blue Plymouth that Hassel drove between the houses. They had Tom's coat wrapped around her. Her head was still covered up with redsplotched towels. Then they chugged off down the railroad right-of-way, Hassel up front with Uncle Brigham, who was in a lot of pain, Tom and Betty in the back seat holding Brenda. Doyle Ray came out and sat on the front porch step. He didn't have a coat on, even though it was cold. Old

Sam Chernenko, who had come to see what was going on, stood beside him. Doyle Ray said, "I want Dillon. He's my kin. I want to talk to Dillon."

"Dillon's still at work," I said.

Doyle Ray buried his face in his arms. I walked away and left him with Sam. My mother would be at Winco bottom soon, waiting to pick me up, so I walked the railroad track. The cold air burned my cheeks where I cried—although I couldn't recall when that had been—and I held a gloved hand across my face.

I reached the bottom just as the hearse pulled in. My mother was standing beside the old Plymouth. When she saw me, she ran at me and held me tight to her.

"Thank God it wasn't you," she whispered in my ear, and I felt ashamed to be so important to anybody. She let me go. "I'm going to ride to the hospital," she said. "You go on back to Dillon's and spend the night."

I went over to the blue Plymouth where Hassel and Tom stood watching the two funeral home men load Brenda into the back of the hearse. My mother climbed in beside her. After they drove away, we got in the Plymouth, all three of us in the front and me in the middle. The heater didn't work and I was shivering so bad it was hard to breathe. Tom put his arms around me and laid his cheek against the top of my head.

"I should have done something to keep this from happening," he said. "Those are my afterschool kids. Both of them are my kids."

"It wasn't your fault," I said.

He rubbed my arm, laced his fingers through mine, and squeezed. Hassel reached over and grabbed Tom's arm. He drove the rest of the way with one hand and all three of us holding onto each other.

Doyle Ray has been sent to the reform school at Pruntytown for two years. Arthur Lee says it is for his own good. Tom testified in Doyle Ray's behalf but it didn't help. The judge, who is a buddy of Arthur Lee's, said the shooting was an example of Tom's "disruptive influence on the young people of Number Thirteen." When he said it, Tom took a step like he would punch the judge, and Hassel grabbed his arm. I had one more reason to hate Arthur Lee.

Brenda was in a coma for two weeks, then she woke up. When I visited her in the hospital, she had stitches puckering her forehead like a black bug stuck on her skin. After six months she came home. Now she is in her wheelchair on the front porch, slumped over like she is made out of rags, sniffing at the summer breeze. She lays her head to one side and stares straight ahead. The pure white lines of the scar mark her like a brand.

I stand in front of her. "Brenda?"

Brenda swallows loudly. "Hi."

"How you doing?"

"Hi. How—" Her mouth moves in circles like she is swigging mouthwash. "Hi."

I hear steps behind me, and a clanking sound. Toejam Day is out with his gunnysack collecting pop bottles. He is shirtless in the July heat, wet with perspiration, and his ribs show smooth like his chest has been polished.

"Hey, Toejam."

Toejam stops.

"Brenda," Toejam says. "Hey, Brenda."

"Hi." Brenda moves her mouth. "Hi."

Toejam grins and looks at me. "Hey, Jackie. She's doing good, aint she?"

I can't stand to be around him right now. I turn and run toward Dillon's trailer. When I look back Toejam is watching me with his head ducked down like his feelings are hurt.

― ― ― ― ― ―

Rachel, 1966

I dream I am in the middle of the river again and the ice is coming. I slip from my mule's back into the cold water. Then Dillon has me around the neck and is hauling me to shore, only I don't want to go because I am safe in the river. Dillon pulls me onto the bank and I wrestle him but he sits on my chest. He is so heavy I can't breathe and I try to scream but he only presses harder. He is looking out over the river toward the mountains, and he is smiling.

I sit up in bed and Arthur Lee holds my arms. I gasp for breath and he is saying, "Rachel, Rachel are you all right?" I strain to see his face but it is too dark. After a while I breathe easier. I lean against him.

"Jesus Christ, you scared me," he says. "I thought you were having a heart attack."

"No," I say. "It's just heartburn."

"Heartburn! That's a damn bad case of it. Maybe you ought to go to a doctor."

"I've been."

I shut my eyes. The doctor has already explained that I had rheumatic fever without knowing it when I was a child, that the heart muscle has grown weaker. I am taking digitalis, and I have told Jackie and Arthur Lee that I don't eat fried food because I am on a diet. I won't tell them any more unless it gets worse. Arthur Lee would only get mad and attack the problem like it is a seam of coal to be dug, would want to call in every specialist, waste his money over something that cannot be made right. Jackie is having a hard enough time with what happened to Brenda. I don't want her fretting about me. Maybe I won't get any worse.

Besides, Jackie would tell Dillon. He might come for me again and I am not strong enough for that.

DILLON, 1966

My people were from the Black Mountains in south Wales. Mommy had it from my daddy, who heard it from his daddy and his daddy before him. Daddy told Mommy a little of the Welsh stories he heard growing up, about the good fairies and the bad fairies, only one bunch was so purely good and the other so purely bad that they were both perilous. It was their purity would kill a person.

There are mountains in Wales. I wanted to go there during the war but I never got a long enough leave. I have seen pictures in books at the Justice Public Library. They are like our mountains only bald of trees. You can look at them and tell, even in a picture, that they are not just piles of rock, they are ancient spirits. The old ones believed that way, my people used to say, and so do the Indians in this country. I knew it myself when I worked in the mine. I could hear the mountain above me groan and cry out, mourning its losses, screaming with pain when we cut away its bones. I knew when the roof fell and took a man it was no accident but the mountain lashing out like a wounded animal.

I can hear the mountains talk at night. It is a gift I have from my great-uncle Dillon the hermit. I lie on my bed with the window open and hear the cries coming off Trace. I have seen what they are doing above Lloyd's Fork. Once when all the television sets in Number Thirteen went blank, Hassel and I drove up to see what had happened to the antenna. "Bears probably knocked it over," Hassel said. I smiled at his foolishness. We took my truck up the old road past the remains of Winco camp on the mountainside where the black people once lived. Most of the houses were caved in and scraps of curtains hung from the windows, caught on jagged edges of broken glass. They are ghostly dwellings, looking as though you could thrust your arm right through the wood. We drove until the first fall of timber blocked the road. I stopped the truck and said, "I don't think they's much doubt what's happened, do you?"

Hassel looked up the mountain and shook his head, his eyes narrowed against the sun. "Damn it," he said, "they're supposed to just be stripping the other end of Lloyd's Fork. I seen their permit in the newspaper at a Concerned Citizens meeting."

"Reckon Arthur Lee can't read a map," I said.

I let off the emergency brake and started backing down the mountain, pulling on the steering wheel, twisting my head back and forth until my neck ached. I forgot Hassel was there. All I could think was, *Goddamn VISTA and his Concerned Citizens, and don't that name sound like a passel of idiots sitting around with their foreheads puckered up. Goddamn silly boy that thinks he knows more than we do, pissing around with food co-ops, like a few crates of tomatoes and cucumbers will end poverty, while the American Coal Company kills men underground and rips apart these mountains. Every goddamn kid on the hollow mooning after him. Goddamn Jackie mooning after him and won't give me the time of day.*

I like the Robo. Wouldn't have thought a car wash would be satisfying, but there are a lot of moving parts to keep up and I like working with machinery. A machine is interesting as a puzzle but predictable enough so while you work you can let your mind roll anywhere it wants to. When the wash is running, Sim and I talk, or if I am by myself I will read a book. At the end of the page I look up at the sheets of water and soap, the whirring green brushes, and feel the muscles of my back relax. After a car leaves there is a clean wet smell like a swimming pool.

At four-thirty I walk to the pay phone by the highway and call my trailer. Jackie answers.

"Got much homework this weekend?" I ask.

"No," she says.

"I aint seen you in a 'coon's age. Let's pack a lunch, go up on the mountain like we did when you were a youngun. I got a hankering to see that hermit's cabin again."

Maybe it's cruel because I can guess what we will find and I haven't warned her. But I want to see for myself and I want her there. I want to see what she will do.

"All right," she is saying on the phone. "Can Tom come too?"

Goddamn VISTA. But I can't think of a good reason to say no. So the next day I have to walk the mile of track with him to Winco where my truck is parked. It is October, the leaves are speckled brown like russet apples, and the clear air seems as crackly as the leaves. we make small talk about the weather, about the car wash.

Then I say, "You see a lot of Jackie."

He smiles and says, "Jackie's a good kid. I'm glad she can hang out at Number Thirteen."

He keeps his head down, watching where he is walking, not looking at me.

I say, "I hear tell you're going to be a Catholic priest."

"That's right," he says. "In a year or so."

"Here a while and then gone."

He notices the edge in my voice and glances at me.

"Something wrong with that?" he asks.

"We seen too much of it."

I have said enough to keep a distance between us, so I walk a while in silence. The railroad has laid new gravel along the track and it grinds beneath our feet.

Then the VISTA says, "I've been aware for a while that you don't care for me. You're pretty cool whenever we run into each other. Anything you want to talk about?"

Goddamn college kid, trying to use some kind of psychology on me.

I walk a while longer without saying anything, trying to make him uneasy. Then I say, "We take care of our own problems down here. We don't appreciate the government sending us a bunch of outsiders that come in here like it's some big adventure, showing off in front of the poor hillbillies, and then taking off when the notion suits them."

He stops walking. "Maybe I shouldn't come today," he says, "if you feel that way."

"There's something I want to show you," I say. "I don't have to like you to think it's important for you to see it. Besides, Jackie would be heartbroke if I show up without you."

He looks at me funny but doesn't say anything and starts walking again. We reach my truck and ride most of the way to Annadel in silence.

Jackie is waiting on the street below Arthur Lee's house, beside the boarded-up Roxie Theater. She lights up when she sees us, and I know it's not because of me. The VISTA gets out of the truck so Jackie can sit between us. She gives me a peck on the cheek and then ignores me, keeps turning her head to look at the VISTA and poking me in the arm with her elbow.

I turn on the radio, Porter Waggoner singing "In the Pines." Jackie slumps on the seat, says, "You don't still listen to that hillbilly stuff do you?" Her voice is low and pleading.

I flick the knob off and grip the wheel with both hands, fighting off the impulse to smack her.

"Sorry," I say, "I forget I'm traveling in sophisticated company."

"You don't have to turn it off," the VISTA says. He sounds uncomfortable.

"No," Jackie says then, her voice so low I can barely hear her, "you don't have to turn it off. I didn't mean anything."

We pass the Jenkinjones camp houses, the company store, empty since Arthur Lee built a fancy new office out of cinderblock and glass. At the burning slate dump I roll up my window against the acrid smell. The slate has almost reached the far side of the hollow. The VISTA looks out the window.

"What happens if they fill in the whole hollow?" he asks. "Won't water start to back up there?"

"Behind that pile of bone?" I say. "Sure. No place else for it to go."

"I ought to look into it," he says.

"You do that."

I keep my voice low and even but he glances at me anyway. Jackie squirms and pokes her elbow into my ribs, this time on purpose.

The road is rougher than I remember. The truck rocks back and forth across the ruts, climbs over rocks and roots.

"Bad road," the VISTA says.

"Looks like it washes out every good rain," I say. "That's something new."

Then we reach a tree fall. There is a clearing to leave the truck.

"Want to walk it?" I ask.

"Why not," the VISTA says, trying to sound cheerful. He gets out and stands a little ways off.

Jackie sits on the edge of the truck seat like she doesn't want to get out.

I lean back inside the cab and ask, "Something wrong?"

"It's all muddy and tree trunks everywhere," she says. "I'll get my new tennis shoes dirty."

I want to grab her wrist and jerk her up straight. "Stay here if you want to, princess. But you aint making a very good impression on your boyfriend."

"He's not my boyfriend," she whispers," and you have been embarrassing me all morning. You better stop, Dillon, or I won't speak to you ever again."

I slam the truck door and she gets out the other side. I start climbing over the tree trunks and the VISTA is close behind. The ground has been chewed up by heavy machinery. Jackie slips from a trunk and steps in mud up to her ankle. The VISTA pulls her out by the arm but her tennis shoe comes off. "Dil-lon!" she wails like it is my fault. I ignore her and keep on. We are getting near the turn-off where the narrow track should run straight through the laurel up the mountainside. But when I round the curve of the hill there is no laurel, no mountaintop to climb, no hermit's cabin, only a highwall, sharp like a knife, and a slice of empty sky.

Jackie and the VISTA come up behind me. It is worse to see it than to imagine it, and I can't speak for the tightness across my throat. I look at Jackie. She is standing with her arms folded across her chest, looking down at her muddy shoes. I wait but she doesn't look up.

"Jackie," I say, "there's your heritage."

She doesn't say a word. She doesn't care about a damn thing except her silly crush on the VISTA, and I think, *You are not mine.*

"I wish there was something I could do," the VISTA says.

I say, "That's a joke. You work for the government, and the government and the company, they're the same. They didn't send you in here to get anything done. They sent you in here to make folks think they care. It saves their asses until they can think up something else.

And you, son, you're like a fish on a line. They'll give you some slack, let you run for a while, but then they'll haul you up on the bank to die."

"I know that," the VISTA says. "I'm just trying to push things as far as I can, see where the limits are. I'm not naive, Mr. Freeman, and I don't like being patronized by you."

"Is that so?" I laugh and light a cigarette, grind the match under my boot, no danger of starting a fire here. Jackie is tugging hard on my sleeve.

"I'll patronize you if I want to," I say. "I earned the right."

"Because you blew up a railroad bridge?" the VISTA says. "Because you went to prison? So what? People here talk about you like they admire you, but I don't see why. You just hide in that trailer all the time. It's a fucking waste, man."

I pinch the cigarette between my fingers, blow smoke, feeling mad as hell and pleased at the same time.

I say, "You're telling me my life is a waste? And you want to be a priest? Pretty boy like you and can't touch a woman? Now that's a fucking waste."

As soon as the words are out of my mouth I know I've gone too far. The VISTA's face is red and his fist comes up like he might slug me. I raise my hand, start to apologize, but Jackie has slogged through the mud and grabs my arm.

"Stop it!" she yells. "Stop picking on him, you stupid old backward old hillbilly! You don't know anything!"

I pull my arm away and she strikes out, the heel of her hand catches me across the cheek. Then she staggers back across the mud and over the side of the spoil bank, headed for the truck.

The VISTA and I look at each other. He grins suddenly and says, "Hardheaded as she is, it's obvious who she's related to."

Number Thirteen, 1963–1968

—————————————————————

JACKIE

My shoes are cased in heavy mud but I run anyway. I climb over the tree trunks, ignoring the bits of wet bark that stick to the palms of my hands and knees.

When I reach the truck I stop to scoop up mud, throw it splat across the windshield. Then I run on down the mountain, gaining speed, faster than I have ever run, feet pounding, a roller coaster cut loose to run free, taking the curves, feeling the jolts in my shoulders and neck, breathing hard, and I trip finally near the bottom and slide on my stomach to the edge of the road. I lie still for a moment. Smoke from the slag heap curls up through the trees.

The stinging pain rouses me. I turn slowly onto my side. My arms are raw and red, my knees are bleeding, and the skin of my stomach burns. I lie still and then I hear the truck motor somewhere above me. I haul myself up and try to run again, but my ankle is sprained and I can only hobble. I sit in the road and pick bits of red dog and rock out of my wounds.

They drive around the curve and stop the truck. I stand up and limp around to the back like I will climb in there but Tom is out, he has me by the arm and leads me to the cab. I start to cry and he gets in beside me, puts his arm around me and lets me sob on his shoulder. His chest moves up and down when he breathes.

Dillon and Tom are talking. Their voices are low and calm, as if they have been talking peaceably all the way down the mountain.

"I've been following the strip mine permits," Tom is saying. "I don't think American Coal has one for this end of the mountain. We could sue them."

"You hear tell of the overburden?" Dillon says.

"No."

"It's what they call the land over a seam of coal. It's the mountain they're talking about. Overburden."

"Poor mountain," Tom says.

He takes out a handkerchief and dabs at my bloody knee. Dillon is watching with this suspicious look on his face, and I am tempted to stick my tongue out at him but I don't because I am grown up now.

HASSEL, 1966–1967

We finally went door to door to raise money for that food co-op and bought our first batch of groceries. We set up in what used to be a store when Junior's people had it. Still yet has the little white coolers with sliding doors where they kept the cold CoCola, only the coolers don't work no more, so we have our stacks of paper bags inside. The old wood sign that says Tackett General Store is still yet nailed onto the wall outside. We put up a new sign says Lloyds Fork Co-op.

The *Justice Clarion* had this article in the newspaper that said a cooperative was communistic and un-American. Said next the Concerned Citizens would be calling each other comrade. We didn't pay them no mind and it was Opening Day but our permit to take food stamps hadn't come from the government. We cut the ribbon anyhow and Louelly prayed and the gospel quartet from the Holiness Church sang "Just A Little Talk With Jesus." I read out a letter from Sargent Shriver that said, "Congratulations, you have the first War on Poverty Food Cooperative in the Nation," and then most folks went home without buying anything because we couldn't take their food stamps.

Tom got on the telephone and called the Agriculture. Me and Betty Lloyd was sweeping up. Betty was supposed to run the store and we was going to pay her a little salary only it didn't look like they'd be any money.

"What are you telling me!" Tom was yelling into the telephone.

"None of this screwing around. We got a letter of congratulations from Sargent Shriver. Now you're telling me we're out of business before we get started?"

Betty Lloyd leaned on her broom, rolled her eyes at me and lit a cigarette.

Tom told the telephone, "All our customers own the store. That's how a co-op works, damn it."

Then he hung up the phone and said another cuss word, which is something else Catholics can do. He said, "The Agriculture Department won't give us a permit to accept food stamps. They say it's a conflict of interest because food stamp recipients own the co-op."

So Arthur Lee's congressman had been talking to the Agriculture. I stayed awake all night thinking on what to do. I reckoned I was the one should come up with the answer because I studied Arthur Lee enough when I pumped his gas and I know how he thinks. Tom, he don't think crooked thataway. He will look for what is right and how to stand up for it. He wanted to take the Concerned Citizens to Charleston to hold protest signs outside of that federal building where the Agriculture office is. He wanted to write back to Sargent Shriver and ask for help to get that there permit.

The way I seen it we had done spent our little bit of money on a load of fresh vegetables and fruit. The tomatoes would be rotten by the time anybody noticed all them picket signs and letters. And the way I seen it, Arthur Lee's congressman knew Sargent Shriver too. I hear tell all them fellows in Washington drink their liquor at the same places. I said to Junior Tackett, "Now what would Arthur Lee do if he was us? Arthur Lee would kick some rear end, and he would kick it fast."

"That's because he can," Junior said.

Well, I have got some things done in my time, too. Next morning I drove the Batmobile to the food co-op. Betty Lloyd was setting at the counter twiddling her thumbs. She has a metal box to keep her change in, on the counter beside the big jar of dill pickles, and it was shut tight.

"No customers?" I say.

"Woman from up to Felco that hadn't heard about the food stamps.

I had to turn her away. It about killed me because she had three younguns with her, so I give each one of them a dill pickle."

"That's all right. I thought what to do but you're the treasurer of the Concerned Citizens and I need you to come with me. Lock up the store and bring the checkbook."

I drove the Batmobile to Justice town with Betty setting up beside me and explained what I had in mind. First thing we done was go see one of them new poor people lawyers that the government sent in. That is one thing about the government, it is so big that for a spell the right hand won't know what the left hand is up to. It usually don't last and you got to move fast to take advantage. So while Arthur Lee was calling all his government buddies, here was this lawyer with a bushy beard and a bow tie and blue jeans, and I could tell he wouldn't be with us long but while he was he'd dearly love to help us.

I told that there lawyer what had happened. Then I said, "Arthur Lee Sizemore has the Pick-and-Pay up to Annadel. But they got them Pick-and-Pays other places too, because I seen one over to Logan and one at Oceana. I reckon Arthur Lee don't own the whole thing, so he must just have himself a lease like he does at the Esso. And I reckon that Pick-and-Pay is a big outfit that sells stock."

That lawyer had on them glasses with the wiry rims, real shiny, and he got this twinkle in his eyes. "I reckon you may be right," he said. He got on the telephone and when he called the stock exchange in Huntington I knew him for a man that could think crooked like me. He handed me the telephone.

"Yes sir," I says to that stock man, "this here is Hassel Day, president of the Number Thirteen Concerned Citizens, and I have with me Mrs. Betty Lloyd, our treasurer. How much is a share of stock in that there Pick-and-Pay groceries? $25.50? I would like to buy one share in the name of the Number Thirteen Concerned Citizens. Wire you the money? Yes sir we can do that right now."

While Betty run down the street to the Western Union that lawyer smiled at me. He says, "I assume I should be suing the Agriculture Department to revoke the Pick-and-Pay's license to accept food stamps on the grounds they are owned in part by food stamp recipients."

I rubbed my chin. "And you better call that Pick-and-Pay headquarters too. Tell them hit's Arthur Lee's fault they're getting sued."

We shook hands on it. I said, "What do I owe you?"

"Oh." The lawyer held out his hands and humped his shoulders. "Uncle Sam pays my fee."

Me and Betty stopped at the Dairy Queen for hot fudge sundaes, then we went home and told Tom what we done. On Thursday our food stamp permit come in the mail and we started selling groceries. Tom said, "Hassel, I sure as hell am glad you aren't a coal operator. You'd have every bit of Justice County carted off by now." Which set me to thinking maybe it's a good thing I didn't go past the eighth grade after all.

Tom reads a lot of books about God. It is what I mean about him standing up for what is right. It aint enough for Tom that the Bible is thick as a doorstop and hard enough to live up to by itself. He has got to add onto it.

They are big old ugly books with covers as drab as potato skins that he keeps in a box beside his bed. One time I went in where he was stretched out on his bed reading, and asked him what was in the book.

"It's by a German minister named Dietrich Bonhoeffer," he said. "He was plotting against Hitler so the Nazis hung him. Listen up." He flipped a few pages and read, " 'When Christ calls a man, He bids him come and die.' "

"It aint too cheerful," I said.

"No," Tom said. "You got to be crazier than hell to be a Christian," and then laughed about it. He will laugh at such things, like he wants to show he aint scared of nothing. But one night I woke up before dawn to take a pee and seen a gold bar of light at the foot of his door. Then I heard him mumbling out loud, but I couldn't make out what he was saying. And I thought he sounded like he was in pain. So while I peed I tried to think if I should check on him. Finally I reckoned I'd better in case he might be sick, so I tapped on his door. Right off, he said, "Come in."

He was in his underwear, kneeling on the floor with a book laid open on the bed. It weren't a Bible that I could tell but it called one to mind, all thin-papered and with red ribbons to mark the place. Tom looked up at me and I seen he wasn't hurting in his body but he was still yet in misery.

"You all right?" I said.

"Yes," he said and looked away.

"Sorry, I didn't mean to come in on something private." I started backing out of the room.

"No," he said, "come on in, if you want to."

I stood still, not sure what to do.

"I get up every morning at three and pray," he said. "It's a kind of discipline. But this is one of those nights when praying seems to hurt more than it helps. I could use a break." He slid down to where he was sitting instead of kneeling. "You know, I can't stand those ministers who tell people praying to Jesus will make everything all right. They're the worst kind of lying sonsofbitches."

"I reckon," I said, not sure what he was aiming at.

He leaned against the bed and laid his head down on his arm, his face turned away from me.

"You're not married, Hassel. Is it hard for you? I don't see you dating any women. Is it—"

Then he said "Oh!" and looked up at me like he'd just thought of something. I took a step back and said, "It is hard sometimes for a fact." I thought how I was talking too fast and he would notice.

"You—" He stopped again. Then he said, "Can I tell you something? I think you'd understand."

I swallowed hard. "Sure," I said.

"You know priests are supposed to be celibate? That means no sex, period. And I—   Sometimes I want a woman so bad I don't think I can stand it. And I'll get fond of someone and everything's fine except those feelings come on, not just love but—"

"I know," I said.

"When I was in college I had girls hanging all over me, because I was on the football team. Most of them wanted to sleep with me and I wanted that but I was afraid of it too because then it would mean I would be stuck with them. I'm not the kind of guy who can sleep with a girl and then drop her just like that. Guys who do that are shits."

"I wouldn't think you were like that," I said.

"Finally I decided on this one girl. She was real religious, so it was a while before we slept together. And when we did, I liked it a lot. I couldn't get enough. But she couldn't get enough either, not sex but me. She wanted to be with me every minute. I couldn't shake her. So we split up. She was real hurt. I wouldn't want to do that to somebody again."

"No," I said.

"Anyway, I decided to be a priest. So marriage is out of the question."

I said, "Do you have to be a priest?"

"Yes. I don't know why, but I have to."

"They's some things you can't change," I said. "You just got to go on and do the best you can."

He nodded and took a deep breath. Then he said, "I didn't mean to keep you. No need for you to stay up."

Next morning he was like nothing happened and I thought maybe I'd dreamed it. Then when we was washing the supper dishes he said, "I'm glad to be here, but it's good to know I can pick up and leave if I want to. I'd hate to lose that freedom to some woman."

He started whistling, hard and low, and scrubbing the crusty scales off an iron skillet.

A month later Tom and me was sipping our breakfast coffee when we heard the whopping sound of a helicopter. It got so loud the trailer started in to shake. I pulled back the curtain and we could see the copter, white with a gold seal on the door like a police car will have, settling down on the ninth hole of the golf course. Two men in suits climbed down and run toward the houses. Somebody knew they was coming because a man from the golf course unlocked the gate and let them through.

"Uh-oh," I said. "Wonder has Dillon been getting in trouble again?"

"No," Tom said, and straightened up his shoulders. "They're here for me."

"Good Lord," I said, "what have you done?"

"Nothing you don't know about," he said. "But it appears it doesn't take much."

He sat down on the couch, real calm looking. I jumped when they banged on the trailer door, even though I was expecting it. When I opened the door one of the men held out a piece of paper.

"Agent Temple," he said. "Federal Bureau of Investigation. I have a search warrant."

He pushed right past me and another man followed him. Tom stood up.

"What do you want?" he said.

They didn't pay him no mind and went on to the back of the trailer. "Which bedroom's yours?" Agent Temple said.

Tom pointed to the right. They went in and hauled out drawers, threw Tom's clothes in the floor and rummaged around, stacked the boxes where Tom kept his books and his work files.

The telephone rung. While I answered it, Tom leaned against the wall.

I put my hand over the mouthpiece and whispered, "Hit's Betty. They's another FBI man over to the co-op and he wants the ledger. She says she's setting on it and he'll have to haul her ass off it before she hands it over."

"No," Tom said. "Tell her to give it to him. It's over, Hassel."

"Tom. Naw."

Tom put his hand on my shoulder. "Hassel," he said real gentle, "it's over."

"Tag these boxes," Temple was telling that other FBI agent. "We're taking them with us."

"Do you mind telling me what you're looking for?" Tom asked.

Temple come out in the hall. "Do I mind, son? I don't mind. You'll be goddamn lucky if you don't end up in front of a grand jury. Misuse of federal funds is serious business."

They toted them boxes to the helicopter. Another man was waiting for them with a brown ledger stuck under his arm that looked like the co-op books. The blades of the helicopter whipped around slow, then faster until they blurred. After the copter took off they was chunks of turf scattered all over that golf course green.

Tom stood quiet for a minute. Then he went in his room and shut the door and he didn't come out for hours.

Dillon, 1967

The VISTA is standing on the front steps of the Holiness church. He looks through the door but doesn't go in. I watch him from behind the curtain of my trailer on the Free Patch. He has on blue jeans and a white T-shirt with grayish damp spots between his shoulderblades.

I light a cigarette and step out my front door. Cigarette smoke is useful on a summer evening, it will keep away the gnats. As I climb the steps to the church, I can hear the clinking of the out-of-tune piano through the open door. Jackie is playing for the Vacation Bible School. She doesn't go to the Holiness church, but the regular piano player works the evening shift at Number Five so she is filling in to help Louella Day.

I stand beside the VISTA. Louella is directing the children, and they are practicing for their program on Sunday, singing, "Everybody Ought to Know Who Jesus Is."

I say, "You watching the younguns, or you watching Jackie?"

The VISTA turns his head but he doesn't look straight at me. He puts his hand on the door frame.

"What kind of question is that?" he says.

"The kind you don't like to answer."

Then he goes a little way down the steps. I say, "Come on to Hassel's place. I want to talk to you."

He doesn't say anything and I walk down the steps to the Dew Drop, wondering if he will follow me. He comes behind me and when we go inside he heads for a booth in the far corner. There are two men at the bar talking to Hassel. I buy a pitcher of Stroh's and carry it to the booth. The VISTA is leaning forward with his hands on the table, fingers laced tight together like he is praying.

"You heard what happened?" he says.

"Of course I heard."

"They were going to send the Selective Service after me, then they found out I'm 4-D. That really pissed them off so they decided on criminal charges. They say they'll drop charges if the co-op shuts down and I scram."

"Never let it be said the government don't take a personal interest in folks."

"Louella Day got a notice her food stamps have been cut off," he says.

"Shouldn't surprise you. You come in here and stirred up a pot of shit, now these people are stuck with the smell."

"You're a fine one to talk."

"That's different. I knew I was coming back here. You aint never planned to stay."

"This isn't the only place in the world with problems, you know. There are places that need me worse."

"Need you? Nobody needs you. Who the hell do you think you are?"

He blinks like I hit him. "You can be damn cruel," he says.

"Never mind," I say. "It's Jackie I want to talk about. She's upset at you leaving."

He rubs his finger around the rim of his glass mug. "I know it, and I'm sorry. It's a schoolgirl crush that's worried me for a while now. But I didn't want to hurt her feelings."

I say, "You want to sleep with Jackie."

"You're crazy! I told you, she has a crush on me. She'll get over it."

"Maybe she will, maybe she won't. I aint talking about her right now, I'm talking about you. You've known right along you were going to be a priest, and you've known how she feels about you. You aint done a thing about it. And I'll tell you why. I think you enjoy it. Makes you feel good, don't it? Makes you feel like a man."

He stands up. "Goddamn you," he says.

I stand up with him. "Why do you want to be a priest? I see how you are with her. You ought to be moving heaven and earth to have her."

"Why are you talking like this? God, Jackie's your relative!"

I say, "You think my relatives don't make love?"

"She's just a kid."

"Old enough to feel," I say. "Old enough to love. But you turn away from her, you don't deserve her."

"My feelings for her are not like that," he says.

Fool, I think. *I know what I have seen, how you held her in my truck, how your fingers moved up and down the soft flesh of her arm.*

He pulls a wrinkled dollar bill out of his jeans pocket and tosses it on the table, then goes to the door like he will leave. But he stops in the doorway, black against the evening light. I come up behind him.

Jackie has come out of the church and is walking toward the Dew Drop, slim, her hair long and dark brown. She has new contact lenses so the thick eyeglasses don't hide her large green eyes anymore. She waves her hand slowly in front of her face as clouds of gnats rise from the dandelions. She is almost sixteen, the age I saw her mother stretched naked before the Homeplace hearth, and that breaks my heart.

She sees us standing in the door and stops. She holds her mouth tight like she is about to cry.

"I'm sorry, Jackie," says the VISTA. "I've got to go pack."

He turns and walks away toward Hassel's trailer, leaves her standing.

Fool, I think again.

"Honey," I say, "he aint worth it."

Her face goes hard.

"Don't you talk to me," she says. "Don't you. I hate you because you're mean to him. And I hate Arthur Lee for running him off."

She turns and walks down the railroad track. She will sit by herself in the bottom at Winco and cry until Rachel comes to pick her up. Or perhaps it will be Arthur Lee. They say Arthur Lee drives her places sometimes, takes Rachel and Jackie to the movies. It won't do any good now. Jackie will always despise him.

And will despise me too, but that is different. It is hate and love together, and nothing is stronger.

DEATH BY WATER
1969–1971

Tom left and things went downhill for a spell. Louelly lost her food stamps and the government was threatening to take my liquor license if I didn't behave. Then Arthur Lee organized his own Concerned Citizens, only he called it Citizens for Good Government, and them fellows in Washington sent all the Poverty money to them. Arthur Lee dug out the hillside behind his house and put in a swimming pool.

Me and Junior spent a lot of time in front of the TV set. We watched them Smothers Brothers until they got took off the air for being too sassy. We watched Martin Luther King and Robert Kennedy get shot. The Russians was beating up on folks over in that there Czechoslovakia and the police was beating up on younguns up in Chicago. They all wore helmets that looked just alike. Junior said it

was a whole passel of coal companies running things all over the world, so we was just as well to set tight.

But around here, there is always something. Uncle Brigham had the black lung bad. He'd take a hard breathing spell where the fluid would build in his lungs and go in the hospital to be hooked up on all them machines. Then he'd come home and get around on a metal walker and several times a day Betty would strap him into some portable oxygen machine.

One day when he was feeling stronger, we drove him to a demonstration in Charleston. We went in the Batmobile which is doing fine, although I haul an extra radiator in the trunk just in case. It was Sim and Dillon and me took him, and Louelly's Ethel skipped school and went too. Uncle Brigham was too weak to go on the protest march, but he set in a lawn chair beside the fountain at the capitol building and held a sign. It had a skull and crossbones, and said "Black Lung Is Killing Me."

We had Uncle Brigham wrapped up because it was a cold day. They was thousands of coal miners there, all shivering in their old coats and hunting jackets. Some had on them caps with the ear flaps or brown hats with little feathers in the band. Some didn't have on no hats at all and their ears was red. I had me on a red toboggan said Davidson High Coaldiggers, and I was glad for it because my hair is still yet crew cut. Junior cuts it by running one of them electric razors over my scalp. I don't have to worry about being took for no hippie.

While we was standing there listening to the speakers, a man come up that said he was a doctor from Beckley. He carried a jar with a dead miner's lungs inside that had turned black like the leavings in a iron skillet.

He said, "Aren't you Dillon Freeman?"

Dillon looked him over a minute, then said, "I might be."

"I know some people would like to meet with you," that doctor said. "There's still a union needs cleaning up."

"I tried once," Dillon said.

"You've got more friends now," the doctor said.

So they went off together to talk, that doctor with the jar of lungs tucked under his arm. It is a marvel what this world is coming to when they are doctors carrying on like that. Junior says it is the sixties for you.

Ethel was looking around. She has been in trouble, Ethel, getting in fights at school and wanting to drop out.

"You know what," she said. "I want to be a miner."

Uncle Brigham laughed and coughed. "Aint no girl can be a miner. It's hard work. Besides, a woman is bad luck in a mine. Causes roof falls."

"That's silly," Ethel said. "You already got roof falls without women."

"They'd be more," said Uncle Brigham.

"Why would you want to be a miner?" I said.

"I like all these men," she said. "I like being with them. They put me in mind of Daddy."

After more speeches at the capitol we went to Shoney's for coffee and hot fudge cake. That is the best stuff you'll eat, hot fudge cake, the sauce all gooey and the ice cream between the layers of cake, and the coffee was so hot it felt like I was pouring it all the way down to my toes. Uncle Brigham tucked his paper napkin into the neck of his shirt like it would really cover him.

"Damned if I wasn't in one of them demonstrations," he said. "Reckon I'll just have to be a hippie now. Reckon I'll grow my hair long."

"You aint got no hair," Ethel pointed out.

"I'll get me a wig. Get me a necklace with one of them peace symbols."

We laughed at that, because Doyle Ray Lloyd went straight from the reform school at Pruntytown into the army and now he's in Vietnam. Uncle Brigham gets real mad when he sees one of them peace demonstrations on the TV.

On the way home I kept looking in my rear mirror and seen Ethel talking to Sim Gore. Every time I looked she was still yet talking to him. Uncle Brigham was asleep beside me and after while Dillon was snoring too. Ethel and Sim kept talking until we dropped Sim at the Robo. When we got to Winco it was dark. Uncle Brigham was plumb wore out so I drove the Batmobile all the way into Number

Thirteen, tilted sideways on the railroad bed. They was no trains running because the whole mine was out in a wildcat over the black lung. Dillon went to eat beans and cornbread at Brigham's, and I took Ethel home. I was wanting to watch that TV news, looking to see if we was on, but Ethel said, "Let's go for a walk, Hassel. I got to talk to you."

"It's late and kindly cold, aint it?" I said.

"Please."

So we went out and walked a ways up toward the tipple and set on the track. That rail was so cold it made my butt numb real quick. Ethel took out a box from inside her jacket and was digging around inside it.

"What's that?" I said.

"Pot," she said.

"Ethel Ann! Where did you get that there?"

"Bought it myself with what I make at the car wash."

I knew she was working weekends at the Robo, her and Sim Gore's boy Leon.

"Aint that a waste of money," I said.

"You can't preach, Hassel. You sell liquor every night except Sunday. This aint no worse."

"Maybe," I said. "But it's against the law. And it's hippies smoke it."

"It aint just hippies."

I had to admit I was interested watching her rummage that box. I am curious turned. She was raking out what looked like little BBs, only she said it was the seeds. She stuck the seeds in her pocket and rolled the rest in a cigarette paper.

"Try a joint?" she said.

I shrugged and took it. I will try anything oncet. I smoked it down to the nub, until the little bit of paper was hot against my lips. Then I dropped it.

"No!" Ethel said. She felt around in the dark. "You got to save them roaches, Hassel. Keep enough of them and you got another joint." She peered at me. "How you feel?"

"I don't feel a goddamn thing." I rolled my shoulder blades around.

"You are wasting your money on that there pot. Give me a beer any day."

Then I started to giggle.

"Hassel," Ethel says. She slaps her knee. "Hassel, you are stoned and don't even know it."

"If Louelly finds out about this, she will have a conniption," I said.

Ethel was smoking her own joint. "Hassel, I'm pregnant," she said.

I giggled again. "Well, shit, Ethel." Then it wasn't very funny. I looked at her. All I could see was her nose and mouth lit orange by the joint.

"Mommy will kill me," she said.

I couldn't stop staring at her orange-lit nose, it was that pretty, like a Christmas light.

"Ethel," I said, "they's something you don't know, but maybe you should. Hit aint no shame to be pregnant. Your daddy and mommy had to get married because Louelly was pregnant with you."

"I figured that out a long time ago," she said. "I can count, you know."

"Well then, it aint the end of the world. Only thing is, you be sure and finish school. You only got until June. Then you can marry your fellow and raise that there youngun."

"It aint so easy. The daddy is a colored boy." She blew out some smoke, white like her breath. "Sim Gore's Leon."

"Oh, Lordy," I said.

"Hassel," she said, "Uncle Brigham's dying, aint he?" Then she busted into tears.

Louelly cried and carried on when she heard Ethel's news, and I heard tell that Sim and his wife wasn't too pleased neither. Leon was set to go to Bluefield State in the fall and Sim wanted that education for him. I didn't blame Sim, and none of us was looking for a marriage after all. Ethel said she didn't mind because she wasn't in love with Leon Gore. They had just been fooling around. So she had baby Tiffany and me and Louelly are helping to raise her. She is a pretty baby with brown eyes and skin like a good suntan. Ethel has kept on working at the Robo, although she don't make much.

Death by Water, 1969–1971

Now it is fall again and the leaves have turned the trees to puffs of red and orange so bright they like to put your eyes out. I can set outside my trailer and see the green golf course and the creek and the mountains beyond like piles of patchwork quilts, and I declare Number Thirteen is the prettiest place on God's earth. I keep thinking on that trip to Charleston for the black lung rally and making plans. I am thinking why do I have to mess with Arthur Lee? One day I will go back up there and ask that state government to build a bridge.

DILLON, 1970–1971

Some say there is a curse on these mountains. When I was a boy, a map hung on the wall of the Scary Creek School that showed where Indians once lived—pink for the Iroquois, green for the Cherokee, orange for Shawnee. There was a gray blank over these coalfields, and the word "Uninhabited." The Indians came to hunt in these hollows but never settled. It was a spirit land, sacred and dangerous. You can feel it still.

Summer is kind. The green hills rustle gently in the warm breeze. But then winter strips the leaves from the trees and the gray mountains are revealed, grizzled and hoary, their ridges edged with jagged stone teeth. In England I saw the burial mounds, the ancient stones set in circles by long dead sorcerers. The mountains are great barrows, the tombs of a long lost race, crowned by megaliths placed by God.

We have had hard winters of late, each with its own disaster. In 1967 a bridge collapsed and killed two score. The next year a mine blew and seventy-eight men burned alive. In sixty-nine, another mine explosion. Now I am listening to my truck radio on the way to Annadel. Yesterday, Marshall University's football team was killed in a plane crash at Huntington. I am thinking of Jackie, who goes to Marshall now and writes for the school newspaper.

I pull into the parking lot of the Pick-and-Pay and I see Rachel. She stands beside her car, looking small in her black coat, while a boy loads the trunk with bags of groceries. Her face is as gray as the mountains and has a look as tired as death. She looks up and sees me. we stand for a moment, watching. Then I walk over.

I say, "Jackie's all right?"

"She's upset," Rachel says. "A friend of hers was killed. But she's all right. She had no reason to be on that plane, thank God."

I nod at the trunk, say, "How you going to get all those groceries in the house?"

Her breath comes in short white puffs. "I'll manage," she says.

"I'll follow you up the hill and tote them in for you."

"That won't be necessary," she says.

"Rachel," I say, "I know we aint been on speaking terms all these years. But I'm still yet kin if I aint nothing else. Up on Trace Mountain I told you I'd always be there if you really needed me. I meant it."

"Right now," she says, "I don't really need you."

Then she gets in her car and drives away.

They say Arthur Lee is good to her. He took her to the Grand Ole Opry and to the Greenbrier Hotel in White Sulphur Springs once or twice. Things I could never afford.

I hear she is having heart problems, that she is having tests done, that she tires easy and Arthur Lee hired a woman to cook and clean for her. And since I saw Rachel at the Pick-and-Pay, I hear she quit her job. She never quit for me, she would never have quit for Arthur Lee, and I know it can only mean one thing.

I had been living as though she was already gone. I watched the ice floes carry her down the river and banished her from my thoughts. Now she's started dying by bits, far away where I cannot reach her.

Sim and I are traveling all around to meetings of miners, planning how to get rid of the crooks running the union in Washington. We meet in peoples' houses, because the union halls are closed to us. We drive at night, the headlights follow close behind us, and I wonder. I carry a loaded pistol in the glove compartment.

Hassel finds me by telephone at a house meeting in Whitesville.

"Jackie called," he says. "Rachel's took to the Grace Hospital. It looks real bad."

It is not him talking, it is her.

Sim is watching me. He sees my face.

"Sim," I say, "can you thumb back to Blackberry?"

"Sure," he says. "Is someone sick?"

I can't say her name. I leave without a word.

She is going back to the Homeplace and she is going without me. It isn't what I wanted. I planned on dying first and I would roam the earth for her, grab her by the neck and drag her back with me.

Three hours to Justice town. Headlights from oncoming cars slap across the windshield.

I try to think what will happen. Jackie will be there, and my mother. And Arthur Lee. What will Arthur Lee do? He will let me see her or I will have the place down about our heads.

At the hospital I run from the parking lot and up the steps. It is after midnight. The lobby is dark except for a single light at the information desk. No one is there.

I run my finger down the list that lies open on the desk. Room 316. The old elevator is goddamn slow and I hear it clank as it descends the shaft. I lean against the door, willing it to open.

The room is empty.

A nurse walks down the hall, holding a tray. Her glasses flash as she passes under a ceiling light.

She says, "They took her to Charleston in a company helicopter. There's a new cardiac unit there and Mr. Sizemore managed to get her in."

I am already heading back to the elevator. The nurse is behind me saying, "They only have three beds. Mr. Sizemore was on the phone for an hour, I think he had to pull some strings," and I can't listen to her, can't wait any longer so I take the stairs two at a time.

Three hours to Charleston and I take every curve as fast as I dare. I wrestle the steering wheel. My tires wail as though they are mourning.

Arthur Lee can't let her go without turning her dying into a way to show what a big shot he is. Goddamn him to everlasting Hell. If Rachel dies before I get there, I will strangle him.

The lights in the hospital lobby are dim and the waiting area outside the cardiac unit is in shadow. Arthur Lee is dozing on one couch, his head resting on his rolled-up jacket. My mother lies on the other couch. She sits up when I come close.

"Thank God," she says.

"Where is she?"

She nods toward two double white doors. "Last bed on the left," she says. "Jackie's with her."

I start for the door.

"We have to go one at a time," Mom says. "Send Jackie out."

Hell with that. I open the door quietly and glance around. Most of the space is taken up with white curtains hanging from metal rods. At the end of the room a nurse sits at her desk, writing on a chart, her head resting in her hand. I can see the white-clad legs of another nurse under the curtain to the right. I tiptoe in the opposite direction and pull back the last curtain. Jackie looks up.

"Stay there," I whisper.

A bank of machines stands guard over Rachel's bed like metal men with eyes all blinking green, or waving black arrows back and forth like long lashes. Rachel's arm is wrapped tight with bandages holding an IV needle, and her hands lie at her side, palms up as though she is pleading. Her breath comes in short wet gasps. A plastic oxygen tent covers her head and shoulders and her eyes are shut.

I take her hand. It is hot.

Jackie says, "The doctor thought she'd be gone by now, but she keeps holding on. Do you know how she's dying? Her lungs are filling up with water. It's like she's drowning slow in her bed."

Drowning. I raise the oxygen tent and touch Rachel's face. The skin is drawn tight across her forehead. I run my finger along her taut brow, brush the hair from her temple.

Jackie is behind me. "I don't know what I'll do without her," she says. "But I can't bear to see her like this."

She goes out.

Rachel breathes more slowly. I look around, afraid Arthur Lee will wake up and come in.

"Rachel," I say.

She opens her eyes. I turn her head, turn it ever so gently on the pillow, so she looks at me.

"Rachel," I say again.

She says, "Dillon."

She shuts her eyes and gasps, opens them again.

"You been waiting for me," I say. "I know you have and I know what it's cost you. You're my brave Rachel."

She squeezes my hand. The crooked finger she broke in the mule's harness lies across my palm. I bend my head and kiss it.

"You can go now," I say. "You don't want to die with Arthur Lee. I punished you, and then you punished me, but that's done with. You want to die with me, Rachel, not with him. I'll unplug these damn machines if I have to, but I'd rather you did it yourself."

I put my arm under her shoulder and lift her close to my chest. Her hand falls across my arm and she holds my shirt sleeve between two figners. I brush her hair back.

She smiles.

"Go on, Rachel. Go on now. Wherever you're going, I'll come after. I swear I'll find you."

She never takes her eyes off my face. And then she stops breathing.

I hold her that way for a moment, then I close her eyes and lay her back down. I fold her hands, palms flat, across her chest. Then I walk to the door.

"Nurse," I say.

The nurse stands up and comes toward me. I go out into the hall. Jackie and my mother are huddled together on the couch. Arthur Lee is sitting up and rubbing his eyes. When he sees me he starts forward.

"You're too late," I say. "She never was yours, and she never will be."

Book Four

EXILE
1980–1982

JACKIE, 1980

When my mother died, I knew something had passed between her and Dillon, something I had no part in. When Dillon told us she was gone, his face was strained with grief but also filled with a triumphant pride that both puzzled and frightened me. Arthur Lee sensed it too and looked on Dillon with pure hatred. I turned away from them both to weep on Aunt Carrie's shoulder.

We buried my mother at the Homeplace cemetery. We went against Arthur Lee's wishes. He wanted her in a plot he'd bought in the large new cemetery at Justice town. But she told him before she died where she wanted to be buried, and I had it in writing, in a letter she sent me at school. Arthur Lee could do nothing but stand to one side in a black coat and gray hat, head down and hands clasped tight behind his back, while her bronze coffin was set in the Kentucky earth.

Dillon was the first to arrive at the cemetery, had helped with the digging, and took for himself the place at the head of the coffin. Arthur Lee left as soon as the service was over, but Dillon lingered to help fill the grave, so possessive I thought he might climb in with her. I couldn't bear to watch him.

So I left the cemetery alone, drove back to school empty and forlorn, with no plans to set foot in the mountains again. My mother had staked an early claim to me, she had made her life a fortress to protect me, and she was my safe place. I thought she suffered Arthur Lee only for my sake, and with her gone, I wanted no part of him. I still loved Dillon, but I couldn't bear the way he wore her death like a badge. I wanted to escape for a while to places unfamiliar to my people. It was easier that way to pretend she and they had never existed.

I took my journalism degree, studied in England for a year, and then signed on as press secretary to a West Virginia congressman. I saw Dillon only once in all that time, at Aunt Carrie's burial at the Homeplace cemetery. Again he stood beside an open grave and I could imagine he had never left the cemetery, had remained there through the years and weathered, so old and beaten did he look. He was only fifty-three then, and it may have been the grief that aged him so. I thought it might also be loneliness, but I didn't want to admit it for the guilt I might feel. I blamed hard work. The union had been cleaned up, the mines were working full blast thanks to the energy crisis, and Dillon was running a continuous mining machine underground. A man his age had no business going back down in a coal mine, and I said so.

He said, "Work underground and leave, it calls you back. Just like if you live in the mountains and leave, they call you back."

"Maybe," I said, and got away from him as soon as I could. There was still an uneasiness between us. I kept remembering how he always seemed disappointed in me and my Mom but never said why and how they went their separate ways. Mom never tried to turn me against him, but I always assumed he had done something to hurt her terribly. And I still recalled the way she died with him, and the sight of him brought back the bad memories.

I would have tried to clear the air if I'd known how. But our lives were lived too far apart. I wept for Aunt Carrie, then returned to Washington and tried to close the door on my past.

I was no better with boyfriends than I was as a teenager. After years of running scared in college I finally got the nerve to sleep with a staffer for an Iowa senator. I didn't think he was really interested in me, but he was good-looking and I was curious so I took my clothes off for him on the first date. It was over so quickly I wasn't sure if I was technically still a virgin, and I never heard from him again.

Then I got drunk at a party and invited a *Post* reporter to my apartment. I enjoyed the kissing and snuggling and rubbing, but when he rolled on top of me the awkward rearing and wild gyrations, not to mention the sounds, were so funny I forgot to feel anything and started giggling. I decided men don't have a sense of humor about sex and I didn't care if he was offended. In the morning I was glad when he left for good so I could read the newspaper in peace.

And there was the musician who turned out to be gay, which I had guessed all along, but I still spent a year pursuing him. And the two friends at the office who I thought might be attracted to me but were also happily married. I was still my mother's daughter and wouldn't have dared proposition them for fear her ghost would visit me in the middle of the night and tell me how disappointed she was. I guessed they would have turned me down anyway.

I've always been a sucker for parades, so I went to Ronald Reagan's inauguration even though I despised him. I got off the bus at Fourteenth and Constitution wearing my heaviest coat, a knit hat, and a scarf wrapped around my nose and reached Pennsylvania Avenue just in time to see Reagan ride by, waving his arms and grinning, surrounded by Secret Servicemen going at a half-trot and the looks on their faces saying the whole thing was a big pain in the butt. I thought of Arthur Lee. The only time I ever remember him is when I see some politician showing off. It's more nostalgia I feel than anything else.

As I walked down Pennsylvania Avenue the show changed from block to block. Anti-abortionists carrying jugged fetuses emerged from subway elevators at the National Portrait Gallery, Young Spartacists ranted at the FBI building, vendors sold Uncle Sam hats and jars of red white and blue jellybeans.

I turned back in the direction of the White House, searching for a place to watch the parade, but people lined the street four and five deep. Finally I reached the National Theater and found a gap in the crowd. The Marine Corps band was passing, resolutely playing "From the Halls of Montezuma." Across the street a group of Hare Krishnas moved in the opposite direction, clad in saffron robes that quickened the gray stone buildings behind them. The Krishnas went to a lilting drumbeat sprinkled with tinkling bells, *ta-ta ti, ta-ta ti, ta-ta ti-ta-ti-ta-ti*. They leaped in unison on the last ta-ti and their ponytails flew into the air. The ponytails reminded me of Louella Day. Krishnas and Marines met, refused to notice one another, and went on in opposite directions.

Then I noticed the demonstrators in the open area across from the theater. I waited until a high school band from Sheridan, Wyoming, passed by and crossed the street to hear what was going on.

"Ronald Reagan doesn't care about human rights," said a long-haired woman with a bullhorn. "And he's proud of it. But we're here to say No to the CIA war on the Third World." Gloved applause. People held color-coordinated posters for different countries where the US supported repression—red for Chile, green for Iraq, blue for South Africa, purple for South Korea.

The demonstrators were chanting "No more imperialist war, US out of El Salvador." I noticed a priest, his white collar showing above his coat and his dark hair flecked with gray, holding a brown sign for Honduras.

I went up to him, said, "Excuse me, but you look like someone I knew a long time ago."

The priest stared, then said, "Jackie?"

It was Tom Kolwiecki.

We took the bus to a bar on Eighteenth Street called Millie and Al's, a shabby place with dark wood booths and a pastel jukebox. We ordered a pitcher and a pizza. Tom was tall and still slim, with dark hair cut short above his ears in a style that looked almost medieval except he didn't have a tonsure. He was a Jesuit, although he had not yet taken his final vows and would not be ready to for several more years.

He pulled the white plastic tab out of his clerical shirt and waved it.

"This is not the real me," he said. "I hate these dog collars. But for demonstrations it's good to dress up. It calls attention."

He unbuttoned his shirt and I noticed dark brown hair straggling over the top of his white undershirt.

He said he was the director of a place called the Cervantes Center.

"I thought priests had churches," I said.

"Jesuits do lots of different things," he said.

"So what is this Cervantes Center?"

"We organized that demonstration," he said. "We're into tenants' rights here in the city, lobbying on the Hill, sending food and supplies to Central America, stuff like that. But to tell you the truth, I'm not sure anybody's paying attention. Last winter I drove a truck full of medical supplies down to Honduras. It opened my eyes for damn sure. That's where the real work of the Church is being done. I've been thinking about asking for a transfer."

"It's dangerous there," I said.

"Yeah, it is." He said it like I'd paid the place a compliment.

The beer worked on me, warming me. I studied his fingers resting lightly against his mug, the nails neatly trimmed, smooth and oval. Rivulets of water ran through the frosting on the glass and wet his hand.

He said, "What about you? You like your job?"

"It was exciting at first," I said, "but not any more. I trained as a journalist, but I spend all my time making a mediocre congressman look good. I feel like a fraud. And sometimes I'll see something in the news, about a mine accident or a flood in the mountains, and I'll think, What am I doing here?"

"Why don't you move back to Justice County?"

"I don't know. I'm afraid to. For one thing, my mom died several years ago, and it wouldn't be the same without her."

"I'm sorry," he said.

I shrugged. "Anyway, I love it there, but I hate it too. I despise it. I'm afraid it would take too much out of me to live there, especially without kin. Dillon's all I've got left, and he's so hard to get along with sometimes."

"Same old Dillon, huh?"

I told him Uncle Brigham had died of black lung, that Doyle Ray Lloyd had come back safe from Vietnam, and Hassel was still trying to get a bridge built.

"Good old Hassel," Tom said. He refilled our mugs from the pitcher. "What else?"

We ate the pizza, drank more beer, talked, odds and ends of catching up. I told him in college I'd been an exchange student in London.

"In seventy-two? I was studying in Rome the same time. Just think, if we'd known, we could have met halfway in Paris. Wouldn't that have been something?"

I didn't like to imagine it. It made me feel how much of life we miss while time passes. Then neither of us could think of anything to say for a while. Someone put coins in the jukebox and the blowsy voice of George Jones crooned "Take Me" with Tammy Wynette. I looked up to find Tom's dark eyes on me, and he looked down quickly.

"Do you like being a priest?" I said.

He smiled and his face warmed with pure pleasure. "I love it. God knows I hate the Church sometimes. But I can't imagine being anything else. It's the most challenging life there is."

I tried not to show I was disappointed. He looked around for a waitress and asked while he was turned away, "I suppose you've got a boyfriend?"

"Oh," I said. "Not right now. I'm probably too picky. Or busy. Or something."

He looked back at me. "These guys around here must be crazy."

"Thanks," I said, and blushed.

"You get lonely sometimes?"

I didn't like to admit it. "A little. My job doesn't leave a lot of time for socializing."

"That's one thing about the Jesuits. You can have people around when you want them. It's like a built-in family."

"I wish I had something like that."

We went outside. The street lights glowed in the early evening dark. Tom said, "Where do you live?"

"Townhouse in Alexandria, just off Seminary Road."

"I live a few blocks from here. I'll round up one of our cars and take you home."

He lived near Malcolm X Park in a gray stone building he shared with five other Jesuits. I waited in the long hallway, bare except for a coat rack, chair, and a telephone on a stand, while he fetched the car keys. The air smelled of varnish and musty carpet, as though the windows were never opened. Once a man came down the stairs and looked surprised to see me standing there, said Hello, and went out the front door. Tom came soon after with the key.

"Lucky," he said. "Nobody signed for it all night."

The car was a dark green Ford Pinto with a dent in the passenger door. We drove out of the city, past the Pentagon and along a freeway that glowed with a gaseous orange phosphorescence.

"Hey," Tom said, "since we're out here, can I show you something?"

I thought of my empty apartment. "Sure," I said.

We escaped the freeway past gray office blocks and turned into a Catholic cemetery. An immense slab of concrete, an image of Jesus in hollow relief, stood guard in the floodlit circle at the far end of the drive. Its right hand was raised in a forbidding gesture, but the drama was ruined because the statue's face had been fashioned with cartoon-like features. Tom slowed the car. He was grinning.

"Watch Jesus' face," he said.

It was a trick of the lights. As we drove past, the round face seemed to turn and follow us with an angry expression. Tom put the car in reverse and backed up. The face still watched us carefully.

"It looks like Grumpy of the Seven Dwarves," I said, and started to giggle.

Tom put on the brakes. The face stopped moving and glared at us.

"I call it the Jesus of Washington," Tom said. "It's my comic relief. When I'm feeling bad about the Church and having a hard time praying, I come here. I look at that stupid statue and it's so damn tacky it makes me laugh. Then I can pray. I sit right here in the car and pray."

"Pretty risqué," I said.

He laughed. "Yeah. One time the caretaker came up to check on me. I think he was disappointed when he found out I was by myself."

He eased the car a little farther down the drive, then stopped and cut off the motor and lights.

"I think about Number Thirteen a lot," he said. "I remember Hassel and that damn bridge. And Louella Day's poems."

"There were bad times too," I reminded him.

"Sure, but the bad times were part of it, like tacky statues are part of the Church. If I'd never lived at Number Thirteen, I'd be a different sort of priest." Tom leaned back. "You know, that was the happiest time of my life, those VISTA years."

"Me too," I said.

"You were part of that," he said. "I liked having you around. And now to see you all grown up, well, it's pretty amazing. You're just like I thought you'd be."

He touched the sleeve of my coat, turned his head toward me. His face was half light, half dark.

"I'd like to keep seeing you," he said. "It would mean a lot to me."

"Me too," I said.

He smiled and didn't look away. I still felt lightheaded from the beer, and it was all I could do to keep from throwing my arms around him and burying my face in his neck.

I said, "This is the moment you'd kiss me if you weren't a priest."

He stopped smiling. "I am a priest," he said.

I felt my face grow hot and I looked out the window at Jesus, who glowered back.

"Sorry," I mumbled. "I can be real stupid sometimes."

Tom let off the brake. "Where do you live?" he asked. "I'll take you home."

I felt like crying. Tom pulled down the driveway and drove silently. I wouldn't look at him, leaned against the car door, ready to bolt as soon as we reached my apartment. When we stopped in the parking lot I turned away and grabbed the door handle. Tom put his hand on my arm.

"Wait," he said. "I've got an idea. Why don't you come work at the Cervantes Center? We decided to hire another lobbyist for the Hill. With Reagan in town things will be a hell of a lot harder. And we need someone to put out our newsletter."

I froze, tried not to show my surprise. "I don't know," I said.

"You'd be perfect. We could pay you twelve thousand a year."

"Twelve thousand! You expect someone to live in Washington on that?"

"There are lots of group houses in Mount Pleasant. You could move into one of those."

He walked me to my door. I was afraid to invite him in, afraid he'd think I was being forward again.

"Call me if you want the job," he said. He scribbled his phone number on a scrap of paper, leaned over, and hugged me goodbye, patted my shoulder.

I went inside, flicked on the stereo, flicked it off, opened all the drawers and closets, opened the refrigerator and kitchen cabinets, stared at the jars I never opened, the clothes I never wore, the records I never played. Junk. I sat without moving until he'd had time to get home. Then I called him and said, "Where is this office of yours anyhow?"

When my mother and I lived at Number Thirteen, we would have been struggling by most Americans' standards. But we had so much more than everyone else, it sometimes felt like we were rich. Then my mother married Arthur Lee, and we lived in the brick house on Annadel hill with the swimming pool and all the latest appliances. At Christmas, Arthur Lee always gave me some expensive piece of jewelry, even though I never wore jewelry and would have been embarrassed to show off such costly stuff if I had. Money was Arthur Lee. Money was my father, distantly remembered and vaguely threatening, gloating about making wampum.

So when I donated all my furniture except for my books and bookcases to the Salvation Army, sold my car and gave the proceeds to a soup kitchen, it felt like shedding a suit of armor. I wrote Arthur Lee the only letter I'd written in three years to tell him what I'd done, just to infuriate him.

I moved into a Catholic Worker house on Eighteenth Street just off Mount Pleasant. It was a brick row house, four floors high. When Raymond, one of the people who lived in the house and ran a homeless shelter, escorted me into the dark basement kitchen and turned on the light, roaches burst like spilt brown rice across the counter tops.

"Sorry," Raymond said. "We sprayed last month but it doesn't seem to do any good."

"I don't mind."

It was true. The gloomy kitchen thrilled me. So did the sofa covered with a worn blanket and the rummage sale lamps, like Louella Day's living room, and grimy Mount Pleasant Street with paper cups in the gutters and bits of squashed food on the sidewalk and old posters plastered over brick walls.

Tom and I spent a lot of time together, going to cheap movies on week nights we weren't working late, and Millie and Al's on the weekends. We would order beer and scout the other tables. Lots of people left a couple of slices of pizza, and Tom would swipe the leftovers while I kept an eye out for the waitress.

I could almost pretend it was a relationship. We did the same things every other couple did on dates, except for the sex. He told me things about himself I hadn't known.

Once I asked, "Do you see much of your mother?"

"No," he said. "My dad died when I was kid, you know. My mother and I aren't close."

"I figured she'd be proud to have a son who's a priest."

"Hell, she didn't even come to my high school graduation," he said.

"That's terrible!"

"Yeah, well, she's an alcoholic. I was an only child, and my dad and I were real close. I think she was jealous of what we had. He did everything with me. He was a football coach, so he was always proud of what I did in sports. And devout as hell, typical Polak. Went to Mass several times a week."

"How did he die?"

"Heart attack. It was my first junior high football game. I was only in the seventh grade but I was already starting, wide receiver. Dad was so proud. It was all he talked about the week before that game. Anyway, I dropped a pass in the first quarter. I could hear my dad in the stands yelling 'Tomacz! Tomacz! That's OK!' It's what he called me to let me to know he loved me. I wanted to catch one so bad for him, but the quarterback didn't throw to me again until near the end of the game and we were down by four points. I was in the end zone and the ball hit me smack in the chest and I held on to it. The defender nearly took my head off but I still held onto that damn ball. I was lying there with guys piled on top of me, listening for my dad. But I didn't hear him. And when I stood up and looked at the place he'd been sitting, I couldn't see him, just a bunch of people standing with their backs turned.

"Nobody could tell me if he had had the heart attack before I caught the pass or after. My mother got tired of me asking about it and said, 'Is it important?' " Tom shook his head. "It was the most important thing in the world to me. When she said that, I think I hated her. And she knew it."

"Where is she now?" I asked.

"Still in Paterson. She remarried, not very long after my dad died either. My stepfather owned a steak house and drank too, used to raid his own bar. The house would be empty when I got home from school, and I'd cook my own supper. Then they'd come in from the restaurant around ten while I was doing my homework and go to their room. I used to pretend they didn't exist."

"I'm sorry," I said.

He shrugged. "It was a long time ago. Anyway, the Jesuits are my family."

"I used to want to ask you about your family," I said, "but I never had the nerve. I had this hero-worship thing about you, like I didn't dare ask you something personal. Silly."

"Yeah," he agreed, "but you were just a kid."

When he shared things like that I wanted to hold him, to comfort him. But he seemed to sense it, and afterward weeks would pass without me seeing him outside the office. When I asked about a movie, he'd make an excuse, say he was tired or had to take work home. I wasn't sure I believed him. Sometimes when we stopped by his house, I thought the other Jesuits treated me coldly. I imagined they were warning him away from me, that they saw me as some kind of temptress, which seemed like a big joke because I couldn't tempt my way out of a paper bag.

Then I would be bent over my desk, pasting up headlines on the newsletter, and he would stick his head in the door.

"How about a flick at the Circle tonight?" he'd say.

And I'd say Yes, right away, even if I was tired or had seen the movie before, because in those days I had no pride when it came to Tomacz Kolwiecki.

JACKIE

I travel Blackberry Creek in my mind at night as I fall asleep. Memories melt into dreams of black coal tipples and curving stone walls, of dusty summer weeds and the wail of a train as it swings through the hollow. Before I sleep, I remember the time I went on a home nursing visit with my mom to see about a woman who had tuberculosis. We drove up Trace Mountain until the road turned to mud and then we walked. Mom told me that long ago people lived in log cabins, but then the timber companies took over the land the coal companies didn't want and people couldn't get wood without trespassing, so they covered their crumbling old houses with cast-off roofing material. Better-off people called the houses "tarpaper shacks."

I went inside the consumptive woman's tarpaper shack with my mother. The floor was part blood red linoleum, part splintered wood. Blackened newspapers covered the wall behind a pot-bellied stove. The only furniture in the main room was a threadbare chair and a small table. Mom whispered that I shouldn't sit on the chair. She disappeared into the bedroom to bathe the sick woman. The woman's husband was dead, killed in the mines. I sat on the floor with my knees drawn up under my chin. A blonde girl sat across from me, her back against the wall, silent. We stared at each other. I was afraid to say hello. When Mom was done, the girl's mother wobbled out of the bedroom in a tattered pink housecoat. She was thin like Louella Day and coughed a lot like Betty Lloyd. Mom was trying to convince her to enter the tuberculosis sanitarium in Beckley.

"What would happen to my younguns?" the woman kept asking.

Then I dream. The woman keeps asking the question. No one answers her. She goes back and forth from me to my mother, her face closer and closer, her breath damp and contaminated, *what will happen to my younguns what will happen to my younguns what will happen to my younguns?* Her nose touches mine, I feel a fine spray across my face, and I try to pull away. Then I wake up in Washington and the woman is a million miles away. I want her close again. And I want my mother.

JACKIE, 1982

Raymond, who lives in the bedroom above mine, is tall with thinning gray hair and a full beard. He used to be a Republican, but then he met Daniel Berrigan at a parish pot luck in Falls Church during the Vietnam War, had a religious experience, and took to throwing blood at the Pentagon. Raymond plans the meals for the Catholic Worker house, usually things like Swiss chard casserole or sweet and sour soybeans. A lot of the food comes from the dumpster behind the Safeway. Raymond keeps a crock pot going all the time. Leftovers go into the pot along with a bit of water. Vegetables about to go bad also go in. Everyone else—mostly kids fresh out of college who work at the homeless shelter—calls it perpetual soup. The soup was started before I arrived and no one can remember what the original ingredients were. Over time it has taken on a light chocolate coloring that grows darker if nothing new has been added for a while. I stay away when the color gets toward black, but usually it isn't too bad with crackers in it.

When the telephone rings, Raymond is eating breakfast, Cheerios in powdered milk because we are sending all of the dumpster milk to the soup kitchen. I am having a slice of toast and jam instead. Powdered milk is where I draw the line. I will die before I drink it.

I pick up the phone and Dillon is on the other end, his voice shaky and faraway like he is calling from inside the coal mine.

"I can barely hear you," I yell. "Bad connection."

"I said I'm coming to Washington for a demonstration. Riding on a bus tomorrow night that will get there Monday morning."

"What kind of demonstration?"

I make out black lung budget cuts and Reagan and sonofabitch in between pops on the line.

"Where?"

"Union headquarters. Try to find us. It's been too long since I set eyes on you."

At the office, Tom finds the news item in the *Post*—"Coal Miners Rally against Reagan Black Lung Cuts."

"I ought to invite Dillon to stay a while," I say.

"If he stays overnight he'll miss the bus home," Tom points out.

"I could drive him back to West Virginia. I'd love to see Justice County again."

"But you've got those hearings on the Philippines coming up on Wednesday," he says.

"Shit," I say.

I am sick of hearings. Washington is more and more depressing. Dillon and the other miners think if they come all the way here and hold a rally, someone will actually care. Or maybe Dillon is just along for the ride. He never had many illusions where politics is concerned.

"I'll come to the rally with you," Tom says.

"If you want to," I say.

• • •

I crave the mountains. They invade my dreams, and so do my kin, living and dead. Last week it was Dillon I saw while I slept. He was walking along the bank of Blackberry and he fell in. I jumped in and hauled him out.

I tried to interpret the dream to Tom. I said Dillon in my dream was not Dillon, he was all my people, and I should go back and help them because if I don't, who will? Tom says I am a romantic, that it is my childhood I miss, not the mountains. He says if I went back I would be disappointed.

But he shares my restlessness. What he will say is, "I'm too safe here. Maybe I should talk to my provincial about a transfer to Central America."

So I think, Why should I listen to you, when you talk about leaving, as if I didn't matter. Slowly I am coming to accept that my life will never belong to a man, not even to Tom. Especially not to Tom. I am my own planet and constellations. And I am making up my mind.

At McPherson Square, Tom and I watch the men climbing off the buses. They are in their shirtsleeves, some in blue jeans and large belt buckles, but most are older men wearing polyester pants. It is a hot, sunny day, and the grass in the park is dry and yellowed. People from nearby office buildings hurry along the sidewalks, men in white shirts and ties with jackets hung over their arms, women in cotton dresses and heels. Only a few stop to read the signs, and the miners who tentatively hold out leaflets are waved off.

We stand in the shade of an oak facing union headquarters, a large stone building that resembles an old bank. A disembodied voice on a loudspeaker drifts toward us: "Ronald Reagan doesn't care if you have to breathe on a respirator. He doesn't care if your wife and children are left behind without financial support while you go to an early grave. We're here to tell him we won't stand . . ." then disappears in an amplified screech. I stand on tiptoe with my hand shading my eyes and look for Dillon, finally see him on the edge of the crowd, in olive green work pants and a faded plaid shirt. I slip away from

Tom, sneak up behind Dillon, and touch his arm. He turns part way, sees me, and hugs me to him. He smells of Old Spice.

"Hey, girl," he says. Then he notices Tom. "Well, lookee here! If it aint the VISTA!"

They shake hands. Dillon says he is tired, that he didn't sleep well on the bus, "but I aint never been to Washington, and I wanted to see this youngun." He squeezes me again.

It is getting hotter and we fan ourselves with the leaflets the miners pass out. Senator Byrd is on the platform saying how much he has done for the miners. The men applaud politely.

"How much time you got?" I ask Dillon.

"We're supposed to meet the bus behind the White House at three-thirty."

"Anyplace you want to visit?"

"I just want to visit with you," he says. "And I'm starved to death." He waves his hand to take in the crowd. "This here is just pissing in the wind anyhow. Let's get something to eat."

We find a deli on I Street. Glass cases that hold blocks of meat and cheese line one wall, and the tables are slabs of white formica. I sit beside Tom, with Dillon across from us. We order beer and hot pastrami sandwiches, because Dillon has never eaten pastrami and wants to try it. I ask about Number Thirteen. Dillon says Hassel and Junior are fine, that Toejam is courting Brenda Lloyd, that Betty Lloyd lost her black lung benefits, and the government says she owes it back thirty thousand dollars. He says American Coal has put new machines underground and opened more strip mines, so the coal is going out but there aren't as many jobs. Tom is quiet, watches Dillon and me carefully as we talk.

"So," Dillon says, "what do you all do with your time?"

When Tom tries to explain about the Cervantes Center, Dillon looks blank. Finally he says, "It sounds like a lot of talking to me."

"We do more than talk," Tom says. "Last month we had a demonstration against contra aid. We had our biggest crowd yet."

"So what?" Dillon says. "There's a demonstration right over yonder and a hell of a lot of good it's doing." He fishes a pack of Camels from his shirt pocket, taps the bottom, and chooses a cigarette.

"Don't you read all the news reports about smoking?" I say. "It's really bad for you."

He pauses with his lighter in his hand, a look of irritation on his face.

"Sorry," I say. "I don't mean to be bossy."

"Actually we're in a nonsmoking section," Tom says.

Dillon sticks the unlit cigarette in his pocket, takes a wedge of dill pickle from a red ceramic jar on the table, and sucks on it. Dillon keeps looking at me. A waitress brings our sandwiches. Then Dillon says, "You like it here?"

I glance at Tom. "It's okay," I say.

"You go to these demonstrations?"

"She got arrested in front of the White House," Tom says.

Dillon keeps looking at me like Tom never spoke. Tom daubs mustard on his sandwich.

"It was no big deal," I say. "We cleared everything with the police ahead of time."

"You mean you told the police what you was going to do?"

I shrug. "Yeah."

"That's the dumbest thing I ever heard tell of."

"It was moving," Tom says. His voice is low and tight. "We held candles and called out the names of people murdered by the Contras. Then we sat down in front of the White House gate and linked arms."

"I bet that ruined old Ronnie's evening," Dillon says.

"He was in California," I say. I am starting to smile.

Tom says, "You got a better idea? We thought about blowing up the Memorial Bridge, but we decided there were too many police around."

If Tom thinks he's making Dillon mad, he's wrong. It's like they're playing cards and Dillon knows he's got a full house. He keeps talking to me, ignoring Tom. "So you went to jail? For how long?"

"Overnight. They put us on probation."

"That's play jail. Like Monopoly."

"It was a damn powreful witness," Tom says. He leans across the table at Dillon.

"I want to see somebody witness, I'll go to church," Dillon says.

"I guess you would have made fun of Martin Luther King, too?"

"Martin Luther King didn't stand around singing hymns and inviting the police to some tea party."

I poke Tom with my elbow. "You say the same thing yourself. You're always wondering if we're doing any good here."

Dillon turns to me. "Things are getting rough again back home. You don't have to look for a cause there. Just set still and something will run over you."

"That's a lot more true of Central America than Appalachia," Tom says.

"You aint in Central America," Dillon says. He asks me again, "You like it here?"

"No," I say.

Tom glances sideways at me and a muscle jumps in his cheek. He says, "Why the hell are you hanging around then?"

"I could ask you the same thing. You're always talking about wanting to be some martyr in Honduras."

He starts to answer back, then mutters "Shit," under his breath. He reaches in his pocket, looking for money to pay the bill. Dillon is watching us with his eyes narrow.

Outside, Dillon takes out the pack of Camels. "You know that *Justice Clarion?*" Dillon says. "Always been a terrible newspaper. Some fellow in Lewisburg just bought it, but he don't want to move to Justice so he's looking to hire an editor. Aint had much luck from what I hear tell. Hired one fellow that didn't last a month. He didn't care for the coalfields."

"It's not for everybody," Tom says. He is walking fast. Dillon refuses to hurry.

"Why are you telling me this?"

"Because I'm getting old. Because I miss you." He takes out a Camel, studies it, then drops it on the sidewalk. "Tell you what. You come home and I'll quit smoking."

He takes the pack from his pocket, crumples it and throws it in a trash can. Tom doesn't notice. He is already crossing the street, heading for the subway station.

. . .

We left Washington about the same time. I took the job at the *Justice Clarion;* Tom went to the Yoro province in Honduras where the Jesuits were working with campesinos. We didn't have much of a goodbye. Right after I announced I was leaving, Tom got arrested for occupying an apartment building with some tenants fighting eviction. I wondered if he did it on purpose, so he would be shut away in the DC jail while I packed my bags.

Before I left, I took a cab past RFK Stadium to the modern stone dungeon isolated in a moat of throbbing light, set my hand palm flat against the screen between us and tried to get up the nerve to say I loved him. But his face was set in an expression of studied disinterest, as though my visit were part of the day's routine. He glanced at a guard, then at the clock on the wall and back at me. I lost my nerve and only said I would write.

"I'm going for language training as soon as I get out of here," he said. "It will be a few months before I have a permanent address. Maybe I should write you first."

"OK," I said, and felt everything slipping away.

He didn't write for nearly a year, then sent me a letter from Honduras. He said he was doing the most important work he'd ever done. The banana workers at a nearby plantation were on strike, and the campesinos were trying to form a cooperative. Living conditions were hard, he ate beans and rice every day, and worked in the fields in the hot sun alongside the campesinos. He slept in a hammock and banged his shoes against the ground before he put them on, looking for scorpions. He wasn't complaining, he was bragging.

I wrote back in care of the Jesuits in Tegucigalpa and heard nothing for six months. After a second letter, he stopped writing.

So he was beyond my reach and there was nothing I could do except remind myself that I was the one who'd decided first to leave Washington, that I had not lost him because he was never mine to lose.

BRIDGES AND DAMS
1985–1986

HASSEL, 1985

I still yet have in mind to build that Homer Day Memorial Bridge, but I have been bound to play Cupid first. It is something I like to do. I believe different from Louelly, who says that God has made somebody for everyone, but bad luck can get in the way. Like she thinks Ethel aint never got married because the man God picked out for her got killed in that Vietnam War before Ethel had a chance to meet him.

Me, I think love is something that has got to be worked at. And sometimes a person needs a little help. I always reckoned Toejam would be that way. He won't push hisself on nobody, and they is more push in finding a sweetie than anything else.

Still yet, Toejam's situation was special. It wasn't bad luck nor shyness nor even tall mountains and broad rivers that stood between

him and his true love. It was that Ronald Reagan.

Nobody in Number Thirteen voted for Ronald Reagan in nineteen and eighty. I seen it in that *Justice Clarion* where they list how every precinct in the county voted. Only precinct that went for Reagan was Justice town itself, where the lawyers live. At Number Thirteen precinct it was Jimmy Carter 72, Ronald Reagan 0.

Now I don't care what nobody says, a voting machine looks like an upright coffin with a shower curtain hanging on it. We are free to vote but you have got to be careful of it just the same, like picking up a copperhead. When I seen it was just Georgia and West Virginia voted for Jimmy, I told Junior, "Lordy how we stick out. They won't be nothing out of this government but trouble."

Sure enough Betty Lloyd lost her black lung check that come after Uncle Brigham passed away and the government said she owed them back the thirty thousand dollars that she'd got from it. But worst of all, Brenda's disability check was took. I say worst of all because that stood between Toejam and his love.

Toejam has been courting for several years now. It started when Louelly's TV went bad. Toejam would go to Uncle Brigham's to watch his "Rockford Files" and his "Mork and Mindy." Then he got to going every night, even after Junior put Louelly in a new picture tube.

Brenda don't care a bit that Toejam is shy, and she didn't mind when he dropped out of school. Toejam always sets on a kitchen chair beside Brenda's wheelchair. She nods her head and laughs a lot. Sometimes Toejam holds her hand. She twines them skinny fingers through his and squeezes so hard his knuckles turn white. If he catches me watching he will duck his head and grin.

I am watching him now, hauling Brenda on his back, her legs tucked tight under his armpits and her arms wrapped around his neck. It is easier than pushing her wheelchair on the red dog. Louelly is having her Sunday school class over for Kool-Aid and cookies and Toejam is taking Brenda. He stops and waves at me, picks up Brenda's limp hand and makes it wave. Brenda grins and calls out something I can't figure out.

·   ·   ·

Toejam used to be the janitor at the Felco grade school. He loved that job. He liked to wash the green chalkboards and see them come clean. He liked the way the first graders would holler "Hey, Toejam!" when they seen him in the hallway. He didn't even mind to clean the bathrooms, said the younguns weren't bad to mess. But the schools was going down because more and more people was moving away from Blackberry Creek. Then Ronald Reagan stopped the school money coming. So the Felco school closed and the younguns had to bus to Davidson. Toejam lost his job right before he was set to marry Brenda.

It had been hard enough to get Betty Lloyd to agree to a wedding. One Sunday after church, Toejam took me and Louelly to call on Betty. We set around the living room and drank coffee.

"Toejam don't make much," Betty had said. "And Brenda needs doctoring now and then."

Toejam sank back in his chair and looked pitiful.

"Toejam has got medical from the school board," I said. "Brenda has got that disability from the government. And I still yet have the Dew Drop. I can help out if need be."

That clinched it. I have the coldest beer on the creek and the psychedelic light, except now I call it a disco light. I have a boy sings on Thursday nights as sweet as Eddy Arnold and a band on weekends called the Drive Shaft that can play Alabama songs and Bob Seger too. The Dew Drop has gone down some, like everything else, but it still does a trade. And someday I will have that car bridge.

"I reckon it's all right with me," Betty said at last.

Then Toejam smiled and grabbed Brenda by the hand and Brenda laughed. When Brenda laughs, she throws her head back in that wheelchair and cackles like a chicken.

But then Toejam lost his job and the Lloyds lost the black lung and the disability. Betty said the wedding had to be put off. She wasn't hateful about it, just said it was her responsibility to look after her youngun, and while Brenda was still yet single she could keep her daddy's Social Security.

Toejam was heartbroke. He tried to get on at the mines but he couldn't pass the tests and by then they wasn't hiring no ways. Then he tried caddying at the golf course and he could haul them bags of clubs all right, but he never could keep straight all the different kinds of irons and putters. So the manager put him to janitoring the clubhouse.

The first day after work he come straight to the Dew Drop, where I was mopping the floor, and asked for a beer. That took me back because Toejam is churchgoing and aint much for drinking. I peeled open a Bud and set it on the bar.

"Hit's different at the country club," he says.

"Now, Toejam," I says, "aint janitoring the same everywhere?"

"Naw it aint," he says. "They done had a big party Saturday night. People throwed up all over the bathrooms. And guess what I found in the closet?" He leaned forward and whispered, even though they was nary a soul around. "It was a pair of panties on the floor. And one of them rubber things, all sticky and wadded up."

"Son, that's life."

"They was some men drinking up there when I left. They was cussing out the miners."

I nodded. "That's life too," I said.

He ducked his head. "Hit's only part time. I asked about the medical. They said it won't be none."

He took on other chores. He cleaned the Dew Drop and I paid him for it. He walked the highway looking for aluminum cans, the way him and his mommy used to pick up pop bottles in the old days. He said the cans was lighter and easier to carry, but he missed the way the bottles clinked together like music.

I couldn't bear to see him so downhearted and mopey, and it like to broke Betty Lloyd's heart too. She said Brenda was so tore up she wouldn't watch TV.

"I don't like to be mean, Hassel," she says.

"You aint mean. You're looking after your own."

"You reckon we could do something about that disability? Maybe go to Arthur Lee?"

I laughed.

"What about Jackie Honaker?" she said. "She's at that *Justice Clarion* now."

"And writes them editorials that run down Arthur Lee."

"He's still yet her stepdaddy."

"Still yet," I agreed. "But I don't see that she can do a thing."

They was another election and I thought that might do it. We all vote at the country club because they won't bring the voting machines into Number Thirteen. We have to walk all the way around by Winco bottom, and by the time you traipse up that hill to the clubhouse, you feel like you done accomplished something, but that's what voting is for.

The two machines was set in the middle of that slick ballroom floor across from the white French doors. Folks tiptoed across careful to keep from slipping on the wax. Toejam peeked out from the kitchen, real nervous. Sometimes he had to come out and mop where somebody tracked in coal dust but he always went back to the kitchen.

Folks nodded when they seen him, said "Hey, Toejam." They all knew what they had to do. When the votes was counted, Number Thirteen went for Walter Mondale 49-2. I reckoned the two was Doyle Ray Lloyd and his wife. Doyle Ray come back from Vietnam different-turned, and I will tell about that later. Anyway, our 49 votes wasn't enough and Ronald Reagan tromped that there Mondale.

So we went to see Jackie Honaker. She has got an office across from the courthouse, and it is strange to see her all growed up and her name on the door with "Editor" underneath of it. She is not as skinny as she was, and she must be in her thirties, but she still yet wears blue jeans and sweatshirts and not much makeup that I can tell. I reckon you don't have to dress up when you set around and write all day.

When Jackie come home a few years back, I hadn't laid eyes on her since her mommy died. I'd said, "Law if you don't take more and more after Dillon."

She had looked surprised and then smiled and said, "I was always afraid I took after my daddy's people. I'm glad to hear someone say I look like Mom's side of the family."

When me and Betty went to call, she set us down on a beat up old couch and give us cups of coffee. It was real bad coffee, bitter like the pot hadn't been cleaned in a year. Then I told her what we come for. First she looked sad and shook her head. "I barely speak to Arthur Lee. He never has forgiven me for burying my mom in the Homeplace cemetery, and he hates my editorials." Then she sipped her coffee and got a hopeful look on her face. "I've got a better idea. I used to work for that congressman from upstate. I know him and I know people on committees in Washington who might do a favor. I'll call them."

And that is what happened. Next month we heard tell one of them judges would look over Brenda's case, and he put Brenda back on that disability. So we set the wedding date.

Betty said, "Doyle Ray will want to do the marrying."

It is hard to think of Doyle Ray Lloyd as a preacher, but he come home marked. When a person shoots his sister, does time at Prunty-town, and survives driving a tank in Vietnam, it will take something to save him. Some in Doyle Ray's shape would become drug addicts. If he was rich, or if he come from someplace else, he might have climbed barefoot up one of them holy mountains in foreign countries or gone to one of them shrinks like everybody does in New York City. But we don't have none of them, so Doyle Ray become a mean kind of Christian. During the week he drives a coal truck, hauls from the strip mines up on Trace. But on Wednesday nights and Sundays he pastors the Church of God (Prophecy) at Spencers Curve.

I went to a service one time just to be neighborly. It was aggravating because they prayed to save me and called me by name. Doyle Ray don't even hold with the Holy Rollers. He says they have too good a time, and besides it is un-American to speak in foreign tongues. I tried not to mind all that and just paid attention. When Doyle Ray preached about Hell his face was all twisted up like he was already there. He screamed and beat on that pulpit until he was soaking wet with sweat. He hollered about drugs and rock music, and the alcohol he claimed had killed his daddy, and the Commie hordes that come at him in Vietnam and would get us all if America didn't turn to God. When he was done he seemed to feel better, like he was safe for a little while, and the congregation seemed to be wore out like they'd been worked hard and to feel better too.

So Doyle Ray did the marrying for Toejam and Brenda. Louelly's Ethel claimed it sounded like he'd preached a funeral instead of a wedding, they was so much hellfire strowed about. But Toejam and Brenda didn't notice, they was that much in love.

JACKIE, 1985

I bought a camp house in upper Felco with firm wooden floors and a deep front porch. It had once lodged the store manager and so it was built solid. From the porch I could see the shell of Arthur Lee's Esso that had become an Exxon and then closed for lack of business as people moved away. A line of close-together houses for black miners stretched beyond the low concrete blocks where the gasoline pumps once stood. The white people still called this Colored Row.

Some of the camp houses that remained on Blackberry were in better shape than I recalled from my childhood. Over the years people had worked hard to spruce them up, covering weathered boards with aluminum siding, adding storm windows. But many camps had been torn down. On my first day back I drove up Blackberry Creek and would round a curve expecting to see houses and find a weed-choked bottom instead. It was like returning to a city that had been bombed and learning which neighborhoods had gone up in flames.

Each day I drove the hollow to work, past Number Ten bottom that once hosted the carnival but now held a nursing home, past boarded-up brick schools and the crumbling houses at Carbon camp, to Justice town. I walked to my office past the gaping hole filled with scattered brick and broken glass that marked the spot where the Pocahontas Theater burned. The Flat Iron Drugstore was still open but the soda fountain had been ripped out and the store was filled with jumbled shelves of toiletries and pills. A rusting padlock clasped the door of a barber shop across the street. When I was a child the shop boasted a revolving striped pole held in a frame of gleaming brass. I recalled watching the barber cut Dillon's hair, the dark locks falling like feathers to the green linoleum floor. The stacks of white towels, the room-length mirror, and the shoeshine stand supervised by a bent old man had spoken to me of sophisticated big cities. Now the barber pole was dented and crusted with coal dust. Looking through the clouded glass of the door was like squinting through an old camera.

Two chairs stood empty, yellowed cloths draping the arms. A shaving brush lay beside the sink. Bits of litter were scattered over the floor. I saw my ghost reflected dimly in the mirror.

At Number Thirteen, the company store had been gutted, its roof caved in, girders exposed naked to the sky, brick walls streaked black. Some people had left and their houses had been reduced to piles of wood and cinderblock by American Coal. But most of the houses still stood. Boards salvaged from torn-down houses and collections of useful auto parts were stored on the porches and in former outhouses as Number Thirteen went about the business of taking care of itself.

Around the bend on Lloyds Fork, the American Coal tipple, crenelated like a castle and engorged by coal from the strip mines all around, had expanded toward the houses like a giant octopus. I often sat on the porch of Dillon's trailer. I could see the new buildings and conveyor lines, but I tried not to look in that direction. It was spring when I returned to Blackberry Creek. The new leaves were out and smelled strong in the gray evening. A chorus of peepers cried loudly from water-logged ditches topped with green scum. Past the black walls of the Dew Drop Inn, past the wood and wire fences, past Hassel Day's submarine trailer, the green grass of the golf course had come alive in the warm rains. A lone golf cart skirted a white sand trap. I sat with a long-necked beer, waiting for Dillon to come home so we could visit, and was happy despite Tom's absence. I knew the romantic songs that moaned "just can't live without you" were lies. On Blackberry Creek I would gain strength and color, like a starving person fed rich broth.

My office was a storefront on the hill below the courthouse. There were two rooms, the back room with cabinets filled with advertising files and a board for layout, the front with a computer and printer and a desk for Betty Lloyd, who I hired to take care of subscriptions and phone calls. We could look out the window and see the courthouse steps where my Aunt Carrie's preacher husband was gunned down by coal company thugs. Sometimes when it was dusk and I had been working a long time I would look up and think I caught glimpses of ghostly gunmen, their coattails flapping as they moved toward the steps.

One hot September evening as I was leaving the office after working late, the phone rang. Tom Kolwiecki said, "Hello," as clear and familiar as if I'd only seen him yesterday.

"You sound close," I said, and felt my throat get tight.

"I am. I'm at the Pizza Hut."

"Here in Justice? In the United States of America? Good God! Why didn't you tell me you were coming?"

"Spur of the moment trip. Tell you more when I see you. That is, if this is a good time."

"Be there in five minutes."

The Pizza Hut was on a narrow lot at the edge of town where the mansions of Edgewood run up against the ragged edges of Carbon coal camp. I picked out his car, an old orange Datsun with Maryland tags. He was waiting inside on a dark brown bench, wearing jeans and a Georgetown University T-shirt. He swept me up in a hug. I held on tight and he sighed, his mouth near my ear.

We huddled over frosted mugs of beer, our elbows sticking to the plastic checked tablecloth. We could look through the smoky window glass across Blackberry Creek at swaybacked houses in an abandoned section of Carbon. It had been sunny outside, but the gray glass made it appear a storm was brewing.

"You're looking well," he said.

"It's done me good to come back."

He watched me closely. "Has it?"

"Yes. Somehow I'm more myself here." I started to tell him he was also looking well, but I wasn't sure it was true. He was fit and tanned, but his face was deeply lined and there was something wary in his eyes that I had never known before, like an animal unsure of its surroundings. Instead I said, "How long are you in this country?"

"A while," he said. "I've been kicked out of Honduras. It happened so fast I'm still trying to get my bearings."

"When?"

"Three weeks ago. A jeep pulled up with some Honduran military officers. Except the driver was American, and the jeep was American. The Hondurans handcuffed me and took me straight away, wouldn't even let me get my things."

"Tom, they could have killed you. You could have just disappeared."

He was turning his beer mug round and round and not even aware of it.

"I wouldn't have been the first," he said. "A Honduran Jesuit disappeared the year before I got there. He's never turned up."

"Where did they take you?"

"Don't know exactly. They put a blindfold on me. It was dark when they took it off." He looked away. "They were pretty rough."

"What happened?"

He shook his head fast like he was trying to wake himself up. "I'd rather not talk about it. But when they were done with me, I ended up in the waiting room of the Tegucigalpa airport with a one-way ticket to Miami in my pants pocket. I was a mess, blood on my clothes, cuts and bruises on my face. People sat as far away from me as they could."

"I'm sorry," I said. "But I'm glad you're safe."

"Safe," he said bitterly. "Yeah, I suppose I'm safe now."

I poured beer in his empty glass. He picked it up but his hand shook and beer sloshed onto the table. He set the mug down quickly.

"Sorry I filled the mug too full," I said.

"Will you stop apologizing for every damn thing!" he snapped.

I looked down, hurt. The pizza came, thick and studded with bits of green pepper and black olives. He chewed slowly, not like the old days in Washington when he would eat two slices to my one. After a while he picked up the glass of beer carefully and sipped off the top. I watched him closely, like a mother whose child has fallen and hit its head.

He said, "How's everyone at Number Thirteen?"

"Struggling," I said. "Nothing much has changed."

"You don't know what struggling is. I had a friend in Yoro who reminded me of Hassel. President of our farming co-op. He was shot in the back three months ago. The landowners call it deer hunting."

I opened my mouth to say I was sorry and shut it again. Instead I said, "Are you going back?"

"I don't know," he said. "The Honduran bishops don't want me and the Jesuits are trying to put pressure on them, but it's—" He shook his head, seemed like he wanted to say more, then repeated, "I don't know. It doesn't look like it."

He was drinking beer steadily. I waited.

"Day before yesterday I went to see that statue in the cemetery in Arlington. Only when I got there, the lights were out. The caretaker said some teenagers broke out all the bulbs. It was so dark I couldn't even see the stone unless my headlights were right on it. And then it was like Jesus was staring into space and didn't even see me. So I thought, what the hell, I'm on my own." He leaned back. "I don't pray any more" he said.

"You need some time," I said.

"The Jesuits assigned me a spiritual adviser and that's the same damn thing he said. You know what else? He says, 'Can't you go home and take it easy for a while?' I said, 'Where the hell is home?' "

"Here," I said.

"Sure." He laughed. "I'm forty-three years old and I spent a couple of years of my life here. That makes it home all right."

"Why'd you come, then? If this isn't home, get in your car and go on back to Washington."

He stared at me.

"Go on," I said. "I'm not going to beg you to stay."

"You're getting mean in your old age. Must be from hanging around Dillon."

He stood up, pulled a twenty out of his pocket and tossed it on the table, then headed for the door. I followed him. When he reached his car, he stopped and leaned his elbow on the roof.

"I didn't want you to misunderstand my coming back here," he said.

"No," I said.

"Sometimes I used to think you expected certain things from me."

"I loved you," I said. "I still do and I won't apologize for it now. It's a natural human feeling, in case you haven't noticed."

"You loving me has nothing to do with my life," he said. "It's irrelevant. If that sounds cold and arrogant, I don't care. God put me here for a purpose."

"Except now you're scared to death what it might be," I said.

"No. I'm at a dry place spiritually, that's all. I keep questioning how God could allow a place like Honduras to happen. I can't go back there until I'm sure about my vocation again. But I'm not scared."

"Like hell," I said.

"Don't tell me how I feel."

"You drove over here looking for some kind of comfort."

"Not from you. I wouldn't ask for that from you. It's been a while and I wanted to say hi. That's all."

"You could have sent a postcard."

I left him. When I drove away, spinning my tires in the gravel of the parking lot, he was still standing beside his car.

Three weeks later, he came by my office with a red rose stuck in a white bud vase. He set it on my desk.

"I want to apologize," he said. "I was an asshole when I was here last time."

"It's okay," I said.

He sat down. "I'm back for a while."

"What?"

"Honduras is still up in the air and the provincial thinks it will be good for me here, a place I was happy before. The local bishop says okay. The only catch is, he wants me to hold Mass on Sundays, try to get people to come."

"Can you do that? You said you were having trouble praying."

"The Mass is still the Mass," he said. "It doesn't depend on my faith. That's about all I've got left right now."

I said, "I'll come to Mass."

The wariness was back in his face. "Why? You're not Catholic."

"I went to Mass at the Catholic Worker house in DC," I reminded him, but I promised myself then I'd not go near him on Sunday morning without an invitation.

He moved into the empty half of old Sam Chernenko's double house with the whitewashed rocks in the yard. He decorated the rooms with posters of Martin Luther King, Dietrich Bonhoeffer, and Sandino, taped a brown sign on his refrigerator that said "Pray for the dead and fight like hell for the living—Mother Jones."

A battered wooden table in the living room held thick brown candles, a plate and chalice of slate blue pottery. Tom nailed signs to telephone poles at Annadel and Felco and Number Ten that announced

Catholic Mass
10:00 A.M. Sunday
St. Francis's Mission
Number Thirteen

Each Sunday he lit the candles and set out wine and bread. No one came.

He told me that he celebrated by himself. I hoped the Church was right, that the bread and wine did become the body and blood of Christ and would be strong medicine for Tom.

HASSEL, 1986

I never did think of Tom Kolwiecki as a drinking man. When he lived with me, he always enjoyed his beer and would have a couple while he watched the television or when folks come to visit, but I never seen him drunk.

This time back, though, he's took to drinking hard. I know because he gets his beer from me. I meet the beer trucks at Winco bottom in an old pickup of Junior's that is so far gone it will not hurt it to drive the right-of-way regular. So Tom buys a twelve-pack from me instead of going to the store and hauling it up the railroad hisself. It seems like he gets a pack real often, and he will pick up a fifth of Jack Daniels to go with it.

Then he took to visiting the Dew Drop around six o'clock. Mostly the place is empty. Business is so bad I am only open four nights a week now. Tom set on a stool, all leaned over the bar, and would drink five or six Rolling Rocks without stopping except to toss down a shot of whiskey. He left wet circles all over the bar where he set the bottles down. When he has had too much, he don't get crazy or silly like a lot of people will. He just gets real quiet and when he does talk, his words are a little blurry. But the first time or two, he didn't say much. It was like he'd got something on his mind but wouldn't say what it was.

The third time he come drinking in the Dew Drop, he set on the bar stool and drank three beers without hardly a word and asked for the fourth. When I give it to him, he said, "Hassel, maybe I shouldn't be doing this. My mother has got a drinking problem, you know."

I said, "Want me to take it back?"

"No," he said. "This is just temporary." Then he said, "Hassel, why am I here?"

"Because we want you here," I said. "And you do a lot of good."

"Like hell. I don't do a goddamn thing, and neither does anybody else around here. It's like everybody's asleep."

"I don't know," I said.

It kind of hurt my feelings because I still yet try to help folks out, and I have been trying again to get that bridge built. But it is true Tom has tried to start a Concerned Citizens again, and nobody has been much interested. I reckon they have been disappointed too many times before, and it is all most people can do to figure out where the next paycheck is coming from. They will not talk against the strip mining like they used to, because that is about all the jobs left any more. Number Thirteen and Jenkinjones are the only deep mines working on the hollow. So Tom sends out his notices about Thursday night meetings at the Holiness Church, and only me and Junior and Louelly will show up. Tom will say, "No point in wasting our time," and we just go on home.

So Tom drank more beer and said, "Here I sit. I offer a Sunday

Mass that nobody's interested in. I call meetings nobody comes to. I lie safe at night in my bed. I should be back in Honduras."

He stared into the mirror behind me. When I turned to get a rag to wipe the counter I seen his face looking old and drawed out in the glass.

"Hassel," he said, "I'm a coward."

"Why ever would you say that?"

But he just shook his head and wouldn't answer. When he left I stood in the door and watched him walk up the road. He stumbled once but then he walked straight. After that he took to drinking in his house again.

I am going to Charleston and ask that state government to build the Homer Day Memorial Bridge. They was a time I would have been scared to try and talk to the governor of the whole state of West Virginia, but I am more confident these days. Back a few years they was a little library built up to Annadel, before Ronald Reagan stopped such things. I put in my time there. First I read that *World Book Encyclopedia* all in alphabetical order. Then I went through them Time-Life home fix-it books and the *Nations of the World.* Now I am plowing through the novels. I even read that there *War and Peace* last July, although I don't recommend it in the summer time. Anyway, I reckon now I can handle that state government.

Besides, they is something in Charleston I have aimed to see, ever since I read about it in the *Justice Clarion* last month. It is a pair of dressed fleas. Some Russian fellow dressed them back in 1909, and they was in the museum in the state capitol basement since World War I. Then they built a fancy new museum across the street and them fleas wasn't good enough for it. They wanted paintings and sculptures and such, and they was going to throw the dressed fleas in the trash can. But the secretary of state, he rescued the fleas, and he keeps them in his office. I read about that and tried to figure how you would get clothes on a flea and what a dressed flea might look like. So I reckon I will look them up after we see to the bridge.

I invited Tom. I know his heart aint in it, but I reckon the trip might do him good, and he said he would come along for the company. He has got on that black shirt and white collar like priests wear, and you would think them state people would be afraid not to listen to him.

But no, the highway people say, We done spent all the money we're going to spend in Justice County this year. Pleased to meet you.

So there is nothing to do except find that governor's office. The first room where you wait has got a big chandelier and a thick blue carpet that makes you just want to walk slow and be quiet. The receptionist is blonde and looks like Cheryl Tiegs on the magazine covers.

"No," she says, "the governor is in Fairmont. One of his assistants will be back from a meeting in half an hour if you'd like to wait."

We set and wait for the assistant. That receptionist tells us how much the crystal chandelier weighs, how many prisms of glass is in it, how they clean it one piece at a time, and how long that takes. She tells us who all the dead governors are that have their pictures hung on the wall. She says, "The carpet you're standing on is the largest piece of seamless carpet in the world."

Then a young fellow comes in. He says he is on his way to another meeting but he will talk to us for five minutes. He is real neat with a fresh shaved neck and a yellow tie. He shows us in the big office. That governor surely does have a big desk, but they aint nothing on it except a statue of a soldier and a lamp, so I can't see what he uses all that table top for.

The young man looks real sad when I tell him we need a bridge. "I'm afraid it wouldn't be a priority project," he says.

"It don't have to be a big bridge," I say. "One lane to drive a car over. We'd build it ourselves but the creek is too wide. Hit wants an engineer and concrete. It would help the old people and the folks fetching groceries and the sick people. Somebody gets sick or hurt, we got to carry them a mile to meet the ambulance. We got businesses too, a restaurant and a repair shop and two churches." I look at Tom. "We got a Catholic church. Some big towns don't even have a Catholic church. This here is the priest."

The young man nods his head at Tom. "Father," he says. "Of course you understand we just don't have the money. Things are tight all over and the feds are really cutting back the highway money." Then he looks at his watch.

And that is that. We go outside and set on a bench to eat the sandwiches we brung with us.

Tom says, "You better forget about that bridge, Hassel."

I am feeling pretty gloomy myself. I brush the bread crumbs off my hands and stand up to leave. Then I recall what I read in the newspaper.

"Long as we're here," I say, "they's something else I been wanting to see."

I take Tom to the secretary of state's office where the receptionist gives me a decal of the state flag for the Batmobile's windshield and a blue plastic pin shaped like West Virginia. Then I ask about the dressed fleas and she points at a glass case over against the wall.

I set my eye to a magnifying glass. They are real fleas all right, stuck on a little card. You can see their pointy black heads, and sure enough, they are wearing little red jackets. One has on trousers, the other has on a blue skirt and you can see her skinny flea legs sticking out underneath of it.

"I swan," I say, and move over so Tom can take a peek. He don't look very long and I know he is ready to leave. But when he is done, I look again. It is strange to think them fleas was alive, maybe living on a dog, and Teddy Roosevelt or somebody else old was president. That boy flea is going to pot, you can't hardly make out his britches no more. But them fleas is still yet a fine accomplishment. I feel real peaceful, like I read about in that *Nations of the World* that people are in Tibet when they visit a holy place. I make a vow that I won't never give up. If a fellow can dress two fleas, I can build a bridge.

―――――――― ―――――――― ――――――

DILLON, 1986

I tend the graves at the Homeplace in Kentucky, scythe in hand, rooting out the weeds, raking the dirt. My daddy's grave is sinking some, and Rachel's and my mother's have lost their rawness although the granite headstones are shiny and sharp-cut. I try not to think on what has happened to Rachel inside her coffin. I don't fret about such changes for myself, for I believe there is something beyond this world. But I don't want her too far ahead of me, and I pray that broken finger will remain so whatever part of me lives on may grab onto it when I lie beside her.

And I cut the grass in Winco bottom where my house once stood, though all that is left are three concrete steps that end in midair. I recall how I walked down those steps on my way to Rachel's house or held her hand while she came up them. I tend a wild rosebush that grows beside the remains of the wire fence. I cut the red roses and lay them at the corner of the fence where the red fox and the Japanese skull are buried. If I had incense I would burn that too.

Once Jackie found me there, laying the roses. She stared at the flowers on the ground, then at me, and looked surprised.

"I got things buried here," I said.

She raised her eyebrows. "Things?"

"A Japanese skull your mother brought back from the Philippines. I thought it ought to have a proper burial."

"Oh," she said. "I reckon you were right about that."

"Your mom was young and foolish," I said. "She didn't mean anything."

Jackie smiled. She said, "I like to think of her as young and foolish. I wish I'd known her then."

I started to tell her about the red fox. I started to tell her who she is. I knew, standing there with her, that she was mine. But she had turned away from me before, like her mother did, and she would be angry I had waited so long. So I was afraid to tell her and turned my face away from her. She went on down the railroad track, on her way to visit Tom Kolwiecki at Number Thirteen. She spends more time with him than with me.

I watched her walk away, her shoulders thin and her hips starting to broaden, like her mother's did at that age. I thought how time has passed. I recall when you could drive through these mountains and meet a funeral procession, and every car on the road would pull off and wait until the mourners had passed, whether they knew the dead person or not. It was a way to show respect, like those Japanese, the way they bow. Lots of people don't pull over any more. I would like to know the year and the day when people stopped pulling over, and I would like to know why.

Once a year, on the anniversary, I drive through Jenkinjones and up Trace Mountain where Rachel and I first made love, where Jackie ran from me and I knew she loved the priest. Only I cannot go far now, for a fence stops me halfway up the mountain and beyond lies a flat wasteland, the core of the mountain barely concealed by saw-grass and the sprayed-on green fertilizer that Arthur Lee will call reclamation. I stop at the sign and read the words: PROPERTY OF AMERICAN COAL COMPANY   OFFICIAL TRAFFIC ONLY BEYOND THIS POINT   VIOLATORS SUBJECT TO PROS-ECUTION. Then I turn and drive back. I will not find the place again until I am dead.

I stop at the foot of Trace and study the pile of bone. Now the slate fills the head of the hollow and has become a dam, holding back the waters of Pliny Branch and sludge from the strip mine. I know the company has been adding to the pile, and yet the water looks closer to the top than before. The rains have been heavy lately. I get out of my truck and walk out across the top of the dam. The bone crunches beneath my boots. The water carries a black scum like skin. It is absolutely still, no insect would dare disturb the oily surface. I stop and listen, kneel and place the palm of my hand flat on the bone. It is warm as flesh.

"So," I say aloud.

On the way home I stop at the American Coal office in Jenkinjones. The office is no longer in the brick company store, which is a roofless ruin, but in a cinderblock building at the edge of the camp. Inside there is green carpet everywhere and wispy green plants. Certificates cover the wall, reclamation awards from the state. A woman sits at the reception desk.

"I want to see Arthur Lee," I say.

She takes my name and when she says it in the telephone she listens a moment and looks at me. When she hangs up I say, before she can speak, "I'll set here as long as it takes. And if he slips out the back, I'll speak to him on his front porch."

She picks up the phone again, hits a button, and says something real soft. After a while Arthur Lee opens a door in the back and holds it open. He stands away when I enter and doesn't offer me a seat.

"I aint any happier to be here than you are to have me," I say. "It's about that dam at the head of the hollow."

"What about it?" he says.

"You got a permit for it?"

"I reckon we do."

"You reckon?"

"Charleston office takes care of that."

"Sure," I say. "And even if you don't have a permit, who's going to do anything about it."

He sits at his desk and glares at me, says, "Is that all you come for?"

"Y'all just dumped that bone," I say. "Just piled it loose."

"They's a clay core under the new end," he says. "I made sure they put it in."

"What about the old end?"

He looks down at his desk and shuffles some papers. "Don't know," he says. "That was started before my time."

"We had a lot of rain," I say, "and the water is highest I ever seen it. I been taking note, even if you aint."

"You think I don't pay attention? I got a measuring stick in one end of that pond. Besides, it's holding, aint it?"

I lean over his desk. "I felt that bone," I say. "It was something there. That bone is uneasy."

He stands back. "Dillon, you always was a crazy sonofabitch. Don't you come in here trying to spook me."

But I see it in his eyes. He knows. He does not like to know, he does not believe it would really happen, he cannot imagine it like he cannot imagine the end of the world so he doesn't think about it, but I have reminded him and he knows.

"I'm going," I say, and I turn and leave but already his hand is moving toward the telephone and I know he will call some of the boys and have them take a look at the bone, and then he will call Philadelphia and say he is worried, and they will say there is no money for that and there's nothing to worry about and how are your production figures this month, Arthur Lee? And they will talk among themselves later, say, That Arthur Lee, he's getting a little long in the tooth and he didn't go to one of those fancy business schools, did he?

Whatever else I think of Arthur Lee, he lives here. He will stay awake the nights.

JACKIE, 1986

Dillon called me about the slate dam above Jenkinjones, and I went to look for myself and take pictures. The oldest part had stopped burning and green shrubs grew there. But the slate now stretched across the hollow from Trace Mountain to Peelchestnut, and a lake the size of several football fields had collected behind it. The water was a bluish black and looked solid enough to walk on.

I tried to get a quote from Arthur Lee but he wouldn't talk, so I ran a thick headline across the page, "Slate Dam Unsafe?" Hassel and Tom called for a meeting at the Felco VFW hall, where people had their say and signed a petition to send to American Coal headquarters in Philadelphia.

About a week after the petition went out, I woke to my telephone ringing on the bedside table.

"Jackie? Jackie? Honey? This is Arthur Lee."

His voice was so slurred I could barely understand him. I had heard rumors that Arthur Lee was drinking hard, like he did when he was younger.

"Arthur Lee?" I said. "Are you drunk?"

"Naw! Honey, naw! I aint had a drink for twenty year. Not for twenty—" the line banged where he had dropped the phone—"Shit" he said from a distance, then, "Honey, you still there?"

I fell back on the pillow. "I'm still here, Arthur Lee."

"Honey, I knew your daddy long before you was born. I loved your mother dearly and never raised my voice to her the whole time we was married. I know you never cared for me. But Philadelphia is on my ass, honey. You know how it is. They can always bring in a young man and—"

I interrupted, "So this is about the dam?"

"I'm saying don't write about it no more. Please. Tell them buddies of yours not to send any more petitions." He stopped to hiccup. "The boys in Philly say that dam is fine and they don't want to hear any more about it."

"American Coal can't tell me what to print in my newspaper," I said.

"It aint your newspaper," he said. "I know the boy in Lewisburg that owns it."

I took a deep breath. "I won't tell anybody you called me," I said. "I won't tell anybody the shape you're in right now or the clumsy way you're trying to threaten my job. But I'll write what I want to, Arthur Lee, and you can't tell me different."

"Honey, your momma was the finest woman I ever knew. She was a lady. She wouldn't want—"

"Good night, Arthur Lee."

I hung up.

I wrote several more articles. The newspaper's owner called and told me he'd had some complaints, but then a *Charleston Gazette* reporter came to investigate, so the story was out. But nothing happened. Tom sent my articles and pictures to Charleston and Washington. Nothing.

Then we had a dry spell, the water went down, the mines at Davidson announced another big layoff, and people forgot about the slate dam.

KUDZU JESUS
1986

HASSEL

Louelly still testifies in church. Last Sunday she stood up and hollered in tongues for a while, something that sounded like Tweedledum and Tweedledee, then she dropped down into English.

"They will be a miracle," she said. "They will be a miracle right on Blackberry Creek and Lloyds Fork."

Preacher said, "What kind of miracle, sister?"

Louelly just shook her head. "I aint been give to know that. But hit will be soon."

Doyle Ray Lloyd pastors at the Church of God (Prophecy) up near Annadel, and he is hauling for the strip mines during the week. His truck is a black Mack with an orange cross painted on the cab and the name HELLFIGHTER underneath. Doyle Ray has got a CB in the

cab so he can witness all day to anyone that don't turn him off. He is making good money and he takes it for a sign that God has blessed him because that's what they say on that there "Seven Hundred Club." They will not hear about the rich man and the eye of a needle.

For a while, Doyle Ray and his wife Sandra lived in a double house at Number Thirteen. Then Louelly's Ethel got on as a miner at Number Thirteen back when they was still yet hiring and bought the other half of the double house. Doyle Ray has never cared much for Ethel. It goes back to Ethel beating up on him when they was younguns.

Ethel is partial to pink and covered her end of the house with that color of aluminum siding. She said she seen pictures in that *Southern Living* magazine of pink houses in Florida. She tried to get Doyle Ray to put the same on his half so they would match, but he said pink wasn't no color for a Christian home. He put up olive green aluminum siding, so it is a funny looking house. You can spy it from across the creek.

Anyway, Doyle Ray put in a double-wide trailer at Winco bottom, near where Dillon's house used to set, and moved his family into it. His wife claimed she got tired of climbing all the steps after she had her younguns, but we all reckoned they didn't take to living beside a sister-in-law who worked in the mines and had a half-colored youngun without even being married. And they didn't care for Ethel setting on her front porch drinking a beer on a summer evening. Besides that, Doyle Ray is driving for a nonunion outfit and Ethel is strong union.

Doyle Ray walks the track to Number Thirteen every clear evening except prayer meeting night. He'll go see his mother first, because Betty smokes and cusses and aint never been a churchgoer. Doyle Ray thinks his daddy is in Hell and he frets over his mommy.

Then he'll take out after somebody else, inviting hisself in for a cup of coffee and interrupting whatever television show a body is trying to watch. He's even been to see Ethel oncet, but she threw him right off her porch. He won't go see Tom. I do believe he is scared of a priest.

So me and Louelly and Ethel and Toejam, with Brenda hoisted on his back, are on our way to Winco bottom, walking to the Batmobile so Louelly and Ethel can trade for groceries at the Pick-and-Pay. It is one of them pale summer evenings when the heat has been burned away, the gnats are rising, and the cool air feels just right. Kudzu grows thick up the hill beside the track, like a green rug throwed over the maples and dogwood and poplars.

Off in the distance, Doyle Ray is coming toward us, black Bible stuck under his armpit. He don't see us because he is looking at the mountainside, then he stops short, drops that Bible right on the ground, and puts his hands to his mouth. He sinks down on his knees and bows his head.

"Lord God almighty," Ethel says, "Doyle Ray has lost his mind."

"Hush!" Louelly says. "He seen something."

When we reach him, first he acts like he don't know we're there.

Louelly says, "Doyle Ray?" real careful, like he's made out of glass and her voice might bust him. He twitches his shoulders.

"Come on, Doyle Ray," Ethel says.

Doyle Ray looks up. His face is shiny with sweat. "I see the Lord," he says. "I see my sweet Jesus!"

"You see Jesus?" Louelly says. "Here?"

Brenda says, "Yee-sus!" She throws back her head and laughs.

Doyle Ray points behind us. "I see Jesus in the tree yonder! He's in the kudzu!"

I look where he is pointing. The kudzu has swallowed up a tree that hangs over the railroad cut back toward Number Thirteen. The tree is so covered up you can't tell what kind it is. But with the evening light behind it and the leaves taking on darkness, it does look like the head of a man with a big nose and a beard.

Ethel folds her arms across her chest. "Where?"

"It's the Lord!" Doyle Ray cries. "He's clear as day. If you can't see Him, you aint saved."

"Hit does take after a man's head," Toejam says.

Louelly's face is shining. "Hit's my miracle," she says.

"Come on!" Ethel says. "It could be Abraham Lincoln. It could be one of them Smith Brothers off the cough drop box."

Doyle Ray is furious. "It aint a thing to make light of," he says. Then he leaves us standing.

When we get back from the Pick-and-Pay, I head straight to see Tom, who has been so down in the mouth I am anxious to cheer him up. He is out on his porch, leaned back in a chair and his feet propped on the bannister, holding a can of beer. Jackie Honaker is setting on the steps with her arms folded across her chest and a hurt look on her face. They don't even say hello when I come up.

"Tom," I say, "Louelly prophesied a miracle and it looks like it's come to pass. Maybe hit's something to do with you. Just because the Word come in the Holiness service, that don't mean it can't be a Catholic miracle."

He looks up. "Miracle?" Then he laughs, but it aint a happy sound. "I need a miracle," he says. "The bishop's coming Sunday. Says he wants to see what progress I've made. Wait till he sees my one-person Mass."

"Sunday?" Jackie says. "Why on earth don't you call him and tell him you're not ready yet? Tell him it takes more time. He'll understand."

Tom just ignores her. "So, Hassel, what kind of miracle do we have today, a bleeding statue of the Virgin or just a simple faith healing?"

I can tell he has been drinking too much again because Tom just don't act like that when he's sober.

I say, "They's a tree over yonder that's covered up with kudzu and it appears to be Jesus. It's a big head that looks at you."

"Where?" he says. "Can you see it from here?"

I point way off to where the tree hangs over the railroad. "Over yonder," I say. Then I notice that from this angle it looks even more like a head.

Tom stands up and looks where I point. "I see it," he says. "God, it does look like Jesus. What do you think, Jackie? Maybe Jesus is following me."

Jackie says, "It's not even looking in this direction."

"No, but it might swing around this way any minute now."

"Very funny."

"I'm not trying to be funny."

I can't figure out what they are talking about. Tom says, "No offense, but could I ask you to leave? Both of you? I need some time alone with old Jesus there."

"You need time with Jesus or Jack Daniels?" Jackie says.

"Never mind."

"Fine!" She sighs great big and then looks at me. "Come on," she says, and tugs on the sleeve of my T-shirt. We walk down the street toward my trailer.

She says, "Something's wrong, Hassel. Something's been bad wrong ever since he came back, but he won't talk about it."

"Something happened there," I say.

"Yeah," she says. "It was dangerous for him. They've got a saying in some of those countries, 'Be a patriot, kill a priest.' "

"Good lordy," I say. "No wonder he don't want to go back."

She looks at me hard. "So you think that's it, too?"

"He told me he's a coward."

And after Jackie leaves, I keep thinking on what she said and why Tom is so scared. And it comes to me all at once. When that West Virginia bishop visits and sees Tom aint done no good here, he'll say Tom has to leave Number Thirteen. And maybe them Jesuits will want to send him back to that Honduras. And it will be our fault, his neighbors, because we didn't stand up for him.

So I know what I have to do.

It does take some planning. I aint never seen a Mass and neither has anybody else I know except Jackie. But I don't want to ask Jackie because she might tell Tom and spoil everything. Still we have got to know what is going on like we been through it before. So I go to the library and copy that service right out of a book. It is easy because the Catholics, they have got everything wrote down. Betty takes my notebook to the newspaper office and types the whole thing up, then runs it off on the Xerox.

In the meantime, you can look at that kudzu tree from either side and still yet see the head; it's only straight on that it's just a tree. Doyle Ray says that's the way it should be because a sinner can't face up to Jesus head on. Doyle Ray has been on the telephone and called every preacher he knows, then the Bluefield TV station. Now there are three hundred people standing out on that railroad track, clutching them Bibles. If you stand behind my trailer you can see them alongside the fence beside the seventh hole of the golf course. They wave their arms and testify at the men in plaid pants who drive the little carts across that there green. There are so many cars in the bottom I have to park the Batmobile half a mile above Winco.

The crowd aint done me no good. If they was Catholics they might like a cold beer after they seen Jesus, but they are not Catholics, and that is my luck.

It comes Tom's big day and I peek out my window until I see him walk the track on his way to pick up that bishop in Justice town. I call Jackie and when she answers, real sleepy sounding, I say, "This is Hassel and I got a surprise. Why don't you come on over to Tom's for that Mass this morning?"

She says, "Hassel! What are you up to?"

"Never you mind," I say, and laugh and hang up. Then I go to Tom's house and let myself in the front door, which aint never locked. I carry folding chairs from the Dew Drop and set them in the front room.

Everybody comes at nine o'clock, like they promised. All my people are here, and Junior and his mother and Betty Lloyd. Dillon Freeman comes in quiet and sets in the back looking strangled in a dress shirt and tie, but he's got a smile on his face like the whole thing is real funny. And after while here comes Sim Gore who is a widow man now and living with his son Leon at Felco. Now that is something that aint been seen around here, white people and black people setting in church together. I don't know what Betty thinks about that, because her family has always been real prejudiced, but maybe that bishop will be impressed.

Then there's my best customers from the Dew Drop, who I have promised two free beers for showing up. There is Clennis Marcum who is disabled and walks on a cane. There's Rodney from Jenkinjones that drives the Stroh's truck. There is Howard who works the Robo Car Wash since Dillon sold out. And there is Luther Beasley who is still yet the town cop up to Annadel and has let bygones be bygones where Tom is concerned.

I hand out the Xeroxed programs and they have the prayers in them that you read, even the Lord's Prayer that everybody knows by heart anyhow, and the program tells you when to stand up and when to kneel down. The librarian said when the Mass calls for kneeling we have to hunker right down on the floor, and Louelly has brung a pillow for the arthritis in her knees. We practice with me reading the preacher's part.

Then we get to where there will be a cup that we all drink out of. Clennis says, "I hear tell it's real wine instead of grape juice."

"That's right," I say.

"I don't hold with that."

"Now Clennis. You get drunk as a skunk at the Dew Drop."

"That's a Saturday night," says Clennis. "This here is church."

"Well just pretend like you're taking a sip. Or else don't take none at all. You don't have to act like you're Catholic. We just want the bishop to know that you like Tom and you're interested in what he's doing."

"Don't know Tom," says Howard from the Robo.

"Just be quiet, Howard," I say. "Just set still."

Howard pulls me aside. "What if that bishop asks me a question, Hassel? I don't know nothing about Catholics."

"Just say you're studying on it. You get stuck, I'll help you out."

"Hardest beer I ever earned," Howard complains. "Think I'll pay for it next time."

After we practice, I decide it would be the mayorly thing if I walked to Winco and met Tom and that bishop. When I start down the railroad track, I see Jackie coming.

"Hassel," she says. "What's going on?"

Then I tell her.

"Oh lord," she says. "Oh lord."

I say, "I know we're fooling that bishop, but hit's Tom's life at stake. You don't want them to send him back to Honduras, do you? You see how he's scared to death of it."

"But they aren't sending him back," she says. "He told me the Honduran bishops won't have him so he's stuck here."

"Then what's he so scared of?" I say.

"I don't know." She looks back toward Kudzu Jesus. "I don't know."

"Well," I say, "hit's too late now. We done practiced and everything. I'm going to meet the bishop."

"All right," she says. "You go on. I'll try to figure this out."

When I reach Kudzu Jesus, Doyle Ray Lloyd is gathering his congregation from the Church of God (Prophecy) for a service.

I say, "Doyle Ray, that Catholic bishop will be here pretty soon. We don't mean to disturb your service, but we got to bring him by here."

"Bring him on," says Doyle Ray. "Jesus has come to judge him."

"Y'all be polite," I warn.

"My people are wise as serpents and gentle as doves," says Doyle Ray.

I wait about ten minutes at Winco bottom and then I see Tom's green Toyota come bumping over the bridge. Tom says the bishop drives a Lincoln Continental, but they will have left it at the motel. When Tom sees me, he stops the car and gets out.

I tell him I was going to save him a parking place, but Doyle Ray's people have took up all the space.

"That's all right," he says. "The bishop doesn't want to walk that far anyway. There won't be any trains on Sunday so it should be okay to drive the right-of-way. Hop in."

I get in the back seat and that bishop half turns and says hello. He has gray hair and a round face like someone that would make a good Santa Claus.

"And your name is?" he says.

I tell him. Then I say, "We been looking forward to your visit, Bishop."

"We?" he says.

"All of us," I say.

The bishop gives Tom a funny look. "I'm glad to hear it. Father Kolwiecki made it sound like he hasn't been very successful here."

"Oh, Tom's real successful," I say. "I reckon you'll be surprised."

Tom glances around at me and makes a face like he's saying *What the hell is going on?* then starts the car. We tilt sideways when we mount the right-of-way and that bishop holds onto the door handle to keep from sliding into Tom's lap. Chunks of gravel rattle around the axles and bounce off the oil pan.

"You picked an out-of-the-way place." The bishop has to holler to be heard above the racket. "Wouldn't something on the main road be better?"

"I wanted to be in Number Thirteen," Tom says. "It's where I lived before and besides I like a challenge."

I seen my chance then. "Bishop, we wouldn't be so cut off if we had us a bridge. I been trying for years to get one built but the state won't help us. Maybe y'all could see fit to help now that we got us a Catholic church."

Tom's ears are bright red and he turns part way round to look at me. The bishop laughs kind of short. "I don't believe the Church is in the bridge building business, Hassel."

So I don't say anything else about it because I figure we got enough on our plate. We round the last curve and there is the congregation of the Church of God (Prophecy) of Spencers Curve, eighty strong, dressed neat in their suit coats, their frilly dresses, the little girls in shiny black patent leather shoes, standing on the railroad ties, in the ditch, on the river bank. Kudzu Jesus is leaning over them.

Tom stops the car and Doyle Ray Lloyd walks toward us, looking like an undertaker in his black suit, Bible held to his chest like a shield. Tom sticks his head out the window.

"Sorry, Doyle Ray. We didn't mean to interrupt your church service."

"We was waiting for you," Doyle Ray says.

"Oh." Tom looks at the bishop.

"We're concerned for your immortal soul. We are praying that Jesus will deliver you from the whore of Babylon, the beast of Revelation, the Roman Catholic Church. We are standing here before Jesus, and we want to know if you can see what we see in that tree."

The bishop is looking at Doyle Ray like he is crazy.

"Bishop?" Tom says real low.

"Father, I don't know what's going on here. Maybe it's best if you handle it."

Doyle Ray is standing calm and, hot as it is, his forehead aint even moist. I can see part of Tom's face in the rearview mirror. He looks like a man you see in a war movie that is holding a grenade and waiting for it to go off.

Kudzu Jesus, 1986

"We love you, Tom," Doyle Ray is saying. "But the hellfire is dreadful and we don't want to see you suffer it. My own mother is at your house this very minute and in danger of being dragged into the flames with you."

"At my house?" Tom says. "What's she doing at my house?"

"She is tempting Satan, that's what she's doing. Now you look at that tree and tell me what you see."

I stick my head out the window and holler, "He sees Jesus all right. He even seen Jesus from his front porch the other day."

Tom holds onto the steering wheel and stares at the tree.

"I don't see anything," he says like he's gritting his teeth.

"I aint surprised," says Doyle Ray. "We'll pray for you then. And I'd be obliged if you'd send my mother away from your house."

Doyle Ray backs up and motions his people to move off the right of way and let the car go by. Mavis Samples that used to come to our Concerned Citizens meetings sticks her hand in the open window. "God bless you," Mavis says. Tom grabs hold of her hand and squeezes. A breeze kicks up and when we pass under Kudzu Jesus it's like the leaves ripple and whisper pleasant among themselves.

"Father?" That bishop's voice is real soft. "What was that all about?"

I can tell Tom aint in the right frame of mind to stick up for hisself, so I jump in and help out. "Hit aint nothing," I say. "Some folks around here see Jesus in that tree covered up with kudzu. Hit's like them Catholics in Texas that seen Jesus in a burrito shell."

Tom don't say a word and bishop don't ask another question, but his forehead has got thinking lines in it. When we get to the house, he climbs the front steps, looks around at the wood porch swing and weathered floor boards, opens the screen door. We follow him inside and Tom sees all the people. He holds tight to my arm.

"What the hell is this?" he says in my ear. "Hassel? What have you done?"

"See here," I say, "at all the folks that love you. And we want you to stay and we don't want them to send you to that Honduras."

Tom looks like he is about to cry and turns away. Everybody has stood up and they look real nervous. The bishop don't seem to notice, he is going around and shaking hands, asks everybody's name. When he gets to Brenda he puts one hand on her head and waves the other one around like he is drawing a cross in the air. He stops in front of Howard from the Robo, who is uneasy at having his hand held, and just beams. It is like the way a cat will get in the lap of the one person that hates cats.

"Well, son," the bishop says, "Have you been enjoying this fellowship?"

Howard looks at me real pitiful and I nod my head hard. "I'm studying on it," Howard says in a croaky voice.

"Ah!" says the bishop.

Tom comes up to him. "Father," he says, "this is not—" He stops and tries again. "This is—"

"Don't worry," says the bishop. "It's not a large group, but very impressive for the time you've been here. Now, shouldn't we prepare?"

So Tom takes the bishop into the bedroom to put on what you call the vestments, and he don't look a bit happy. Jackie comes up to me.

"He looks more upset than ever," she says. "It's like he wants to fail. What are we going to do?"

"We just got to keep going," I say. "That there bishop is nice enough. Maybe he'll still yet cheer Tom up."

Jackie lights the candles, and when Tom brings the bishop back out, we sing "Amazing Grace" which everyone knows, even Howard. Ethel's Tiffany plays the old beat-up piano in the corner. The bishop is wearing this big purple tent with gold leaves sewed all over it. Howard and Luther and the Dew Drop boys are staring at that and at Tom in a long white robe like a wedding gown.

We say what you call the Gloria and everybody does just fine. Then Junior gets up and reads the scripture. It is about Jonah and the whale, how God sent Jonah to preach repentance to Nineveh but Jonah didn't want to go and run away from God. Then Jonah was on a boat that got caught in a storm and the sailors figured out it was Jonah's fault. They carried on and said, *Tell us, we pray thee, for whose cause this evil is upon us, What is thine occupation? and whence comest thou? what is thy country? and of what people art thou?*

Tom sits up front. At first his face looks blank, like his mind is far away. Junior keeps on reading. He has got a strong voice, Junior.

"Why hast thou done this?" For the men knew that he fled from the presence of the Lord, because he had told them.

Then I see the fear creep across Tom's face, and the shame. And I know we have done wrong, not because God will mind that we have tried to help Tom, but because we haven't helped Tom at all, somehow we have made him go back on hisself and broke his heart. He has to read the Gospel and I try to catch his eyes, but he won't look at any of us. He keeps stumbling over the words. That bishop is watching him like a hawk. But Tom makes it all the way through and sets back down.

The bishop's sermon is a real snoozer and I hope that will calm Tom down. But his hand is shaking when he pours the wine. I pass around the basket we are using for a collection plate and everybody puts in a dollar. When I come to Jackie, who is setting in the back beside Dillon, she whispers, "We've got to do something!"

"I'll try to talk to him when I go up front."

I take the collection up and give it to Tom and when he starts to turn away, I put my hand on top of his where he's holding the basket and squeeze real hard. "I want you to know, we didn't mean no harm," I says. "We are truly sorry. You do what you have to do."

He stares at me, then turns away and sets the basket on the table. Then the bishop launches into what you call the Sanctus, he is barreling right along and we are standing and kneeling until Louelly's knees crack.

The bishop says, "Lamb of God who takes away the sins of the world, have mercy on us."

"Oh God have mercy!" cries Tom. He leans way over and covers his face with his hands. He drops to his knees.

The bishop grabs Tom by the arm. "Shall we go in the other room, Father?"

"No," Tom says. "I have to confess. I'm a liar and a coward. I can't pray anymore and I don't have any faith. I'm a terrible priest. I'm not worthy."

The bishop starts to say something, but then Louelly calls right out, "The Holy Ghost is here! The Holy Ghost is speaking to his servant Tom! Praise the Lord! Praise Jesus!" She leans way back in her chair and waves her arms in the air. "Wheeeee! Whoooeee! Labitibi-ta!"

The bishop drops Tom's arm and Tom leans against him and stares at Louelly. Then Louelly is hollering *Non nobis domine domine non nobis domine domine sed nomine sed nomine* and the bishop says, "That's Latin! Where did you learn Latin?" and Louelly stops dead and hushes, which I have never seen her do at anybody's bidding once she is speaking the tongues.

"We don't even use Latin any more," the bishop says, like he can't figure out where he is.

Louelly says, "I speak whatever the Spirit gives me to speak. And I am a Holy Roller, but I fellowship with anybody the Lord gives me to fellowship with, even a preacher that wears a quilt."

"I'm pleased to hear it," the bishop says. Then he looks at Tom. "Father, I'm totally confused. I allowed you to come here because I thought you felt called. That's what you told me and that's what the Jesuits told me. Then when you picked me up in Justice you told me you were failing in your mission. But we arrive and I find—" he waves his arm "—this."

Tom speaks real quiet. "I lied. I lied to my provincial and I lied the you. I lied to my friends here." He looks at Jackie. "I want to go back to Honduras. It's more home than here. But I'm scared. I don't have the strength for it."

The bishop puts his hands together and turns his back to us like he is praying what to do. He walks to the window and looks out. Then he says, "Hassel, would you read from the thirteenth chapter of Corinthians?"

When I stand up to read I see Jackie has gone out on the front porch and Dillon has followed her. The screen door slams shut. I read, " 'Though I bestow all my goods to feed the poor, and though I give my body to be burned, and have not love, it profits me nothing.' "

Then the bishop says, "I think we should continue with the Mass. Father Kolwiecki, you have confessed and are absolved. We'll talk more about this later. You should feel free to take communion and so should anyone here who's been baptized. This is just what the Mass is for."

It is real interesting, that Mass. It does seem holy, the way that wine burns your throat when you swallow. After it is over, the bishop takes Tom off to the next room to pray. When everyone else leaves I sit on the couch and listen. I can't make out their words but it is the same thing over and over, like when the Holiness speak in tongues only low and soothing. I get down on my knees and shut my eyes and ask the Lord to keep Tom safe.

JACKIE

I didn't feel like going home so I went to Dillon's trailer, threw myself full length on the couch, and cried myself out. Dillon sat in a chair across the room and watched. When I was quiet, he said, "Go talk to him."

"No," I said. "He doesn't want me. I don't mean a thing to him."

"Why did he come back here? He didn't come back for Hassel or for me."

I rested my head on my arm. "It looks like he came back to hide."

"He could have hid anywhere," Dillon said, "but he picked here."

"He wants to go back to Honduras," I said. "You heard him. He *wants* to go back."

I thought of all the Hondurans he knew, people I would never meet, whose lives he'd shared more closely than mine. I hated them. I turned my face away, shut my eyes, and pretended to nap, nursing my anger. After while, I did drift off to sleep. The telephone rang and I sat up with a start. It was almost four-thirty. Dillon was standing by the door with the phone in his hand. He held it out and said, "For you."

I spoke into the receiver.

"I had to drive the bishop to the motel in Justice." Tom's voice was quiet. "Then I came back and did some thinking. I need to talk to you. Can you come to the house now? Please?"

I said, "Are you drinking? I don't want to talk to you if you're drinking."

"No," he said. "No drinking from now on. I want to face this with a clear head."

"All right. I'll come."

I set the phone in its cradle and thought I might be the one who'd need a drink before the evening was over. Dillon stood in the kitchen and sipped a cup of coffee.

I said, "You be here all evening?"

"Wasn't planning on going no place."

"Good. I may need a shoulder to cry on again."

"You going over there?"

"Yes. I think he wants to say goodbye, probably for good."

"Go on," Dillon said. He followed me to the front door and opened it. "But don't you go afraid. And don't you get to be an old woman and wish you'd said or done something you never had the nerve to."

"Dillon, don't expect—"

He shut the door in my face. I turned away, blinking back frustrated tears, and walked to Tom's house. He was sitting on the front porch steps and when he saw me coming he stood and held the door open, then followed me inside. The room seemed empty after the morning's crowd, the metal chairs folded and stacked against the wall, the bread and wine gone. I sat on the edge of the couch and Tom stood in the center of the room with one hand on his forehead.

"I'm sorry I lied to you," he said. "I want you to know it's nothing to do with you. I've lied to everyone."

"I'm not mad about that," I said. "I just want to understand."

He started to pace. "The first lie was to the Jesuits. After I'd been back in the States a little while, they started making inquiries. The Honduran bishops aren't pleased with what the Jesuits are doing there, but most of them want to keep some kind of relationship. I won't go into all the church politics, but the provincial told me they'd pulled some strings and I could go back if I wanted to. I said no. I said I felt called to come back to West Virginia."

"And you didn't."

"No. I love this place. I love it a lot. But it's not where I'm supposed to be now. I can't explain how I felt in Honduras, but it was just right, even when things were tough. It's a lot like here, you know. They've got mountains that have been stripped for their mahogany trees so they have mud slides and the land looks torn up and beaten. And the people, they need so much."

"I see."

He sat on the couch beside me. "I lied to you second. I told you the bishops wouldn't let me back in Honduras. The only person I told any kind of truth to was Hassel. I told him I'm a coward, and that's true."

"Tom, you should be scared. You could get killed."

He started talking again like I hadn't said a word. "The third lie was to the bishop. Actually it wasn't really a lie, it was a setup. It's like I wanted to be a fraud and a failure here, so I'd have no choice except to face up to Honduras. I've been drinking and feeling sorry for myself. I haven't done much of anything for anybody and I haven't invited people to Mass. I didn't tell the bishop any of that until he came down. I figured he'd be pissed and call my provincial and tell him to pull me the hell out of here." He ran his hand through his hair. "I didn't figure on Hassel recruiting a whole damn congregation, or Louella witnessing in Latin."

"Or Jesus showing up in a kudzu tree," I said.

"No," he said. "God, no. It's been looneytunes around here, hasn't it?"

Then he started to laugh, and I started to laugh. He laid his head back against the couch and watched me. I stopped laughing.

"Is that all?" I said.

He looked quickly at the ceiling, chewed on his lower lip. I couldn't tell if he was thinking or about to cry.

"No," he whispered, "there's more. In Honduras they tortured me. They—"

He turned his face away.

I reached out and touched his hand. He didn't pull back. I turned his hand over and laid the soft flesh of my palm against his. He straightened his fingers and laced them through mine. His eyes were shut and tears slipped down his cheeks.

"For a while they beat me," he said. "They took off my shirt and burned me with lit cigarettes and cut me with a razor. They held my head under water until I almost passed out. And the last thing was they"—he took a deep breath—"they pulled down my pants and they hooked a wire from a battery to me—to my testicles—and they shocked me. They only did it once. The pain was so awful and I screamed. They laughed. They said, 'See father, we can make you a eunuch if we want to. We can preserve your vows for you, we can keep you from sin.'

"They stopped after that. For a while I was numb there, then the feeling came back. But they talked to me in the jeep on the way to the airport. They said, 'Come back here, Father, and we'll poke out your eyes. Come back and we'll cut off your dick.' "

"Oh God, Tom."

"When they were torturing me I didn't pray. I didn't think about the Church. I thought about you, Jackie. You're what I held onto. I saw you just as clear, and I tried to talk to you. Once I even called out your name."

He leaned close suddenly and pulled me to him, put his mouth on mine. His lips were dry. He held me so tight it was hard to breathe. Then he opened my mouth with his tongue. He kissed my ear, my neck, moved to my mouth again.

"I need you," he said. "I need you so much." He ran his fingers through my hair. "I took a vow of celibacy. God knows I've hated it, but I've never broken it. I take vows seriously. But I can't do what I have to do without a touch of human kindness. I can't be a priest without breaking that vow at least this once. Do you understand what I'm asking? I'm asking more than I have a right to ask you. I'm asking you to send me back to Honduras."

"You're asking me to send you back loved," I said.

His face was close to mine, searching. "Yes. Are you strong enough for that?"

For answer I unbuttoned his shirt, slipped my arms inside, and stroked the flesh of his back. His fingers tightened on my arm. I pulled his shirt off his shoulders, slid down his chest, and tickled a nipple with the tip of my tongue.

He lay back against the couch and pulled me with him, opened my blouse. I leaned over and kissed him and his hands moved down my front.

He said, "You don't wear a bra?"

"No, silly. It's too hot in the summer. Are you disappointed there isn't one to take off?"

He smiled and shook his head, touched one breast as though he were studying it. Then he took it in his mouth and I arched my back and gave my body up to the pleasure of him. He pulled down my shorts even as I unzipped his jeans, but before I could touch him, he turned me so I lay full length on the couch. He ran his hands over my body and his mouth followed his hands.

Then he stopped, stood, and turned his back to me. I was afraid he would say, "No, I've changed my mind, you're ugly, this is wrong." Instead he took off his jeans. His skin was pale orange in the evening light.

"When they were hurting me, I wanted so much for you to touch me. I wanted you to touch every place they did."

He dropped the jeans and turned. I took his wrist and pulled him to me. When he lay still I explored every inch of him, found the small round spots across his shoulders where he'd been burned, stroked three long white slash marks on his abdomen, then traced them with the tip of my tongue. He lay with his eyes shut and his arms flung above his head. I held his erect penis, nuzzled it against my cheek, combed the fine fur of hair at his groin, and gently explored until I found the single thick scar across the loose skin. I leaned close and covered the scar with kisses.

He pulled me back to his chest and our eyes held. His were dark and flecked with gray light.

"Thank you," he said.

"I should thank you. You're so beautiful."

He smiled, and his hand moved across my thigh, between my legs. He kissed my neck, whispered, "This is for you now." Later he moved on top of me and we slid together, bodies slick with sweat, and began to rock gently. We moved more and more quickly until I rose and moaned and fell back. Tom held on longer, an ecstatic loath to reenter the world, then he cried out and I held him until he came to himself at last.

I spent the night in his bed. The sheets bore his scent, and I stayed awake as long as I could, touching him, sniffing, tasting. In the morning we sat naked in the middle of the living room floor, surrounded by pillows, sipped hot tea, and ate blueberry muffins. Then we lay close again and loved, then tickled one another with the tips of our fingers until he stopped and held his hand against my cheek.

"How can I leave this?" he said.

I put my hand on his. "You love Honduras and you love being a priest," I said. "And that's how you'll leave." I started to smile to show that was okay, but my throat tightened and I hid my face against his neck.

"You've got to go on and live your life," he said. "No holding back with someone else because of me."

"No," I whispered.

"I'll be fine. I'll write you this time. And I'll be back, I promise. They give us leaves sometimes."

I said, "We won't be able to do this again."

"No," he agreed. "This time will have to be enough."

"Will you confess what we've done, as a sin?"

"I'll confess the breaking of my vows," he said. "But what we've done was no sin. I've never been more sure of anything in my life."

He stayed another week, making arrangements for the house and saying goodbye. He gave his car to Ethel Day, who was laid off from the mine. We loaded his couch in the back of Dillon's truck and took it to my house. Tom left with only a shoulder bag of clothes and a few books.

We walked to my car at Winco bottom, passed beneath Kudzu Jesus, which had grown so fast it resembled nothing at all. Then I drove Tom to Charleston to catch his plane. We sat side by side on plastic chairs and held hands. When the flight was announced, Tom shouldered his suitcase and turned to me.

"We're not done yet," he said.

He held my face in both hands and kissed me. Then he walked up the carpeted tunnel and disappeared.

GOD'S BONES
1987

JACKIE, 1987

Dillon was sifting through a box his mother left him when she died, a cardboard box with white roses on the lid and tied up with a pink ribbon. Inside were journals she had kept, family letters, newspaper clippings brown and brittle as wood shavings. Dillon was taking notes and trying to write the story of his mother and father. Sometimes he brought his work to Felco for me to edit. He was a blunt writer, with no gift for subtlety or the sinuous twists of storytelling, but he was surprisingly open to criticism. He sat meekly at my kitchen table, hands in his lap and coffee cup in front of him, while I marked pages with a red pen.

Once he said, "You ought to write this. You're better than I am."

"No," I said, "it's your story."

"Then what about your own stories? I recall when you was a youn-

gun, you was bound you would write some day."

"I do write," I said. "I write every day for a living."

"That's different," he said. "There's too many rules with a newspaper. I'd like to see you cut loose."

One winter's evening I was eating warmed over pizza and watching TV when he knocked on the door. I thought he had come to show me more writing, but he held a letter typed on American Coal Company stationery.

"It's from Arthur Lee," he said. "He's finally got his revenge."

I offered him a slice of pizza, but he waved it away and gave me the letter. It informed us that American Coal had purchased the mineral rights to the Homeplace from the Imperial Land Company and had begun to strip the mountain. The cemetery would soon be covered by a hollow fill and the graves were to be moved at a date to be set at the family's convenience, but no later than March 1, 1987. Signed Arthur Lee Sizemore, Superintendent of Mining Operations.

"You go there to tend the graves," I said. "Did you know they were stripping?"

He shook his head. "Last I was there was September. They must have been back up on the mountain then. I didn't even see the permit notice because they run it in a Kentucky newspaper. Come this time next year, that cemetery and most of the Homeplace will be under five hundred foot of rock. And there's not a damn thing we can do about it."

"There must be something," I said, but I knew there wasn't.

Dillon rocked back and forth on the chair, holding his knees. "You know, in the old days when they stripped a cemetery, they just scattered the bones. Didn't tell the family, didn't think nothing of it."

"I reckon things are more civilized now," I said.

"My daddy and mommy wouldn't have stood for this."

"They couldn't have done anything if they were alive," I said. "They'd be as powerless as you and me."

"What are you saying? Are you saying this don't bother you?"

"It bothers me," I said. "I'll write an editorial about it, and I'll call whoever is in charge of strip mines in Kentucky, and people will read the editorial and say isn't that too bad, and the Commonwealth of

Kentucky will send me a letter saying the permit is in order and referring me to some book of regulations, and that will be that."

He wouldn't look at me, took a cigarette out of his pocket.

"I thought you gave up smoking," I said. "You promised you would if I came home."

He paused, then found a lighter and flicked it. "What do you care?" he said.

"I don't want anything to happen to you. You're all I've got."

"Is that so?" he said. But he stubbed the cigarette out on my empty pop can and dropped it inside. He stood up. "I'm going to be there," he said. "I'm going to watch them dig up them graves. I'll understand if you don't want to come."

"I'll be there," I said.

The first Saturday in February was a gray day that promised an icy rain. We drove across the Levisa to Kentucky in Dillon's pickup truck. In the pale light, Dillon looked old. The skin of his face was rough, white and flaking in the cold air, and the muscles of his cheeks and neck had sagged into pouches.

We didn't talk for a long time, across the old iron bridge at Justice town into Kentucky, dodging the potholes on Pond Creek Road, over the twists of Johnnycake Mountain and down Marrowbone. Dillon asked for a cup of coffee, and I opened the red thermos he'd stuck under the seat.

He sniffed the white curls of rising steam, sipped a while, then said, "You hear from that Tom?"

"Last letter was about a month ago," I said. "He was pretty sick in September, one of those stomach amoebas that gives you diarrhea for days, but he says he's all right now. He moves around a lot in case the landowners come after him. He's got two banana cooperatives going and he's working with kids, too."

He'd enclosed a photo, Tom grinning at the camera, surrounded by excited dark-haired children waving their arms, turning to look at him and laugh, so much like we were long ago. I had taped the photo to my refrigerator.

"And you aint seeing nobody else?" Dillon asked.

"I told you before, if I meet somebody I like, and he likes me, I'll spend time with him. Until that happens, I do just fine on my own."

"Letters from Honduras won't keep you warm at night."

"Is that so? Since when did you start giving advice?"

"You're kin. I got a right."

"Yeah? What if I started bossing you about those trashy women from Justice town you sleep with?"

"What do you know about that?" he said.

"I hear. It's a small town, you know. You better watch yourself, Dillon, you'll get some social disease."

"Never you mind." He actually looked embarrassed. Then he said, "I don't mean to give you a hard time. I know how you feel about Tom. Maybe I understand how you feel better than you realize."

"Maybe you do," I said. "It's funny, when I was a kid, I used to think my father was the only person who had sex. I couldn't imagine my mother doing it with someone, or you either for that matter."

"Your mother raised you to think bad of it," he said.

"I know. I'm not sure why."

"She was in a bad marriage with Tony," he said, "and she was scared."

"Of what?"

He didn't answer.

"Well," I said, "I was always a little scared myself. Maybe because she was. It's like something I had nightmares about when I was little and I couldn't quite get rid of them. At least not until Tom. It was different with him. You know what I think? I used to be scared of my dad. I know it's not natural for a child, but I think I hated him. These last few years though, it's like I think of you as my dad, and that's different. I mean, I can even talk about sex with you."

I thought that would please him, but he frowned and didn't say anything.

"Dillon," I said, "were you ever in love?"

He changed the subject.

"I watched a TV show last week," he said, "on that public station. It was about moving graves. There's some old church in London where they used to bury people in the basement, and now they're moving the coffins so they can build something else. Funny how we think like a grave is a permanent thing. But I reckon there's nothing permanent, not even death."

"I'm not sure I want to hear about it," I said, feeling cross because he had brushed me off and brought up just what I didn't want to think about.

He ignored me. "They opened them coffins," he said. "Doing some scientific study. Three hundred years ago them people died. They showed on TV what the bodies looked like. Some was dry skeletons. Some still yet had the skin and hair on, all parched and shriveled, and the clothes stained. But most coffins just held this black liquid with the bones."

"Dillon, it's our own people we're—"

"You know what they called it? Body liquor. Aint that some way to think of it? Body liquor."

"Shut up!" I said fiercely.

"It was right on TV," he said. "Nobody alive knows them people, you see, so no one cares any more. Get far enough away from a death and it don't mean a thing."

"If you don't shut up," I said, "you can stop this truck right here and let me out. I'll thumb home."

"I'm just preparing you," he said.

But there was something in him that enjoyed it, that wanted to see those graves opened so he could set eyes once more on whatever remained to be seen. I shrank away from him, pressed against the truck door, and looked out the window.

We parked at the mouth of Scary Creek. A dirt road had been cut into the hillside past the Aunt Jane Place, but we walked the railroad track like we always did. Boulders the size of small houses had toppled down the mountain into the hollow behind the cemetery, and the slope above the hollow was littered with broken tree trunks and mud slides.

The road ran right up to the grave sites. Arthur Lee Sizemore and two other men waited beside a backhoe and a panel truck that would carry the caskets to the Justice Cemetery.

"Dillon," Arthur Lee said. "Jackie."

We didn't answer.

"This will all be done professional," Arthur Lee said. "I know you aint happy about this. I can't help that. The company needs this coal, and we done good by you here. Even got new coffins for the old graves, and we didn't spare no expense on the coffins neither. I'll treat these here graves like they're my own kin. Hell, one of them is."

"Get on with it," Dillon said.

Arthur Lee waved at the man with the backhoe and sidled over like he would stand and watch with us, but we moved away. He went to stand beside the truck instead.

My mother's grave was first. The men removed the marble head-stone, wrapped it in burlap and hoisted it into the back of the truck. Then the backhoe tore out the dirt alongside the grave. It was brown clay, moist and cold-looking. The backhoe operator was jabbing the blade, methodical and vigorous, like a hungry but self-controlled man going after his evening meal. The second man followed him with a shovel. Watching, I thought, there will be nothing there. My mother is not buried, she went off someplace years ago, and someday she will return or else I will go find her. Deep down, it was what I had believed all along. The harsh scraping of the shovel against metal proved me wrong. When they raised the casket, it was as though she had died a second time and I had just learned of it. I began to shake. Dillon stood perfectly still, his hands thrust deep in his coat pockets, but the muscle in his cheek twitched.

The coffin was smooth as new-buried, except for one corner that had rusted the color of dried blood. I glanced at Arthur Lee and saw he was weeping. I cursed him under my breath, a man who would cause himself such pain for the sake of money or pride. He took out a handkerchief and wiped his nose, stuck it back in his pocket, and took out a roll of masking tape and a black marking pen. He knelt beside the coffin, smoothed a strip of tape onto the end, and wrote RA-CHEL SIZEMORE in large black letters.

Dillon's thinning gray hair was plastered against his forehead by the winter dampness. His face was deeply lined and set in the clearest expression of hatred and longing I had ever seen. He stared at the dark hole in the ground, then at the coffin in the back of the truck, his body bent slightly forward as if he held himself back with great effort.

And watching him I knew there was something of his soul in me, something that disturbed me and yet I hungered for it. The backhoe gouged out the graves of my grandmother and grandfather; two more coffins came out of the musty ground, and as I saw all my people torn from the earth, I glimpsed something of the future as well and knew everything had come to an end with me, for I would never produce a child unless I met a man who disturbed me as Dillon did and there had been no one except Tom who could touch me that way.

The backhoe reached the edge of the cemetery and stopped at the grave of Rondal Lloyd, Dillon's father.

"That's one of the old graves," Arthur Lee said. He had composed himself and walked toward us again, as though he decided his presence was so offensive he would use it as a weapon. His voice held a hard edge. "Won't be nothing left of the pine boxes. That's what we brought these empty coffins for. Wait until you see this. It's real interesting, like what them archaeologists do."

He glanced at Dillon as though he expected an outburst, but Dillon ignored him. The backhoe dug alongside the grave as before but more slowly, with shallow, mincing bites. Suddenly a wide streak of dark brown, rich and coarse like a fallen tree limb that disintegrates beneath a pile of wet leaves, cut through the drab clay.

"There he is right yonder," Arthur Lee called over the engine noise. "Careful now."

The streak grew to a depth of three feet. The backhoe stopped and the man with the shovel carefully removed the heavy clay on top, uncovered more brown like a pile of damp coffee grounds.

"What is it?" I said.

"It's the coffin and the body," Dillon said. "What's left. They'll put the whole thing inside that empty coffin."

I took his hand and he squeezed mine so hard it felt like my fingers would crack. The backhoe scooped up a mouthful of the dark loam and swung round toward a coffin lying open on the ground. The soil fell in with a clatter, and spattered against the white satin lining. The backhoe swung around and dipped up more soil. Then Dillon cried "I see a hand!" and pulled me toward the grave. The backhoe operator glimpsed Dillon moving toward him and hit his brake too quickly.

The machine swayed. Some of the soil dropped into the coffin, but a portion of the mortal remains of Rondal Lloyd fell in a shower onto the ground. A skeletal hand landed beside a clump of spargrass.

Dillon said, "Goddamn, Arthur Lee, I'll kill you sonofabitch," and he grabbed Arthur Lee by the front of his jacket and dragged him to the ground.

"Let me go!" Arthur Lee screamed. "Leroy, help me!"

Dillon pushed Arthur Lee into a pile of dirt. Arthur Lee tried to stand up and Dillon pushed him back with his foot. Leroy grabbed at Dillon's arm but Dillon hit him in the mouth and he backed away. The man on the backhoe sat with his mouth open. Dillon picked up a shovel and began flinging the contents of his father's coffin at Arthur Lee.

Arthur Lee raised his arms while Dillon kept pelting him. "You're crazy!" he yelled. "You done scattered your daddy all over creation!"

Dillon flung down the shovel and leaped on top of Arthur Lee. He had Arthur Lee around the neck and tried to choke him. Then the two men pulled Dillon away. He kicked out but they were younger men and they pinned him to the ground.

Arthur Lee was clutching his throat and croaking, "I ought to have you up for attempted murder!"

"Do it!" Dillon screamed back.

"I'll get on the CB and call the goddamn state police right now!"

But Arthur Lee was so whipped out he just fell back against the pile of dirt and lay panting. Dillon quieted down too, and the men loosened their grip on him. He sat up. We were all silent and listened to the distant rush of the river, then I said, "Come on, Dillon. Let's go home."

He leaned forward and rested his head on his arms for a moment, catching his breath. Then he said, "It's yourn, Arthur Lee, land and bones," like he was tired to death. "Do what you want."

He got up slowly, stood at the end of the truck and looked inside. "Rachel," he said, "I wish I could carry you out of here myself, but you see how it is." Then he went down the road, walking stiffly, without looking back.

We didn't say a word until we got back to the truck. By then a cold, light rain was falling. Dillon turned suddenly, his face stricken.

"My daddy's hand! I left it lying!"

I touched his arm and he looked around. "I've got it," I said, "in my coat pocket."

I drew it out slowly, for it was brittle and the end of one finger had already fallen off. It lay in my own white palms and stained them with dirt.

I said, "You can take it to Winco bottom and bury it with the Japanese skull."

Dillon reached out and touched the thumb. "I was holding his thumb when he died," he said. He leaned against the truck and began to wail, a deep guttural sound that frightened me.

I pulled a bandana from his coat, carefully wrapped the hand in it and put it back in my own pocket. I put my arms around his shoulders.

"Get in the truck," I said. "Here, on the passenger side."

He didn't protest when I opened the door and helped him in, as though he were very old or a child, as though I was the strong one. I got in the driver's side and turned the key he'd left in the ignition. Grapevine Road was dark and wet. I took the curves slowly, pressed the button for windshield wiper fluid, banged on the dashboard to jog the balky heater.

Dillon slumped beside me.

"Do you recall," I said, "How you used to play that Civil War game with me when I was little? You were the only one who would play it with me."

After a moment, he said, "I recall."

"That's when I first started wishing you were my dad."

"Pull off the road," he said.

I swung the truck onto a wide shoulder at the crest of Johnnycake Mountain and turned off the ignition. We listened to the ticking of the engine.

"I am your daddy," Dillon said.

I held the steering wheel, felt the shock move up my arms. "How can that be?" I whispered.

"I should have told you a long time ago, but your mother was against it. Then there was a distance between us. And what it come down to, I wasn't sure for a long time. I thought you might be Tony's and I wasn't sure I'd want to claim you and it seemed best to let it all go to the grave with Rachel. I don't know if you can forgive me for that. I wouldn't forgive it if I was you. But I know you're mine. I see it in you more and more every day. I saw it in the way you held my daddy's hand."

Then he told me how he had pursued my mother, how she had resisted but finally given in, how they had loved one another and torn at one another for years before the final break. He told me about the red fox, and the top of Trace Mountain, and what happened there, of blowing up the bridge and how that drove them apart for good. While he spoke I studied his face and hated it and loved it and saw in it what I had been longing for all my life. The truck cab grew cold but we didn't turn on the engine. Dillon poured coffee into the thermos cup and we took turns sipping. Once in a while, I placed my hand over the bulge in my coat pocket to warm the bones.

WAITING FOR LECH
1988–1989

DILLON, 1988

I have been in a war and I have been in prison. A coal mine is like them both. You are always confined, always expecting a bullet to tear you open or a roof to fall.

I was raised on the stories of the old days. My mother told me how the coal companies came into the mountains and took our land, how our people died in the mines, or of illness or hunger, how they were beaten or shot for joining the union, how they froze in tents, even little children, when the companies turned them out of their houses.

I always expected coal would kill me, like it did my daddy and his daddy before him. But I never had an accident after the roof fall when I was a young man. And although I am short of breath when I climb, the black lung does not seem to bother me as much as it does some, those who suck in air as though their lungs are eating their breath.

Probably it is because I laid out all those years when the company had me on the blacklist. Now I am retired, and I am lucky because my child is a daughter who will not work in the mines. So it seems I have escaped.

But there is no rest. American Coal has been taken over by the International Oil Corporation and they have made Arthur Lee retire. They have laid everybody off, brought in new machines that rip and tear even bigger chunks of land, and hired nonunion miners to run them. I have had my notice in the mail, on the official American Coal stationery with the red, white, and blue stripes at one end and "A Member of the International Oil Family" in small gold letters in the right-hand corner, that says my medical benefits have been cut off. Louella Day has her widow's notice, and Betty Lloyd has hers.

So it is a strike, though no one here has looked for it. We have put up plywood picket shacks at Jenkinjones and Number Thirteen. We have nailed an American flag to the door frame beside a sign that says POLAND, WEST VIRGINIA.

Jackie is writing about this strike for her newspaper. Together we walk to the new cyclone fence the company has built between Number Thirteen and the tipple. Rolls of shiny barbed wire with sharp curved spurs hang over the fence top like metal vines. A man in a black uniform and sunglasses films us with a video camera from a new guard tower. Another man in black stands at the foot of the tower and watches us through binoculars.

The company has built a barracks inside the fence where the scabs sleep and eat their meals. The scabs are not from around here. They never come outside except to go into the mine. They must be poor men that they will be made prisoners willingly. The only way they can leave is if the company takes them out by helicopter. The helicopters fly low over the houses at Number Thirteen and the noise and vibrations make you feel your veins will pop out of your skin.

Jackie has a folder with her. She takes out a brochure and holds it up. The front says "Property Rights Defense Team. We defend your assets."

Jackie says, "That's the guards dressed in black."

She opens the brochure and reads, " 'Our trained personnel are equipped with M-16 rifles, grenade launchers, tear gas, and K-9 kennels. We have available, on request, an armored personnel vehicle.' "

"They're talking about a tank," she says. "And I've been doing research. Some of those guys have flown drugs from Columbia and guns to the Contras in Nicaragua. Some of them have prison records."

'That's okay,' I say. "I got a prison record too, and I aint afraid of this bunch."

She squints at me. "What are you saying?"

"I'm saying we'll handle this our own way."

"Times have changed, Dillon. I hear the union is going to use nonviolent civil disobedience."

I laugh.

"Times have changed," she says again.

"How? What's the difference between them bastards over there and the Baldwin-Felts gun thugs in my daddy's day? Bucky Collins up to Felco has sent his younguns to his brother in Ohio. You know why? Somebody drove by and shot out their front window. One bullet hit two foot above his little girl's bed."

The guard on the tower raises a bullhorn. He calls, "Get away from the fence."

"Bullhorns and video cameras," Jackie says. "They've even got an outfit that specializes in catering for scabs. That's what's different. They've gone slick, and everything they do looks good on the TV news. The union has got to go slick too."

"Get away from the fence!"

The bullhorn voice sounds like the man eats metal for nourishment. The guard on the ground is walking toward us. He carries a pistol on his hip.

"Can't you fucking hear?" he yells. "Get away from the goddamn fence!"

"I'm with the press," Jackie says. She pulls an ID card from her jeans pocket.

"I don't give a fuck who you are," the guard says.

"We're on our side of the fence," she says.

"That's still company land," the guard says. "Every fucking shack over there is on company land. Now get the hell away, bitch. You too, old man."

"Shut your goddamn mouth," I say.

He rests his hand on his gun butt. He has fleshy cheeks and bruised eyes under the bill of his black cap. Jackie steps back a few steps. She spreads her arms.

"Is this far enough?" she says. She takes two more steps. "Is this?"

The guard glares at her.

"Don't tell me where I can go!" she yells.

Then I see two more men walking our way, and a Bronco with dark tinted windows pulls out of a new building of corrugated steel. It is not like me to back away from a fight, but I'm terrified that all these men will have a close look at her. They drive the roads at night in their Broncos, three and four together.

"Let's go," I say.

She walks backward, hands on hips, then turns abruptly and follows me. "Sons of bitches," she says. "They treat us like we're some kind of subversive."

I say, "We are."

We hold meetings in the union hall up at Raven. I hate to drive there. The company has put up floodlights on both sides of the creek so that the tipple on the far bank shines white as a fairy castle at night, and Lloyds Fork Road is lit brighter than a football game. The inside of my truck flashes from pitch dark to white to pitch dark again in a matter of seconds, and I guess my picture is taken in that bright second. I raise my middle finger in front of my face whenever I pass.

I am not the president of the local anymore, it is a boy from Daisy Creek, but they look to me for advice. I don't say much. I am still trying to figure out the nonviolent civil disobedience. The boys at the meetings say it like it is one long word and I know they haven't got it nailed either. It is what Martin Luther King did, and some say it is the Christian way to do. But Martin Luther King was killed dead like Jesus was. The union says we must use it or the newspapers and the

TV will call us violent. But Phil Vivanti has already been on the CBS News and called the strike violent because we have flattened the tires of scab coal trucks with nails that Junior Tackett welds together in his tool shed. I have never yet seen a truck tire bleed red blood, but the TV news will weep over ruined rubber. Or they will not notice us at all.

Doyle Ray Lloyd is driving scab, running his truck named HELL-FIGHTER across the picket lines every day with coal from the Trace Mountain strip job. He is the only local boy crossing the picket line. I hear the talk, that we should rock his trailer, that we should crack the windshield of HELLFIGHTER or cut the brake lines. I decide to talk to him because Doyle Ray is kin—his Papaw and my daddy were brothers.

In the evening I climb Doyle Ray's cinderblock steps and knock on the metal door. It is a double wide trailer. Between what he makes driving and the extra he gets from his preaching, Doyle Ray is doing all right. He could probably afford to build a house, but the company still owns all the land hereabouts and they will not often let you build. With a trailer, if the company wants you gone, you can move quick enough.

Doyle Ray doesn't say a word when he opens the door, just stands back and lets me in. I haven't been in the trailer much. Neither has anyone. The narrow living room is tidy. I sit on a brown plaid sofa. The walls are fake wood. A large flat cross and a picture of Jesus hang on one wall. Another wall holds a hen and a rooster made of different kinds of dried corn and beans. Doyle Ray's wife Sandra and the two boys are watching television. She is a small woman with wispy brown hair and teeth that stick out a little ways.

"Hey, Dillon," she says, but she doesn't smile.

I nod toward the chickens. "That's real pretty. You make them yourself?"

That brings a smile.

"I glued on every piece," she says, and starts to tell me how she drew the patterns out of a magazine and painted on the shellac to make the chickens shine. It is not something I am interested in, but I can listen polite as anyone.

"Go to the kitchen, honey," Doyle Ray says, "and take the kids."

"Aw, Daddy," says the oldest boy.

"Ronnie!" says Doyle Ray, sharp. They go into the kitchen without another word. I think how Jackie would act if a man ordered her out of a room, or even how Rachel would have carried on, and smile to myself. Doyle Ray is looking at the TV. Pat Robertson is on, talking about the Communists taking over Central America.

"This is serious," I say.

"I reckoned," Doyle Ray says, and turns down the sound, but Pat Robertson is still on, the camera never goes off him so I look away.

"There's a strike on," I say.

He doesn't answer, just watches the TV like he can read lips.

"I know we aint had much to say to each other all these years. We gone our own ways. You're a preacher, and I aint one for church. You drive nonunion. But your papaw was brother to my daddy. We're kin. There was a time when kin counted for something in these mountains."

"I aint joining no strike," Doyle Ray says. "I got younguns to feed."

"So does everybody. The boys draw eight hundred a month from the union, strike benefits, and that won't last. Aint much when you got kids."

"That's more than I'd have if I quit driving."

"You could drive independent. Or I got a buddy has a union outfit on Island Creek, hauling for union mines in Logan County. He says they'll take you on, and that is a big favor to me because you know how jobs are. Only thing, you'll have to drive farther to get there."

"If I'd wanted to drive union, I'd have got on union when I first started."

Then I see where we are going and that it will do no good to talk, but I have a need to try.

"What's wrong with union?" I ask.

"They're resisting the authority God set over them. They got no right to tell the company how to spend its money or tell a man whether he can work or not. It's communistic. God give the authority to the company."

I say, "Doyle Ray, you are letting them ride you for a mule. It's plain stupid."

He leans forward with his knees spread apart and his hands clasped in front of him.

"Is that all you come to say?"

"No. I come to warn you to watch out for yourself. When a man gets desperate, he might rock your trailer, or tamper with your truck. If I hear anybody talking against you, I'll try and warn you, but I may not hear."

He looks at me for the first time.

"Why you telling me that?" he says.

"Same as I said earlier. You're kin."

"Kin," he says. "You know something? When I was a youngun, I worshiped you. My daddy was a drunk, but everybody on Blackberry Creek looked up to you. When you blowed that bridge, I thought it was the greatest thing in the world. I wished you was my daddy."

"Oh no," I say.

"Wished you was my daddy and wished he wasn't. Wished he was dead sometimes, when he beat me. Did you know he beat me? Know he beat Brenda? I reckoned you didn't or you would have done something about it."

"I knew he took a strap to you," I say. "Most men whip their younguns now and again."

"Spare the rod and spoil the child," he says. "That's in the Bible, and I believe it. But he whipped hard. Didn't you know that? I reckoned you didn't and when you went to jail I knew you couldn't help no way. It was up to me. And I looked at what you done and I thought, Dillon aint afraid of nothing and I aint neither. Dillon fights back and I will too. And I shot—"

His breath hitches on him and he stops. Then he hollers, "Don't you tell me about kin! My kin is Jesus! Jesus says you will call no one father except God! Jesus says if you put your kin before God you are not fit to enter Heaven! Jesus says—"

Sandra runs into the room, says, "Honey?"

Doyle Ray stops dead. "You better leave," he says.

He walks to the door and opens it. When I go out I nearly fall down the wobbly cinderblock steps, and he slams the thin trailer door behind me.

This will be a long strike. It may have no ending. Families will keep on drifting away as they have these thirty years. They will come back to visit. Already I see them on the weekends. They say the companies in North Carolina or Tennessee where they have gone tell a fellow when to take a crap and the boys down there just sit back and take it. They say it's not the same as home, and they can't stay away from the mountains. I have heard of people in South America, religious fanatics, who cut themselves and whip themselves until they bleed and even nail their hands to boards. I think the boys who leave are like that, returning to the place that is no longer home, coming back again and again until they are cut and bleeding and the pain of loss is all that binds them to these hills. Those of us who stay are like that too, holding on to what wounds us like picking up ground glass.

Some day there will be nothing left. Kin will die, the mountains will be ground down to dust. Wooden coal camp houses were not built to last the ages.

HASSEL, 1988

Brenda thinks her brother Doyle Ray's coal truck is in love with the Batmobile. You cannot explain to her that cars and trucks don't have no feelings. When we go to where the cars is parked in Winco bottom, she sees HELLFIGHTER setting beside Doyle Ray's trailer. Doyle Ray tilts the truck bed back to keep the water from collecting, and HELLFIGHTER looks like an elephant on Wild Kingdom about to mount the Batmobile, which is usually parked nearby. After Brenda married Toejam she learned about such things. Now when she sees the Batmobile and HELLFIGHTER, she rears back and hollers, "Wuv! Wuv!"

The Batmobile is an old car. If it was a person I reckon it'd be over a hundred. I was ready to turn it into scrap metal years ago, but Louelly wouldn't hear of it because it was Homer's car. She thinks the Batmobile is blessed. Once her and Ethel's Tiffany was near killed in it. A pickup truck come round a curve at them and Louelly slammed on the brakes. That there truck just grazed the car door before it flipped into the creek and the driver, a drunk fellow from Jolo, died. I put up a white wooden cross on the spot beside the road, and Louelly painted a red cross over the scratch on the Batmobile's door.

So I got Junior to overhaul the engine one more time, as a wedding present for Toejam and Brenda. For his own wedding present, Junior wired the inside with four horns. That way anybody setting in that car can honk at someone they know when they ride up and down the creek. The button on Brenda's horn is red, and when she pushes it the horn plays "Raindrops Keep Falling on My Head."

The scab trucks has been hauling the coal out of the hollow every day, just like they done back in the sixties. I have an idea that we should block Lloyds Fork road with our cars. I don't mean to brag, but I can think up plenty to do for this here nonviolent civil disobedience. If Martin Luther King was alive, he'd be glad to know me.

So we meet in Winco bottom like in the old days of the Roving Pickets, only now Doyle Ray's trailer sets there instead of Dillon's house, and Sandra Lloyd watches us from the porch with her face all drawed up like we are some kind of varmints. I can't stand to look at her, she's so sour. Doyle Ray is on the road, but he will be coming through, hauling a load in HELLFIGHTER.

We drive up the main highway below the golf course, take Lloyds Fork off to the right, and then stop. We fill up both lanes and leave spaces so cars can go back and forth slow-like between where we parked, but the coal trucks will not have room to come through. I stand at one end of the line with a red flag to direct traffic, and Junior stands at the other end.

Ten minutes later, a line of coal trucks arrives. The Property

Rights boys lead the way in them Broncos with the dark windows. But they stop when they see the trucks can't follow them and pull off the road. The men in black get out and stand in a bunch. One of them has got a telephone, and I reckon they are calling the state police, but it will take a heap of wreckers to move us and jail cells to hold us. Twenty coal trucks set with their engines idling, shaking and grumbling while them drivers get impatient and stamp their gas pedals. The drivers stick their heads out their windows and cuss, except for the truck in front, which is HELLFIGHTER. Doyle Ray Lloyd will die before he will cuss.

I am standing with Louella and Toejam beside the Batmobile. They have stuck a sign on Brenda's wheelchair that says American Coal Stole My Medical Benefits. The Batmobile is the first car in line. Its flat black paint does not catch the early morning sun but it is a wide old car, and with its high back fins it looks like a wild creature out of one of them Saturday afternoon Japanese movies on TV. Louella has wiped the bumpers clean of mud and coal dust, and GOD IS LOVE stands out red and clear.

Brenda wants to blow her horn. Toejam holds her in the open door and she stabs the red button twice with her finger. After "Raindrops Keep Falling on My Head," Toejam carries her to a pile of railroad ties beside the road and holds her on his lap. I am thinking Doyle Ray must see his sister there, her head limp on Toejam's shoulder as she stares at the car and smiles. Perhaps the sight will make him turn around.

Then Dillon Freeman walks over to HELLFIGHTER. He stands up on the running board and holds the side mirror. Some boys from Jenkinjones see them and think Dillon is giving Doyle Ray a hard time. They move closer, waving their arms and yelling *Scabbie Scabbie Scabbie*. A spray of tobacco juice covers Doyle Ray's windshield like old blood and runs down over the wipers. Then a rock hits the windshield.

Doyle Ray has been leaning out the window, talking to Dillon, but he starts back and hollers "Lord!" when that rock hits the glass. HELLFIGHTER gives a big lurch forward and keeps going. Dillon jumps down just in time and lands hard in the gravel beside the road.

Doyle Ray has the door half open and yells, "The brakes is gone!" and the front wheels twist around. One tire lifts off the ground and the truck spins like some big awkward animal. Then HELL-FIGHTER settles with a big crunch on top of the Batmobile. The car's roof collapses and that windshield crumples like white crepe paper. HELLFIGHTER blunders on into a red pickup truck, dragging the Batmobile and crushing it under its tires.

After HELLFIGHTER comes to rest, everything gets real quiet. Then Brenda, setting in Toejam's lap beside the road, starts in to scream. Doyle Ray has hit his face on HELLFIGHTER's door and is slumped over the steering wheel. When we haul him out, he is unconscious and the blood runs from his smashed mouth. An ambulance comes from Annadel and takes him to the Grace Hospital.

Doyle Ray has what they call a broken mandible and all his front teeth are gone. His jaw is wired shut and his face looks like the laced side of a football. I go to his trailer to ask how he is doing and that Sandra shuts the door right in my face.

And Brenda is so upset she won't say a word, not "wuv" nor "hi."

JACKIE, 1989

One night Ethel Day was on picket duty at the shack outside Number Thirteen tipple when there came the sharp whine of a bullet and her hand resting on the door frame opened up like hot melting wax. Ethel saw the taillights of a Bronco vanish around the curve before she fainted. Junior Tackett found her there when he stopped to bring her a thermos of coffee. He wrapped her hand in a red bandana and drove her to the hospital where the doctors picked out the splinters of metal and wood, and formed tendon and bone into an unyielding claw.

Junior called me at three in the morning. I grabbed a camera and flash and drove to the picket shack. It was still several hours before dawn and no one was around. Night creatures keened high up on Trace, as though the mountain itself was alive and lamenting. I took pictures, then drove slowly back toward Felco, lightheaded from want of sleep. A vehicle with high bright headlights pulled in close behind me. I speeded up a little but the headlights stayed with me. At a wide place below Felco I pulled off the road. In the same instant I saw the vehicle was a black Bronco and it was pulling off the road behind me. I pumped the accelerator and pulled onto the road at full speed, rear end skipping back and forth as my tires caught the rough edge of the pavement. The Bronco followed.

I flipped my rearview mirror to dim, taking some small comfort at reducing the relentless lights to pinpricks, and tried to think. It seemed best to go on home. They probably knew who I was and where I lived, so there was no use playing games. My neighbors at Felco had dogs, some were light sleepers, and many of them had guns. I would be safest among them.

I passed the boarded up Exxon station, pulled into my street, and sat with my motor running and my lights turned off. The Bronco sat behind me, its lights still on. Minutes passed in the glow of my dashboard clock. Then a porch light came on at the last house in Colored Row, and a man stepped out wearing a housecoat and holding something in his hand. I turned off the ignition, got out, and walked toward the Bronco to show I wasn't intimidated. Out of the corner of my eye I saw Sim Gore walking down his front steps with a pistol. The Bronco pulled away from the curb, gunned its motor, and sped away.

Hassel showed up in my office with two CoColas from the lunchroom down the street. He set one Coke on my desk.

"You heard the news?" he said. "Lech Walesa's coming."

I sat up straight. "Here?"

"That's right. One of Dillon's buddies called from the union in Charleston. He's coming to support the strike. Won't that be something?"

I knew Walesa was on his way to the United States, hoping to get aid for Poland now that the Communists were on their way out.

"When?" I said.

"Supposed to be Wednesday," Hassel said. "That gives us five days to tidy things up. And we got to figure out what to do with him when he gets here. Wouldn't hurt to find somebody who talks that Polish."

"Don't you think he'll bring his own interpreter?"

"Sure, but it would be neighborly if we had somebody here too."

I smiled. "You wouldn't be wanting somebody who could ask him about bridges, would you?"

"I thought on it," Hassel said. "But I don't reckon Lech Walesa's got any money. That's why he's coming here, aint it? I hope he does better with that President Bush than I did."

I knew Hassel had sent a letter to the President and asked for help building a bridge.

"So you heard back?" I said.

"Oh yeah, last week." He opened his wallet and took out a folded piece of paper. He read,

> Dear Young Friend,
> Thanks for taking the time to write and share your kind thoughts with me. I appreciate your warm words of friendship.
> It's a wonderful privilege to be in the White House. You can be certain as I begin my first term that I'll try my darndest to live up to what you expect of me as president.
> I treasure your thoughtfulness and wish you all the very best.
> Sincerely,
> George Bush

"They didn't even care enough to push the right computer button," said Hassel, "but I'm saving this anyhow. That signature might be worth something some day."

"It's done by machine too," I said.

"Oh." He looked at the letter a moment, then dropped it in the trash can. "Maybe if Lech Walesa gets money from somewhere, he can give me some pointers. You know who I wish was here to help talk to him is Tom. Aint he Polish, and don't I recall he can speak a few words of it?"

"Yes," I said. "I don't think he speaks it very well." I looked out the window.

"Damn, I miss him," said Hassel. "It's been three years now. They ought to let him come back."

"Sorry, Hassel. I don't think the Jesuits would send him all the way from Honduras just to translate for you."

"I reckon not," he said.

There was a strangely cheerful note in his voice. I said, "Hassel, you don't know something, do you?"

"Know what?" he said.

"You haven't heard from Tom?"

"Naw. I aint never heard from nobody in a foreign country in my entire life."

On Wednesday morning, everyone was working hard to get ready for Lech Walesa's visit. The Dew Drop Inn had been closed six months for lack of business and the little building was in bad shape—the concrete floor streaked with coal dust and damp where the corners leaked, the psychedelic light pulled loose and dangling from the water-stained ceiling like a ball of old tin foil. Boxes of pipes and wire were stacked behind the bar where Junior Tackett had stripped the building of old fixtures to sell for scrap.

But people were cleaning up, scrubbing the floor, tearing the black shutters off the windows so the light could come in, stringing red and white crepe paper all over everything. They hung a SOLIDAR-NOSC banner across the back wall, set up tables and folding chairs from the Holiness church to hold the fried chicken and links of Polish sausage and sauerkraut and potato salad and rows of little waxed cups filled with melting ice.

I was beginning to worry. The *New York Times* had arrived at the newspaper office with Walesa's schedule. He was to address Congress on Tuesday and receive an award at the Kennedy Center on Wednesday night. I showed the article to Dillon.

"That doesn't leave much time for the coalfields," I said.

"No," Dillon agreed, "but he could get here by helicopter easy enough. I talked to the union in Washington and they still hear that he's coming. But they did say there's pressure on him not to because it would make the American government look bad."

I went on about my own task, which was to take flowers to the old cemetery at Number Ten. It was the cemetery I used to see when I visited my Italian grandmother years earlier, or rather the woman I thought was my grandmother, the cemetery where the Italians and Russians and Poles had been buried long ago. The graves had been neglected for years and you could barely see the stones at all for the weeds. But Dillon thought it would be a good place to take Lech Walesa, to let him lay a wreath on the grave of a Polish coal miner. He had spent the weekend clearing the weeds. I helped him on Sunday afternoon, watched him move slowly, head down and back curved, while he traced the edges of the old stone fence with a gas-powered weed cutter. It was autumn and the air was crisp, smelled of dry leaves and mud.

I drove to the florist in Justice town and back to Number Ten with my car seat filled with orange and red marigolds, past the shells of abandoned company stores, boarded up schools, the foundations of houses peeping through sheafs of sawgrass. I passed the church with the gold-leaf dome that had once been Orthodox but now housed the Abyssinian Baptist Spirit-Filled congregation and might soon close because the Baptists were also dwindling.

At Number Ten I parked on the dirt road beside the cemetery, climbed the broken stone fence, and wandered among the graves with my arms full of flowers. I picked up a piece of broken bottle we'd missed and tossed it aside, then laid flowers, stems laced together, beside several Russian markers engraved in Cyrillic. Next were two inscriptions in what I guessed was Polish. A glass oval was set at the center of each stone. One oval was smashed, as though someone had pounded it with a rock, the thick glass crushed white and shot through with lined shards. Beneath the second oval was the copper-brown photograph of a sturdy woman in peasant dress, her hair pulled severely back from her face.

"Need an interpreter?" a voice asked from the road.

I turned. Tom stood beside my car. He climbed the fence and walked toward me, caught me up in his arms, and swung me around.

"I stopped in Justice and called Hassel. He told me you were here, and he hopes you aren't mad at us for keeping this a secret. It was pretty sudden anyway."

I kissed him for answer. "I can't believe it! Let me look at you. God, you look wonderful!"

"You been getting my letters? I sure do look forward to yours. And the kids love the books you sent."

"I'm glad. How did you get away?"

"My mother was really sick for a while, and she just died," he said. "I came back for her last few days and I did the funeral."

"Oh, Tom, I'm sorry."

"Me too. I've got her to grieve for, and mostly I miss what we never had. But her liver was shot. She told me she was ready to go and I was with her when she died."

We walked together, arms around each other's waist.

"I started to call you first thing when I got back to the States, but the Jesuits decided I should go on a tour of parishes since I'd be here anyway. We're raising money for a new school and medical clinic. So I asked if I could add some leave time onto that. I wanted to surprise you."

"But Hassel knew, that rat!"

"I called Hassel to make sure you'd be around."

"How long can you stay?"

"Just a week to start. Then I have to leave, but I'll be driving back and forth across the country and I'll have lots of chances to stop in. Plus I'll spend Christmas and New Year's here, and I'll be here the whole month of February and part of March."

Crows yawed far up the mountainside and a brisk wind ran through the leaves at our feet. I took Tom's hand and led him back to the grave with the photograph.

"Tell me what it says."

He leaned over and studied the grave, wiped the glass oval with a red bandana handkerchief.

"Kielce," he said. He straightened and sighed.

"Kielce?"

"It's where they came from, in the south of Poland. This woman died young. Her husband too—the stone says the roof fell in the mine."

We walked some more and Tom translated—beloved daughter—lost in the Great War—taken in the mines—St. Kazimierz—beloved, beloved.

"My Polish is rusty," Tom said. "I'm having enough trouble getting back into English. I haven't used Polish since my dad died and that's a hell of a long time ago."

"You'd better practice up. Lech Walesa's coming."

"Uh-oh," he said.

"What?"

"When I called Hassel this morning, he said they just got the word from Washington. Looks like Walesa's not coming after all. Sounded like everyone was pretty disappointed. I guess I'm the only visiting Polak you'll get today."

"I'd rather have you," I said.

He put his arms around me and held me close. "I've missed the hell out of you," he said.

He followed me in his car to Winco bottom and we walked the track together. We met a television crew from Bluefield, hauling their equipment back down the railroad track, cursing and scowling. At Number Thirteen, people milled around in the October sunshine. Hassel's old band had been playing but they were starting to take down their sound system. Everyone looked glum.

But Toejam was the first to spy Tom and cried "Well lookee here!" Soon everyone was crowding around, shaking hands and hugging and talking loud. Then we picked up our plates and stood in line for Polish sausage and sauerkraut, and the band decided to set back up and play a polka.

Tom and I sat on the steps of the Holiness church on the hill. The floodlights at the tipple beyond Number Thirteen made the enclosure look like a baseball field lit for a night game, and the black-uniformed guards patrolling the fence could have been umpires. The full moon was just out of reach beyond lower Trace.

Tom said, "Hassel's getting old. It's funny, I never thought it would happen to him. But his hair's almost gray."

"You've got a few gray hairs yourself," I said.

"Yeah, but Hassel, Jesus. He's somebody you think will be young forever."

I said, "I don't know what will happen to Hassel now that he's closed the Dew Drop. All the Days have coming in is Louella's Social Security and a little pension."

"Hassel will figure out something. He always does."

"I can't see Hassel leaving, that's for sure."

"What about you?" he asked. "Are you staying?"

"I hadn't planned on going anywhere. Why?"

"Because this place is dying, Jackie. Every time I come back it's more clear. I just wonder how long you'll hold on, that's all. I wonder what there is here for you."

"You live in a tough place, too," I said. "You of all people should understand me staying. It's my home."

"I know that. But I keep thinking if you went away you'd have a better chance of meeting somebody, making a new life with somebody."

"I'm fine," I said. "Besides, Dillon's here."

"Yeah. I about fainted when I got your letter that said he's your dad."

"You and me both."

He put his arm around me and pulled me close.

I said, "When he told me, the first thing I thought of was to tell you."

"I'm glad." He nudged my knee with his. "There are things I want to say to you, things I couldn't say in a letter because I'm afraid I wouldn't be clear. I still don't want you to pin any hopes on me."

"Say them," I said. "I don't have any hopes you'll leave the priesthood, if that's what you mean. I wouldn't want it. I can tell it won't happen by looking at the pictures you send from Honduras and studying your face. And if I fall in love with someone else, I won't hold back. I'm learning I've got enough love for lots of people."

"Good. Because I wanted to say that I do love you, that I think about you a lot, and when things get tough, I feel you with me. I remember when we made love. It carries me through. And it would be the same if you were with somebody else."

"I already knew that, but it helps to hear it."

"I do get time off now and then. I don't have the money to travel far, but we could meet somewhere safe, in Managua or Costa Rica. Will you come down?"

I leaned back and smiled at him. "I'd like that."

"Promise?"

"Promise. Now I've got a question. Where are you staying?"

"I figured I'd stay at Hassel's."

"Except Hassel would never tell you this, but you'll be running off Junior Tackett if you stay there. He'll have to go back to his mother's."

"Oh, are they still together? Hell, I don't want to bother them."

"I've got a guest bedroom," I said. "And I'm clear on all the ground rules. Besides, it might be good if I had a man around sometimes. I think those company guards are watching me."

"Actually," he said, "I'd like to stay at your place. I'd like that a lot."

The light was on in Dillon's trailer, and we stopped to say good night. He had the television on and a can of beer in his hand. When Tom left us to go to the bathroom, Dillon nodded after him and said, "So, is he planning on staying a priest?"

"Of course he is. Now you stop matchmaking right this minute."

"Never mind," he said. "The one you catch is the one that bores the hell out of you anyway."

He glared at the TV. Lech Walesa was at a concert in the Kennedy Center, wearing a tuxedo and sitting with George Bush.

"See there," Dillon said. He flipped the channel and opened a beer for me.

TILL HUMAN VOICES
WAKE US
1990

DILLON

Last week it turned cold sudden, and snowed. Then it rained for two days and melted the snow. There was one day that showed a blue sky, then rain again. In the morning when it is coldest the sky will spit snow but that will melt by ten or so. It is heavy February weather, thick with clouds come pressing down to earth. The mountains are slate gray and they throw off wisps of smoke. The ground is black and churned up like dark chocolate.

I keep awake, thinking about that bone dam at the head of the hollow. I have been twice to check on it. The first time the water was high. The rain was falling so hard it seemed to spark and fizz when it hit the flat black water. I looked around for Arthur Lee's measuring stick and couldn't see it anywhere, so I found a long branch and stuck it in the edge of the bone.

I went back when the rain commenced again. I just had time to see that the water had come five foot up on my branch when a gun thug in his black uniform found me. The strike is dragging on with nothing happening, and the gun thugs are still yet guarding the Jenkinjones tipple.

"What you doing up here?" the gun thug demanded.

He had pulled up in one of them Broncos and his partner sitting in the passenger seat showed me his gun, like I didn't already know it was there.

"I'm checking on this here dam," I said. "It's got nothing to do with the strike."

"Hell it don't. This is company property and you're trespassing."

"Everything on this hollow is company property," I said. "Now I am here looking at this water rising because we got a hollow full of people living below this dam."

"I got my orders," said the gun thug, "and they are to keep anybody away except the legal number of pickets allowed up at that tipple. Now get on off, grandpa, before I have to get rough."

I drove home and tried to think what to do. I started to call Arthur Lee, but he has got no say any more. I wasn't even sure he'd be sober when I called because I heard tell he laid drunk all the time since he retired. Finally I called Jackie. She run an article that said Residents Nervous About Slate Dam. The union said the company should do something, and American Coal sent out a press release saying the dam is safe and the union is trying to harass the company.

So I am lying awake again tonight and the rain so hard it is like hammers beating on my trailer roof. Somewhere around three I drift off to sleep, but I dream and the dam looms over me and crumbles before my eyes and I wake up and hear the rain pounding hard on my trailer roof and my heart racing to beat it. I look at my clock and it is six o'clock of a Saturday morning.

I dial Arthur Lee's number on the telephone. When he answers I say, "Arthur Lee, it's Dillon Freeman. I'm calling about the bone dam. I know you aint with the company no more but maybe they'll listen to you. Something's wrong, I know it is, I can feel it."

"Dillon, you sonofabitch, do you know what time it is?"

"The company aint looking after it, Arthur Lee."

"What the hell you telling me that for?"

The receiver clicks in my ear. I cuss softly, "Goddamn bastard that can't be woke up for something this important." Then it hits me that Arthur Lee wasn't asleep and he wasn't drunk. He had answered the phone quick and his voice was clear and alert. Arthur Lee knows what I know.

I call Jackie. She takes a while to answer and her voice is sleepy.

"It's the dam," I say. "I had a dream. There's something wrong and I'm going to check."

She says, "Should me and Tom come?"

"No. But y'all get dressed and get ready to run."

"It's probably all right," she says. "The guards are up there and the pickets. They'll notice if it's looking bad."

"It's dark," I say. "There aint no time for talk. I'm going."

I pull on my trousers and shirt over my longjohns, and my leather jacket that Jackie gave me for Christmas, and walk the track to Winco. Rain pelts my head and shoulders. The vinyl seat of my truck is so cold it freezes me through all the layers, and I shiver until the heater starts to work. The hollow is dark, hardly a house shows a light. People will sleep late on Saturday. I lean forward, squinting to see past the rain and the whipping of the windshield wipers. I wish to God I had a thermos of coffee with me.

At Jenkinjones I stop at Sim's to warn him, then I recall he has been living with his son at Felco since his wife passed away. I leave the houses behind, turn off my headlights, and drive slow so the gun thugs won't see what I'm up to. I park near the ruin of the company store where the road climbs the hill to the tipple. The tipple and fence are lit with floodlights like at Number Thirteen, and the picket shack is a shadow outside the gate.

In the hollow it is still dark. The rain has slowed. I switch on my flashlight. The path up the side of the hill is muddy and pulls at my feet. At the top I stop to listen. A low moan swells from the water—it is the tormented spirit of Trace Mountain torn apart. I hear voices in the moan and I step toward them on the dam.

My leg sinks to the ankle.

I take another step and go in to my knee.

The water sighs. Above me there is no sound.

Then I hear a motor far off. I struggle back to the mountain, my legs coated with sludge and aching from the cold. I slip and fall on the path down the mountain and bang my left knee. When I finally limp to my truck, a gray dawn is lighting the hollow. A Cadillac pulls in beside my truck and a man gets out.

"What the hell!" he says.

"Arthur Lee!" I grab him by the coat. "That dam's gone soft!"

"Soft?" He is looking up at the dam.

"Get in your car and drive like hell to let people know," I say. "It's all there's time to do."

He is still looking at the dam. He pushes me away and starts up the path.

I yell, "If you go up you'll not come back down!"

He hesitates. I jump in my truck and start the engine. Then, comes a rumble. Arthur Lee is running back toward his car and I don't dare wait longer, I have people to save, but Arthur Lee will not make his car, so I drive close to him and he wrenches open the truck door and climbs in.

"Drive!" he yells and I head for the turn, tires screaming through the gravel but I stop before I round the curve and roll down the window of my truck. Arthur Lee quits yelling and we stare.

The bone dam looms black and high as the mountain. Despite the wet, smoke rises from the base where the bone still burns, has burned for generations. A curl of water laps the top and runs like a tear down the front of the dam then the center of the bone pile sags and melts.

The water waits

Then the dull boom when the lake touches the fiery slate and a gray cloud swells, rises far up the mountain, another explosion and another and the rising cloud sweeps away the picket shack and the tipple fence before it falls to earth a whirlpool licks across the bottom, rips out a large electrical transformer

flames shoot to the top of Trace Mountain   the sky crackles

I push the accelerator to the floor and drive.

Arthur Lee is holding onto the dashboard his head bent almost to his hands.

"Jesus God," he says, "Jesus God Jesus God."

I blow my horn through Jenkinjones, but I will not stop for I cannot save them all and I will choose who.

At Annadel I pull up to the pay phone in front of the grocery store and jump out with the coin already in my hand.

I drop in the quarter but the line is dead.

Arthur Lee is out of the truck.

"I'll go on foot from here," he yells.

I say, "You'll never make it."

"Goddamn you to hell," he says, "they are my people too."

He is trotting as fast as an old man can trot toward the fire station, and as I drive the highway below Spencers Curve, the wail of the siren follows me.

———————————————————————

JACKIE

Tom and I are sitting at the kitchen table drinking coffee and wondering if we should be worried when the light goes out and the refrigerator stops humming. The clock on the stove shows 8:01 in the winter morning gloom. The second hand doesn't move.

Tom says, "Maybe we should call the sheriff's office."

He picks up the telephone but sets it back again. He says, "The line's dead."

We put our coats on and go out on the porch. From far up the hollow we hear distant thunder, then an eerie singing sound.

HASSEL

I always get up early, even on a Saturday. It is the way I get things done. So does Louelly. She says she can't sleep in after all them years of getting up at five to get Homer ready for the mines.

A body couldn't sleep this morning no way, what with every dog in Number Thirteen cutting such a shine. They are howling and barking and the ones penned up are pulling on their chains. But while me and Junior are walking toward Louelly's, they stop all at once. It is the blamedest thing I ever did hear.

When we get to Louelly's, Toejam's dog Blue is whining and trying to dig a hole to get under the house. Then we open the front door. I smell the bacon and eggs frying.

ARTHUR LEE

Got a stitch in my side from running and I can't get my breath. My ears are pounding. And I still hear the roar, still I hear it.

Most of the houses in Annadel are on the hillside and I won't get to them. A few people have come on their porches to see what the siren is about. They will think it is a fire up the hollow somewhere. They will turn over in bed and go back to sleep. I want to holler and tell them but I got no air. No air.

I run again, toward Spencers Curve in the bottom.

There is the Church of God. I start to pass it by when I notice the car parked outside. Up the steps and pound on the door. It's a little boy opens it. Doyle Ray Lloyd and his wife are standing in the middle of the aisle with a mop and broom.

Got no air.

"Mr. Sizemore?" says Doyle Ray. "Are you all right?"

"What the hell—got no—what you doing here?"

"This is the Lord's house," he says. "I'd appreciate if you didn't cuss."

"Go home. Get out of here."

"We always clean the church on Saturdays," says that woman. His wife.

Got no air. I turn and point outside. Then they hear it. Doyle Ray comes to the door and looks and the ocean busts around Spencers Curve a wall higher than the telephone poles, and Doyle Ray has a boy in his arms and the woman has another boy and Doyle Ray says "Children, pray to Jesus."

The ground shakes and I am down on my knees never in a church since I got married I try to recall my wife's name and I can't think of it but that Tommie she was little and mean as fire and God I loved her

DILLON

I am behind a slow driver and there are only curves ahead but I pass anyway, honk my horn and pull crossways in the road, yell a warning, and go on. I am driving faster than the water is moving. I sense that, can feel the power grow fainter behind me, and the air is very still, waiting.

At Felco I stop at the first house and pound the door. A little girl in pajamas answers and I see the cartoons on the TV in the living room. "Who is it?" a woman calls from the bedroom. I say, "Get everybody out, the dam has broke," and I leave before I can see what they will do.

I am back in the truck and I don't stop until I reach Jackie's house. She and Tom are standing on her front porch.

I yell, "It's broke."

"God help us!" Jackie cries. She looks old, older than her mother ever did.

Tom grabs my arm. "When?"

"Right after I got there. No time to talk. Jackie, you go up and down this street and knock on doors. When you hear it coming, you climb that mountainside."

"I'll get Colored Row, too," she says.

I grab her shoulders.

"Go wherever, but you climb when you hear it!"

I push her away.

Tom is already in his car. "I'll warn lower Felco," he says, "and if there's time I'll go farther."

I head for my truck. Jackie is already going down the road. She stops but I wave her on.

"I love you both," she calls.

I watch her in my rearview mirror as I drive away. She is running up the steps of a house when I lose sight of her.

T o m

I have reached the end of lower Felco, still knocking on doors, when I hear the thunder and I see the water. It caroms up one side of the hollow, then the other, as though the earth were tilting back and forth. I run for the hillside and climb.

Pieces of buildings are riding the waves, the houses of upper Felco jumbled together like a herd of elephants, jostling, disappearing beneath the roaring surf and reappearing as bits of lumber tossed high in the air. I look for Jackie's house but I can't tell. Low water surges ahead of the moving wall and covers the road and the railroad track, laps at the foot of the hillside. Then the wall passes the sound so loud I cannot think

My arms are wrapped around a tree and I hold it in a death grip though I am above the water that moves so fast I am dizzy and I turn away for my feet want to go from under me it moves so fast

I see the church. It is only part of a church, a steeple and roof. The current pushes it toward me. A tiny figure clings to the steeple. The roof hits the mountainside and the child holding onto the steeple reaches an arm to me and screams. Then the water has the roof again and wrenches it away from the bank, back out into the current.

I leap into the water. Cold. I grab the roof, pull myself up.

He is soaking wet and coated with black muck. I pry him from the steeple and his arms grip my neck.

Hard to breathe.

We are moving whirling and I am dizzy.

The waves wash over us and my grip loosens. The boy screams.

A trailer tumbling end over end   We rush toward it and it raises up to crush us   I let go of the roof and we are free in the water

I go under

Up and the boy screams

Wood is all around   it hits me   stunning

I grab a tire   we ride fast   a shelf smashes against the side of my head

I go under

Wider

The sky is wider

The water slows

I go under

The water slows

The mountain grabs me and lifts me

I hold the boy tight

It is not the boy

The boy?
It is not the boy   it sticks in my chest   wood   hold it tight
Cold

———————————————————————————

JACKIE

Silence. Steam rises from the earth. All the houses are gone, except for one turned upside down like a turtle on its back.

The world is gone.

It is raining again. I am so cold I cannot feel my body.

No one is with me except Sim Gore, who lies beside me, wrapped in my coat. I knocked on his door but no one answered, so I went on until I heard the water. Then I climbed until I had no breath left.

Sim washed up against the mountain on a slab of wood. When he opens his mouth he coughs up black sludge. His eyes are open wide.

"Leon?" he asks when he can talk.

I say, "I don't know where Leon is."

He coughs up black sludge.

"Kill me," he says.

He dies before he can say it again. I cover his face with my coat but I am so cold. At last I put the coat back on. Sim stares at me, his face twisted in a horrible grimace. I try to turn him on his stomach so I don't have to see his face. I put my arms under his shoulders, and the wet soaks my coat. He smells like kerosene and is heavier than he would have been in life, things take on weight when they die.

The earth hisses and smokes.

———————————————————

D I L L O N

I have run ahead as long as I can. I have stopped at houses, trailers. I pass the Lloyds Fork turnoff, drive across the Winco bridge. I cannot reach Number Thirteen and I pray they will be safe because they are a mile up the fork. I park outside Doyle Ray's trailer.

I hear the roar.

I can still make the high ground but I knock on the door, call for Doyle Ray. He is kin, my cousin's boy, his Papaw was brother to my daddy. When he doesn't answer I kick in the door. No one is home.

I stand in the living room and smile at the chickens on the wall. I hear the roar.

I limp outside, my knee paining me where I fell down the hill. As I walk the leg begins to stiffen and I have to drag it behind me. I reach the scrap of fence where I buried the red fox, buried the Japanese skull.

Buried my father's hand.

Would have buried Rachel, but I will find her now.

The water shrieks like all the lost souls, but it carries with it the top of Trace Mountain where I lived my life now dumped and scattered to the wind, the heart of it
is there
    water reaches my thighs, pulls at my legs, I turn to face the wall and stretch my arms wide

---

JACKIE

Night and I sleep beside Sim. He is a comfort there even dead. I take off his shirt and put it on. I sleep again.

Light.

I am walking.

The road is gone, the ground is scored with deep ridges and littered with boards tires garbage odds and ends of twisted metal. Pieces of houses were caught and piled high with electrical poles and railroad track looped like roller coasters.

I see stone foundations.

I see a severed arm lying beside an upturned washing machine.

I see pools of black water.

I see a body covered with black sludge hanging upside down from a tree.

I am walking to Number Thirteen.

I can't feel my feet. The inside of my nose is frozen hard. I breathe through my mouth and the cold cuts my throat.

Tom and Dillon will be at Number Thirteen. Hassel will keep them safe.

The soil has been stripped clean and I am walking on bare rock. Walking on bone.

I reach where Winco bridge should be but it is gone. Then I see Hassel and Junior and Toejam standing on the far shore like angels of the Lord.

I wave at them and sit down. I cannot move. I lie down sideways.

Junior and Toejam carry me. Hassel walks beside and holds my hand. He talks the whole time.

"You wouldn't believe," he says. "Number Thirteen is still yet there. My trailer is washed away, and Dillon's, but the houses just took on high water. We missed the worst, just got a backwash, because we're that mile up Lloyds Fork. And the bridge at the tipple, hit's still yet there. Water took out the tipple fence and the guard towers so we can walk wherever we want to. We'll carry you right on across that company bridge."

"Dillon," I say. "I want Dillon."

"I aint set eyes on Dillon," says Hassel. "I reckon he's all right. That Dillon always could take care of hisself."

"Tom," I say.

Hassel stops talking.

Hassel says, "The Holiness church is on the hill, so it didn't take on a drop of water."

They take off my clothes and wrap me in blankets. They lay me beside the coal stove in the Holiness church.

Tom is already there. He lies on his back, covered by a blanket. His eyes are closed.

Hassel puts his hand on my forehead. "Jackie," he says. "Tom's hurt real bad. You want to hold his hand?"

Yes, I say.

His hand is cold.

"We found him just above the golf course after the water passed," says Hassel. "He had a piece of wood stuck in his chest. We pulled it out but I think he's bleeding inside. He needs you to hold his hand. You got to fight and make it, Jackie, because Tom needs you. You talk to Tom."

Yes. Tom needs me.

Someone pulls the blanket over Tom's face.

"No," says Hassel. "Take it off." He leans over me. "Jackie. Talk to Tom."

Yes, I say.

I start to talk again. I tell him I love him. His eyes are closed. He says, *We're not done yet.*

He tells me about Honduras, about the children. He says Honduras is lush and green with lovely red flowers, and you can pick bananas right off the tree. Oranges and lemons. Coffee beans from shiny-leafed plants. The children are lovely. They run barefoot like we did at Number Thirteen.

Helicopter, Hassel says. Civil Defense helicopter.
Civil Defense, Civil Defense.
We are on the helicopter, but they cover Tom's face. No. I pull off the blanket. Then I try to stand. I can see out the window. I will tell Tom what I see.

The mountains are falling away below us. They are ripped and torn like a rumpled gray quilt where the cotton batting shows through. The crown of Trace Mountain is gone, a flat rocky moon pocked by green ponds of acid water.

I say, *Don't cover Tom's face, I'm talking to him.*

A man turns and says, "Christ get her to lie back down."

THE NEW WORLD

HEADLINE *New York Times*
International Oil Calls Flood 'Act of God'
SPOKESMAN ASKS FOR PRAYERS

Dillon has never been found. The search parties recovered nearly a hundred and fifty bodies on Blackberry, men, women, and children, but Dillon was not among them. I was told his body might have been washed all the way to the Levisa, or the Big Sandy, or even the Ohio.

Perhaps the Mississippi, I suggested.

Of course it wasn't so. He was close. I dreamed of his skeleton stripped and blackened and mired in sludge, becoming one with the bones of the mountains.

I work for a Pittsburgh newspaper, copy editing, concentration, concentration. It is what I need.

At night I remember. I lie on my bed with the window open to the summer breeze and a calico cat at my side. Above the incessant noise of traffic on the street outside my apartment I listen in vain for the lone whistle of a train bearing coal out of a distant hollow. I close my eyes and try to smell a summer evening when the heat has been swallowed up and the fresh breezes blow off the mountains. I imagine the lightning bugs floating by and the peepers calling from ditches green with algae and the root steps that lead to the Homeplace cemetery and the peak of Trace Mountain rounded and unscarred.

And Tom.

And my mother and my father.

I can no more go back than I could dig up a corpse and blow life into it.

The phone rings. It is Hassel.

"Jackie?" he says. "How you been?"

"Fine," I say, short, and nothing else.

He tells me about Number Thirteen. He calls once a month and tells me about Number Thirteen. I don't have the heart to ask him not to call.

He tells me the company has built a new road up Blackberry Creek, straight and broad because now there are no houses to take up space in the bottoms. The coal trucks are running in fleets from the strip mines.

He tells me Winco bottom is filled with drab green-and-white trailers, brought in by the government to house people who lost their houses in the flood.

He says, "They's lots of people to look after. It keeps me hopping. I'll have a person talk to me straight on and then they'll bust out crying for no reason at all, or younguns will take screaming fits."

He says, "Me and Junior are scavenging. We go to old tipples and tear them up for scrap metal, cut up old machinery that's been left behind. Toejam and Louelly help. They pick up chunks of coal off the road that the trucks has dropped and we sell it for house coal."

He says the government replaced the bridge at Winco bottom but not Number Thirteen. He has written the United Nations to ask for help building a bridge.

He asks, "Think you'll be back?"

I say, "I don't know."

"Come on home," he says. "We'll still yet be here."

After I hang up the phone, I lie on my back in the darkness while the traffic flows away below me and try to see pictures on the ceiling.

DATE DUE			
JUL 0 8 2009			
SEP 0 1 2009			
OCT 1 1 2008			
OCT 2 5 2008			
FEB 05 2009			

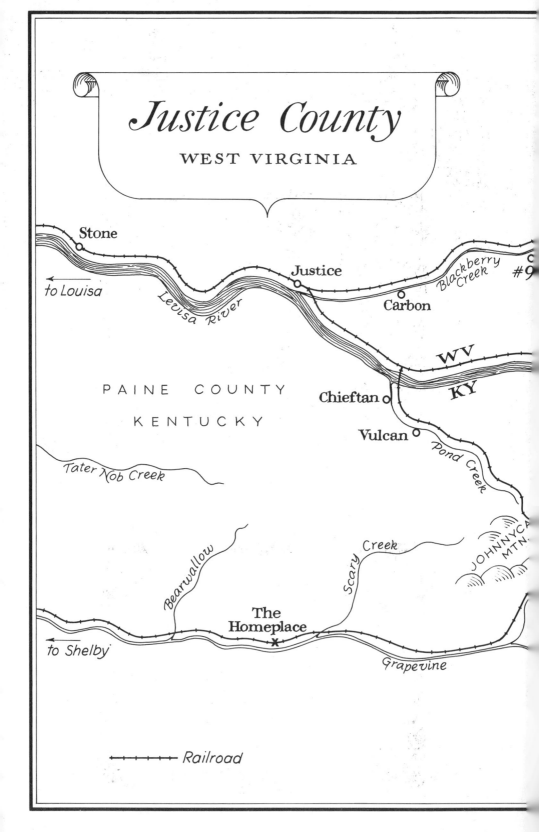